WALKING BESIDE MUDDY CREEKS

Wanda Hancock

Order this book online at www.trafford.com
or email orders@trafford.com

Most Trafford titles are also available at major online book retailers.

Printed in the United States of America.

ISBN: 978-1-4269-6455-8 (sc)
ISBN: 978-1-4269-6456-5 (e)

Trafford rev. 04/26/2011

 www.trafford.com

North America & international
toll-free: 1 888 232 4444 (USA & Canada)
phone: 250 383 6864 ✦ fax: 812 355 4082

CONTENTS

THE EMERGENCY ROOM

It was late afternoon and the ER was rather quiet. Kari's partner had gone to dinner and Kari was looking out the ER ambulance doors and enjoying the view of the trees that were just beginning to turn color.

Kari went back into the ER to prep for any emergency that might come in. One of the rules was to leave trays and IV'S set up for the on-coming shift.

The small community hospital rarely had severe trauma. However, there were cases in which the hospital was the closest around and the ambulances came there. Joey, Kari's partner, had come back from break and Kari was supposed to take her break. Just as they were reporting and chatting, the emergency radio came on and announced they were bringing in a gun shot wound. They called the ER doctors and prepared for a surgeon to come in too. By this time the ambulance was at the back doors and the medics were rolling the gurney up the ramp into the #1 ER. The patient was covered and only the top of his hair was seen.

Joey and one of the doctors were intubating the patient. Kari was starting a large bore needle for fluids and blood. One of the aides was cutting the clothing off the patient in order to get a good look at the wounds. Kari hadn't looked up from the IV; however Joey and the aide took in a sharp breath.

That caught her attention. She looked at the patient and stood stock still. It was her husband on the gurney and she knew he was dead. She looked closer and realized he had a head wound as well as a chest wound. There was blood leaking from several areas. Frank was pronounced dead. Kari dropped the IV and went into another room. She came back to get his wedding ring, but it was gone.

When Kari went into #2 ER, the doctor and Joey followed her. The other doctor called the police and they were there within minutes. They took notes on Frank, took his belongings, and during that time one of the doctors told the police that he was Kari's husband. They went into the room with Kari and asked numerous questions, about his job, where he worked, and if he too did shift work. She told them everything she knew. They had been married only a few months. They asked curious questions again about his work. Kari told them he worked under cover for a federal agency, but could tell no one which branch or department, not even his wife. Sometimes he had to go undercover and be away for several days. He left home in old, sloppy clothing without shaving or combing his hair.

The shock was beginning to tell on Kari's face, regarding her husband's traumatic death. Who could have done this to him and why would anyone want to kill him? They were living in a nice neighborhood. The neighbors knew Kari very well and that she worked as an RN in the hospital. The officer kept asking her questions that seemed irrational and confusing. The last of the officers said they were going but she was to continue her usual routine, until her grieving and the hospital thought she could come back to work.

Kari was so in shock that the doctor suggested she stay in the hospital that night. Kari was tough and took hard work and messy work in stride, without having any problem. Nursing was her calling, she often said. When they got her to her room, she became so upset with crying that it seemed the entire crew decided she needed sedation.

The next morning she felt groggy and bewildered, but she knew she must prepare for funeral arrangements. She called one of the nurses up stairs, whose husband owned a funeral home. Kari told this nurse which church he attended. Frank was Catholic, but rarely attended Mass. The Father had to be told. Her nurse friend called her husband and he came over and took care of the arrangements for her.

The police had to have an autopsy to determine what and how he was killed. When they finished that, they allowed the funeral to be completed.

There were many friends and several people she had never seen at the Service.

Kari went to Church as often as she could but she was not Catholic. Her Pastor (Rev. Joe and his wife, Camille) came to see her fairly often. She always felt better after they left because they would hold hands and pray for her. A couple of friends spent a few nights with her, just for comfort.

She decided to go back to work in about a week. She reflected on what happened, what the police asked and wondered why they were so inquisitive. Kari found herself becoming weak and scared. What now!

Kari had heard nothing from the police as to the autopsy report. There was no sharing of information of anything. The Priest hadn't come to see her either. Had the police started to find whoever did this? She couldn't understand. She slept fitfully and soon gave up on what others might or might not do. She began to go on-line to find any available information on the Federal and State Governments. After a rather slow search, she became tired and went to bed. However every day she learned more about people who did illegal drugs.

The next day Kari began to go through the house to find anything that related to Frank. She went through his closet and chest of drawers, looking for anything she could give to Goodwill. She found some change in several pockets, but nothing more. She began to fold shirts and pants, but kept his suits on the hangers. One afternoon she went into the garage to just look at his 'stuff'. Besides the usual tools and lawn mover, she found a small tool box about the size of her make-up box. The tool box was locked so she began looking around for the key. She found the key taped to the bottom of the tool box. When she opened it she found papers she didn't understand and in a language she did not know.

While she wondered why a large envelope had her name on it, she became concerned. The envelope said, To Kari: In the event of my death. She opened the envelope and found what looked like insurance papers.

She began reading and realized that Frank had taken out a large insurance policy for her in the event he died. When she realized what this probably meant, she began to cry and then she began to pray. What should she do and who should she contact who might know what this meant. She cried and prayed through out the night. Since Frank's death, it seemed a number of friends stopped calling or visiting. At times she thought she had become paranoid. Finally she went to sleep.

When she awoke, she realized she needed an attorney, but not one from this small town. She went on-line and found a reputable law firm that was located in a larger city about 150 miles away. She called and made an appointment to see one of them. She had investigated the law firms in that city and had picked this group.

On the day she had the appointment with the attorney; it seemed she was being followed. Since the car did not follow when she left town, she thought little more about it.

The lawyer met with her and said the insurance papers were valid, but she would need a financial adviser. He also told her, after she met with the financial advisor, she should take the tackle box from which the insurance came and take it to the police. She refused.

Her attorney (Wayne) called the insurance company to determine the process. The company wanted to know her identity. At this juncture, she asked the attorney if he could represent her with whatever legal matters came. He would act as her representative when the check came in. Kari had learned quite a bit about attorney's authority and responsibilities. She had bought a cell phone with a new number from the one she had at home. She instructed him to use only the cell number when contacting her. She also asked the attorney to keep the tackle box in his personal bank and he agreed.

In about two weeks her attorney called and told her that the insurance check came to him. She had asked him to personally take care of it until she could come and get it. He (Wayne) advised her to see a financial advisor, which she did. She had already checked to insure the financial advisor was reputable. She met with Wayne and her financial advisor. She found three banks and bought a deposit box in all three of the banks. She also kept a rather large amount of money in each bank box, in the event she needed it.

She opened a savings account and checking account in each of the banks. She also instructed her financial advisor to have each bank find gold and buy a specific number of ingots, and put the same number of ingots in each bank box. She had each piece appraised to ensure the value. She

4

checked on-line for some appraisal firms to be sure the one she chose was reputable.

She took a few more days off work to visit different friends and what family she had left. She told her supervisor she was having some flash-backs and needed extra time off. The supervisor understood and told her to take the time off she needed.

KARI GOES BACK TO WORK

However, when she started back to work, she thought she was being followed again. Several cars came by her house whose owner she didn't know and followed her to work. How could they know she worked the ER? Perhaps some neighbor told them. Her routine never changed; groceries were bought on Thursday, laundry was done on Tuesday and supplies for neighbors, who couldn't get out, were done on Wednesday. She continued to see one of the same cars following, but they never stopped or spoke to her. She finally told Joey and he suggested she call the police to see if they were checking her and if so, why. The police had no knowledge of anything like what she described, and they did not make available to her the autopsy results. Soon the cars stopped showing up and Kari continued with her work and chores.

Kari had a strong belief that whoever had caused Frank's death, one or more of the police were involved. There seemed to be a cloud of mystery surrounding her. How would one know? She talked briefly to her pastor regarding being followed and that the police didn't seem interested in giving her any information. She needed someone she could trust to 'keep ears and eyes' open for anything that seemed unusual in the community.

Kari realized for the first time that things didn't 'feel' right at the hospital. There was nothing concrete on which to base her feelings. There was less cheerfulness and fewer people stopped by to chat. As time progressed she knew 'something' was not right in the atmosphere at the hospital.

Kari had grown emotionally since Frank died. She spent some time on the internet to find information on each branch of the US bureaus. She found access to one bureau that dealt with international drugs and human trafficking. As she began to study, she realized her previous naive nature had not served her well.

Kari became more aware of people's body language, speech, laughter and other characteristics of those she was around at work and the patients who came into the ER. Since the hospital was small, the ER usually had the same people or families with multiple complaints. She also noticed that since Frank's death there were new patients that came to the ER, usually with an ailment that required some type of narcotic injection.

Kari decided to move away. She told no one at the hospital and continued to work. She had a plan in her head. She also kept her lawyer aware of her belief that someone was following her. On her days off from work, she worked her plan.

She began to look around for some property she liked and planned to build a log or cedar cabin in which to live. She found 3 acres that were thickly wooded. She decided to buy the property. It was located at the foothills of the mountains around the city. There had been no legal hassles when she had the property surveyed and the lawyer had checked as far back as necessary to ensure there was no lien on the property, or anything that would later cause problems. She put the bill of sale and papers into her security box in the first bank.

There were many house planners and builders. So after checking on line for the reputation of the various planners and builders, she chose one who did log cabins. She looked at many log cabin styles, but finally decided on one she really liked. She talked with the builder and asked for a few changes. She wanted a balcony on the back side of the great room and a bathroom that would also have a door in the end of the balcony and office, which would make another exit. There would be steps leading to the ground. This would make a perfect library, if she could get the builder and architect to put specific shelving in the balcony.

Finally the plans were made and Kari instructed them to begin work on her house. She made stipulations on viewing any wood or other things needed for the house and when she was satisfied, the builder went ahead with her plans. Her lawyer was the only one who could contact her as her legal advisor.

She went back to work and chores. She still kept in contact with her attorney via cell phone, as to the progress of her house. She had already established his fees and thus far had no reason to doubt him. Kari knew she was becoming very un-trusting of others. She was a pretty auburn haired girl with big grey eyes and was outgoing in her personality. Kari knew her inside self had changed. No one seemed to notice anything except outgoing Kari was a bit more reserved in her demeanor. Since her husband had been killed, who could blame her? She still went to Church when she had Sundays off. She also kept a closer watch on her home and community.

Kari took her shower and was preparing for work one afternoon. She could not believe it had been about three months since Frank was killed and she had heard nothing from the police. Earlier than she needed to get to work, she went to see her pastor, and briefly explained that she needed him to keep her cell phone until she picked it up. He asked how she was doing and she told him she was becoming more un-trusting of people. Pastor Joe and Camille assured her they would do anything she needed. Pastor Joe and Camille had lost their only daughter a couple years back and so it seemed they thought of her as if she was a daughter.

No one ever mentioned Frank's name and she again became afraid she was being followed. She laughed and told Pastor she might be ready for an 'I love me jacket'. They laughed together and Kari realized she was really laughing at one of the 'nursing – isms', most nurses used when it had been a very difficult day. Her Pastor was pleased to see the 'old' Kari on the way back to living. Of course he would keep her cell phone until she was ready for it.

Kari went on to work and the evening progressed as usual, cuts and bruises and sick children came in for treatment. It was busier than normal with more patients coming in for severe headaches or backaches that required narcotic injections. She and Joey kidded around more and he was so glad to see his 'old' Kari back to her usual self, even if still a bit reserved. When the shift was almost over they set up trays and IVs as usual for the on-coming shift. She told Joey that her head hurt and asked if he could manage for a while; she'd like to go home. Joey said, "Oh sure and you take something for that headache." Kari had known for a long time that Joey was gay, but he treated her as his big sister.

Kari gathered her things together, purse and car keys in her hand on the way to her car. Before she could comprehend anything a large man with a ski mask jumped from between two cars. Although she had her keys with the alarm, she mashed the button. The man was large and knocked her down. She thought he was black, because she did notice his hand as he reached out to hit her. Her head hit the asphalt parking area and she passed out. When she began to get her senses back the man hit her hard on her face and side of her head. She was out again. When she began to come to, she realized he was violently raping her. She pretended to be out for another minute or so and tried to get up. He began kicking her in the ribs, hips, and pelvic area. By this time she thought he was planning to kill her. He suddenly got up and ran to a car in the parking lot and the car moved on.

She looked around again for her keys and pushed her alarm again. The shift change had started and nurses were coming in for third shift. Joey's replacement had already arrived, and he was on his way home. Joey saw her and called to the other nurses coming to work. They picked her up and took her to the ER. By the time she got in the ER, the nurses saw what had happened. They took her vital signs and started some oxygen to help her wake up and told her to take deep breaths, she started crying and said she couldn't. She looked at herself and saw the clothes she had on, on the ER floor and she was wrapped in a warm blanket, usual protocol for one going in and out of shock. She didn't know how she got on the gurney, or who started the IV but Joey and several nurses were with her. The doctor had ordered x-rays of the pelvis, ribs, legs and skull. She seemed to hurt everywhere. When the doctor read the x-rays he found a fracture of her upper left leg.

As soon as they could, they washed her down and put a hospital gown and warm blanket on her, the doctor asked her, "Who did this to you?" All she could tell him and the nurses that the man was large and had a ski mask on. She related to them that she thought he was going to kill her. The doctor said, "He could have, had that been his motive." He asked her if the man said anything. Kari could only remember him saying, "Where is the money bitch," along with more profanity.

They decided to hospitalize her for the night, but before she was taken up stairs, the doctor did a DNA swab. Kari was so afraid to stay by herself, that she asked one of the nurses to sit with her that night and she would pay them for the shift. The doctor and other nurses saw how angry Joey was at someone doing this to his friend, that he should go home and get rest. He said, "I'll rest right here and if I dose off, wake me when you make rounds." Nothing happened during the night, but nurses came around rather frequently.

The next morning Kari sent Joey home, assuring him she was fine. When the doctor made rounds, he said, "You will need   side splints on your femur and they would do a cat scan on her head to be sure you don't have a hematoma." After all those procedures were complete, the doctor said, "You must have a hard head", and smiled at her. She knew this doctor well and they chatted a while. She told him that one more night in hospital would be enough. She wanted to go home. Then she asked, "Where are my purse and the car keys?"

The doctor said, "They found her purse and keys, but she probably didn't want to use it again." It had been searched, her wallet torn up and the bag had been tossed across the wall at the parking lot. She told them the only credit cards she had was one for gas and one for the department store she used. She asked for her car keys and noticed that one to her house was gone. She told the doctor she had friends to stay with, but she would never again be in that house alone. She also asked if one of business office ladies would cancel the credit cards for her. They were pleased to help her anyway they could.

The nurse brought her belongings, but Kari said, "Only my keys." After she and the nurse talked a while, Kari called her pastor and asked him to come get her at the hospital. She had been discharged, but had to use a crutch for a while. She went home with her pastor and his wife. They treated her as if she belonged to them. She knew she had to have clothes but could not possibly go shopping. The Pastor's wife was a little larger than Kari, but she gathered some of her clothes, mostly snap up model's coats for Kari to use, since it was summer with a few cool days. The clothes felt good and big enough she could work her legs, when she got into bed.

Kari began to practice walking with the crutch, but had no idea how difficult that task could be. She would work a while and rest a while and then repeat the process. In a few days she asked Pastor Joe and Camille to take her to her house. She remembered that Frank had kept another house key on a shelf in the garage. They found the key and went inside; the place was a disaster zone. What had whoever did this been looking for? She told Camille that she needed underwear and some of her own clothing. She and Camille went to her underwear drawer and retrieved bras, panties, and socks, as well as some shoes and clothing. Pastor Joe said, "Anything else?" Kari told him she wanted some of her doll collection and especially the doll with red hair. The doll was dressed in her communion dress and was posed to take her First Communion. Frank was Catholic and said when he got the doll for her, that some day they might have a little girl who would want it.

They boxed up what she wanted and they went back home. When they got back to pastor's house, Kari knew she had to tell them the ordeal that caused the leg fracture and her black and blue face and arms. Again they hugged her and prayed for her. She also told them she would be moving, but not where lest someone decided to harass them. She was so tired after the afternoon's experience that she was ready for a bath and bed.

Kari had not wanted anything to eat in days, but they made her eat at least one balanced meal at dinner. The rest of the time she ate snacks.

In about two weeks it was time to take the splints off and get a good check-up. They all three went to the doctor's office and he put a soft splint on and wrapped it with ace bandages. She would need to use the crutch for another few weeks.

Kari felt a lot stronger and decided it was time to move. She called her attorney and checked on the progress of her house. It was almost ready for inspection. Kari decided to take her belongings and go to her new house. She could use an air mattress until inspection was done. Pastor Joe and Camille would not hear of it. They insisted on moving her themselves and stay in a motel for a few days and see her every day. Again she reminded them of possible problems for them. "Oh, stop it," Camille said, "We are grown ups with the ability to deal with whatever might come up." They were not willing to let Kari go without some way of checking on her occasionally. It was almost fall again and they needed a vacation. So Pastor Joe made arrangements with the Church leadership for a vacation. Of course, that was fine.

THE MOVE

In a couple days, she decided it was time to move, but her car was still at the hospital. She had no intention of keeping that car, so she signed it over to Pastor Joe to sell it or keep it, or whatever he wanted to do with it. Kari realized there was so much to do, such as, get a U-Haul and box the things she needed to take with her. She called her attorney and told him she was coming up to her house. He said, "The house and property had not been totally completed." Kari also asked him to get her a phone installed and with several jacks for phone usage with one being in her bedroom. He assured her that he would have that done.

Kari and Pastor Joe and Camille planned to have breakfast the next morning and have the U-haul delivered. They would leave that afternoon, Pastor Joe and Camille had already reserved a suite of rooms, because she would be sitting up for the three hour trip. They would go out to dinner and have a good night of rest. When they finally got to the motel, Kari was really grateful for her dearest friends, thoughtfulness and common sense. Before they went to bed she told them about her house, its design and where it was located. As they were getting ready for bed, she asked to leave her door open so they could hear her, of course they did.

The next morning they had breakfast, but Kari only wanted juice and coffee. When they finished eating, Kari called her lawyer and asked him to meet her at her house about 11:00 o'clock. He agreed and they prepared to go on to the house. It was a bit difficult to get in the car with the crutch, but she did it.

She, Pastor Joe and Camille, went to her house. It really was beautiful to Kari. Kari enjoyed very rustic things and had hoped she and Frank could build a house just like this one. It had several chimneys. There were about three steps up to the small porch, but she had told the builder to place railings in case someone needed help coming to see her. She never dreamed she would be the first to need them. Her lawyer and builder arrived a few minutes later. They each had a key and wanted to be sure she was happy with the house. She introduced them to Pastor Joe and Camille and everyone seemed cordial and they went in.

The great room was beautifully covered with logs and planks that she really liked. There was a fantastic fire place ready to go and it was primarily made of rocks. She looked at the balcony and it was exactly what she wanted. She had difficulty getting up the steps with her crutch, but she was determined to go to her office and library. The bathroom off the end of the back wall had been done like she wanted. While she looked around on the balcony, the four below chatted quietly. She got down the steps and realized she was already tired again. They all went into the bedrooms downstairs, one on each side of the great room. Her bedroom had another beautiful fireplace. When she had looked out front from the balcony, she noticed how much light was present through the long windows that went from top to about three feet off the floor. They had put window seats in each window of the great room and that seemed so warm and inviting without her having to go outside to see anything.

They went into the kitchen and the large wrought iron pot hanger and rolling island for prep of food, was ready in place. She was really happy. The kitchen had plenty of room for refrigerator/freezer, round table, chairs, open shelving for storing china, platters and other things. There was room underneath the open shelves to store any foods or cans she wished. She had planned for every thing in her kitchen with flat space to be granite. All of her other equipment would be stainless steel, cast iron, or copper. She had an alcove for her washer and dryer at one end of the kitchen. The other end of the kitchen had another alcove for larger pots and whatever she wanted. From both alcoves there was a granite shelf from one side to the other wall to hold her coffee pot, large mixer, blender, meat grinder, etc. There were also drawers under the shelves at each end.

After every one had seen the house with her, they all were pleased when she said, "Yes, This is what I want." She signed the papers that her lawyer had brought and Pastor Joe was a notary. Everything was signed, sealed, and paid for with all the warranties in place. The lawyer then took them to the courthouse so they could see that the proper papers were registered and now Kari had a home on the property she had purchased. Although they had accomplished so much, Kari was more exhausted than she thought necessary.

Pastor Joe and Camille insisted she come back to the suite of rooms for a while. She did. For the next couple of weeks the routine continued. They went on line for the kind of refrigerator, freezer, and range she wanted. Pastor Joe and Camille helped her order bedroom settings and furniture for the great room, as well as, a desk she wanted for the balcony and for her bedroom. Kari also wanted a new computer and copier for her office. All the materials were delivered while they were all three present. The beddings, pillows, blankets and quilts for both bedrooms were ordered on line. The great room had shelving that could hold her doll collection and figurines. Kari told Camille to pick what she liked because she and Pastor Joe had a free place to stay when they wanted to go anywhere. There was a nice bathroom in each bedroom, again with granite shelving, tub and shower. Under the granite sink there was shelving to put towels, bath clothes and all toilet needs.

Pastor Joe and Camille helped her unload all the things she had packed up to come to her new home. It started to look like her. When she and Camille were making beds and chatting, Kari told Camille that she needed to see about a hospital that she might like to work in. She had previously looked into the phone book for physicians and a dentist. Kari would check the doctors on line. Pastor Joe and Camille planned to leave the next day. That night after they all had supper, she told them she wanted to stay at her house that night. They asked if she was sure and of course she was. They brought her to her house with all the keys, but she had given them a key to enter anytime they wanted. During the previous days she had purchased many cans of vegetables, staples and food for the freezer and refrigerator, for an entire month or so.

Before they left her that night, she asked Camille to come to her bedroom. She and Kari went in and Kari told her she thought she might be pregnant from the rape. She wasn't sure, but her constant fatigue and inability to eat made her think so, plus she hadn't had a period in 4 to 5 weeks. Kari could not remember if she had told Camille that she had a glance at the man who raped her and as his fist was coming toward her face, she thought he was black.

Before they left she asked Pastor Joe to check for a good Church she might attend. She knew she would be unable to work for a while, but she wanted to find a group of Christians with whom she could worship. He said, "Absolutely." However, he and Camille were really worried about her, if she was pregnant who would take care of her? This time it was Kari's turn to tell Camille, "I'm a big girl now and am no longer afraid." She knew her Heavenly Father would protect her. Pastor Joe and Camille left and decided they would also keep an eye on her through the lawyer. The lawyer or builder had not kept a key, but the lawyer was on retainer for Kari and had what he needed.

She rested that night, but kept a light on and the fireplace on low. When she felt stronger the next morning, she called her lawyer and asked if one of his staff would come take her to get a car. He asked if Sandy would be okay. Kari had met Sandy several times and was pleased they could check out car places and get to know the city a bit. Kari knew what she wanted, a 4-wheeled drive mini van that was pearl white or a pretty red.

Sandy and Kari chatted and began to get to know each other. They found the very mini van that Kari wanted. They took it for a round about town. She took it back and told the dealer she wanted to buy the car. She told the dealer to determine the costs, warranty, and licenses. They gave her the information and she had them prep the car. She and Sandy went to the first bank and took out a cashier's check. Wayne, Kari's lawyer, checked to be sure all was well. Kari and Sandy went back to the dealership and picked up the car, making sure the oil and gasoline was filled. Kari completed the paper work and asked Sandy to come over if she'd like to see the house. They stopped and got burgers and fries and took them home to eat. Sandy was finishing school in order to teach, but her husband wanted her to go ahead and get her lawyers license as well.

Kari asked Sandy where they went to Church and she told her. Sandy offered to take Kari to her Church and meet the Pastor and office workers. Kari agreed and they went to the Church and met the pastor and staff workers. It seemed very much like the Church where Pastor Joe was pastor. They talked a while and Kari needed to go home. She could not remember being so very tired. She picked up the phone book and looked for an obstetric group of doctors. She then went on-line to check their background. After writing the number down, she prepared to go to bed. She again left the fireplace on low and a light on and went to sleep.

The next day she called and made an appointment to see the doctor. She had already prepared her medical history, which was short, but included the rape and fractured leg. She saw Dr. Little in the group. She checked Kari and tested for pregnancy, the result was positive, about seven weeks. Dr. Little asked Kari if she wanted an abortion due to the circumstances of the pregnancy. Kari made it very clear that for her, this was not an option. Dr. Little understood. She gave Kari routine vitamins, etc. and a schedule for routine appointments to ensure all was well as the pregnancy continued.

Well, she had her confirmation, so she went to a store and bought a few baby clothes, diapers, bottles and Pedialyte in case she needed it. She went home and ate a light dinner, took a shower and made an early evening of this day. She had a long prayer asking God to teach her what to do in the following months and when her baby arrived. She also called Camille and told her about the things that occurred since she and Pastor Joe had gone. She told her about the Church she had visited and asked them to pray for her and right choices she may need to make regarding any or no explanations when she delivered a mixed race baby. Camille assured her they would, but she was sure Kari had made and would make the right decisions.

Kari still did not feel up to going back to work at the new hospital. She had checked with the Director of Nursing and was assured there was work, especially with Kari's background. Kari told the Director she would contact her when she felt able to come to work.

Kari spent the next few days tidying her house, putting her doll collection in place, and mostly resting. She decided to take a short walk outside her house about lunchtime. She found a small, muddy creek fairly close to her house and she wondered why it was muddy since there had been no rain for a while. She made a routine of walking about every day to gain strength and see her property and the beautiful trees while just enjoying the outdoors. The creek stayed muddy, which was unusual since it had a bit of running water, however it stayed muddy.

KARI'S PREGNANCY
AND
THE UNEXPECTED VISITOR

One afternoon when she was coming in from her walk, a car drove into her driveway and stopped. A rather nice looking woman got out of her car and told Kari her name. She had a very young baby with her and she asked Kari if she would look after her baby until his father could pick him up later in the afternoon. The lady (Kelly) said, "My sister is seriously ill and I must go to the hospital to be with her." Kari asked her where she and her husband lived and how she knew Kari. Kelly told her that she had spoken to Sandy and learned that Kari lived here not very far from their home. Sandy had not called Kari or if she had, Kari missed the call while she was walking. Kelly seemed in such a hurry that Kari took the baby and Kelly pulled a couple of boxes of 'supplies' out of her car, which were for the baby. She said she really must leave and left.

Kari looked at the baby and it being a rather chilly afternoon, decided to take the baby inside. She finally got the boxes into her great room and went to check the baby. Kari was a bit concerned when she really checked the babe. He seemed a bit feverish and his lips were dry. Kari undressed him to check him; perhaps give him a bath and clean clothes and a bottle, if the lady had left one in the boxes. The baby was sick. The dry skin indicated some dehydration and a very red bottom, which indicated that he at some time that day or previous night had diarrhea. She bathed the baby, he smelled as though he had not been bathed, and wrapped him in a large warm bath towel, which she hung at the foot of bed. Afterwards she then turned the fireplace up. She laid him on her bed and went to look for his bottle.

Kari was shocked! The only belongings that seemed for the baby were dirty one pieced gowns, socks, and a few small diapers. She found two bottles of formula, but when she opened them the milk was sour. Kari realized this woman 'Kelly' had lied to her and probably may have abandoned the baby. At this point Kari knew she could do nothing except look after the little one. She was glad she had started to get a few supplies for her own baby. She put her baby's new things in the dryer with softening sheets and ran it for 15 minutes. That would make them soft and as germ-free as she could make new baby clothes. The baby had whimpered and cried while she bathed him. While the dryer was going, she picked up the baby and fed him some pre-warmed Pedilyte. She also checked his bottom and put some petroleum jelly on his little reddened bottom.

When the dryer finished Kari took the baby clothes, diapers, socks and a baby blanket out and dressed the baby. She began to rock him; she already had a rocking chair in her room and the baby quieted and slept. She continued to rock him for quiet sometime. Then she thought of what Kelly had told her about Sandy telling her that Kari would be glad to baby sit until his father came home. Kari checked the phone, but there was no message. She phoned Sandy and told her what had happened. Sandy didn't know such a person, but told Kari she would try to find out what was going on. Sandy called Kari back and said there was no young woman seriously ill or dying at the hospital and really no one was dying there. Here we go again, Kari, you have not become as untrusting as you thought!!! It was getting late in the afternoon and Kari knew she had to prepare something for the baby to eat. She was afraid to give any milk, so she washed what would have been her own baby's bottles and used distilled water with one teaspoon of 'gator-aid' to try and keep his electrolytes in balance, at least until the morning and she would take him to the emergency room. She had forgotten that she had Pedialyte in the shelves.

Kari was truly exhausted by this time. She drank the rest of the gator-aid and lay down beside the baby who was still asleep. Kari awoke to the doorbell and knocking on her door. She wasn't asleep, the doorbell really was ringing. She had not changed clothes to rest and so she went to the front door. She had worked so hard with the walk and baby care, she needed her crutch for safety to get to the door.

When she got to the door, there was a rather tall man and he asked her about his baby. Kari was becoming angry and asked him, "Who are you and how do you know me?" The man was nice-looking and clean cut. He pulled out his wallet and showed her his picture identification, and more quietly asked if she knew where his baby was. Standing in the door, blocking his entrance, she realized this was silly. Had he been inclined, he could have picked her up and moved inside very easily. She opened the door and motioned him inside. He came in and appeared not to notice her crutch. Kari asked him the sex of the baby and how old the child might be. He, of course, realized she was still a bit angry and scared. He again told her his name, Daniel Meyers and that his baby was a boy with dark hair and was about seven weeks old.

Kari took him to the bedroom where she and the baby had been resting. He gently picked the baby up and began to talk softly to him. Kari was growing less afraid and could hardly stand, so she sat down and asked him if she could hold the baby. She began to rock him in her rocking chair. She asked him to please have a seat in a chair opposite her at the fireplace.

Daniel knew some talking had to take place. He told her he had been married to Kelly, but when she got pregnant she planned to have an abortion. He begged her not to do that and he would pay her for total custody of the baby. She had a greater greed and concern for her figure than anything else. She agreed on a large sum and signed legal forms to such an arrangement. She would never try to take the baby and would leave him total custody and, by the way, she wanted an annulment of their marriage. He readily agreed and had used the same attorney that Kari had used. He told Kari they had met Sandy during the process.

He and Wayne had only seen the baby at birth with all the legal matters on hand. The legal forms were signed and he had seen the baby only once since his birth. Knowing that Kari was still nervous Daniel told her to call Sandy and see what she said. Kari did and he seemed to have told the truth. Sandy also told Kari she did not have to be afraid of Daniel, as he was the Chief Chaplain for the police force in their town. Kari hung up and thanked Daniel for his honesty. She asked him to hold the baby until she could get her dinner out of the oven, that she was very weak and tired. Of course he was pleased to do so.

Before her walk, Kari had prepared a pot roast and left it in the warmer for dinner. She thought possibly that Daniel had not had dinner, so she prepared the table for two, made coffee and called him in the kitchen for dinner. He did not expect to eat until he could go to a diner, but was pleased she felt she could trust him enough to eat dinner with him across the table.

While Daniel had held the baby, he gave him a bottle of Pedilyte that Kari remembered she had, and the baby went to sleep. He also noticed Kari's stethoscope lying on the bed and by the way in which she spoke, he thought she was a nurse, which of course was true.

While they were eating, they chatted and Kari began to relax more. The small amount of supper she could eat had given her some strength, as well as, additional gator-aid. They talked about his work and how he would manage, now that the baby was with him. He looked straight at Kari and said, "I'd like you to be his nurse as long as it is not too much work for you." He told her that he had seen her stethoscope and books and believed she was a good person who would treat his son well.

As long as we're talking there are some things you need to know about me and you might also check with Sandy or Wayne, her lawyer. She was an ER nurse and had undergone some severe trauma, emotionally and physically, so she did need to rest. However, if he felt the baby would be all right with her, she would love to keep him. She told Daniel that she did not go out at night and rarely during the day, except to take a short walk. She said she had no idea he lived so close to her. She had never seen a house on her walks. She also said that she could rest when the baby rested. By the way, "What is this child's name?" Daniel laughed and said 'Daniel', but he planned to call him Danny. For the first time in a long while Kari actually giggled like a school girl. She surprised herself and told him she couldn't remember giggling since she was a girl and she was far passed being a girl. She was twenty-four years old. They talked for quite a while and the conversation was light, but enlightening as well.

Daniel asked why she had a bassinet in her bedroom and she showed him her doll collection, some of which were baby dolls. She had kept the baby dolls in the bassinet, but would make it into a bed for Danny. She reminded him that as Danny grew he would need a larger bed. She would make him a list of essentials to pick-up for the baby. She also asked who

Danny's doctor would be. She needed to know formula and vitamins, thus Daniel would need to take him to the doctor for a baseline. Daniel said he would do that tomorrow about eleven o'clock. Kari asked him to ask the doctor to please do a good check-up because Kari was afraid he might be dehydrated.

It was soon time for Daniel to leave and he told Kari he might drop by in the morning to see how he was doing. Kari said, "Fine, and I'll have him ready by eleven o'clock to see the doctor."

DANNY SEES THE DOCTOR

The next morning about eight o'clock Daniel stopped by to check Danny and chat with Kari about the night with him. Kari told him she had only given Danny Pedialyte and kept him clean and dry. He had slept fairly well. Kari asked if Daniel needed her phone number in the event the baby was sicker that she thought. They exchanged phone numbers and Daniel gave her his home and work phone as well. Daniel told Kari he would see her about eleven o'clock and left.

Daniel came back about eleven o'clock and Kari had the baby ready and also had the list of essentials she would need for Danny. When they had gone, Kari lay back down for a while. She was still experiencing fatigue in the mornings. She slept about two hours and awoke feeling much more refreshed. She ate a light breakfast with her coffee and juice. She then tidied the bedroom and kitchen. She was still a bit afraid to go to the balcony without someone being present, so she turned the T.V. on and watched the news and weather.

She also began dinner with the intention of asking Daniel to eat. Kari was a good cook, but she did not like to cook for only herself, plus she enjoyed the conversations. She prepared pasta with meat sauce, a salad and a small pound cake to be eaten with blueberries and ice cream from the freezer. About an hour later Daniel and Danny came in. Daniel handed Danny to Kari and began unloading the supplies she needed, as well as, a car seat for Danny and a 'swinger-jumper' with a canvas bottom with a seat belt so he could use his legs more.

The doctor said the baby was fine and that Danny weighed eight and one-half pounds. He said the doctor agreed that Kari had done the correct protocol with the Pedialyte, because the baby was a bit dehydrated and had been rather ill with a stomach virus. He ordered the formula to be taken between the Pedialyte, for the next two days, and then to formula alone. Daniel gave Kari a list of instructions for Danny and was so thankful that Kari requested he check the baby.

Kari started though the bags of goods Daniel had brought. There was a small chest in which to keep his supplies and a larger chest for clothing he had bought. He had bought a good supply of diapers, baby clothes with feet, undershirts, toys and blankets. By the time all the things had been put away, it was time for Daniel to go back to work. He asked Kari if there was anything else she needed and there was not at this time. Again, Daniel turned to leave to go back to work and maybe grab a burger for dinner. Since it was later than they realized, Kari invited him to stay for dinner, which he accepted. Daniel asked Kari why she cooked when she ate so little and she told him she enjoyed cooking and conversation. That was a wonderful thing for Daniel because when he got off work, he was usually very tired and needed dinner. He usually grabbed a sandwich for lunch.

Daniel told Kari that he would appreciate dinner if Kari felt like it but he would buy all the groceries and bring them to her. He told her to make a grocery list plus routine supplies needed for the house or anything she might like. They agreed and both enjoyed a good dinner. Daniel said, "You are a good cook", and that he enjoyed the food she made very much. And so, a routine developed. Daniel bought whatever Kari needed and she cooked and looked after Danny. Every evening they developed a deeper relationship.

The next morning, Kari looked at her calendar and realized that she had an appointment with Dr. Little about eleven o'clock. She got herself ready to go and then gave Danny a bath and clothed him. She put the car seat into the car and came back to get the baby. She went on to see Dr. Little and explained that she was baby-sitting this baby.

Dr. Little checked her, did a sonogram, and seemed a bit concerned that the baby was not growing like she had expected. Kari told the doctor she did not eat much herself, but would certainly try harder to take in good nutrients for herself and the babe. Dr. Little could not determine the sex of the baby and Kari said, "That's fine, it really doesn't matter." She wanted a healthy child. She soon left the office with additional instructions.

Kari and Danny started home and she remembered it would soon be Danny's three month birthday. She stopped by a shop and picked up some invitations, stamps and table-setting for a party. She bought napkins with small, cute, baby animals on them and party plates to match. She planned to have a surprise birthday party for Danny. Since she knew so few people, she would invite Daniel, Sandy and Bob, and then she decided to invite Pastor Joe and Camille, her lawyer Wayne and his wife Linda. It might be silly to have a birthday party for a three month old, but she was going to anyway.

She planned the menu and put the birthday supplies beside her bed. She planned a beef roast, mashed potatoes with rutabaga, string beans and salad. She was planning a chocolate cake with coconut frosting for the party.

After the morning work-out with the doctor, it was time for food for herself and Danny. She fed Danny and he went to sleep. She ate the most nourishing food she could and took a nap.

When Kari woke up from her nap, she made a meatloaf with turnip greens and baked sliced sweet potatoes. She decided against a dessert since she had ice cream in the freezer if Daniel wanted dessert. She then checked on Danny and they played a while and he let her know he was hungry. He had started to grow and had become more active. After he ate, she put him in his swing. He began to jump and noticed the wooden tools on the bar in front of his swing. Soon he would get tired so Kari turned on soft music and they both dozed.

When Daniel came in for dinner and to check them both, he noticed that Kari had her crutch out again. He also noticed her eyes had dark circles and wondered if she was sick. Danny was in his swing and playing with his tools. When Daniel and Kari sat down to have dinner, the table was already set. Kari asked Daniel if he would serve their dinner, which he was glad to do.

As they began to eat, Kari soon put her fork down and told Daniel she had to talk with him, either during mealtime or afterward. She seemed a bit nervous so Daniel said, "Well, let's just eat and talk." Kari seemed to relax and took a sip of water and told Daniel that she had seen Dr. Little today. Kari told Daniel that she was pregnant, the baby was not growing well, and Kari wasn't eating enough. She started crying and told Daniel that Dr. Little had asked if she wanted an abortion under the circumstances of rape. She told Dr. Little that was not an option for her. She would carry this baby and love it and rear it the best she could, no matter if the baby was mixed race. Kari told him about the Church she had attended before she moved here.

Her previous pastor (Pastor Joe and wife Camille) knew about all that had happened. They had taken care of her as if she were their own daughter. Daniel asked if they caught the man that did this to her and she said, "I don't know." The rapist had kicked her in the pelvis, cracked her left leg and bruised her face and chest badly. The rape, beating and grief/shock over her husband being killed, had caused her some rather severe emotional problems. She was working when the ambulance brought him in. They were only married a few months, but had gotten along fine. She had also been followed for a while wherever she went. The police seemed to know nothing and they gave her no report of the autopsy, although she knew he had been shot. Frank had left a large insurance policy to be paid to Kari in the event of his death.

Occasionally during the supper talk, Daniel would ask a question which didn't seem unusual to Kari and therefore she answered. They finished dinner and Daniel told Kari to go lie down a while. He would clean up and take care of Danny. She said, "Okay but don't forget to feed him and change him into his night clothes." She also put on her night clothes and kept a small light and the fireplace on. In a few minutes, Kari was sound asleep with a childlike snore.

While Daniel had tidied the kitchen and took care of Danny, his mind was racing. Kari had told him more than she knew. As Chaplain for the entire police force, he had access to the Chief of Police and had a good relationship with him. He would find out about what had happened to Kari. She had mentioned the small town and hospital where she had worked. For some time, his Chief of Police had heard rumors of drugs that were being smuggled in to the counties around. Kari had also told him about her house being 'a war zone'; when she, Pastor Joe, and Camille went back to get Kari some clothing and things she wanted. Kari said, she would never again enter that house, plus she gave her car to Pastor

Joe to do with whatever he wanted. Daniel began to make a plan that he would keep quiet about except with his Chief and her lawyer, Wayne. By this time of night he knew he would not go out the door and risk awaking Kari, so he put Danny and the bassinette into the other bedroom and slept on top of the covers. He cared for Danny all night and loved it. He also knew he was in love with Kari, but he definitely wouldn't tell her that until the time came.

When Kari awakened the next morning she felt so much better, and she remembered she had not fed Danny all night, nor had she changed him. She turned over and saw Danny's bassinette gone. What happened? Then she smelled coffee and Daniel came out of the kitchen with Danny on his arm and smiled, Danny said to tell you 'Good Morning Sleepy-head'. "Did he tell you to get me a cup of coffee too?" "As a matter of fact, he did and here it is. You also have eggs and toast on the table." She asked Daniel how he got into her house, since she didn't remember giving him a key. "You didn't, but I haven't left. I slept on top of the covers in the other bedroom and got to know my son a little." "He is great! Yep, he sure is." Daniel left for work and to begin his plan to find out what happened to Kari and what he could find regarding drugs in the surrounding counties.

Since Kari was feeling so much better today, she found the instructions from the doctor who saw Danny and made sure of his birthday. She then began to address a few invitations. The birthday party would be next Saturday, at her house at 3:00 p.m. She began to make little place cards for each plate. She sent Daniel, Wayne and Linda, Sandy and Bob, and Joe and Camille a card.

Kari played with Danny, got his bath, dressed him and fed him again. He was beginning to show his own little personality. She knew when he needed changing, was sick or just plain cranky. It was time for his morning nap. She also took a rest before making dinner. She decided to make baked chicken breasts with cranberry and blueberry sauce. The side dish would be sweet corn mixed with pasta shells. She had the basics ready, and then took her rest.

When she and Danny awoke, they played for a while then changed him and gave him a bottle. Kari placed him in the swing he had begun to enjoy. He bounced and played with his tools, and occasionally 'talked and laughed' with them. Kari finished dinner and put the chicken breasts with sauce in the warmer. She put the pasta and corn on the counter and planned to put the spicy, white sauce on it just prior to serving.

While Danny was occupied, she tidied the house and put some clothes in the washer. When the washing cycle completed, she put the clothes in the dryer. She was beginning to get tired again and noticed that Danny had gone to sleep in his swing. She knew she would hear him if he awoke, so she took a rest on her bed. She almost always had soft classical or Christian music playing. That seemed to help her emotional status, which she understood might take a long while to become normal again. She was so easily frightened she knew her music helped her relax. While she was lying down, she thought she felt her baby move. She was thrilled at this sign of life.

Danny let her know he was awake and ready for her attention. She smiled thinking about him and got up to attend to his needs. They were simple enough, changing and a bottle and then some play time. She made a pallet on the floor in the great room and they played 'kick her hands'. She had placed some toys on the pallet, which she gave him, and got up to put the dried clothes away and finish dinner.

Daniel came in about six-thirty. He had an emergency because she noticed some blood stains on his trousers. He saw Danny on the floor pallet with all the toys, and got down to play a while too. Kari told Daniel that Danny could talk and Daniel looked at her sharply. Kari began laughing and told Daniel, "Well it sounded like talk to me." Daniel then started laughing as well. He seemed more relaxed than when he first came in. Kari began to tell him about Danny and her playing 'kick her hands' and talking to one another. Sometimes, she sang to him and he definitely listened. They got up from the pallet and Kari told Daniel that dinner would soon be ready. The table had been set and she told Daniel to sit down and she would serve their plates as soon as she could get the sauce on the pasta. That was fine with him.

He began to tell Kari about his day, a suicide of a young man and how horrible it was to see a young man who was so desperate. He also began to tell her about some of the things he wanted to see started at some Church or Community Center. Projects that cost little, but could show the younger people that life was a gift from God. If they could get some wise Christians to volunteer to be at the center, let the young folks know they had a friend and an opportunity to play sports or talk without being afraid of judgmental attitudes, it might save other lives.

Kari was listening intently, but it seemed Daniel had forgotten she was in the room, almost as though he was talking to himself. Kari stirred the pasta a little harder than needed and began serving them. Daniel looked up at Kari and asked, "Was I boring you?" "Absolutely not," she answered, she would love to know others with such deep compassion and care for the youth.

Daniel got up to leave and turned to Kari with a key to his house. She still did not know a house was nearby. Daniel asked, if she wanted to see some of the countryside? He would be home early tomorrow and they could all three take a ride. When Daniel came in early, she had Danny dressed for his first real outing. She also had a small cooler for his formula. She had purchased a diaper bag when she saw Dr. Little. It had essentials and she wanted to be sure that Danny wasn't bored or hungry. Daniel smiled to himself; she sure did act like a mother.

Daniel put the car seat in the car and strapped Danny in. No fuss, no bother. He seemed like a very contented baby. They began their ride and Danny was soon fast asleep. They chatted while Daniel showed Kari around the property past her own, told her about a few of the neighbors close by to him and then they arrived at Daniel's house. Daniel invited Kari inside, but Danny was still asleep and she knew she would not leave him and that she knew not to try to lift him in the car seat. Daniel noticed her slow response and realized she was not going in without Danny. He went around the car, un-hooked the car seat with Danny and they went inside. Kari had to use the key that Daniel had given her. His house was much larger than hers and had a more modern look, but she liked hers better.

While they were checking his house, Danny awoke and was demanding something. Kari took him out of the car seat, put a small blanket on Daniel's couch and took Danny's very soiled diaper off. She put the dirty diaper on the floor and carried Danny to the bathroom and cleaned him really well. She brought him back, wrapped in one of Daniel's hand towels. She put him back on the couch and put a fresh diaper on. Danny still wasn't through fussing, seemed he also needed his formula. Kari always ran the bottle under hot water to take any chill off. Danny was more and more displeased with his arrangement. Kari talked softly to him and found a chair and sat down to feed him. This quieted him and soon he began talking to Kari. Kari looked at Daniel who had a slightly bewildered expression. "How did you know what Danny needed?" "I told you we talk a lot." Daniel started laughing and said she had a better understanding of baby language than he did.

Daniel went home and Kari began to think about what he said about wise adults who would be non-judgmental with the youth and young adults who were often neglected. Kari decided to call Camille and tell her what Dr. Little had said about her baby. Camille wanted to know how Kari was doing. Kari told her about baby-sitting two and half month Danny. She also told Camille about the baby's dad. "He is the Chief Chaplain for the entire police force of the town."

Kari's phone call told Camille more than she had known and could tell that Kari probably cared about him, as well as the baby. Camille interrupted and told Kari they had received a birthday card from Danny Meyers. Camille thought that was such a great idea and asked what she could do to help Kari. Kari said, "Just come up and visit and meet Danny." They chatted a few more minutes and Kari asked Camille if anyone had heard about who attacked her and the end result of Frank's autopsy. She nor Joe had not heard or seen anything out of the ordinary. They soon said good-bye and Kari prepared herself and Danny for bed.

Danny was sleeping for longer periods at night and awoke very in-frequently. They got up and Kari dressed, she noticed she had lost weight instead of gaining. She also had not felt her baby move in a while. She did have a small bulge in her tummy.

She dressed Danny and they ate breakfast and Kari decided they needed to take a walk. It was a bit chilly, but they both had coats and hats. Daniel had bought a covered stroller for Danny. That made it easier for Kari to push him along and they could both get fresh air and enjoy the view. They strolled along a while and Kari again noticed her creek. It was still muddy; she wondered why it seemed to always be muddy. Danny didn't know, so they started back home. Outer garments came off and they played on the pallet a while. Kari did some washing and planned dinner for tonight. When the washer went off she put the clothes in the dryer. She been thinking of the menu for Danny's birthday party and began to write the necessary ingredients, plus she wanted another side dish. She planned on corn and pasta with a spicy white sauce. She really liked that dish.

Kari hadn't noticed the time, but Danny let her know he was hungry and needed a change. She dried him and fed him and they both took a rest. He was so precious; she wished she could keep him forever. However, if wishes were horses, we could all take a ride. She napped a little while Danny was asleep. When they got up she changed him again and put him in his swing while she prepared dinner. She prepared a meat and red bean casserole. She also roasted broccoli, brussel sprouts, and carrots with spices in olive oil. She made a bread pudding for dessert.

Kari began to finish her place settings for Danny's birthday party, even if the adults didn't want a hat, well Danny might. She called Sandy and chatted a few minutes and they were all coming to the party. Sandy thought that was a great idea. Kari also checked her camera. She had been taking a few pictures of Danny, but she especially wanted one at his party. She made sure that she had tidied the bathrooms, bedrooms and kitchen and put the clothing away.

It was only two days before his party, so she made sure that Pastor Joe and Camille had clean sheets and towels. She had planned to get a vase of flowers to put in their room and some chocolates, but forgot to put them on her list. Well, maybe tomorrow, she would ask Daniel to bring a small vase and chocolates. The great room and kitchen were spotless except for Danny's pallet. He had not turned over by himself yet, but he definitely tried and scooted around on the pallet. She had never liked the idea of a playpen for him, so she had not mentioned it to Daniel. They had not talked about getting a larger crib, but he was growing well and probably would need one soon.

When Daniel got home, everything looked good and smelled awesome. He again thought about the love he felt for Kari, but still had not told her. She had not indicated any feeling toward him except a friendship that was growing warmer. Kari came out of the kitchen to say "Hi" and Danny was 'talking' too. He went over and patted Kari. He said, "Something smells great." Then he went to pick up Danny and said, "And it sure isn't you big man." Kari realized she hadn't changed him in a while and took him to change him and clean him up. Daniel felt bad that he made that remark, it might sound to Kari that he was complaining. So, he went into the bedroom and took over that process and told Kari to relax, he was only making a feeble joke. They both laughed together, when Daniel had failed to put a diaper in front of Danny, he gave his daddy a good 'spray'. "Well," he said, "I'll know better next time." He asked Kari if she wanted him to run home and change clothes. "Of course not," she said, "Even Danny's pee is perfume." Now let me finish here and we will have supper, still laughing all the time.

They sat down to eat and Daniel said he got a cute card from his son for his three month birthday. "Who do you suppose sent that, he can't reach the mailbox?" Kari said, "Well, maybe I helped a little, but he thought it was a great idea and he needed a bigger bed." She told him that when Danny was kicking, the little bassinet would wobble. Kari asked Daniel if he minded that she planned this party without his permission. "Of course not, I hadn't even thought of that but it's a great idea." Kari told him that Sandy and Bob were coming, as well as Wayne and Linda and Pastor Joe and Camille. She told him that Pastor Joe and Camille might stay a few days for a visit. She was quiet excited about them staying. They were the closest thing to parents she had and that she loved them.

Daniel helped her tidy the kitchen and asked what he could do to help. She asked him to get a small vase with some flowers and a box of chocolates for their bedroom. He readily agreed. When it was time for Daniel to leave, he reached over and kissed his son and gave Kari a hug and a thank you. She didn't pull away, but she didn't respond either. As he opened the door to leave he said, "I'll see you guys tomorrow." Kari smiled and said, "Goodnight."

THE BIRTHDAY PARTY

Kari and Danny awoke about the same time the next morning. "Oh, Danny today is Saturday and we are celebrating your three month birthday. Isn't that great?" Danny just babbled. She stayed in her night clothes until after she cleaned and dressed Danny. She decided to leave him in some dry pajamas until closer to the party. They ate and Danny swung and Kari began preparing for the dinner party. She had most everything ready, just needed to put some things in the oven and set the table. She had already decided she would serve buffet style and they could all enjoy the great room with the fireplace. By the time all the preparations were done, it was time for her to dress and put on some make-up, which she hadn't done in a good while. She put on a pretty sweater and skirt and flat shoes. The sweater was a robin's egg blue with some small flowers around the neckline and her skirt was navy. Everything was clean and the food smelled wonderful. She realized that she had not taken a break all day and Danny had taken a long nap after lunch.

Daniel came in about one o'clock with the flowers and chocolates and put them on the dresser in the other bedroom. He then turned to Kari and asked, "Does that look all right?" Kari smiled and said, "Just right." That was the first time Kari had stood so close to Daniel and he hugged her and this time she hugged him back. Daniel said, "Before we dress Master Danny, I have something to tell you." "What?" Kari asked. Daniel answered and said, "Kari I love you, and I would like to marry you. You don't need to answer, just please think about it." Kari shook her head yes. They got Danny dressed in a little outfit Kari had picked up when she planned the party. He was so cute; she just had to take a picture. Daniel was holding him and she snapped the picture. Daniel looked up rather surprised that Kari had taken a picture. Kari told him she had kept a record with pictures and notes on his progress.

Just then the doorbell rang. Kari moved quickly to the door to be enveloped in Camille and Pastor Joes arms. They began chatting away and Kari introduced Daniel and then smiling broadly then introduced Danny who took it all in stride. They sat down in the great room and began to get to know Daniel and Danny. Camille couldn't keep her hands off Danny.

In a few minutes, Sandy and Bob, Wayne and Linda came in and began to admire Danny. They talked together for a while and then Kari announced dinner would be buffet. So everyone got a plate and came back to the great room and ate and talked quietly for a good while. Then it was dessert time. She took the cake out of the refrigerator and they served themselves along with coffee. Kari also had prepared a tiny spoonful of ice cream and cake for Danny. She put his hat on, but he would not have it. He was more interested in something he had never seen. Kari gave him a tiny bite and, of course, he chewed, spit and seemed to want more. They were all laughing and it was a grand scene, at least for Kari. She took more pictures and went to put the camera down.

TO THE HOSPITAL

Kari came back into the room to join the conversation, but first she had to refill her coffee cup. All of a sudden Kari cried out, blood was gushing onto the floor and she knew she was losing her baby. Camille and Daniel were by her side in a flash. Daniel asked Camille to please take care of Danny, that he was taking Kari to the hospital. Sandy and Bob, Wayne and Linda followed him. Daniel wrapped her in a large blanket, picked her up and Wayne drove them to the ER. Sandy, Bob and Linda followed in another car. Kari wept silently the entire short trip to the ER. Daniel took her right into an ER and asked for Dr. Little. Almost everyone in the ER knew Daniel because of his work. They immediately put her on a stretcher and started an IV and oxygen due her blood loss. The ER nurse called Dr. Little and she was on the way over. The ER physician checked Kari and she asked him, none to pleasantly, please save her baby. He didn't answer, but knew the baby was beyond saving.

Camille and Joe stayed with Danny and prayed for Kari. How could one young woman endure so much? Of course they both knew God has a plan for every life and He would see her through this as well. The phone rang and Joe picked it up. It was Daniel and he told Joe, it looked like Kari was definitely losing the baby. Her doctor had just come into the ER and knew Kari had to have a D&C. She was bleeding too much and might need blood. He signed the release form and they took Kari to surgery. Daniel followed close by until the Operating Room was open and then they scooted him out. Wayne would stay with him and the others went home to wait for any information.

Daniel called to report on Kari and told them that she had lost the baby and they had her in surgery now. He told Pastor Joe, "I know you and Camille love Kari, but I do too. I have asked her to marry me, but she has not given me an answer." Joe smiled at Camille and while Daniel talked on, Joe told him not to worry one bit about Danny. He told Daniel some of the emotional trauma Kari had been through. Daniel said she had told him some of the things, but he had no idea how emotionally frail she was, but he had kept a close eye on her. He again told Pastor Joe how much he loved Kari and asked for their prayers.

After he got off the phone, he went into the waiting room where Wayne was still waiting. Daniel told Wayne that he really loved Kari and, no matter what, he would look after her. Wayne smiled and said, "Seemed everyone including the Police Chief knows that and assured him of all the best wishes." Wayne told Daniel how badly Kari looked when she came to see him. He knew she didn't trust anyone and that he was very gentle with her, and handled as much of the legal work as she needed. Wayne told Daniel he had seen a remarkable uplifting of her spirit, but he wondered what this latest trauma may do to her.

In about forty-five minutes, Dr. Little came out and talked to Daniel. She told him that Kari had had a miscarriage, however she had stopped bleeding. She was coming out of the light anesthesia and asked if he wanted to see her. Daniel was on his feet like a bullet and went to the recovery room. Kari looked so small and frail on that bed. She was about five feet five inches tall and weighed approximately one hundred ten pounds; but Daniel felt as if his heart was breaking. The recovery room was almost ready to transfer her to her room and Daniel followed them. They transferred her to her bed and she moaned softly. Daniel held her hand and told her that he was here, and would not be leaving until she did. She looked at him for a long time and then said, "Thank you." Daniel asked the nurse to tell Wayne that he would be staying the night with Kari and that Wayne could go home if he wished. He would need a car to take Kari home the next day, when she would be discharged.

Wayne said okay and left. He went back to Kari's house to give Joe and Camille an update. They were glad to talk with him and asked how Daniel was doing. Wayne smiled, and said, "He's a wreck." They all laughed gently and said he had almost demanded that they understand he loved Kari. Wayne said Daniel was a good man, but had no idea how much he was cared about with the entire police force. Most of the officers knew about his concern about Kari, as well as his unspoken love for her. They had made several un-noticed visits to ensure she was okay.

When Kari was settled, she began to speak softly and Daniel could barely hear her and he realized she was praying and reaffirming that God had a plan for every life and that He had her little one in His arms. They had not told Kari the sex of her baby, because they were unsure. Kari prayed and told God she would have the baby cremated at the hospital and to please let him or her know Kari loved them. Her fatigue and anesthesia took over and she almost fell asleep. She looked at Daniel and asked if he would mind lying beside her. "Of course I will," Daniel replied. Through out the night the nurses kept check on her and smiled at Daniel. They noticed him lying on top of the covers with his arm protectively around Kari. Daniel was a tall man with a large frame and he was barely on the bed, but he would not sleep in the lounger in her room. "I'll be fine," he said.

BACK HOME

The next morning Dr. Little came in and discharged Kari, but gave some instructions which included not lifting anything over ten to twelve pounds, and take specific rest periods through out the day. Kari looked at Dr. Little and said, "Well I can't take care of baby Danny." Dr. Little said, "Not for about a week, but still no lifting until I see you again." She looked at Daniel and asked if she could still see Danny. "Of course, but you might have to fight Camille for him." She kept the hospital gown on and Daniel wrapped her in his big coat and off they went. "Do you think Danny will have forgotten me?" "Of course not, he's as smart as his father you know."

As soon as they got to the house, Daniel noticed that Camille had made a bed on one of the sofas for Kari to rest on. Kari smiled when she saw Camille and Joe, but her face fairly beamed when Pastor Joe brought Danny in. Danny started wringing and twisting to get out of Joe's arms to Kari. She hugged him, while still in Joe's arms, and talked to him and he began his own welcome home babble. Everything soon settled down and Camille went with Kari to put some of her own clothing on, some sweat pants and sweat shirt, with socks and bedroom shoes. Kari told Camille that the only pads she had were from the hospital and she'd need some tomorrow. Camille assured her that she would get some. Kari told Camille she wasn't allowed to lift anything over ten pounds for about a week and asked if she would put Danny in her arms when she got back to great room? "Of course!"

When they got back to the great room someone had put a large soft pillow in the rocking chair and Kari headed straight to it. She looked up and Daniel had Danny in his arms and handed him to Kari, and she whispered,

"Thank you." They all talked a while, but everyone knew Kari needed her bed. Camille came over and picked up Danny and had a bottle with her. She carried Danny, with Daniel right beside her, into Kari's bedroom and laid him with her and asked her to feed him. It was time for each of them to nap.

When they got back to the great room, Daniel told Camille and Joe how much he appreciated them. He told them that Kari felt by them as if they were her parents. They both smiled and said, "Yes she's that dear to us as well." They chatted a bit and then Daniel asked Joe if he had service on Sunday. He would not take Danny away from Kari and he would sleep on the couch all night and take care of them during the next week, but he needed to call the Police Chief and make him aware of where he was. Joe told him that he did have service tomorrow, but would be back the next day.

Camille would have none of it. She would stay with Kari and look after Danny, but Daniel was still welcome to sleep on the couch. Daniel laughed and said "Yes, and I won't wet the couch." They all laughed and they felt so much lighter in their spirit. Camille had already made dinner, but was finishing the last few things. They would have a late lunch and early dinner combined. When time came they all ate well. While Camille was in the kitchen, Joe and Daniel talked quietly.

Daniel told Joe that his Chief of Police had heard rumors about illegal drugs in several counties around where they lived. He said his Chief was checking with the SBI to see if they would intervene with the homicide of Frank and possibly find out if Frank was killed because he was involved. He told Joe the Chief would keep him informed on the progress. Joe told Daniel he was hearing rumors, but nothing definite, so he wasn't going to mention that to Kari or Camille. Daniel agreed. He reminded Joe that he was willing to wait for Kari to answer him as long as it took regarding marrying him. "No matter," he said, "I'm staying close." Joe smiled and asked if he could do the ceremony. "Of course, not a better man around, that I know of."

Daniel then told him about his own dream to get help for the youth and teenagers in a setting in which the 'kids' would feel safe with non-judgmental people around. He was still looking for a place in which they could do something productive with their time and also provide as much education as they needed to graduate from school. He asked Joe and Camille to really pray that this could happen.

In a moment they heard Kari scream. What on earth had happened? They all three rushed into the room and Kari was screaming and did not appear to be awake well. Danny decided to join in about that time. Camille picked Danny up and Daniel sat on her bed and gently lifted her up. She awoke then and wrapped both arms around Daniel, crying all the while. Joe quietly left the room.

Daniel held her and rocked her as a child until she could calm herself. She finally stopped sobbing and tried to find a tissue and could not find anything, which started another round of sobbing. Daniel got her the box of tissue and talked quietly to her, telling her again how much he loved her. She quieted and seemed to relax. She looked straight at him and told him that she thought she loved him too. But she had thought she loved Frank and after the initial shock and trauma of his death, with no actual knowledge of what happened to him and why; she couldn't be sure she knew how to love. However, she thought she really did love him. He kissed her and his own heart was about to jump out of his chest. Daniel said, "Yes, you do love very deeply and I understand that the shock of losing Frank, the rape, and miscarriage was indeed a reason to doubt yourself 'a wee bit'," but he indeed loved her and believed she would grow to love him, without the fear. "Daniel, there is one thing I need you to tell me." "What?" he asked. "Do you love me or feel pity, there is a huge difference." He smiled and said, "Oh yes there is a difference and my love for you is until the Lord takes me home." Kari looked at him and he thought she could see his soul, Kari looked so straight at him and said, "I do love you and yes, I know the difference as well".

Kari looked up at him and said, "I ask this one thing from you, don't ever lie to me." Daniel looked straight back at her and said firmly, "I don't lie!" She reached up to hug him and this time she kissed him. When she did her stomach rumbled and she started to giggle. "Wonder if Camille might have a 'crumb of supper'?" Daniel laughed and said, "Let's go see." They came out of the bedroom holding hands and Daniel said to Camille, "Kari is hungry and she wants to know if you have a 'crumb of supper' left." Camille certainly had 'more than a crumb' and she better eat. There was still birthday cake and coffee to finish.

While they were having cake and coffee, Danny let it be known that he was hungry too. Joe had played with Danny on the pallet for a long time. When he picked him up, Joe said, "Oh my, how do I fix this?" Kari started to get up and realized she wasn't supposed to lift him. That almost brought on another crying episode. Daniel said, "Oh, Kari taught me how to handle this, come on and I'll show you." They took Danny into Kari's room and proceeded to change him and put another outfit on him. Daniel said to Joe, "You know, I had no idea what a fantastic job Kari had done with Danny. I've paid her nothing, but bought all the groceries and supplies she needed. That's the way Kari wants it." "I feel bad that I didn't insist, but you know how reserved Kari can become if you push, so I've done what she asked." Joe assured Daniel that Kari wanted to take care of Danny. Anyone could see how she lit up when Danny was around. I think Danny has and will help Kari through this latest trauma.

They went back to the great room and Daniel took his now dry and clean son to Kari who was already in the rocking chair. He placed Danny in her arms and Camille had his bottle ready. They talked and relaxed for a long while and Joe finally got up to go. He turned to Kari and said, "You have a double or triple job to do until I return. I'm leaving my wife here with you and Danny will help look after her and his dad. Your only job is to supervise with Danny's help. Your "Papa Joe" will take care of these older babies, if they don't behave." Kari looked at Camille and Daniel and they were both grinning from ear to ear. Seems they had pulled a 'fast one' on Kari and she looked at Danny and asked if he was involved in this arrangement. Danny just babbled and went back to his eating. When it was bedtime, Kari and Danny slept in her room, Camille went to her room and sure enough, Daniel slept on the couch.

THE CHIEF NEEDS TO SEE DANIEL

On Sunday morning, Daniel told Camille that he needed to go see the Chief for a while today. Kari asked, "On Sunday?" "Yes," he said back. "I'll be at the Chief's home," and he gave Camille the number if he was needed for anything. They finished breakfast and another cup of coffee. Danny let it be known that he needed attention. Daniel went over and kissed him and Kari and on the cheek, since it was time for him to go.

Daniel got to the Chief's house about ten-thirty that morning. He told the Chief the latest he'd heard from Joe and asked if the Chief had heard anything from the SBI. "First of all, Daniel, my name is Carl, when we're at work, the name is just, 'Chief'." "Understood," Daniel replied. Carl asked about Kari so Daniel told him what had occurred and how she seemed stable at present. Pastor Joe was coming back tomorrow and would tell Daniel anything he had found regarding the investigation.

Wayne has in his private bank box some information that Kari asked him to keep in the event it was needed. She did not know the language and could not read it. The material was in the tackle box where she found her insurance papers. "Wayne did not tell me, but Kari did. You might, at sometime, mention it to Wayne."

Carl reminded Daniel that things had to be kept quiet for now; however, he thought there might be a break rather soon. Carl did not know, until last night, that one of the agents had a big lead that might result in an arrest of the police chief and one of his deputies; regarding drug running in Kari's old neighborhood. Daniel knew better than to ask Carl any details and he really didn't care to know, except anything that might cause Kari pain. "Well, this much I can tell you; Frank was a 'big man' in the drug smuggling." He assured Daniel that Kari was innocent of everything, except making the wrong judgment in her choice of husband. She had been checked thoroughly by the SBI. Her background revealed that she was without parents or siblings, but her uncle and aunt had reared her and educated her. She was an honor student in her nursing classes, worked hard as a nurse, mostly in the ER, and was more involved in her Church than she made known. She seemed to gravitate to the youth in the Church and community. Carl figured it was because she looked like most of the youth around and seemed to like most of the activities in which she was involved. "Kari is not a saint, Daniel. She has a fierce temper and she disagreed with a speeding ticket she got. She chose on her own to go to court and told the judge just how much she was speeding. Seems like she was singled out to be ticketed or warned about any minute violation she committed, but after demanding to go to trial for the driving/speeding ticket and shouting at the policeman, the subtle harassing stopped."

Daniel laughed out loud. Carl said, "What's so funny," and Daniel told him that he had been on the receiving end of her temper when he came to get his baby. She definitely was not intimidated by his size or demeanor. She stood in the doorway and refused to let him in until she showed her his ID picture. He said that he never mentioned that she was using a crutch, to her. She finally stepped back and motioned him to come in. Carl said that Kari had really been badly beaten, besides the rape. The man could have easily killed her, but that was not his motive. It was a short time after Frank was killed and the man wanted to know about the money. It seems Frank had told someone that he had a large insurance policy on himself for her, in the event of his death, along with some 'insurance for himself'.

Daniel got up to leave and thanked Carl. He told him that he would be back in his office tomorrow, because Camille was staying with Kari and Danny. He stopped by the store and bought flowers for Camille and Kari; he also picked up a large box of 'sanitary napkins' that Camille had asked for. He went on to a furniture store and bought a small crib for Danny. Seems like he forgot something and the sales lady told him, "You might need sheets and a 'bumper pad' for the crib." She got all the things she thought a four month old would need for visual stimulation, music and more 'tools' for Danny. Daniel told the saleslady that he had never been a father before; he had no idea that babies needed so much stimulation. The saleslady laughed and said, "Well, they don't need it so much as most mothers think they do." She told Daniel she had three children and one grandchild and that it shocked her when her daughter felt her baby needed all this. They smiled at each other and Daniel was outfitted with everything the saleslady thought necessary for Danny and Kari.

He got home and first of all, went into the kitchen where Kari and Camille were having coffee and talking. He brought the flowers in, gave Camille hers and then gave Kari her flowers and a kiss on the cheek. He told them he had something else to bring in, so he went back to the car and lifted the trunk and brought out a big box and two large bags of something. Kari asked, "What in the world have you got there?" "Well, wait and see Daniel answered." He asked where Danny was and about that time, Danny let out a whoop and of course he was on Kari's bed.

Daniel handed Camille a smaller sack and asked them to come into the great room. He unboxed the crib and began putting it together but stopped short and asked Kari if this was what she wanted for Danny. Kari said, "Yes, that is perfect." Daniel finished setting up the crib and had to go back to the car for the mattress and other necessities that the saleslady told him he needed. He took out the bumper pads, chimes, and tools that were supposed to stimulate Danny's awareness of things around him. Kari was so happy that she hugged Daniel while Camille just smiled. That must be one smart saleslady, she thought to herself. He opened the sheets and started to put them on the mattress and Kari said, "No!" "They have to be put through a dryer cycle to insure no germs and for softness." Camille took all the sheets and put them in the dryer with a fabric softening sheet, all the while chuckling to herself. They already acted as a couple.

While Camille was working with the sheets, Daniel told Kari he almost bought a playpen, but the saleslady told him that he better check with his wife first. "Some young mothers did not want their off-spring 'caged'." Kari said, "That's absolutely right, Danny is not some little pet or animal, he is a baby that needs freedom to be on his pallet and learn to turnover and crawl." She completely missed the statement about young mothers. Daniel was glad, because of her miscarriage and because he wanted to please her. Kari began to play the chimes and inspected all the tools and toys and smiled. She also thanked Daniel for the flowers.

Danny let out another cry and this one was different, at least to Kari. She almost ran to her room to pick him up, but Daniel got there first. "Please,

Kari, remember what Dr. Little said about not lifting anything over ten pounds." "I'll pick him up and even change him if that's what he needs. I couldn't tell the difference from what sounded like an Indian whoop he let out a while ago, and the cry he just demonstrated." "Well, there is a difference," Kari said. "He was playing a while ago, now he is wet and probably hungry." Daniel smiled and said, "Oh, well then I'll change him and bring him to you in the rocker." Kari said, "Fine," but she stayed close by and cooed at Danny, who talked back. Daniel decided it's now or never, so he told Kari that they celebrated Danny's birthday beautifully, but Danny turned four months instead of three. Kari's face fell, how could she have made that mistake? Daniel said, "Probably because I forgot his exact age until I got home and looked at his birth certificate." "Oh Daniel, I'm so glad you saved the info from the hospital so now I can put it in his baby book that I have in which to put his progress and pictures."

Daniel picked the now dry, but fussy Danny into Kari's arms. She rocked him and talked to him, but Danny started to whimper again. "Well I guess you really are hungry." She asked Daniel to bring her Danny's bottle, but please run it under hot water for a few minutes to take the chill off. Daniel went into the kitchen to get a bottle for Danny out of the refrigerator. He asked Camille, who had almost finished with the sheets, if all new fathers felt pride and bewilderment at the same time. "Of course!" Camille said, "You have had a total change in your life now. Not only do you have a new baby to care for, but probably a new wife. That takes some 'getting used to'." The crib sheets were done and they really were soft. Camille and Daniel took the sheets into Kari's room and put them on his new bed. Kari was rocking the now sleeping Danny and she looked as if she was falling asleep as well. Camille picked Danny up and placed him in his new bed. Daniel suggested that Kari take a rest too. She agreed and lay down on her bed. Daniel and Camille had some coffee and talked a while. It was about bedtime for all of them. Kari and Danny were sleeping in her room and suddenly, she called Daniel and Camille to come. They found Kari lying on her stomach staring at Danny. He had scooted around and had almost turned over all by himself. He got twisted in the leg of his pants and began to really yell. Danny had a temper! Kari got her camera and took a picture. Seemed that camera was close by at all times. They all laughed and congratulated Danny, who cooed and took everything in stride. Kari had been awake a while watching him struggle, but she knew he could do it.

She smiled and let him play and went into the great room. After they talked a while, it really was getting late. Daniel had to work tomorrow, so they all got ready for bed. Kari went into her room to change into bed clothes and changed Danny and put him into pajamas. She asked Daniel to make sure the crib sides were secure and please bring her a bottle, in the event he decided to eat again. Camille had heard and came in with the bottle. The crib was close to Kari's bed and she could reach through the crib slats to feed him or pat his back until he went to sleep. They all went to bed, Camille to her room and Daniel to the couch.

The next morning Daniel went to work and Camille and Kari had a good time with Danny. They were sitting at the table in the kitchen and Kari asked Camille if she could ask her a personal question. Camille answered, "Of course Kari, what's troubling you?" Kari said that Daniel had asked her to marry him, but she honestly didn't know if she loved Daniel, or what she felt was gratitude for all his help. "Also, while I love Danny with all my heart, I don't want Daniel to think that is the only reason I'd marry him, if he still wants me. You see, Camille, I know that a marriage will work when both partners love the Lord and each other." "A perfectly wonderful baby is 'icing on the cake'. Can you tell if Daniel truly loves me or needs a mother for Danny----that's not what I meant! Camille, I still don't trust myself to make right decisions. I know that I'd truly give up if I made another bad judgment call. I don't want to ruin anyone's life." "You and Joe seem to adore one another, and has even grown in the last few years that I've known you. Do you think that might be the way Daniel and I could love one another?"

Camille looked straight at Kari and said, "I do know how Joe and I feel, but I also believe that you have a more mature love for Daniel than for Frank. Joe and I have been told by Daniel quietly and directly that he loves you and it would last until God called him home. Joe and I believe that Kari."

"One afternoon, when Daniel comes home early, why don't the two of you take a long walk and tell him your concerns. You have also indicated you love your house more than his and ask him if he would be willing to sell his house and maybe add a couple rooms to yours?" "The room Joe and I sleep in is very large, with a fireplace and long windows with window seats. I noticed your room is equally large with long windows and window seats. The bathrooms are really spacious and the walk-in closets are great. Seems you could have a room added to the top of you room and the room we sleep in as well. The windows of the sink in the kitchen have a wonderful well of light and the windows in the great room also have good light." Kari gave Camille a hug. "Your balcony could still be yours in which to read, write or study as you see fit." "Thanks Camille, I really appreciate your help, more than I can express."

Danny had just gone down for a nap and so Kari went to sleep. She wondered, as she dozed off, if she would ever be able to bare her soul to Daniel and not worry about what he thought of her. She also wanted to know him more deeply. She went to sleep with a slight smile on her face. Things were very quiet in Kari's room for a long while. Camille checked them both and Kari had one of Danny's hands in hers and he was sleeping like the baby he was.

KARI'S EMOTIONAL STATUS NOTED

Daniel and Joe got home about the same time. Camille had dinner almost finished and told them they could eat when Kari woke up. Daniel asked if she had been sick today or if she simply needed the rest. "She's not sick Daniel, but she has taken a pretty long nap with Danny doing the same." Daniel went in to check on both of them and Danny was awake chewing on Kari's hand. She woke up and asked Danny if he was going to eat her hand off. Danny babbled and Kari laughed. Daniel cleared his throat and they both looked up at him. By this time Danny knew his daddy's voice, as well as he did Kari's. Daniel said, "Well, I'll change you big boy, but no eating anyone's hands." Kari said, "I have to go to the bathroom and I'll be out shortly." When she came out, Daniel and Danny were waiting on her. Kari said, "Daniel, when you have some time one day soon, I'd really like to talk with you, but I need us to take a ride or walk." Daniel said, "Well, why don't we go over to my house and you can lie on the couch and I can use the recliner and we can talk, have coffee or I'll get some dinner brought in." Kari answered, "That might be best, but we'll have dinner with Danny, Camille, and Joe. Okay?" "Yep!" While they had been talking in Kari's bedroom, Joe told Camille that the two of them needed to talk. He found some information that affected the two of them.

Danny, Daniel and Kari came out and joined Camille and Joe, who had been talking quietly. "Well, supper is ready and we can eat now." Kari began to help Camille and they all sat down to eat. Daniel spoke up during dinner and said, "I'm coming home early tomorrow and Kari and I are going to my house for while, if the two of you can stay here with

Danny." Joe said, "That would be great," and that he needed to share something with Camille too, and that arrangement would work well.

It was almost time for Joe and Camille to go home, so Daniel would have to make arrangements for a while to have someone stay with Kari and Danny. Joe said, "Daniel it's no big secret, but my Church is having concerns about some rumors they are hearing regarding Kari's old house and possibly ours, so Camille and I need to go home to make some rather large decisions." "We would appreciate your prayers. Kari gave me her car and I've kept it at our house. Seems folks think that's pretty strange. We'll talk more with both of you once we get back."

The nest day was Friday and the week was rapidly passing. Both Kari and Daniel knew that whatever Pastor Joe had on his mind was serious and he needed his wise wife with him. So, about two o'clock, Daniel and Kari took a drive over to his house. They took a good look around his house and Kari had not changed her mind about the modern décor. She had not told Daniel how she felt about it. She asked if he had some juice in the refrigerator and he checked to see. He brought her a bottle of juice and himself a soft drink. Kari was on the sofa with her head next to Daniel's chest. Whatever Kari had to tell him, Daniel knew it was serious. She started talking rather softly and then more firmly. "Daniel, I know that I love you and if the offer is still open, I'd like to accept."

Daniel got out of the recliner and lay beside Kari. He knew there was more she wanted to say but he couldn't resist hugging her and kept his arm around her. Kari began talking to him and said, "Daniel, it is you I truly love, but please don't think I said this just because you have been so good to me or because I love Danny so much." "I have grown a lot in the last few months and I know the only way a marriage will work is for both partners to be dedicated first to God and then to each other." "I asked Camille if she thought I could make a sound, stable decision considering the past traumas. She assured me that I was a much more stable young woman now." "You see, I had contemplated suicide after the rape, police harassment, and Frank's death. The primary reason I didn't was because of the possibility I could be pregnant. Although I couldn't prove it, I felt the man who raped me was black, but even so, I would never destroy my child."

"I need to take a rest from talking for a while to get my thoughts together to continue." Daniel hugged her again and sat up beside her. "Listen Kari, I definitely do want to marry you and I really love you, and I am definitely called of God to do this Chaplain work. You don't have to be concerned about my thinking you would marry me because of Danny, because I know better!" "I love you for so many reasons; none have to do with pity or Danny, except my deepest thanks for your love for him. "When his own mother was going to destroy him, I thought I would die. There is too much innocent blood being shed. I thought I loved her, but very soon realized it was a mistake to marry her. She was interested only in the house and money."

At one time I was fairly wealthy, but decided to go out of business to serve the Lord. When I told her that, she was already pregnant and intended to abort 'this thing'. I begged her not to and told her I would give her whatever she asked to carry the baby and give him to me with no 'strings attached'. When she heard the sum of money I was willing to pay, she decided she would take it. One condition was to get prenatal care and send the bill to me, which she did. When Danny was born she didn't even want to see him. I had already talked to Wayne about what she wanted and asked him to deal with all legal ramifications. He was with me when she delivered and signed everything over to me. She never asked me over to see her or the baby, for about five weeks. The only reason then was to confirm her monetary state and her annulment. I even offered her the house, but she no longer liked it. It reminded her of this unpleasantness. I've never liked it because it reminds me of something I definitely am not.

"Oh, Daniel that was the next thing I had to talk to you about," Kari said. Kari told him she felt the house was rather cold looking and that her taste was exactly what she had built. She also asked Daniel if he felt by 'his' house the same way. "Absolutely not! The first time I saw your home, after you finally let me in, I thought how warm and comforting it was." This was not the time to begin hugging and kissing her, but he couldn't help himself and she kissed him back. "Well, Kari said, "If we are to marry, there are some additions we'll need on my house; which is, of course, our house. We will need two additional rooms. One like mine and one like Camille and Joe sleep in. They can be added on top of the two bedrooms, and never damage the look of warmth."

Daniel noticed that Kari was looking tired. He asked when she was to see the doctor again, she told him in another week, but would still be unable to lift anything over 10 to 12 pounds. "Also, Daniel, I'll be unable to have sex for at least 6 weeks, maybe longer because of some internal damage I had." "My dearest Kari, when we are married, it won't be just for having sex, it will be for making love and only when you are emotionally ready." Kari looked at him and knew then, there was only Daniel she loved. She said, "Well, I still like to be held and kissed occasionally. Danny kisses me all the time, but it just isn't the same," she said laughing. "That would be wonderful," Daniel replied.

Kari asked him if he thought he could sell his house and never go back in it, since he too had been hurt badly. Kari told him she had some money from the insurance Frank had left and they could live on that, but when they married she would like to be his wife and Danny's mother. She enjoyed cooking, and having occasional visitors for dinner with them. She said she had rather not go back to work unless it became necessary. She also reminded him that while he was looking for a Center to help kids and youth, to please keep on looking. She was sure they could find something and arrange for purchase. "You can talk to Wayne about the money, but that is unimportant to me except to help us with the things God would have us do."

At that time Daniel lifted her up and hugged and kissed her. He reminded her that he too had some money and a job that was adequate for them. Now, I think perhaps we need to get back home before Joe and Camille think we've abandoned them. They put on jackets and went back to the house.

When they got home, Kari went immediately to Camille. She knew she had been crying. "Okay, out with it!" "Camille you know I'm a good nurse and I love the both of you, so nothing can anymore shock or damage me." Kari glanced over at Danny who was asleep on his pallet. "He's been wonderful while you all were gone but I'm worried about you Kari when I have to leave you." "Oh, Camille I will hire a home care nurse to stay with us during the day, until Daniel gets home." Kari began to comfort Camille and told her they all loved her.

THE CHIEF NEEDS TO
SEE DANIEL AND JOE

Daniel and Joe were not needed in their conversation and so the two men went outside on the porch. Daniel got both of them a jacket because it was cold. Joe said, "Thanks Daniel, I'm going to tell you what happened while I was gone. When I drove into my driveway, I knew something was wrong. I looked over at Kari's car and it had the seats ripped open, the trunk open and the entire car stripped. Also, when I went into our house, or rather the Churches house, our dwelling had been ransacked. No one at the Church knew anyone who could do such a thing to the parsonage." Joe loved his elders and staff and believed them. The group went over to the parsonage and looked around and told Pastor Joe, they had to call the police and report this for insurance purposes. Joe did not disagree. It seemed as if their personal clothing and other things had not been disturbed. He went into his study and found his favorite Bible torn and cut; the first one Camille ever got him. Joe's voice cracked and he composed himself and said, "This is malicious. Why would anyone desecrate a Bible?" Some of his books had been thrown on the floor and a couple had their back spine split. "I know things can be replaced, but if my Camille suffers because of this, Well, I don't think I can bear that."

Joe told Daniel that he would like to see his Chief, even if it was Saturday. He needed to know what had happened to the parsonage and Kari's car. Daniel put in a call and sure enough the Chief wanted them to come over. Daniel told the 'girls' he and Joe were taking a ride, they would be over at the Chief's house. By this time, Camille and Kari were talking and even smiling some. Daniel asked, if you girls feel up to it, "I'm a mite hungry and I think Joe is too. Would you all make dinner and Joe, and I will be very grateful; or I can have dinner sent in?" Camille said, "Absolutely not, Kari and I need to cook, we're both pretty good at it, you know." "Oh yes," Daniel replied. Before he left he went over and gave Camille a kiss on the cheek and hugged and kissed Kari.

They arrived at the Chief's house and were warmly received. His wife had made them some hot chocolate and cookies were on a small plate. She quietly left the room. As they were enjoying the hot chocolate and cookies, Chief Carl asked Joe if Kari had ever mentioned a nurse she worked with called Joey. Joe said, "Oh yes, he was one of her closest friends and coworker. Why?" asked Joe. "Well it seems that Joey was so furious over Kari's insults and injury that he decided to play detective. It seems that since Joey was gay, he got into places that others would not normally frequent. He listened and observed and remained unnoticed, probably because he made no secret of his life style. He was approached by one of the guys and wanted to know if he wanted some 'good drugs'. Joey said, No, I'm not into that stuff, it'll eventually kill you. Joey laughed and drank a beer with several of the guys and said, he better hit the sack, he had to work tomorrow. He went to a friend's apartment and asked to use his phone." "Sure, I'm going out, crash here if you want to." Joey said "No, but thanks, my own phone has quit and I want to make a few calls." His friend left and Joey looked up the SBI and FBI numbers and called both. They wanted to meet him as opposed to speaking on the phone. They made an appointment for coffee in the morning. When the arrived; they questioned him about Kari, himself, and Frank, plus a few of his friends. Joey is not a stupid man, and he was frank with both representatives, however, he had a tiny micro-recorder in his shirt pocket. Joe asked if Joey was all right and Carl told him yes.

Carl told them about the SBI investigation into drug running in the local communities and counties. It seemed this was a large underground distribution area. The SBI had already infiltrated and was able to purchase several rather large deals of cocaine, heroin and other street drugs. They were not interested in the street runner except to use him to turn on the next man up, to save himself. Apparently Frank had been a rather high man in the operation, and was probably killed because of cheating the upper guys out of their cut. At any rate that's as much as he could share at present.

Joe said, "The reason I came to see you today, is to make you aware of things I found when I went home to hold services last weekend." Joe repeated his story to Carl and told him what the Church leaders had told him to do. The local police were notified and inspected the premises and assured them they would keep in touch. Joe and the Church leaders called the insurance company regarding the parsonage. No one even glanced at Kari's car or they would have seen damage done. Joe said, "I've heard and seen this dog and pony show so long, I'm fed up. I handed in my resignation as their pastor, effective immediately. Now my wife and I will find an apartment here to be near Kari and Daniel." They were not sure of progress from that point, but they knew God had a plan for them. They stood up to leave and Daniel thanked the Chief and asked him to keep in touch.

When they got in the car, Joe told Daniel he thought this officer was quite different in a positive manner. Daniel told him how long he had worked with the Chief and he had always been straight with him.

They got to the house and walked into a warm, great smelling house. Seemed Camille and Kari had spread a feast; they were both hungry because they hadn't eaten in a long while and because of their concerns. They all greeted one another and Master Danny decided he needed greeting too. "Oh, he's probably wet," Kari said and got up to go pick him up. Daniel took her hand and kissed it and said, "No, I'll lift him up." They took him to his bed and changed him and brought him to the table too. Camille brought Kari a bottle for him and then the men started eating. Camille and Kari ate some too, while Danny gulped his bottle. When Kari took the bottle away, Danny screamed at her. "Well I do know darling, you have a big appetite and a big temper." Kari had some dry rice cereal for baby Danny and she mixed it up. It was really a show watching him eat. "This might be a bit early with the dry cereal, but I've noticed the last few days that he still seems hungry." She decided that next week she would have the home care nurse she had hired, to take herself and Danny to the doctor. His office was just down the street.

They finished supper and dessert which was this marvelous coconut cake. They had their coffee in the great room in front of the fireplace. It was time for Danny to go to bed. Daniel and Kari took him to his bed, changed him and put on his pajamas. With a bottle, Daniel fed him and Kari lay on her bed until he was asleep.

When they got back, Camille and Joe had been talking and had apparently decided to tell Daniel and Kari what their plans were. Joe spoke to Kari and told her she needed to know what had happened to her car and the parsonage. Kari found it hard to believe, she said, "Joe if my problems have caused you and Camille hardship, I am deeply hurt and mad! You both have been so wonderful."

Camille and Joe interrupted her at the same time. "No Kari, this is just mean and someone looking for drugs or money. I did not go see your house, because the parsonage was wrecked." "After the usual calling police, the elders, and staff, I called the insurance company myself. I'm a patient man, but this last insult is more than I can or will stand. I resigned the Church, effective now. Camille and I are planning to move our personal belongings and move into an apartment close by here." Joe had already rented a U-Haul truck and they would pack next week. Some of the Church elders would help; others would not because he resigned. It no longer mattered to him what people thought, he and Camille had prayed until they felt their burden lifted. They knew this was the thing to do. They also knew that the Lord would provide their needs.

Joe told Kari about Joey and his own investigation. He had also told Joey how he felt regarding his lifestyle and he would pray for him. Joey told Joe that was something else he wondered about, his lifestyle. He said Kari knew all about it and told him in no uncertain terms that was against God's commands. She told me to read from the Bible (which I never had) in Romans. She went to her purse and got her small Bible out and found the passage he needed and then the passage on how to be saved from sin. God had provided his own Son to pay the price of sin, for everyone who believed in Him. Joey said, "I've been thinking about Kari a lot and I've read what she told me to. I love and respect her as though she were my sister."

However, "Joe, there is a girl that seems to like me and she is from your Church." Joe told Kari her name and Kari said, "Oh, Joe, she is the sweetest young woman, but won't take any 'guff' from anyone. She teaches school and can handle eighth graders well. Please tell Joey I'm thankful that he has decided to become a believer, and leave that lifestyle." "Joey is a good boy/man at heart, but got involved with a group with that lifestyle. I can't understand the term 'gay' and there were times Joey was very despondent. I'd go give him a hug and tell him he would never be alone, God promised to 'never leave him nor forsake him'; now get your butt in gear and help me with these trays. That was while I still worked there."

Kari then spoke up and told Pastor Joe, that was wonderful news. "You see this beautiful man here has asked me to marry him and I've definitely accepted. Camille told me she felt I was making the right decision this time."

Joe said, "Well, Kari, it seems that Frank had been involved rather deeply in the distribution network and was probably killed because he didn't give his superiors their total cut. At any rate, that is in the past, but I am definitely sure the SBI and probably FBI are now involved."

"When we are back this week, do you want me to sell your house? Even if you never intend to see it again, it is worth a good amount; if not for the house itself, then the land on which it sits." Kari said, "Sell it, burn it or do whatever you think is best." Joe said, "Well I don't think we have to go that far; besides arson is against the law." Kari had already signed over her car to Joe and Camille and then she got all the insurances and deed, and turned them over to Wayne. "Early Monday, I'll turn the house over to you. You need the money and you know I don't."

Camille asked Daniel if that was alright with him. "Absolutely", he replied. "I'm going to sell my house and we are planning to add a couple of bedrooms to this house." He told them that his house had never been to his liking, but his now annulled wife wanted it. He asked her if she wanted the house too? "No," she replied, "It reminds me of this entire mess you got me into." Daniel smiled and said, "Perhaps she was unaware of the money she just threw back in my face. No matter, I've got Danny without any strings and my beautiful Kari has agreed to marry me."

The mood lightened considerably. Joe said, "If I'm to marry the two of you, who will give Kari away?" Camille said, "I will." They had some more cake and coffee and just chatted until Camille saw Kari tried to hide a yawn behind her hand. "Okay, young lady, it's off to bed with you." So Kari smiled and said, "Yes, mistress." They were all laughing when Kari followed Camille into her room to help her get her shower and bedclothes on. Camille came out of the room smiling and told them she thought Kari had missed rest time today. "She was asleep almost as soon as her head hit the pillow."

Joe told Daniel that he and Camille had to leave Monday morning and that he thought Kari had already hired a home health nurse to stay with her and Danny, until she was totally, physically well. "I think she wanted to take that load off of you, Daniel." Daniel said, "It's no load, I'm not destitute and make an adequate salary to support them well." Joe said, "Daniel, don't hurt her pride, she wants to do this and that makes her feel more worthwhile. She told Camille and me that during the days and weeks after the trauma she went through, she thought seriously about taking her own life. She said the only reason she didn't was she suspected she might be pregnant with the child of an unknown rapist. No matter, she said, I could never risk destroying a life."

Camille told them they were having left-over lunch for dinner. "That's great," they both said at once. They heard Kari moving around in her room and soon she came out. "Is that dinner I smell? Seem as though I can't get full lately. Guess Danny isn't the only one who likes to eat." They sat down for dinner/supper and ate. There was light banter between them. Kari mentioned to them all that she had hired a home care nurse to stay with her and Danny until she was well. "The nurse starts at eight o'clock in the morning. She will also take Danny and me to the doctor, because our doctors are in the same strip of offices. I told her I couldn't lift more than about ten to twelve pounds, but I can cook. I told the nurse I would like her to do some light housework and that sometimes I get tired and rest when Danny does. The agreement was fine with the nurse."

Kari looked at Daniel and said, "You know I'm a good nurse and can pick one out who is competent and willing to stay with us until you get home." Daniel smiled at her and said, "I was going to do that on Monday." "Well now, you don't have to. You keep working and looking for that property we talked about. I have a feeling we will have caretakers among us." They both chuckled.

Joe and Camille came out of their room. "Well, young lady, it seems you've already decided what you want done." The food was finished and they took their coffee into the great room, to finish in front of the fireplace. "Every thing was wonderful," said Camille, "But I guess we all need some sleep. Eight o'clock comes early, but we'll be up with breakfast ready before we have to go." Kari said, "I will miss you both so much, however, I know you'll be back when you can." Camille and Joe went back to their room.

Kari looked at Daniel who had said little for a while. "Oh Daniel, did I do something to displease you? I'm truly sorry if I overstepped my border, but I felt like you needed less stress on you. Please tell me if I offended you." But before she could finish, Daniel stood up and reached for her and hugged her snuggly. He also kissed her rather a long time. "No, my dear Kari, I love to see you animated and decisive. It means you are getting over the trauma that you've been through. Oh, by the way, I love you and can't wait to marry you. Joe told me he was serious about tying our knot so tight, no one or anything could break it." Kari said, "I agree and I'm looking forward to our marriage. Please let's keep it simple, there is no need, on my part, for a fancy wedding. I would, however, like to have a new dress." Daniel said, "Well okay, but can I go see it with you in it before anyone else?" "Absolutely and I really want your input on whether the dress is pretty on me, if the color is right and if you really like it." "No problem, Kari, I love you so much, I feel like I might pop." They hugged and kissed for quite a while. "You are the dearest darling in the whole world. I love you, Daniel. Sleep well."

The next morning Kari got up while Danny and Daniel were still asleep. Daniel looked so sweet; she went over and kissed him. He opened his big brown eyes and told her that was a wonderful way to start his day. Kari smiled at him and headed to the kitchen to start breakfast. Daniel said, "I'll give Wayne a report and ask him to see you and Joe early. I know he has court tomorrow afternoon." "Oh, thank you Daniel."

A routine had developed since Camille had been staying. Daniel used her bedroom for a shower and shave. His work clothes were in a box in the closet. He kept thinking, Kari does love me and You know, Lord, that I love her. I pray Your blessing on today and keep Joe and Camille safe. He dressed and came out of the bedroom and headed to the kitchen for a coffee. Kari had made a big pot and was finishing up breakfast that she kept in the warmer. Danny decided to make himself heard and Kari and Daniel went to say good morning. Of course, he needed changing and a sponge-down and a clean set of clothes. They finished with him and got his bottle for Kari to feed him, while Daniel had his breakfast.

Camille and Joe came out of their room and ate breakfast with them. Daniel told Joe and Camille that he had called Wayne. "Wayne can see you and Kari about ten o'clock, if that's okay." "That's fine", replied Joe.

A little before eight o'clock the doorbell rang. It was Sadie, the home care nurse. She presented her credentials and introduced herself to Kari and Daniel. She seemed about Camille's age, but Kari was afraid that Daniel might not like her. They all introduced themselves again and Camille laughed; "Seems like you got a good deal with this nurse, Kari." They all smiled at one another and about that time, Danny decided he wanted an introduction. Sadie had already removed her coat and put her things on the end of the couch. She reached for Danny and he went to her babbling all the time. Daniel smiled broadly and winked at Kari.

Daniel was planning on more coffee with Camille and Joe. He said, "You were right, Joe. Kari needed to make this decision and I couldn't be happier." Daniel reminded him that they had an appointment with Wayne at ten o'clock. "Kari, are you sure?" "Absolutely," Kari replied. Joe, Daniel and Kari got up to go the lawyer's office. Kari asked if Camille and Sadie could look after Danny until they returned. Camille told Kari to 'get on with it'; "Sadie and I can get to know one another and I'll tell her something about his routine."

They met with Wayne at ten o'clock and he had the papers drawn up and two witnesses ready to verify the forms. They were Sandy and another girl that worked in the office. When the work was complete, Kari signed her old house and lot to Joe and Daniel grinned and witnessed too. Wayne told Daniel he didn't have to sign. Daniel said, "Puts me in practice for a far greater signature in a few weeks." They all laughed and left the office

Joe and Camille were ready to go. Kari looked like she would start crying. They both hugged her and told she would be fine, that Sadie and Danny would see to it. Daniel smiled and shook hands with Joe and kissed Camille on the cheek. "We've prayed that God will keep you safe and the trip easy. You are welcome here until you get your apartment, so don't worry about that."

After Joe and Camille left, Daniel asked Sadie if Camille or Danny gave her any trouble. Sadie laughed out loud, and replied, "No, I'm a pretty good fighter if the need arises". Sadie continued, "Of course not, they are both so dear. Camille made me feel right at home and showed me around the house. She said that Kari enjoyed cooking, but still wasn't able to do lifting or real cleaning. I did notice your balcony/office Kari, and it was a mite dusty. I took care of that this morning." Kari told her that she had been unable to get up the steps without her crutch and was afraid if she fell, Danny might need her, so she hadn't been up there. "Thank you, Sadie."

Daniel got up to go to work and bent over to kiss his son, and he kissed Sadie on the cheek. Her beautiful black face fairly shown then he went over and hugged and kissed Kari. "Take care of my loved ones, Sadie," and gave her a big smile.

When Sadie and Kari sat down to get to know one another better. Kari told Sadie why she couldn't do much heavy work. "Sadie, I was raped and beaten before I moved here. My husband had been killed just weeks before and I was an emotional wreck. Joe and Camille have been like parents to me. They cared for me so gently, but still understood I was emotionally frail. He was pastor at my Church and I had known them both for quiet a while. I love them so much and owe them my life." Sadie said, "I wondered why you had that far-away look when you first met me. I thought something bad had happened. I'm sorry, Kari. Now, let's get you a rest while Danny is asleep and I'll finish tidying up before we have to go to the doctors."

Kari went to her bedroom and took a rest period, although this time she didn't think she could sleep. She thanked God for all His blessings and sending Sadie to them. She awoke when Sadie called her to get ready to see the doctor. She had already fed and dressed Danny and put him on his pallet, in case Kari needed help with changing; "No," Kari said, "I'm going in these same clothes even if they are wrinkled a bit." She did touch up her make-up and then coats were put on all of the three and they headed for the doctor, first to Dr. Little for Kari and then to Dr. Lee for Danny.

When Kari saw Dr. Little, She did a complete exam and told Kari that she was healing nicely, but there was one small area near the cervix that wasn't, it would need about three weeks to completely heal. She also told Kari the blood and swabs they had taken revealed no sexually transmitted disease. Kari told her, that she had wondered about that. "Well, that is no worry. However, you will still have to take a rest period in the morning and afternoon." Although her uterus was back to normal size, the trauma she went through, plus the miscarriage had taken a big toll on her pelvic area. While she was asleep, in the hospital, Dr. Little had taken an x-ray to determine if her pelvis bone had been broken. It had not, but they did see a small healing fracture of the left leg. "That must all heal before you are 100%." Kari had gained almost two pounds and that was enough weight gain for the present; also no sex for about three weeks, maybe four, "I'll see you again in about four weeks."

Kari left Dr. Little, then she and Sadie took Danny to his doctor. Dr. Lee looked at Danny and told Kari he could hardly believe this was the same baby that Daniel brought to see him. Danny was sixteen pounds and twenty two inches long. He asked if she wanted his baby shots now and Kari said "No but he can have the DPT vaccination now, but I want to wait a month before the polio and other vaccinations are given." Dr. Lee agreed with her decision, but wondered if she was a doctor or nurse. Kari told him she was a nurse and didn't believe in all vaccines being given at one time. The baby's immune system was not fully functioning and that's why she wanted them given separately. Dr. Lee's nurse gave Danny the DPT and Danny let out a good hearty scream. Kari said, "I don't know if it hurt that much, but I think he was just mad." The nurse left smiling and Danny decided he was okay. Sadie picked him up and they went home.

Kari had turned pale again and looked totally exhausted. Sadie told her to go to bed for a while. "Oh, Sadie, I can't. I need to make dinner for Daniel." Sadie said, "I'm a pretty good cook too, so why don't I make a casserole and leave it in the oven warmer for you and Daniel for supper." Kari told Sadie that she was so tired and that it seemed she could do nothing anymore. "Well, you go to bed and leave Danny and Daniel to me." Kari kissed Danny and went to bed. Sadie told her to get in her night clothes and really rest. Kari did as she was told and almost went to sleep on her feet, but she curled up in bed with a quilt covering and definitely went to sleep.

In about an hour, Daniel came in from work. He kissed Danny and asked Sadie where Kari had gone. "To bed, Daniel, I insisted because when we got back from both doctors visit, Kari looked like she would drop. I told her to take a rest, but she would not. She told me that it seemed she could do nothing for those she loved. I told her I would make a casserole and leave it in the warmer. That way, you can make a salad and have dinner. I've also fed Danny and gave him rice cereal that Dr. Lee said was fine." She told Daniel that since Danny had had his first vaccinations, he might run a bit of fever, however, Dr. Lee told us what to give him. She showed Daniel the medicine and the now sleeping Danny and Kari. "Daniel, she told me about her traumatic history and I noticed today, she seemed to regress into herself. She is less secure than that 'bright' penny I saw this morning."

Daniel thanked Sadie for the meal and information regarding Kari. He told Sadie he knew she was emotionally frail, but seemed fatigued and not feeling up to making dinner had set her back some. Daniel assured Sadie that he was really thankful for her and the work she did. "Now, it's time for you to leave and rest yourself. I'll be right here with the two of them. When Kari awakes, I'll let her tell me what she wants me to know." Sadie smiled and said she hoped the casserole was to his liking. He said he was sure it would be; "Good Night and thank you, Sadie."

Kari awoke about six o'clock and realized she had slept about three hours. What on earth was happening to her? She heard Danny squirming around and whimpering. Kari said to Danny, "Oh, you poor darling, you feel like I do, just plain tired of it all." Daniel heard the talking and went into Kari's room to see her almost on the side of her bed, reaching to Danny. He spoke quietly, but Kari jumped and looked frightened for a few seconds. "Why is my light out? I always leave that small light on and the fireplace on low when it's cold. Did you turn my light off?" "No, Kari, it must have been Sadie; she left a little while ago." "Oh, I guess I didn't tell her to leave the light on."

Daniel spoke to both Kari and Danny quietly, and picked Danny up to put beside Kari. By the time he had picked him up and took him to Kari, she was fully awake. Kari told him Danny might be fretful for a while, because he had his first immunizations that afternoon. Danny was fully awake and yelling. "Poor baby, you are wet and hungry and your little butt must be sore from the shot." Danny was having none of this. He cried and yelled until he was turning red. Kari and Daniel sponged him down, changed him and put clean pajamas on him. Daniel then picked him up and carried him into the kitchen. Kari was already fixing his bottle and while she fed him, she told Daniel that the baby might need that medicine. She showed him a bottle of red liquid that she had placed on the table. After she fed him, he quieted down, but was still fretful. Kari gave him some of the medicine by eye dropper. Danny smacked like he liked the stuff. Kari and Daniel both laughed. "Daniel, if you will bring him into the great room, I'll rock him a while and he'll go to sleep." Kari had Danny snuggled on her chest and Daniel felt a little envious of his own son. My word, Daniel! "get a grip on yourself"!

THE ROUTINE CHANGES

In a little while, Danny was fast asleep and Daniel gently carried him to his crib. He came back to the kitchen and found Kari setting the table. He walked up behind her and gently turned her around and hugged and kissed her. "Now sit down and let me do the rest of the prep for dinner." "Okay," Kari replied. While he was making a salad and finished the table settings, Kari told him that she had seen Dr. Little today. She told him she was almost healed, except for a small 'still healing' area around her cervix. She told him what Dr. Little said about taking a film of her pelvis to insure no hair-line fracture was there. There wasn't on the pelvis, but she saw the fracture on her left leg had not completely healed. She must get some rest off her leg and she was still not allowed to pick up more than ten to twelve pounds, and she could not have sex for about four weeks. "Danny weighs sixteen pounds, and he is a healthy baby who is twenty-two inches tall. He's going to be tall like you, Daniel."

Daniel listed intently to her words and tone in order to learn anything that might help him to help her. He put the casserole on the table and made coffee. They said the blessing and thanked God for the good report. As they ate, Kari said, "I forgot to tell you I've gained two pounds and Dr. Little says that's enough for now. Daniel, I've been thinking backward for a while, trying to understand why I'm tired and emotional so much. I think my hormones have kicked into high gear after the miscarriage and the lack of patience I have with myself. The good Lord knows, I have very little patience to begin with and now to have to be patient a while longer. Well, I don't like it one bit! I can't care for Danny like I want to and Daniel I couldn't even make dinner tonight. Do you think I'll ever be normal again?" Daniel looked at her and chuckled. "Of course, my darling Kari. Your hormones are supposed to be in high gear about four weeks after such a trauma, and yes you are normal and I love you with all my heart. Now, have some dinner with me. I know it's not your cooking, but it is quiet tasty."

They ate quietly for a few minutes and Kari said, "Oh, I'm not to gain anymore weight." "Fine," he replied, "Because there is no dessert, just coffee." Kari finally smiled and told him that she loved him too.

Sadie had insisted she put on her night clothes and Kari had forgotten to change when she awoke. "Daniel, I just realized I came to dinner with no clothes on; let me re-phrase that; in my night clothes." Daniel laughed out loud and replied, "I noticed and believe me it was hard to keep my hands where they belong. I confess, had you come to dinner with no clothes on, my thinking would not have been on completing dinner, and Sadie would have my hide! Now, stop with the fretting and have coffee with me in the great room." "Okay," replied Kari.

They went to the great room and Kari lay on the couch that Camille had made up for her to rest. She heard Daniel tidying the kitchen and placing the dishes in the dishwasher. He came in to the great room with their coffee and they both enjoyed it. "Daniel, did you turn my light off in my room?" "No, dear one, I told you Sadie must have done that when she tidied the bedroom." "Remind me to ask Sadie to leave my light on at all times. This may sound strange to you, but I haven't slept a night without my light since all this stuff happened to me." Daniel said he would be sure her light was on all the time. "I'm sure I can learn to sleep with a small light on," he said, smiling at her.

"By the way, have you heard anything from Joe and Camille?" Daniel said "No, it's still Monday, honey." Daniel had seen the bottle of medicine that Dr. Little had given Kari. The instructions said to take one pill every six hours for rest and relaxation. Daniel wondered how long she would wait to tell him about her medicine. She had probably forgotten it, but Sadie had said she needed a pill tonight, before bedtime. Kari asked him if he had eaten enough dinner and he answered "Yes." "Daniel, I must have asked you the same questions over and over, I'm sorry for that. You see, I'm feeling very nervous and emotional and this is not like me. It seems that I can't do anything right. Poor Danny needs to be held more and rocked and cuddled and I can't even lift him. I'm fed up with this behavior of mine."

Daniel realized that Kari simply did not remember well, since her miscarriage. He had wondered to himself if she would ever be emotionally strong, like the woman who greeted him at the door, with fire in her eyes and pale as death, but she had spunk then. Daniel told Kari that she needed her pill that Dr. Little had prescribed. She said, "Yes, I didn't think I would need it, but Sadie insisted I get it and take it." "Well, my darling Kari, you do need it and I'm bringing it to you." He returned with the pill and a glass of water. In about twenty minutes of light banter with her, Daniel noticed that she was relaxing and her color was good. It wasn't long before Kari was sleepy and was going to bed. Daniel agreed and kissed her goodnight.

In about an hour, Kari called Daniel, rather softly since Danny was asleep in his crib. Daniel went into the room and Kari said, "Daniel, make love to me tonight. I don't care what Dr. Little said. I make my own decisions now." Daniel grinned in his heart; she really was getting spunky again. "Daniel, do I have to ask again, or didn't you hear me?" "Oh Kari, yes I heard, but this is not the time for either of us. First of all, it would be wrong in the sight of our Lord, secondly, we would regret it later, and thirdly, I will not risk your health." "Okay, but would you mind holding me for a while?" "That would be my pleasure," Daniel said. Kari reached for him and Daniel lay beside her and held her closely. Kari said, "Why don't you sleep in a real bed tonight and not that couch? I promise you'll be safe." Daniel laughed out loud at that remark and answered, "That too would be my pleasure." He held her until she was asleep and he too, went to sleep; on top of the covers.

They both awakened the next morning to Danny's cry, and looked at each other. Kari said, "I told you that you would be safe, I forgot Danny didn't make a promise." Kari stretched and tried to wake up completely. Daniel rolled out of the bed very quickly. He went over to Danny, smiling to himself; Kari had no idea how beautiful she looked this morning. He was glad Danny woke them, because with her stretch, she was a most provocative sight. Daniel picked Danny up and went to give him a sponge bath, dry him and put clean clothes on him. It was a good thing he had Danny in his arms, because about that time the doorbell rang. Whew, Daniel thought, just in time son, just in time to keep your daddy out of trouble.

Sadie breezed in the door, removed her coat and said 'good morning' all in less than a minute. Daniel said, "Sorry for not showering and shaving yet, but Danny decided he needed attention pronto!" Sadie took Danny and went to fix him a bottle, but she glanced at the couch and saw it had not been used. Daniel followed her into the kitchen to make breakfast, when Kari came in yawning. "I hope you've got coffee on," to which Daniel replied, "Yes dear." Kari went to the table and asked Sadie if she had a good night. Sadie said that she did. "I guess you want your son to finish feeding him." "Yes, I would love too." She didn't even notice that Sadie said 'your son'. That gave Daniel an idea; he couldn't understand why he hadn't thought of that before.

He ate, drank his coffee and hit the shower and readied himself for work. He had big plans today! He came into the kitchen where Kari and Sadie were talking and getting ready for their day. Daniel smiled and thanked Sadie for the casserole, kissed Kari and Danny and told all three to behave until he got home. They all laughed and Daniel left for work. He checked in and called Wayne. "Wayne, I wonder if you would tell me what it entails for Kari to adopt Danny." Wayne said, "Well, not much really, I'll make the paperwork and have it ready, when the two of you are ready. Why the big rush, Daniel, your wedding day hasn't been set to my knowledge." "Well, it hasn't," Daniel replied, "But I want to surprise her with this information, as well as an engagement ring just as soon as possible."

Things were quiet at the office so Daniel spoke to the Chief and told him what he planned. "That's fine, Daniel, let me know when you need some time off." At lunch, Daniel went straight to a jewelry store. He looked at so many diamonds, but did not have any idea what Kari would like. Kelly had wanted a large ring, but Daniel brought himself up short, Kari was not at all like Kelly. He kept looking and found a ring he liked, a beautiful one-half carat diamond set in platinum; within an orange blossom setting. The clerk asked him if that was what he wanted, and he told her "Yes, but I want the appraisal, along with the ability to exchange it, if needed." "Of course," the clerk replied. "That is a beautiful ring and any woman would love it." Daniel looked at the clerk, who had dark red hair and resembled Kari, to a point. No one would ever be Kari. He kept the ring and papers in his jacket pocket and got a sandwich. He went back to the office and kept looking at that ring; he was as sure as he could be that Kari would like it.

Daniel did some paperwork and decided to go home early. He got home and Kari and Sadie were cooking and laughing. Daniel went on into the kitchen and greeted both of them. Kari was smiling and said, "Daniel, you're home early; what do you need?" Daniel answered her, "I don't need anything, it was quiet today and I decided to bring myself home. I always enjoy seeing my future wife and son." Sadie smiled to herself; she had a feeling what Daniel might be up to.

She told Daniel that Danny had had another bath and change of pajamas. "You might want to put a washer of clothes on and then into the dryer. That will help Kari as she is finishing dinner." Daniel agreed and went to get the clothes basket. He loaded the machine, put the detergent in and walked Sadie to the door. "Thank you, Sadie, for helping Kari today, she seems so much better." "She is," Sadie said and Daniel she told me about the light. "That is pretty special to her and I'll make sure it is on. She also took one of the pills about lunch and took a good nap when Danny was down for his nap." "Thanks for telling me, I gave her one last night and she seemed to relax and sleep well." They reached the door and Daniel helped her into her coat and she said, "I'll see you all in the morning."

Kari and Daniel soon had a routine going. They ate dinner and played with Danny for a while, and then Kari and Daniel talked a while. Daniel thought it still wasn't the time to give Kari the diamond or talk about adopting Danny. She was showing signs of fatigue and he gave her the pill that Dr. Little ordered and Kari took it. "Seems you and Sadie are determined that I get rest. I didn't really believe I needed them and won't take them much longer. I will not get 'hooked' on pills. Got that?" "Got it," Daniel replied, His Kari was getting stronger, it amazed him at how having Sadie had helped her so much.

They had been lying on the couch for quite a while, quietly talking when the phone rang. Who on earth would be calling at this time of night? It was about ten o'clock. Kari said "Hello?" Joe and Camille were on their phone and began talking at once. They wanted to know how she was doing, what the doctor said, how they missed Danny and Daniel, of course. Kari began to laugh; "Number one; Danny is beautiful, weighs sixteen pounds and is twenty two inches long, number two; I'm healing nicely, but I still tire rather easily, number three; Daniel is great! He and Sadie make sure I'm okay. Now, how are the two of you doing?" She asked Daniel to grab the other phone so he too could listen. Joe spoke up and told them that he had put the house on sale with a reputable firm and the selling price would be about three hundred thousand dollars. "Oh, that's fine Joe", Kari said. "Now what did you do toward moving near here? I can look in the phone book for apartments to lease for a short while or with the option of a longer lease." Joe thanked her and Camille did too.

Daniel asked how the gathering their personal possessions and loading them was going. Joe said, "Fairly slowly, but Joey is helping us as much as he can before work. He is a fine young man, Kari. We also met his girlfriend, Leslie, who as you said, is a school teacher. She seems like a strong young woman." "She is," Kari replied, "And she'll keep Joey on the 'straight and narrow'." Camille told them they had help from Leslie as well, she comes in the afternoon and Joey comes in the morning. "It won't be long before we'll be headed away from here." Camille's voice became firm indicating to Kari that there must have been more than the usual packing. Kari said, "Camille, did anything else happen?" "Yes!" "It seems like some of our closest friends no longer wanted to be seen with us. These are people I really thought were our friends. Joe told me to stop letting the devil 'throw his darts'. Our Lord is able and willing to help us." Kari and Daniel spoke almost at the same time; "That's right!"

Joe asked Daniel if he would contact Wayne to be their representative when the house was sold. "Sure will," Daniel replied. "Oh, and have the two of you decided when you'll let me marry you?" Kari said, "Let me check my calendar; it looks like in about three weeks, if Daniel hasn't changed his mind." "Oh, I haven't changed my mind at all. In about three weeks, I'll turn twenty seven years old; think that is the marrying age?" He said laughing. "Just about perfect," Joe said in response. Then poppy-cock, Camille chimed in, "I'll barely have time to get a new dress, but I think I can be presentable by that time." Kari laughed and said, she hadn't got her dress either, but she wanted the whole thing kept very simple. "We'll have a few friends over for coffee and cake afterwards." "That sounds perfect, Kari. Well, we'll have to hang up now; bedtime comes early for old folks."

"We're really getting married aren't we Daniel?" "Yes, my darling Kari, we are." "No matter if I'm an emotional wreck right on?" "Makes no difference, we are getting married. I love you with all my heart." He got up to check on Danny, but he really wanted to get to his jacket. He put the ring in his pocket and came back to Kari, who was lying quite comfortably on the couch. "Kari, I did something without your input today." "What," she asked. "Daniel whatever you do, will be fine, even after we are married. You see, I trust you, Daniel and by the way, I love you too." Daniel lay down beside Kari and said, "Well in that case, I went downtown this morning, without your input and picked up this for you." He popped the box open and there sat the most beautiful ring Kari had ever seen. Daniel said, "I do love you Kari and I want you for my wife until death parts us." "Oh, my word," Kari said, "That's the most beautiful ring I've ever seen and it is even set in an orange blossom. Is it really for me?" "Well let me see, it's too large for Danny and besides he might eat it---yes, my darling it is for you. Give me your hand." Kari did so and the ring fit perfectly and really was beautiful. Kari reached up to hug Daniel and said, "Thank you", but before she could say anything else Daniel grabbed her and hugged her and kissed her hard. "Kari, do you like it?" "Definitely, why did you think I might not, you see it is like me, no one else."

Daniel laughed and almost cried, "I just wanted to please you, but I liked it so much, I really didn't know if you would." He kissed her again and said; "When do you think we can set the wedding? It seems a lot of people are inquisitive about the date." Kari looked down at the calendar and saw she was to see Dr. Little in two and one-half weeks. "I think we could set the date on the Saturday, after my check-up." "That is the best birthday present I could possibly get." "Why didn't you tell me it is your birthday, I can make some goodies for the wedding and your birthday cake as our Wedding Cake too." "That sounds great, my darling." Daniel asked Kari if she would take her pill now. You need to continue the good progress that I've noticed. "Well, okay, but can I wear my ring to bed with me?" "It is now yours, my love, of course." Daniel got her pill and she took it and started toward her room. "Daniel did you sleep okay last night? I did, but I forgot to ask you." "I sure did," he answered. She got to the door way and came back to Daniel and stood there like a little girl, "You forgot my hug and kiss." "Well, I do declare, seems like I did. Let's take care of that right now." He got up from the couch and hugged and kissed her and told her that he loved her. "Also, you don't know what it means to me that you like your ring." She kissed him, looked at her ring and reached up to kiss him again. In about an hour, Daniel had just dozed off, but he heard her call him. "Please sleep in here tonight, same promise is true. You'll be safe." "Okay, my pleasure," he said.

The next morning Danny awoke, mad, wet, and hungry. Daniel got up, took him to the bathroom and gave him a good bath. He was drying him in a great big towel and noticed the tiny bruise on his buttock. "It seems you really did get a shot." Danny did not want any thing, but his food. Daniel finished dressing him in a cute little outfit and was headed to the kitchen to get his bottle ready. The doorbell rang and Sadie was in. "It is really cold outside. They are predicting some snow later on toward the weekend. If you need anything I'll make an inventory and give you a list tonight." "That would be great," he told Sadie. "Well, I have a pretty good idea of what Kari likes to make, but if you think of anything else, let me know." Danny was still having a fuss so Sadie fixed him a bottle, warmed it and poured a small amount of dry cereal. She began feeding him, when Kari came in. While Sadie and Daniel were talking, she heard him making some coffee. "Daniel I would love a cup of coffee while I'm feeding Danny." She gave him part of the bottle and began to feed him his cereal. That had almost become a routine at breakfast time. Daniel hit the shower and shaved and dressed for work. He came into the kitchen and laughed out loud at the mess Danny was making with his 'big man' food. Kari said "I'm sorry; I know you just bathed him but I forgot his bib." Sadie said, "No harm done, I'll get one now." Daniel had heard on the radio last night, something about a shooting, so he knew today would be another rough one. He asked Sadie if she would mind working a little over today or at least stay until he got home. "Of course, I will." Daniel explained that his phone went off from the scanner and there had been gunshots fired. He kissed Danny and Kari and told Sadie he would be back as soon as possible.

Sadie asked if he often had to deal with that and Kari said, "Yes, it seems he is the only Chaplain any of them want. I guess because of his stable personality, it makes the other officers less apprehensive." Sadie said, "My-O- My, what have you got on your hand?" Kari smiled and said "Daniel picked it out and gave it to me last night. Sadie, he really loves me, no matter the garbage I tend to drag around sometimes." Sadie said, "Of course, he does honey. Anyone with two eyes can see he's crazy about you." "Well Frank never gave me a ring, just a tiny wedding band." Sadie said; "I knew his previous wife; she was on the town all the time to flash the big diamond she wanted and had gotten." "Sadie, how do you know so much?" "Because I've lived here sixty years and I read people pretty well. I often wondered what that dear sweet man saw in her. I worked for her for a while, when she left him. She really was bad with morning sickness and was furious about the baby. I think she was also really mad when Daniel left a lucrative job and decided to become Chaplain of the police department. Anyway, she told me if Daniel hadn't paid her an enormous amount of money, she wouldn't be going through this now. But 'he wanted the baby' and paid for her prenatal visits, but she never got excited when the baby moved. She simply didn't care, except it would soon be over." Kari shook her head, "I don't understand that."

Sadie said, "Kari, there are still some women who care little about their babies. My two children are married and one lives in Canada with her husband, and my son lives in west Texas with his wife. They are all Christian and no mother could ask for more, but I do miss them so. My husband died a few years back and that's one of the reasons I keep working. It is so lonely without him, but my Church Family is so close and they love me. Well, that's enough about me. It's time to start lunch and you are to play with Danny, while I get things started." Kari went to Danny's pallet and Sadie brought him to her. They played cars, trains, and 'chase the chicken'; whatever that means thought Sadie.

Sadie stripped the beds, the crib, Kari's bed and the couch bed and put the sheets into the washer. When they finished the washer cycle, she dried them and put the sheets back on the beds. She noticed that Kari and Danny were resting on the pallet, sleeping really, with Kari's arm around Danny who snuggled up like the baby he was. Sadie finished lunch and kept it in the warmer until Kari would awaken. It wouldn't be long before Danny was hungry again and they would both be up.

Sadie proceeded to tidy up the downstairs rooms and bathrooms and sat down to rest a few minutes. She had read the paper with her own coffee when sure enough; Danny began to whimper and then a full-fledged crying. Kari awoke, and Sadie got his bottle out and picked him up for Kari to feed him. Kari began the feeding and then noticed that the cereal was also ready. She put part of the formula in the cereal and fed him. He was really beginning to make less of a mess with food and more cereal actually went into his stomach instead of Kari's blouse or his shirt. Kari kissed him and he cooed. Kari asked Sadie to please put him in his swing, which she did. Danny played and swung for quite a while. "He is growing so fast," Kari said. Sadie said, "That's what babies do. We want to keep them little, but that is not God's plan."

Kari said, "Sadie, have you had lunch already?" "No," Sadie responded. "Well, let's eat then while Danny is satisfied." Sadie served their plates and they began their lunch. "Oh, Sadie, I forgot to tell you, Daniel and I will be married on this Saturday, pointing to the calendar. We definitely want you there. Joe and Camille will soon be back and I do so hope I'll feel better. Actually, since you have been coming over, I feel so much stronger and I want to thank you again. You've made it so much easier to sleep and stay off my leg, as well as your caring for Danny."

"That Saturday," pointing to the exact Saturday, "Is also Daniel's birthday. He'll be twenty-seven. I want to plan a small reception here at the house and have his birthday cake as our wedding cake." "Kari, that sounds great. Let's get some notes made, so we don't forget anything for Daniel to pick up. Get something like finger sandwiches, small petit fore, flower arrangement that matches your bridal arrangement." "Oh Sadie, I forgot all about the flowers I will carry and well as a table arrangement." Sadie replied, "I can take care of that. I do it all the time for the girls who marry at our Church. They seem to want me to make their reception. I never had one that they did not brag on." Kari went around the table and hugged Sadie; "Do you realize this goes far beyond nursing Danny and me?" "Well I want to," Sadie replied. "The week before the wedding I'll bring my own pans and decorating tools over here. Then you can supervise my design for yourself and Daniel. In fact, I can bring you some sketches over tomorrow to get an idea of what you would like." "That would be great, Sadie."

They had developed a good routine for Kari and Danny and it seemed time flew by. Danny rarely changed his routine of play, feeding and changing. He became a bit irritable that afternoon and Sadie said, "It must be from the immunization or it could also mean he is starting to teethe." "Sadie, I never thought of that, he's had a bit of diarrhea as well." Sadie thought he might have some 'bumps' on his gums. Kari checked and sure enough there was a small red bump, just like babies get when teething. "I'll have to tell Daniel, he doesn't know much about babies he told me."

Daniel came in a bit late that afternoon and really looked tired. He kissed Kari, smiled at Sadie and kissed Danny. "Kari, do you mind if I lie down for a bit, before dinner?" "Of course not!" "You must call me when Danny needs lifting." "Yes, dear, rest on my bed." Sadie said, "I wonder why he is so tired." Kari told her about one other time he came in with blood on his trousers. He ate very little and told me he was so in hopes of finding some property for kids and young people to have a place to feel safe and finish their education. It needs to be a complex for an opportunity for basketball and some sports, as well as a room for counseling and spiritual help. "Sadie, do you know of any property that would be adequate for such an opportunity for young people?" "Let me make a few phone calls and talk with some folks at the Church; it won't help much if it is Church related, because most of the ones who need help will not go to Church, period."

They had finished making dinner and put it in the warmer and Sadie told Kari to take a rest while all was quiet. "Okay," she replied. When Sadie left, she went into her room and lay down across the bed from Daniel. They all three slept about an hour and then, Danny was awake and loudly proclaiming the need for attention. Kari sat on the side of the bed and was petting him, trying to get his attention on something besides his tummy, but he would have none of it. Daniel awoke and smiled at them; got up and picked his yelling son up and started to change him. "Kari, I think we need a large pad to put him on; he is a mess." Kari got one of the large pads and went to the sink and got a warm washcloth and came back, took his messy diaper off, washed his bottom, and rubbed it with petroleum jelly to keep the urine from burning. She then put clean clothes on him and got a blanket in which to wrap him. Daniel got up and carried him to the rocking chair with Kari already to receive him. He went into the kitchen and got a bottle and warmed it and brought it to Kari. "I'll probably need that bottle of medicine as well since it seems like Danny is cutting teeth. They get a bit cranky when that happens." Daniel said, "Oh, I didn't know what was wrong."

In a short while, Danny was sound asleep and Daniel put him in his crib. Kari kissed Daniel and told him dinner was ready; it would take a bit to plate everything. Daniel followed into the kitchen and kissed her. He told her he really loved her and sat down at the table for dinner. Kari put dinner on the table, they prayed over it and Daniel said; "This smells great!" They ate quietly for a while and Kari got up to get the coffee. She told Daniel to go lie on the couch and they would have coffee there. He did as he was told. Kari brought their coffee in and sat on the edge of the couch with Daniel. She said quietly, "Daniel if you need or want to talk about today's events, I'm a good listener." Daniel smiled at her and began to tell her about today. "It seems so un-necessary for the trauma kids go through today. There was a drive-by shooting and one young man was killed, another wounded. The mother of one of the boys was wounded severally. The officers with me said it was drug related and they haven't really caught the one who did this." "Kari, I talked to the Chief; I asked him if he knew some space that we might find to start a youth center."

He said, "You know, Daniel I've been thinking along those lines myself. My own Church family might very well be interested or at least know of any available property." He told Daniel he would asked his pastor to be on the look-out for a place that might serve as a youth center. Kari said she told Sadie about it and she was going to do the same. "Daniel, I believe this is the Lord's will and it will work out to bless the youth in this town."

Daniel started laughing and said, "You know sweetheart, you are not only a great listener, but extremely smart. Thank you, my beloved." Kari took the coffee cups to the kitchen and put the dishes in the dishwasher. She only ran the dishwasher every night. Daniel came into the kitchen and asked Kari to come into the great room when she finished, he had something to ask her. "Okay," she replied. When the kitchen was tidy, Kari came into the great room and went to lie beside Daniel on the couch. "Well, I'm waiting!" Daniel laughed and hugged and kissed her. "You are beginning to get your spunk back. Did you rest today?" "Yes dear!" Daniel kept his arm around Kari. "Kari, I know you love Danny and me; would you like to adopt him?" "You bet I would, he could be mine and yours. Do you think Danny would be hurt later in his life when it's time to tell him that I adopted him?" "Absolutely not, Kari you are the only mother he has." "Oh, Daniel when do you think I can adopt him? I love that little boy, even with his red bottom and cranky moods. He is adorable, just like his daddy." Daniel smiled at her, kissed her and hugged her; and said, "As a matter of fact, I've already had the papers drawn up and Wayne has them when we are ready." "I'm ready now!" "It is bedtime now, Kari." "Daniel, I'm so excited, do you really mean it? You want me for your wife and I can really adopt him?" "Yes, my dear, that's exactly what I want."

KARI ADOPTS DANNY

It was getting a bit late, so Daniel asked Kari to take her pill and get ready for bed. "I'll be right here when you need me, remember, don't pick Danny up." "I won't, but I want to hug and kiss him so much." "I'll have to be his substitute then." She took her pill and asked Daniel if she had told him about Dr. Little putting her on birth control. "No, you didn't, but that's a good idea. You certainly don't need another pregnancy right now." "Well, now you know and don't have to worry about anything." "Thank you, my darling Kari, but we still need to wait until you are well." "I guess so, but don't start giving me orders; I'm my own decision maker now." When Kari went to put her nightwear on, Daniel whispered to himself, "Kari, my dear, you don't know what a temptation you are." In a little while Kari came out and stood at his couch and said, "Well, where's my hug and kiss goodnight?" "Coming right up, my dear," Daniel said smiling. They snuggled together for a while. Kari said, "Daniel you know I want to get strong and healthy again. I can hardly wait until I'm able to pick up Danny; and his daddy, maybe." Daniel laughed at Kari, "Honey, you are strong, but picking up Danny's daddy will be a bit tougher." "Oh well, just a thought," she said smiling.

Kari went to bed and right on cue, about an hour later, Daniel who had been asleep, heard Kari call him. He went into the bedroom and Kari said, "This is your side and the same promise applies." "Okay," he smiled. He lay beside her and they both went to sleep. Daniel had been so emotionally drained when he got home, he didn't know what to do except pray, well that's enough; he answered himself.

The next morning Danny again, was their wake-up call. Daniel got up and picked Danny up and took him to the bathroom to clean him up, dry him and put fresh clothes on him. He had Danny in his arms when the door bell rang. Sadie said, "Good morning and how's Danny feeling this morning?" Daniel said, "He was not a happy baby; Kari had to give him some medicine last night." "Oh, he is teething, Daniel." Kari awoke and came out of the bedroom. She asked Daniel to please make some coffee. She and Sadie went into the kitchen and Sadie put some cereal in Danny's bowl and Kari fed him. He ate fairly well, but still remained cranky, chewing on Kari's clothes or his fist. Sadie said, "We'll go by the drug store today and get some teething drops and a chew ring." Kari said, "That's a great idea, I hadn't thought of that." Daniel finished boiling eggs and had the toast ready for the toaster and went to the shower. He came out dressed for work, and reminded Sadie that tomorrow was Saturday and she was to rest. "You know I'll be here with them and besides, you've done so much all ready, I'll never be able to repay you." "Oh, relax, Daniel, you owe me my salary and nothing more except your smile." "You are one terrific lady," Daniel replied.

Sadie told Daniel she had planned to bring over some sketches for their wedding cakes and your birthday, which we will celebrate at the same time; also the suggestions for flowers and dinner setting for the reception. "I hope this takes a load off Kari and you. So many of the girls at my Church have me do their receptions, and not a one has complained."

"Oh, by the way, it has snowed lightly overnight, so be careful when you drive." "The same goes for you all when you go out. Pick up whatever you need and have them send the bill to me." "Oh, please don't pick out Kari's wedding dress; I want to be with her when she does that." Sadie said, "I wouldn't think of picking out her dress but she does need invitations and thank you notes, which we can get today. Neither of us can to be out for long today." "Okay," Daniel replied. Sadie said, "I'll still bring over sketches in the morning and that way you both can decide on what you want." "Thanks, Sadie, I really do appreciate you."

Kari came out of the kitchen just as Daniel was leaving. "Daniel, did you forget something?" "Oh how foolish of me," he said. He went to the kitchen and told Danny goodbye and started by Kari who grabbed his jacket; "No you don't big fellow, don't you start taking me for granted, My kiss is important too!" "I know Kari, but you are so much fun to tease." I love you and he did kiss her, smiled and told them all goodbye.

Sadie told Kari there was still a light snow falling. She said, "Perhaps we need to run into town and pick up anything you might need and those items for Danny. I'll dress him warmly and you can take your time to dress." Sadie tidied the kitchen and then got Danny dressed. He was still a bit cranky, but Sadie rocked him a little bit until Kari came out. Then coats and hats went on and the three of them went to get wedding invitations, thank you notes and a new toy for Danny as well as some drops to rub on his gums and a ring one puts in the freezer for a while. They stopped by a take-out burger place and got their lunch and took it home to eat. Danny was having a fit by this time; so Sadie picked him up out of the car seat and took him inside, undressed his outer layer, dried him, and handed him to Kari who was already in the rocking chair. She had also got the medicine that the doctor ordered, after his immunizations. She gave him a dropper full and then his bottle. Snuggled up against Kari, he soon fell asleep.

While Sadie and Kari were having their lunch, Sadie told her she had told Daniel about the sketches; Kari said, "That's great Sadie, but it is Saturday and you need some rest from us." "Well, I thought the two of you might enjoy looking at them together." "Thank you, Sadie." Sadie told Kari to take a rest while Danny was asleep and she said she would, "I'm a wee bit tired, but I'm really glad we got the stuff we did. The invitations and thank you notes will be great, and I know Danny's teething ring will be helpful. Did you know that Daniel has already arranged for me to adopt Danny?" "No," Sadie replied, "But I think that is great. You're already his mother in my book." "Thank you, Sadie." Kari went to lie down. Sadie tidied things up and started dinner for Kari; she had already told her what she planned.

When Daniel got home, Kari and Danny were just waking up. Kari looked a little tired and Danny was yelling. Sadie was headed for the bedroom and Daniel followed her. Daniel asked Kari what was ailing Danny that he was just yelling; "Well, he's hungry, needs changing and he just bit me." "You're kidding," Daniel said, bewildered. "Oh, it is wonderful Daniel." Sadie had already picked him up to put beside Kari and rubbed his gum and sure enough there was a tiny white tooth. Kari had her camera, she took a picture of Danny and Sadie; and then turned the camera on Daniel, who was literally holding his mouth open. "How did that happen so quickly Daniel asked?" Sadie said, "Once that little bump comes up, babies are fretful for a couple of days and then you find a tooth." Daniel said, "Let me see." He put his finger in Danny's mouth and felt the little tooth. "Kari, it's really a tooth." They all laughed except Danny, seemed he wanted his dinner. Sadie told them good night, and said she would like to get home before the big snow falls. Daniel told her to be very careful; it's not slick yet, but might be later on. They all said, good night again.

Daniel got a warm, wet bath cloth to bathe Danny's bottom and tried to put the petroleum jelly on him like Kari did. Again, Daniel got sprayed well. "Kari said you didn't wrap his front in a towel did you?" "No, I didn't think about that." They both laughed. "Our son is a charmer, isn't he?" "Oh yes, he is just like his daddy." Kari got up and helped Daniel finish drying and getting Danny's pajamas on. She then went to fix his bottle and put his cereal out. He was really into taking his bottle and did not want to stop for cereal. He finished and seemed satisfied for the moment. Kari set the table and put the food onto their plates. She and Daniel sat down to eat, but first Daniel got up and came around the table and picked Kari up and kissed her. "I love you, Kari." Kari said, "I love you too, now sit down and eat with me. I have some things to show you after dinner." They had put Danny in his swing and he seemed more playful than he had in several days. "Oh, he's feeling a lot better now," Kari said. They ate and Kari told Daniel about their day. Daniel smiled and told her how glad he was that she also got a nap. "That I did," she replied. "We're still not having dessert, Daniel." "That's fine; I was getting a bit snug in my pants." Daniel put his fork down and asked Kari when she would see Dr. Little again. Kari told him, next Wednesday, and she expected a great report. "I've been resting more and playing with Danny and we even play on the pallet when Sadie reminds me."

"I haven't walked down the path yet, though; I wonder if that creek is still muddy." Daniel said, "It probably is." "Daniel, you know I sometimes feel like that muddy creek". "How so?" Daniel asked. Kari replied, "Well, I know I'm better physically and I think I am emotionally, because I'm so happy most of the time. Just like that little creek keeps flowing, it still stays muddy. I keep doing what the doctor, Sadie and you tell me, but sometimes I'm muddy inside; almost as if I've done something wrong, but cannot put my finger on it." "Honey," Daniel replied; "You have done nothing wrong. You seem to sometimes dream unpleasant things, because you cry softly into your pillow. If I hold you closer, you seem to relax and continue sleeping."

"Daniel, I'm sorry if I awaken you, but it feels so good to have you by my side. I wasn't aware of dreaming, but I am aware when you put your arm around me." Daniel smiled at her and said, "Always my pleasure darling." They sat at the table and Kari poured their coffee and they drank it. "Daniel, do you remember our wedding is just two weeks away?" "Well seems like I remember something about a wedding and adoption of Danny," he said, laughing. "Is there anything special you want me to do?" "No Daniel, I was just checking. Oh, by the way, where will we be married? I haven't picked a Church yet, with all the things we've gone through." Daniel answered that he usually went to the community Church just south-west of town. "If you want, we'll take Danny for a ride to show off his first tooth." "That's great," Kari replied. "We can also talk with my pastor about using the Church for Joe to marry us, with him performing the 'salt covenant'." "What is the 'salt covenant'?" "Well, you see, at the altar, my pastor will step up to the front and will have a small bag of salt. He will ask each of us to take a pinch of salt and then put it back into the bag of salt. He then shakes the bag and says, 'Just as neither one can find the exact salt crystal they picked up; so may they never let anyone or anything separate them; no more than they can discern what salt is yours or mine'." "Daniel, that is a beautiful part of the wedding ceremony." "I'm also fairly sure we can use the fellowship hall for the reception. If you like the Church and pastor, I'll make arrangements for us to meet with him; that way you can get an idea of the kind of man he is." "Oh, Daniel that would be wonderful. I'd also like to show off our son." "Great!" Daniel replied.

While Daniel made the phone call to his pastor, Kari tidied up the kitchen and put Daniel's swing on automatic, so he wouldn't get too tired of jumping and swinging. She put another toy on the feeding tray and it was a red truck; at least the color was pretty. Danny just looked at it and then at her; she pushed the little truck over his tray and placed his hand on it and they pushed together. Daniel came into the kitchen just as Kari and Danny were busy with the truck and Kari was making a noise like 'voom-voom' and Danny seemed to imitate her. This time Daniel took the picture. They all three played with the truck. Big Daniel and Kari sat on the floor and Danny bounced and slammed the truck on his tray. It seems like he likes his way best, Daniel laughed. "Yep, just like his daddy."

Danny was beginning to tire of the jumper/swing and they took him into the great room and put him on his pallet. Kari took his red truck and lay down beside him, he reached for it and she gently moved it away, Danny began to scoot toward it, and would hold it a moment, and Kari eased it away again. Soon it became a game; Kari talking all the time, come on Danny you can get it and Danny scooting toward the truck. Daniel had put Danny down on his side; he promptly turned onto his stomach. Daniel said to Kari, "I didn't know he could turn over like that." Kari started to cry, "Oh Daniel, you see what I mean by 'muddy creeks'; I forgot to tell you he could now turn over by himself. He started about two weeks ago." Kari was really crying now and Danny was beginning to fret. Daniel picked Kari up and hugged her gently. "Now I think I do have a greater understanding, but that is okay, Kari." He kissed her until she stopped crying and she began to try to find a tissue. "Daniel I've wet your shirt, almost like Danny's spray." Daniel kept his arms around her and gave her a tissue, "Well, so you have, although your tears are not as 'fragrant' as Danny's spray." They smiled at each other and he hugged her again. Danny had settled down to try and reach his truck. He almost had it, when it rolled away a bit. Danny just screamed! Kari quickly got the truck and put it in his hand. The screaming stopped. Quite soon, however, he began to cry differently and Kari got up to fix his bottle and cereal. She would then rock him awhile and he would go to sleep for the night.

After they got Danny settled down for the night, Kari and Daniel sat on the couch very closely. Kari said, "Daniel I'm sorry I wet your shirt; you see what I mean about my brain seems like that creek. One moment I'm so happy and very quickly, I burst into tears. Do you think I will ever get over this? This really isn't like me Daniel; I'm usually much more on an even keel." Daniel answered and said, "You are already much better, Kari and that will improve. The mud will soon be out of your creek," he said, smiling. "You know we have a big week ahead, checking with Chuck about the Church and performing the 'salt covenant' ceremony, but also the fellowship hall for the reception." "Don't be surprised if a lot of my co-workers show up. They've determined to get me married to that "pretty little red head", because she will keep me on a short leash." "There will be less working on off hours and less deep sadness which I seemed to carry. I thought they hadn't noticed how much it hurt to think that Danny wouldn't be here; except for the grace of God, he wouldn't. Also, we must find you a dress you like; I still want to be with you when you find it."

"Now please take your pill and change into nightwear, so you can sleep well." Kari said, "Okay." She went into the bedroom to get her night clothes on. She came back to the great room and sat beside Daniel. She said, "You know Daniel, I haven't called Camille and Joe and checked on them for a while." Daniel looked at his watch and said; "It's still early enough to call them, sweetheart." She went into the kitchen to find her cell phone and brought the portable phone to Daniel, so they could both hear. They sat close together and Daniel had a difficult time not hugging and kissing her to sleep. But, he knew better than to start that, but Oh how tempting his girl was. Kari dialed the phone and Camille answered. "Hello, Camille, how are the two of you?" "Kari, how wonderful you are to call, let me get Joe on his phone, so we can all talk together."

Joe got on his phone and said, "How's our girl?" "Fine," Kari replied. Daniel spoke up and said hello to Joe and Camille. Kari said, "What's going on at the Church and have you finished packing and when can we see you?" Camille answered, laughing she told Kari, "The packing was done; just a few odds and ends to finish. We were planning to see you all sometime next week." "That's wonderful," Kari replied. Daniel said, "Joe did I ever introduce you to my pastor?" "No, I don't think so," he said. "Well, Kari and I are going over to meet him and let Kari look at the Church and reception area to see if she likes it. You see, your job is in two weeks from tomorrow at about three o'clock in the afternoon. I can't wait to have you tie that knot tightly, but Joe do you mind if Chuck does the 'salt covenant'?" "Not at all," Joe replied, "But we need to check with him about using his Church and me marrying the two of you." "Kari and I will meet with him tomorrow and go through all that, as well as telling him about you being Kari's pastor and adopted dad and mom." "That sounds fine. How is Danny?" Daniel spoke up and told them that he was so surprised that Danny bit Kari; Camille said, "Yes, this about the age they start cutting teeth and he started to turn over by himself." "He's grown since you all saw him. He weighs sixteen pounds and is twenty two inches tall." Daniel told them about Kari saying he could talk, but with his new red trunk, he seems to imitate Kari talking. "I'm so proud and thankful for both of them; I just stop and thank the Good Lord for His love and care."

Kari burst in with news about Danny in another area. She said Daniel would let her adopt Danny and the papers have been drawn up, before I even knew anything about it. "Camille, I'm sorry, but I haven't looked for an apartment for you two, but Sadie and I will start looking Monday morning. She has been a jewel, Camille. She volunteered to handle our reception and make the cake. She does that all the time for the girls who go to her Church. She's bringing sketches for Daniel and me to see tomorrow." Camille told Kari for 'us girls' to say goodbye; Joe has something he needs to talk with Daniel about. "Okay, I love you Camille and Papa Joe and can't wait to see you."

Daniel said, "Hello Joe." Joe told Daniel that he had put Kari's house on the market and it sold for about three hundred thousand dollars. "The closing date will be around Thanksgiving. Kari will have to come back here to inform the Judge that this is what she wants. I've never heard of this before, when dealing with selling a house. The money will be deposited in her bank. You see Daniel, Camille and I don't want to take anything Kari worked so hard on. She had it decorated beautifully before Frank died and he expected her to prepare large dinner parties for his guests and then go to work. Daniel, I'm afraid if she sees someone in trouble, she will think nothing of making a substantial check for that person; she is not without insight, she has great insight, but she is still a bit naïve." "Joe do you think it is a set-up to see what she does know about Frank's dealings?" "I don't think so; the SBI did a thorough investigation on her background but it seems to me it's one more way to harass her and maybe find out what the house sold for and why did she sell it." "That's her personal business Joe, but I'll speak to Chief and find out what he has found thus far. Please don't worry, Kari will never be alone again; I'll give my life before anyone hurts her." "I know that," Joe said, "But I thought you needed a 'thumbs up' on what I've heard."

"By the way, Kari and Sadie don't have to look for a place for us. It seems the realtor here has some properties close by you guys and we've decided we are not too old to mow a small yard. Camille has never had a home of her own, and she loves to garden, flowers and fruits and vegetables." She said, "If we can help Daniel find a place, for his youth center, close enough, that she would have the kids, plant and harvest foods and flowers and sell them at a Farmer's Market. We'd split the money fifty-fifty; fifty to the kids and fifty back into the youth center. I bet some of those kids have never seen a garden, nor tasted fresh, organically grown food. She then will have cooking classes and help them learn those skills. A small back yard would be plenty for them to learn gardening skills, as well as cooking skills, and help them in finishing school. You remember Camille is a school teacher. Also, Joey is serious about changing his lifestyle and giving his life to the Lord. I've been tutoring him some, by having him work on mini sermons. He seems like a natural. God Himself will have a plan. In addition, the girl Leslie that Kari told you about is a school teacher and they are planning to leave here sometime in the summer. It seems like things are falling in place for help for the young people, you have such a heart for."

Daniel said, "Joe, I've been thinking about checking with the Community College for teachers who might show them about fixing cars, plumbing, cosmetology and nursing classes they could take to further education. I know that is a big dream, but I still feel the Lord's leading." "Daniel, I hadn't thought of that, but I'll check around here and get a catalogue from this Community College; that will give you some idea of what you would like to see accomplished." "Thank You, Joe, you and Camille take care and we can't wait to see you. Goodnight."

Daniel looked over at Kari and she had fallen asleep on the pallet. She looked at such peace, he was afraid to wake her. He went over and picked her up and carried her to bed, whereupon, she jumped up and looked at him. "Oh, thank you Daniel, I guess I went to sleep on Danny's pallet; it smells like baby." "You did sweetheart. Now go back to sleep." "Nope, you forgot your place, and the same promise holds true, you'll be safe with me." Daniel lay down on top of the covers and had already slipped his shoes off, and Kari said, "Where is my hug and kiss?" "It is coming right up sweetie." He hugged and kissed her and she was asleep before he knew it. That's good thing, because her gown was loose and she was absolutely beautiful. He might have had a more difficult time going to sleep unless she was so soundly asleep. Lord, help me know what to do with what Joe said and please help me take care of Kari and Danny. Father, YOU are God Almighty, nothing is too hard for You. Thank You, Lord.

The next morning was just like the previous week or so; Danny woke up and decided he needed attention. He didn't scream this morning, just his baby jabbering. Daniel got up and sponged him down, changed him and put a cute outfit on him. Daniel had decided he needed boots, which he had picked up yesterday. They were both headed to the kitchen to make his bottle and cereal, when Sadie rang the doorbell and they answered that. Sadie came in smiling and noticed Danny's boots; he seemed a bit bewildered with his new boots. Sadie said, "That's a good idea, they are cute and it is cold outdoors." Sadie prepared Danny's cereal for Daniel and put the sketches onto the table for them to look at. Daniel told Sadie that Joe and Camille were coming back sometime next week, but he still needs her to stay with Danny and Kari. They will be busy looking at the property their agent had selected and getting settled in a new community. "Oh, by the way, here is your check for this week." Sadie looked at it and found it one and a half times what she charged. Daniel said, "No matter, you are also a blessing to us. That won't change when Kari is well, either." Sadie said, "Well thanks. I'll be going; I've got some errands to run."

Kari awoke when Sadie shut the door. What is going on, she thought; she did not hear Daniel or Danny. She ran barefoot into the great room and then to the kitchen. There were her two boys, the big one with cereal on his shirt and the little one 'talking'. Kari went to get some coffee and burst out laughing at Daniel and Danny. They were doing fine and Danny had on boots. "Don't tell me Daniel, that the two of you are going walking or hunting." Daniel put Danny in his swing and he really could swing now. Daniel turned and kissed Kari; "Your laughter is wonderful, but I'd like a good morning kiss." They held each other a good while and Kari asked about Danny's boots. "Oh, those, well, it seems like Danny was telling me he needed some boots." Kari replied, "Oh, so now you understand his language." Daniel laughed and said; "Well it could be that I saw them and I wanted them for him." "That's great Daniel." "Listen, you had better get dressed while I'm able to stay a gentleman; you are a tempting minx, my dear."

In a couple of hours they began to dress Danny in suitable outdoor clothing, as well as Kari and Daniel, in order to meet Daniel's pastor. Kari was a little nervous, but Daniel assured her that he was a fine man, good leader, and great pastor. When they got to the Church, Pastor Chuck was waiting in his office. They went in and Daniel introduced Kari as his future wife. Kari said, "Hello, Pastor Chuck." Daniel then showed Danny proudly to Pastor Chuck who was somewhat choked up; he cleared his throat and told Daniel he had done a superb job in caring for his baby; and to think he might not be here were it not for our prayers. Daniel answered, "That's true Chuck, but God had sent a red-haired angel to help him at the perfect time. Kari has nursed him and played with him and took him to the doctor. She truly is a God-send; but that's not the only reason I love her. She has helped me get out of my depression and I love her because she is the one meant to be my wife."

Kari spoke up and said to Chuck; "I do love both of them, but I believe the Lord led us together and my own pastor and his wife think so as well.

You'll meet then next week and be able to assess them for yourself. They've treated me as their daughter for a long while and I love them. Now, before Danny starts to make his presence known in a big way, could we see the Church and reception hall?" "Of course," Chuck said. Kari stopped and asked; "What do you want me to call you, Pastor, Bishop or what?" Chuck smiled sweetly and said; "Chuck will be fine."

The Church was really pretty, with only one aisle and a prayer bench at the center of the two sides. There was also a balcony. "This is perfect," Kari said. They went to the reception hall and it too would be just right for the reception. She asked permission to take some pictures of the Church inside and the reception hall. "Of course," Chuck replied.

It was getting late, when Kari had the pictures she needed; she would transfer them into her computer for some hard copies. That way Camille and Sadie would be able to refer back if they had questions. Sadie was going to do the cake and goodies for the reception, as well as help Kari and Camille choose flowers for the Church. Kari had told Sadie she wanted the wedding to be simple, but she wanted the Lord honored in everyway possible. Sadie had reminded her that she and Camille could take care of that. Also, while Kari was taking pictures, she remembered that she needed to see Dr. Little on Wednesday for a final check-up. Danny also needed his second round of immunizations. She knelt at the altar and asked God to give her strength and please help her to be the best wife for Daniel. Please confirm Your blessing on this union in a way I can understand. Thank You, Dear Jesus.

Daniel and Pastor Chuck came out of the reception room, followed by a well-dressed, polished woman; she assumed this lady was Chuck's wife. She was; Chuck introduced her to his lovely wife Sharon. Kari and Sharon shook hands and Kari looked deep into Sharon's eyes. She said, "I'm so glad to meet you." Sharon felt as though Kari could see her soul. Kari's big grey eyes were almost piercing; Sharon was an extremely perceptive woman and realized this young woman had some tragedy in her life. Finally, Kari smiled a big smile and said; "You must be a treasure to Pastor Chuck." She said, "I am or else Chuck fibs, because he tells me that frequently."

Kari thanked them for the use of the Church and for their time today. Daniel spoke up and said almost the same thing. He smiled at Sharon and gave her a hug; "Do you like my choice?" "Yes," Sharon said; "She'll keep you straight." "That she will," replied Daniel.

Kari and Chuck had been talking quietly while Sharon and Daniel chatted. Very soon, Danny made his presence known. Daniel had been holding him and he was almost asleep, but decided it was time to go; he wanted food. Daniel noticed that Kari looked quickly at Danny. Daniel, Danny, and Sharon came over to where Kari and Chuck were standing. Daniel also noticed that Kari was somewhat pale and she was now almost limping. He realized she was extremely tired and probably hungry. They said their goodbyes and Daniel and Kari took Danny to his car seat and they left. Daniel knew Kari was not up to cooking or eating at this time. He took them home, gave Danny a bottle and told Kari to take a rest for a while. He would bring Danny into the bedroom when he had finished eating. It seemed Kari had gone someplace in her own head. She took one of the pills Dr. Little had ordered. She had not had to have one in a long while. Daniel wondered what was on her mind, but did not ask. Kari went to lie down, and Danny finished his bottle and went to sleep. When Daniel took sleeping Danny to his crib, Kari was sleeping too, only she seemed restless. Daniel ordered a dinner for two from a local restaurant of grilled salmon, tomato with basil sauce and steamed broccoli and baked sweet potatoes. He told them the delivery time and went in and lay down beside Kari. He took her in his arms, rested her head on his shoulder and she seemed to relax and sleep deeply.

When Kari awoke, she turned to Daniel and looked straight into his eyes for a few seconds, then said; "Daniel, are you really sure you want me for your wife?" Daniel asked; "Kari, what makes you even doubt my love and care for you, you know I've prayed about this and I know you have."

"Daniel, I don't know, but when I met Chuck and Sharon today, it seemed as if I had met them at sometime in the past, almost as if I knew them, and then I think back to my childhood and realize I can't remember much about it, except that my uncle and aunt brought me up and cared for me. I remember once, asking my uncle who my parents were and what had happened to them?" He told me that, they could not talk about that with me, your biological parents are now dead, and you are ours. "I didn't feel neglected or rejected, but I never felt really close to either of them. They are wonderful people, but I don't have any bond with them. Do you think I might begin to feel about you the same way? At this moment, I would die for you and Danny and I cannot see myself ever changing my mind, but based on what I just told you, do you have enough faith for both of us right now?" Daniel answered her, "My dear Kari, you have never told me about your growing up, but I already knew, because the SBI had done a thorough search on you when your husband was killed. You see, Carl told me what the agents had told him, and I saw no reason to bring it up. The fact that you have cordial feelings toward your uncle and aunt, although no real bond; doesn't mean you will ever feel that way about me." "Now you listen to my heart and my words, I have no fear that you will ever be less than the perfect wife and mother, you see, I believe you've undergone so many traumas in your short life and come out of it with only occasional flashbacks is evidence that the Lord is healing you. You must trust me to know my own feelings and beliefs, and I know the Lord has put us together."

Kari had been lying almost on top of Daniel; she looked down at him and said, "I think so too." She bent down and gave him a kiss and Daniel wrapped his arms around her and held her close. "I do love you Kari and I know you love me. Thank you for talking to me." About that time, Kari's stomach rumbled and she remembered she hadn't made dinner, nor had they had lunch. Daniel burst out laughing, "I see the wheels turning in your noggin, and dinner is already arranged. I know you aren't supposed to gain weight, but you have lost some weight." "How do you know", Kari asked. "Because when I hold you I can tell the difference." Kari looked at her watch and asked Daniel how he had arranged to have dinner come to them? "That's easy", Daniel replied, "I called my favorite restaurant and asked them to send out our dinner, it should be here most any time." They got up and Kari straightened her clothes and realized they were really rumpled. Well, I can wash my face and put on some fresh make-up and present fairly well for Daniel to have dinner with me. Daniel had gone into the kitchen and Kari went into the bathroom to freshen up. She realized she felt better, and her leg didn't hurt now.

The doorbell rang and Daniel answered it; he had already set the table for dinner and made some coffee. About that time Danny awoke and let himself be heard, complaining loudly. Kari went over and changed him in his crib. She put his pajamas on and asked Daniel to pick him up for her; she was going to fix him a bottle and cereal. While she was feeding Danny, Daniel finished putting dinner out. When Danny was full, he decided to talk to Kari. Daniel said, "What's he saying now?" Kari answered, "He's asking about his boots and where are they?" He had his pajamas on and Daniel went to get his boots, he then picked Danny up and put him in his swing. Kari, Daniel, and Danny laughed and talked through dinner. "That was wonderful," Kari said. Kari and Daniel tidied the kitchen and took Danny in his swing into the great room. All three of them were thoroughly enjoying themselves quiet a while. Soon Danny decided he was tired of swinging, so Daniel put him on his pallet and Kari gave him his truck with the other toys around him. He played and 'talked' for a while. Kari and Daniel were catching up on the news on TV.

They soon noticed Danny picking up a soft toy, talk to it and throw it; then he would turn himself over and scoot toward the toy he had thrown; he soon became side-tracked to another toy and the process continued. Kari started laughing; "It won't be long before he is crawling wherever he wants. We need to think about a 'baby gate' to put in front of the balcony steps as he might want to crawl up the steps." Daniel replied, "That's a good idea." They continued talking quietly for a while and soon noticed Danny beginning to quarrel at his toys and Kari. Daniel picked him up and Kari moved to the rocking chair; Daniel fixed his bottle and Kari fed him, rocked him and soon he was asleep. Daniel asked, "Do you think I should take his boots off?" "Probably so," Kari replied. Daniel took Danny's boots off and soon Kari said, "Well, it's time for him to be put in the crib." Daniel picked him up and they went to his crib together and Daniel put him down in the crib. He was sleeping soundly and Daniel and Kari went back to the great room.

SKETCHES FOR WEDDING AND RECEPTION

"Oh, Daniel, we haven't looked at Sadie's sketches, nor made any decision. Should we take a look tonight and then make a decision tomorrow." Daniel replied; "That's a good idea." They picked up the sketches and Kari was amazed at the cakes and decorations that Sadie had done. They both looked at all of them and it was pretty easy to pick one they really wanted. The one they both liked was a red velvet cake with cream cheese frosting. She had a few mini cakes as well on a tray that matched the big cake. She had decorated the table with all colors of red, pink and white. The table cloth was white linen with a red and pink runner. The punch bowl showed a red punch with pretty cups that had carved grapes on them. Kari said, "This looks great to me. What do you think?" "That's fine with me, Kari. What color flowers do you want in the Church and reception area?" "I would like tall greens with cream colored flowers woven into them, and some cream candles in stands at each end." "You have already thought this through, haven't you?" "Yes I have, I know this is my second wedding, but the other one was planned for me with no input except Frank and the decorator. This is really my first wedding in which I have any control at all. I hope that is okay with you, Daniel."

"I was married in a Catholic Church with all the pomp that could be done; by a decorator, no less. I know it must have been pretty, but it wasn't me, Daniel. I much prefer what we have planned, although I realize I've been doing the planning and haven't asked what you want." "Kari, this is exactly what I want, as well"

93

"My first wedding was big and showy and without much meaning to me. It was what Kelly wanted and at that time I was wealthy enough to let her have what she wanted. You know, even at the time, it didn't feel forever. I realized pretty soon that Kelly loved the idea of marriage, but not the reality of marriage. She oversaw the building of the house and lunched with her friends and I rarely saw her, except at night and often there was a catered dinner party at night. I worked long hours and didn't really care. This might sound strange to you, Kari, but I feel as though this is my first wedding and what you have mentioned is warm and loving and has a 'forever' feel to me." "Thank you Daniel and I feel the same way. I love you with all my heart and truly believe that God brought us together." "He did, Kari and I love you too."

They put a sticky note on the page they liked and made notes to Sadie. They included what they wanted in the Church decoration and the reception.

Daniel looked at his watch; it was way past Kari's bedtime, because she had not rested enough today, especially with all the activity. "Okay, young lady, it's time for bed." Kari started to giggle, "I thought you would never ask," she said. Daniel answered, "For you to get some sleep, understood?" "Yes Sir," she laughed. Kari went to get dressed for bed and Daniel checked the kitchen and turned the dishwasher on and then he lay down on the couch. He was tired too, but in such a pleasant way. He had thanked God for His watch care and leading of the day, continued with his prayers and was almost asleep, when Kari came out of the bedroom. "You keep forgetting to kiss me goodnight, Daniel." "Well, so I did. That's a shame too, because I like to kiss you." He kept lying on the couch and Kari came over and took his hand and pulled him up to hug him; she didn't have to pull hard. Kari said, "You're forgiven this time but no more forgetting, and besides, I told you your place is beside me and I promised not to molest you." Daniel laughed out loud, "Oh, Kari what a charmer you are." Daniel was so much bigger than Kari; she came almost to his shoulder, but not quite. He hugged her and gave her a long good-night kiss and followed her to his place beside her. She still kept the fireplace on low and he always slept on top of the bedcovers. Soon they were both asleep.

The next morning, the same routine happened. Danny awoke early and started talking his usual baby jabber and then he decided that wasn't enough to be heard, so he became louder. Daniel got up and went to the crib and started talking softly to his son. Danny wasn't interested in talk at this time, he wanted up and his food. Daniel picked him up and took him to the bathroom and gave him a sponge-down, clean diaper and some fresh clothing. Kari came in and said 'good morning' and Danny seemed to talk to her. She went to prepare his bottle and cereal. While Daniel and Danny were busy getting ready for the day; Kari also made coffee. This would be a wonderful day. Her 'boys' came into the kitchen and Daniel handed Danny to Kari and she proceeded to feed him and tell him how wonderful he was. Danny tried to talk too and got milk all over Kari. Daniel laughed and told Kari that Danny responded to her more than to his daddy. Danny finished his breakfast and Daniel put him in into his swing to play. He was a happy little boy.

They made breakfast together and sat down to eat. Daniel spoke up and said, "Good Morning and I love you" to Kari. "Well, seems like I feel the same about you." They chatted over breakfast and had another cup of coffee. Kari told Daniel that she needed to see Dr. Little on Wednesday and Danny needed his second immunization. She told him that Sadie would take them to the doctor. "I don't know when Joe and Camille plan to get here, but surely they will go see the houses that their realtor had talked about." They would know Kari and Sadie would soon be back. "Yes," Daniel replied, but tomorrow he would check with Joe just to make sure they were alright and make him aware of the doctor's visit for Kari and Danny.

This Sunday was indeed a very good day. They talked and played with Danny and Kari made lunch and then put a roast in the oven for their dinner. They talked again about Sadie's sketches and how soon the wedding was coming. Daniel said, "As soon as you feel up to it, let's leave Danny with Sadie and Camille and go look for your dress." Kari said, "Well, I've been thinking about that. I want a pretty cream dress, but I don't know where to start looking." Daniel said there was only one bridal shop that he knew of, but there were several nice department stores they could look into; he felt sure she would find what she liked. "Remember, I want to go with you and see you in anything you try, okay?" "Okay," Kari answered. Soon Danny tired of his swing and wanted out. He reached toward Kari who almost forgot she couldn't yet lift him, but Daniel got to him first. They went into the great room and he put Danny on his pallet. He began to play and 'talk' to his toys. Daniel and Kari watched some TV sermons and had a great morning.

Kari finished making lunch and Daniel made Danny's lunch, so Kari could feed him and the two of them could have their lunch. Afterward, Daniel instructed his two loves to go to bed and rest awhile. Seems they both felt that was a good idea. Daniel put Danny in his crib and Kari lay across her bed. While they slept, Daniel did a long devotion and prayed about the youth facility and a number of other things. Again, he thanked God for Kari and Danny. He went into the bedroom and Kari was asleep, but Daniel lay down on top of the covers and they all slept well.

The nest morning, Danny was again their alarm clock. Daniel got up, gave him a sponge down, and put his clean clothes on. He also put his boots on. Danny was a bit fretful and Daniel thought he had a fever. He called Kari who had already partially dressed; she put her robe on and went to see what Daniel needed. He told her that Danny seemed sick; he is not his usual self. Kari felt of him and realized he must be cutting another tooth. While Daniel prepared his breakfast, Kari had to change Danny again; and Danny was none to pleased, with his situation. He was cranky and didn't really want his bottle. Kari ran her finger around his gums and sure enough, there was a small reddened area beside his bottom tooth, but also a red bump on his upper gum. Oh my, she thought, a double teething. She rubbed his gums with the medication that she and Sadie got and cuddled him. He finally began to settle down and Kari fed him his bottle.

Sadie came in about that time and Kari told her about his teething. "Oh, my poor darling," Sadie exclaimed. Daniel was still somewhat confused; the baby seemed okay to him, except he was a little warm when he bathed him and put clean clothing on him. Sadie confirmed what Kari thought and told Daniel that Danny would be fine; just some extra attention today. "Kari and I will take good care of him; now you shower and get ready for work." "Yes, good lady," Daniel replied. Sadie told Kari that she would take Danny to the rocking chair so Kari could finish giving him his bottle; however, he also needed some drops for the fever and irritability. Kari got the drops and gave him a dropper full and Sadie took him to her in the rocker. Kari cuddled and rocked him and Danny settled down.

Daniel came out of the room, dressed and ready for work. He told Sadie he hadn't had time to straighten things up in the house. He also said he didn't do laundry; they had mostly played with Danny and watched TV yesterday. He reminded Kari to show Sadie the sketches they really liked and thanked her for bringing them over. He told her about seeing his pastor on Saturday and that Kari had taken some pictures for her to check, when she had time. "Okay, now you scoot." Daniel went over and kissed Danny and Kari and smiled at Sadie, and scooted to work.

He went to work and into to talk to the Chief. He told him about their weekend and asked if anything happened over the weekend; that he needed to follow up on. "Yes," Chief answered. "It seems that some of the young people had a drinking party at one of their parent's home. The parents had taken a brief trip to the mountains and left the kids on their own. The parents thought with the big game on that the kids would enjoy free run of the house, eat pizza and have fun. They did indeed eat pizza and everything else they could find, but one of the boys brought in whiskey. He wasn't a regular member of the group, but all the kids welcomed him to watch the game, not knowing he had the booze. After the game, this one boy challenged them to a drinking contest. Two of the group got alcohol poisoning, one of the boys and one of the girls. The girl is still in the hospital and the boy was discharged yesterday afternoon." Daniel told him he would go to the hospital and check on both of them and the families. "That's good, Daniel and keep me informed. We might also give more thought to having a genuine youth center, with an overseer to keep this type of thing to a minimum. I'll also check with the County Commissioners about this project, get their input and perhaps some idea of property available." Daniel told him that Joe and Camille were coming in this week sometime and they were checking some property that their realtor recommended. They are also eager to help.

Daniel went over to the hospital to see the young woman and to find out how she was doing. She seemed glad to see him, because she had known Daniel from the Church. Her name is Lynn. He talked with her for a while and reminded her that God had a plan for her life and He would always be with her. He asked her if she felt like telling him what happened. She said, "We were all having fun and we really don't know this guy, except he supposedly went to school with us. After this happened, the other kids said they had never seen him before and I hadn't either. He seemed nice enough, but he was older than we were, so we assumed he was in college. I guess when he realized what was happening, he left us. He used the name Joe, but now I doubt that is his name. One of the other kids had very little to drink, and he called 911, the ambulance brought Robert and me to the hospital. I guess we learned our lesson, but what will our parents think of

97

us? You know we all go to Church and haven't been in trouble before." She started to cry and said she had really let her mom and dad down. Daniel said, "I think they will be so grateful that they will understand and they do love you, no matter what."

Just as Daniel was leaving to go talk with her parents; they came in and seemed frantic. They immediately went to Lynn and hugged and kissed her. "Are you okay?" they both asked. "Yes, but I'm so sorry, mom and dad." "We'll talk about this later, honey. Our main concern is if you are okay and when you can come home." Lynn said she was to be discharged after the doctor saw her this morning. "Oh, that's wonderful, darling."

Lynn's parents greeted Daniel and told him that when Lynn told them where they were having a get-together to watch a game, they had soon gone to bed. "Lynn is always home soon after the game. When the group comes to our house, we send them home before too late. They have the get-togethers almost quarterly, and so we knew Lynn would be in soon after the game. Daniel you know all of these kids. They are in the youth department at Church, and they're good kids. They have been reared in Church. We all often get together with them for a softball game and hot dogs. There seemed to be no need for us to be there."

Daniel told them that this time Robert's parents had taken a short trip and left the kids unattended. That seemed the opportune time for their 'friend' to show up, none of the kids knew him, but assumed he was in a higher grade or college. He seemed to know them. He said his name was Joe, so they invited him to watch the game with them. "I doubt very seriously that Robert's parents knew the group would be meeting at their house or they would have come home earlier." "Yes, we think that too. As a matter of fact, Robert's mother called us this morning, crying and very upset; she and Robert's dad had taken a trip up to the mountains and would be late getting home. She told us what had happened and we came immediately here to the hospital."

Daniel decided to tell Lynn's parents about his goal for the young people in this county. He said that he had talked to Chief about it, Kari's pastor and his wife, and Wayne and his wife. They need a place to gather with supervision, but not Church related, because some of the kids in the county would definitely not come to a Church. He went on to tell them about possibly having kids come in who needed help to finish school, to learn some basic skills, like working on cars, cosmetology, nursing aide with the prospect of completing their education at the Community College. Lynn's dad spoke up then and said, "It seems like you've really had this type of thing on your mind a while." Daniel said, "I have. I've seen too many young people become victims of drugs, drive-by shootings and other gang-related behaviors. Often the younger crowd gets involved before they realize what is going on and they become isolated and the gangs tell them that they are the only ones who really care about them." "Daniel, that's a great idea, we can probably help with the Community College aspect. John teaches at the college and I work with Social Services, I pretty well know who is really in trouble and those who take the 'county' for a ride, if you know what I mean." "Janet, that's a great idea, it seems that God is preparing the path before us. I'm deeply grateful for your interest and input." They had a short prayer with Lynn and Daniel told them he was going over to see Robert and his parents. John said, "That's a great idea, they are really upset about this whole thing."

Daniel went to Robert's house and his parents were really glad he came. Robert was still recuperating in bed. They talked a while and Daniel had a prayer with them and left. He went back to the office and talked with Chief for a while. Chief Carl asked Daniel if he was falling back into his old routine of working too long hours without a break and becoming so involved with the hurting people that he wasn't taking care of himself. Daniel said, "No, as a matter of fact, I'm going home to see my family now. Thanks Chief."

"Oh, you might check with Wayne regarding some papers that Frank had left in a tool box, that Kari had Wayne keep the tool box in his bank box."

Daniel went home and found Danny really fussing, Kari almost in tears, rocking and trying to soothe Danny; and Sadie finishing the dinner. Daniel said, "What is going on here?" Kari started trying to explain that Danny really felt bad and she could do nothing to help. Sadie spoke up and said, "Daniel, the baby is cutting two teeth at once, he is fretful and senses Kari's unease and becomes more fretful. They both need to sleep a while. I've tidied up the house, did laundry and kept close watch on Danny and Kari. Seems when he quiets down, Kari relaxes, but when it's time for some more medicine, he lets it be known quite loudly." Sadie tried to hide a smile, she told Daniel to come let her show him what she had prepared for dinner; he followed her into the kitchen. Sadie said, "Those two are so close, they seem to sense the other's distress and it makes things a bit worse. You might tell Kari to let you talk with your son and for her to take a rest. I'll get his medicine and a bottle and you can rock him a while. He'll be asleep before you know it. I've already rubbed his gums well, so he will be fine. Kari would not take a rest at all today, even when Danny was asleep, she insisted on telling me about the wedding and what the two of you liked. I assured her that Camille and I would handle everything. She finally lay down on the couch, but I doubt she slept."

Daniel walked into the great room and kissed Kari and Danny. He said, "How about letting me hold our son a few minutes; we'll have 'man-talk'." Kari looked up at Daniel and said, "Okay, but be gentle with him, he's sick." "Okay", replied Daniel. He picked Danny up out of Kari's arms and began talking to him like a little man. He noticed Kari's blouse was damp and she looked exhausted. "Okay, mama, take your place on the couch and let us men talk." Kari smiled for the first time and said, "Well, since, its 'man talk', I guess I will." Sadie came out of the kitchen and told Kari dinner was in the warmer and the clothes were dry and put away. She told Kari she would take the sketches and look at the ones they had chosen, tonight. "Now you get a bit of rest before dinner." "I think I will; Daniel and Danny have to 'man talk', so I'll lie here and supervise, lest they talk about us. I'll tell you if they do, Sadie, and good night."

Daniel and Danny were still murmuring, but Daniel laid Danny across his chest and up toward his shoulder and fairly soon Danny was asleep. Daniel glanced over at Kari and she had too dozed. He really enjoyed the time, holding Danny and watching Kari. They both were so dear to him and again, he thanked God for them.

The great room's fireplace was keeping everything cozy. Daniel rocked Danny while he slept. Danny began to sweat a bit and Daniel thought his fever had probably broken. He watched Kari who really was dozing and went to put Danny in his crib. Then he went into the kitchen and set the table and prepared coffee and put the food out, ready to fix the plates. Before he could accomplish much, Danny awakened crying and fussing loudly. What's the matter now, he thought. He went toward the bedroom and Kari sat up and followed him into check on Danny. His stomach was really upset; he was 'going' at both ends. Daniel filled the bathtub with warm water, Kari undressed him and Daniel came to get him for his bath. Kari changed his crib sheet and got out clean clothing. When Daniel had bathed Danny, he brought him in wrapped in a large towel. He also had the petroleum jelly in his other hand. "It seems Danny has a red butt, Kari." Kari rubbed his bottom with the petroleum jelly and put clean clothing on him. "Oh it's from his teething. This time I'll give him Pedialyte and some more medicine. He probably doesn't need formula at this point." She also got the teething ring from the freezer and laid it on the table to soften a bit.

Kari got the Pedialyte from the cupboard, got the medication and got ready to feed Danny. She gave him his bottle and he soon quit fussing and began to feel better. He seemed to quarrel with Kari and Daniel. Daniel said, "Do you think he should go into the swing for a while? I'll turn it on automatic so he doesn't have to do much pushing and he can play with his toys and that ring you have there." Kari handed the chewing ring to Danny after Daniel put him in the swing. Danny knew exactly what to do with that. He chewed and argued (well his type of arguing) and pushed his swing occasionally.

Kari and Daniel ate the dinner that Sadie had prepared; roasted chicken, green beans and tiny steamed potatoes. She had also made some delicious muffins; that they enjoyed with coffee. They talked about their day and Daniel told her the basics of his day. Kari said, "I'm afraid I haven't done much except hold Danny and rock him and tried to keep him comfortable. You know, Daniel, Sadie is a God-send. She knows what to do and proceeds to tell me when Danny needs something more than rocking. She has also tidied the house and done laundry and made lunch and dinner. How can we repay this wonderful woman, Daniel?" Daniel said, "Kari, Sadie loves us, we pay her a salary, but she does belong here. She knows it, because I told her no matter what, we wanted her to come everyday, as long as she felt like it and wanted too. She said that's enough, Daniel. I love you all too and it's a joy to me to be around 'family' again."

They finished dinner and Daniel picked Danny up and took him to his pallet. Kari came in and lay on the pallet with Danny. They soon began to gurgle and talk and play. Kari put his toys around him, including his truck and went to help Daniel tidy up. Daniel hugged and kissed her and she responded with I love you. "It's still been a great day, even if Danny is cranky. Sadie said those teeth would pop through in a day or two. She also reminded me that Wednesday I needed to see Dr. Little and Danny

needed to see Dr. Lee. I tell you, Daniel, Sadie doesn't forget anything."
"That's great," replied Daniel. They went into the great room and found
Danny on the edge of his pallet with his truck. Kari almost jumped to get
him back onto his pallet. Daniel took her arm and said, "Let's see what
he can do on his own." Kari and Daniel went to the couch together and
watched their son, as well as caught up on news.

In an hour or so, Danny had another stool and spit up some, but not as
violently as earlier. Daniel picked him up and gave him another bath and
Kari went to get clean clothing and made sure the fireplace was on in her
room. She kept it on low, because Danny didn't like covers and she wanted
him kept warm. Daniel came out of the bathroom with Danny nice and
clean and wrapped in a huge bath towel. The same procedure followed
and Danny was again fairly happy. They put him back in his swing and
moved it to the great room, so Kari and Daniel could talk and watch him
at the same time. They had the TV on low, and Danny became interested
and watched with them and chewed his chew ring. That simple action
seemed to soothe him.

After some time elapsed, Danny was ready for a change and dinner.
Daniel took him and changed him, redressed him, and they talked; Kari
couldn't tell if it was 'man-talk' again or what, but Danny seemed to quiet
for a while. Kari mixed the formula with half formula and half Pedialyte.
She also put his medication and teething drops beside her at the rocking
chair. Kari fed him the concoction and rubbed his gums and gave him
the medication. Soon Danny was asleep. Daniel picked him up and took
him to his crib. He continued asleep without further incident. Kari and
Daniel went into the great room and lay on the couch together. Kari was
so tired; she almost dozed in Daniel's arms. He reached down and kissed
Kari's head and told her she needed to change into night wear and go to
bed. She said, "Okay," and got up to put her night clothes on. At the
door to her room, she turned and said; "Don't forget your place." "I won't
Daniel replied." While Kari was changing, Daniel stayed on the couch
and thanked God for the day and His many blessings. Daniel heard Kari
get into bed, he also heard her softly say, "Don't make me come get you,
buster." Daniel laughed and said, "No dear." They both got comfortable
and both were asleep rather quickly.

Danny awoke them earlier than usual; a bit fretful, but mostly wanting
his food. Daniel got up and took him to the bathroom for his bath. Kari

followed them in and knew that Danny was not as sick as yesterday, still grumpy, but not sick. She got his clean clothes out, changed his crib sheet and went into the kitchen to start breakfast. She put the coffee on and made French toast and bacon. Her boys came out pretty soon and she had Danny's bottle ready as well as his teething ring out. Daniel gave Danny to Kari and sat down to his breakfast. "Kari, this is good and good morning, I love you." Kari smiled and said; "Me too!" Danny gurgled and spit milk on Kari's gown and down his own face and clean shirt. "You are a messy little fellow, but so precious to mama and daddy." Daniel smiled and thought that today after Sadie got there, he was taking Kari down to Wayne's office to officially adopt Danny. He spoke to Wayne yesterday and the judge would be in this morning about eleven o'clock. He was going to surprise Kari with this, but when he looked at her, gown wet and sticking to her breasts and half down her shoulder; he figured he better tell her, so she could get a shower and dress before Sadie got there and before he made a fool of himself. Oh my, but she was a beauty and a temptation! When Danny finished his bottle, Daniel took him and told Kari to shower and change into 'town clothes'. He had something to tell her afterward. "Okay," Kari said. I wonder what he's talking about, she thought to herself. She got up to go to the shower and bent down and kissed him and Danny. She showered and shampooed her hair, blew it dry and dressed in slacks, a pretty blouse and got her jacket out. She put on some make-up and arranged her hair; it had grown considerably since she came here.

She went back to the kitchen and ate her breakfast and coffee fairly quickly. She poured Daniel another cup of coffee, as well as herself. Danny was in his swing with his teething ring and toys. "Okay, Daniel, I showered and changed and ate; now what do you have up your sleeve?" Daniel laughed out loud, and said; "If I'd known a surprise was this important to you, I've planned it sooner." "What," she demanded. "Darling, I have arranged for you to officially adopt Danny today. Wayne said the judge would be in at eleven o'clock and would perform the official adoption. Sadie will take care of Danny and I'll pick you up about ten o'clock; is that okay?" "Daniel, that is more than okay, it's absolutely thrilling. I love you and Danny so much and I can't wait to be his real mama. You aren't teasing me are you?" "No, my darling Kari, I already consider you his mother, but we need to make it legal so you will know that he is your own baby." "Thank you, Daniel. The Lord is so good; you know, I've been asking Him to make that happen soon. Well, God answered this prayer with a big yes!" Kari was almost jumping and dancing, but knew she better, not right now. She did go over and hug Daniel and kissed him until he was breathless. "My darling Kari, a man can only stand so much of this love, you need to finish your coffee," he said smiling at her.

The doorbell rang and Kari fairly ran to the door. She hugged Sadie and said, "Sadie, you know what?" "What?" Sadie asked; putting her coat in the closet. Kari said "Daniel and I are going to have me lawfully become Danny's mother, do you believe it?" "Oh, yes sweetie, that's great. Now where is my boy?" "He's in his swing and seems to feel better today." Kari told Sadie about yesterday evening and last night. She told her she gave him his full formula today, but not his cereal. Sadie said, "That's fine. When are you going to court?" "Today about eleven," Kari answered. Daniel spoke up and asked Sadie if she could handle Danny and all this excitement until he could get out of the shower and go to work. "I'll be back to pick Kari up about ten o'clock." "Sure," Sadie answered.

Daniel went to shower, shave and dress. He came out of the room ready to go to work. "Now remember, I'll be back to get you at about ten o'clock." He kissed Kari and Danny and smiled at Sadie.

Daniel went in and checked with the Chief. Anything new, he asked the Chief? "No," Carl answered. "Well, that's good, because I need to leave in time to pick Kari up about ten o'clock. We are to meet the judge for Kari to officially adopt Danny." "That's great, Daniel, Do you need a witness?" "I don't know," Daniel answered. "Wayne said the papers were all in order and the judge could complete this at eleven o'clock. I never thought to ask about a witness." "Well, if you do, there are several officers in court today, I'm sure either one of them would be fine." "Thanks, Chief." Daniel went into his own office, checked his desk and voice mail and decided there was nothing that he needed to attend to until after the adoption. He then left and went to the florist and got a beautiful bunch of flowers for Kari to celebrate the adoption of their child.

He went to get Kari and gave her the flowers. "They are beautiful, Daniel, but why?" "Because you are about to be my son's mother and I love you and appreciate you and your love for Danny, and because I wanted to." "Well, thank you kind sir! They are pretty." Sadie took them and told Kari she would arrange them while they were gone. They arrived at the court house and the judge walked in. They all arose and the judge told them to be seated. The ceremony was extremely short and after a few questions were answered, he put the gavel down and said, "So be it." They all signed papers and now Danny was officially their baby. They got home and Sadie had a small pound cake made and coffee waiting. The table was set and the flowers arranged beautifully. Sadie went to the pallet where Danny was playing, picked him up and introduced him to his mother. Daniel almost cried and Kari couldn't hold back tears. "Oh, Sadie, thank you so much." Sadie said, before she handed Danny over to Kari; "Do you promise to love him, care for him and his daddy for the rest of your life?" "Yes, Yes, Yes," Kari answered and burst out laughing and crying. Sadie handed Danny over to his mother. Daniel hugged Sadie and said my heart-felt love and thanks to you, Sadie. Sadie said, "Good, now you three sit down and have cake and coffee; well maybe not Danny." Kari couldn't resist and she took a tiny piece of cake and put it in Danny's mouth and he chewed and spit it out. "Oh well, you had your chance, darling." All three of the adults had cake and coffee and then Daniel had to return to work. He kissed Kari and his son, and then kissed Sadie on the cheek. Sadie said, "Now off you go."

It was past lunch time, but the cake and coffee had filled Kari; she fed Danny and he went to sleep. Sadie came and put him in the crib and ordered Kari to change and take a nap. "Okay," Kari replied. She was so tired, but so happy. She lay down on the bed and was fast asleep in moments.

THE CHIEF'S NEWS

When Daniel returned to work, the Chief asked him to come to his office. Daniel went to see what the Chief needed and Chief said, "Close the door, please Daniel." Daniel did so and sat down across from the Chief's desk. The Chief said, "Daniel, I got some news from the town in which Kari was living. It seems the SBI had been setting up a 'sting' operation for a good while. They arrested the chief of police and one of his detectives this morning for drug dealing. While that's a good thing, it does not mean the underground is out of business. There is no word on who killed Frank, but it's pretty definite he was in deep with the drugs; and someone involved did the killing. There is also some concern that the group will move headquarters to other counties close by. I'm not too concerned about them coming here, because the word is out that I'm a hard-nosed Chief, and I have some of the best investigators in the state. However, I want you to keep your eyes and ears open for any rumor you might hear. We know definitely the drug dealers are south and east of the town, but at this point, it doesn't seem they are moving any further." Daniel answered and told the Chief that he would certainly keep notice. He also told him about Joe and Camille coming this week. He would make the Chief aware of anything Joe had picked up. "Thank you, Daniel, now it's about time for you to go home. The officers told me that Kari was 'official' now; she is the mother of Danny. I'm really glad; I like that little red-head."

Daniel went home and asked about Kari and Danny. "They're both asleep," Sadie answered. "Well, good," Daniel replied. "Sadie, there's no need to make dinner tonight. I'll call my favorite restaurant and have them send dinner out again. They make good food and it will save you and Kari some time and energy. Now, why don't you go home and get some rest; it's been a long day for you too. Kari said she had to see Dr. Little tomorrow and Danny needs his second immunization. Do you think you can handle that? I've got some work I need to complete tomorrow. Also, when Camille and Joe get here, probably tomorrow afternoon or Thursday, show Camille what Kari wants for our wedding. We are both pretty excited about this, because it seems like the first wedding for both of us. Kari wants greenery and cream colored flowers woven into them, with cream candles on stands at the end of both sections." Sadie said, "I know, Daniel, she has already told me, but she needs reassurance that you want the same." "I do," he said; "Frankly she seems like my wife now. I'm so proud of her and the progress she has made. Has she said anything to you about her "muddy creek" head?" Sadie said that she had mentioned it to her a time or two and she assured her that she was healing. "Daniel, I believe you and Danny are what she has needed for quite some time, so now I'm going home, before my comments give you a 'big head'." Daniel laughed and said, "Okay, no 'big head' from me."

Daniel called the restaurant and ordered steak, creamed potatoes, broccoli and a salad. He again told them when to deliver it and went to lie down on the couch. It had been a long day for him as well, but he needed to think about what the Chief had told him and decide what to tell Joe. He thought Joe and Camille would spend the night tomorrow and begin their house deciding on Thursday. Anyway, there would be time for him and Joe to find some movers and have a talk. He drifted off to sleep and was awakened by a sweet smell and Kari kissing him. "Good evening," she said. "It seems you were tired too. I'll start some dinner in a few minutes but you need some hugging; you looked so sweet asleep." "Oh, yep, I need some hugging and kissing too; 'cause I missed you today." Well, the smooching would have to wait; Danny chose that time to make himself heard. They laughed and got up to check on him. He again had spit up and was cranky. He'd had another loose stool and so the routine continued, with Daniel giving him a bath and Kari getting clean clothing and changing his sheet. Daniel said, "I didn't know one baby could need so much bathing and cause so much laundry that needs doing." "Well, really it's not usual unless he is sick." Kari said, "I'll put something on for dinner and then feed him some Pedialyte and formula." Daniel replied, "No need for that, I've already ordered dinner. We've all three had a busy day and we need to relax this evening and play with our son. Tomorrow you both have doctor's appointments and I believe Camille and Joe will be in late and probably stay with us tomorrow night." "Daniel, you are one terrific man and I adore you"; she hugged him and Danny who was in his arms. "I'll get the formula ready and give him his medicine and rub his gums. He will play with his teething ring a while and then be ready for bed for the night." "Fine," Daniel replied. After he ate, Danny seemed less cranky and Kari put him on his pallet. She and Daniel lay down on the couch and caught up on the news. Danny watched too, but was soon busy with his toys and teething ring.

In about an hour, Danny was getting fretful. They put him in his swing and gave him his teething ring and toys. He played a little while, but was ready for rocking. Kari had Daniel take him to the crib and she changed him and wiped his little bottom with warm bath cloth. She creamed his bottom with petroleum jelly and put on him a clean diaper and pajamas. Danny played with Kari and chewed her blouse and his hand and anything his hand could get hold of; they had forgotten his teething ring, so Daniel found it, rinsed it and gave it to Danny.

Again, her blouse was damp, her hair had been chewed, and her jaw line was reddened. "Danny, you little scamp; why didn't you tell your mama you wanted the teething ring?" Kari said; "He seems to like to chew on me." Daniel thought to himself, smart boy; but, he really needs the teething ring. They put him back into his swing and he was happy, seemed like three minutes; again the crying and fussiness began.

Kari handed Danny to Daniel, fixed his Pedialyte with some formula, dried him and fed him. This time he really was down for the night. Daniel and Kari rested on the couch and soon their dinner arrived. They ate and enjoyed themselves so much. Daniel said, "It's a little over a week until we marry, can you believe that, Kari?" "Oh yes, I know and I can hardly wait. I've got to ask Sadie if she has a vocalist at her church who can sing, or maybe Chuck's Church has a good vocalist. You think that's asking too much of them." "No, I think it's a good idea." They finished dinner and had another coffee and went into the great room. They both lay on the couch and almost dozed off; Daniel turned and held Kari close and almost immediately sat up. "You need to go to bed sweetheart. I love you and I'll be there in a little while." Soon Kari called softly, "I am ready." "So am I sweetheart," but they were not talking about the same thing. Kari was in bed and Daniel was on top of the covers. They slept well.

They awoke the next morning to Danny's talking and then fussing. The same routine applied; Daniel bathed him and Kari changed his crib and gathered the soiled clothes and put them in the washer. She then made breakfast of eggs, toast, and sausage links along with the coffee. Daniel came in with a clean, dry Danny who was yelping for breakfast. Kari had made formula and Pedialyte and proceeded to feed him, while Daniel had breakfast. Soon Daniel got up to shower, shave and change for work. When he came out, Sadie had arrived. He said good morning and Sadie replied. "You know, Daniel that Kari and Danny see the doctor today and, depending on how the two of them feel, I'll take them over to my Church and introduce them to my pastor. She can determine if she wants a vocalist from my church or Pastor Chuck's Church; it wouldn't hurt to have one vocalist from each Church." "Good Sadie, that's what we'll do, one from each Church." Daniel told them to work it out and whatever they decided was fine with him. He went into work and Sadie and Kari began to prepare for the doctors visits.

They went to Dr. Little first and Kari saw Dr. Little. She examined Kari well and said she had healed well. "I'm not sure the leg is completely healed, but you can have an x-ray and get a better idea." Dr. Little had x-ray equipment in her office, as well as a lot of medical equipment. The film showed the leg already knitted. Kari was really happy. She told Dr. Little about her up-coming wedding. Dr. Little warned her that the pelvic floor was healed but the vaginal vault was a bit tight. "That's okay," Kari replied.

The next stop was to see Dr. Lee for Danny's checkup and second immunization. Kari told him about Danny's tooth and his upset stomach as well as him chewing everything in sight. "He is teething again, Kari, but these teeth are about to pop through. He is perfectly healthy and the timing is right for him to start producing teeth. You may start him on one vegetable at a time for three weeks and see how he does with that and then progress to another vegetable or fruit. Try to keep the different foods at least three weeks apart to determine if he is allergic to anyone of them." "Okay," Kari replied.

They left the doctors offices and Sadie asked Kari how she felt about going to see her Church and talk with her pastor. Kari was all for that. She told Sadie what Dr. Little had said and, of course, Sadie was in with Kari and Danny to see Dr. Lee. "That's wonderful, Kari."

They drove over to Sadie's Church and went into the pastor's office. Sadie introduced them and they chatted for a while. Kari asked the Pastor if he had a vocalist who would be able and willing to sing a song at her wedding. "Oh, yes we do. One of the women in the choir has an especially gifted voice." Kari asked if he would ask her to sing THE LORD'S PRAYER and Pastor Charles was sure she would and do a great job for Kari. They thanked him and soon left. They went into town to pick up a few groceries and supplies for home, and then headed home.

Kari decided to make a pot roast for dinner with all the trimmings. She was also planning to make some bran, banana muffins for dinner and breakfast the next day. Sadie reminded her that she still needed to rest a little. Kari said, "I know." Dr. Little said she had lost seven pounds and did not need to lose anymore. They were home by now and Sadie took the groceries in and Kari for the first time; lifted Danny out of the car seat and took him inside. By this time, he was grumbling and fussing. "It seems he needs a bit of food," Kari said. "I think I'll continue with full formula and rice cereal for a while." Sadie thought that might be wise. Sadie took Danny and dried and dressed him in soft pajamas and brought him to Kari, who had prepared his lunch. Danny was hungry; he ate everything and was ready to have a 'rocking time'. He was soon fast asleep and Kari put him into his crib.

Kari decided to go for a walk and told Sadie that she would be back in a little while. She needed fresh air and some time to reflect on all that had happened. Sadie said, "That's a good idea." Kari put her heavy coat on and started down the path she always took, to breathe fresh air and check on her creek. It had rained a few days ago and they had already had a light snow; she wondered if that would make a difference in the creek. She got down to where the creek was and it was flowing, but there was still some muddy water present. Well, there must be something blocking the water flow that was causing it to remain slightly muddy. It's probably a dam the little beavers had made. It had turned rather chilly during her walk and she came back to the house.

As she came up the driveway to her steps, she noticed Joe and Camille coming in. They still had the U-Haul behind their car. They both got out of the car and gave Kari a big hug and told her how wonderful she looked. "Well, let's go in out of this cold," Kari said. They all three went in and Sadie was thrilled to see them, as they were to see her. They began to chat and Joe asked, "Kari, can we bunk here tonight? We've got an appointment with our realtor in the morning and will probably move later tomorrow evening and Friday." Kari said, "I won't hear of anything else. Now the both of you know where your room is and Sadie is such a dear, she's made the room ready, but I doubt Daniel remembers to get flowers and chocolates," she said, smiling. Camille said, "Kari, the flowers and chocolates were great, but we just want to be with all of you. I can't wait to hear all the news, since we last saw you." Kari replied, "Neither can we."

It was almost time for Daniel to be home and Sadie told them all that the table was set and Danny was still asleep, so she was going home until tomorrow. "It's been a rather busy day, but very productive. I'll see you all in the morning."

Joe, Camille, and Kari were talking about all that had happened since they had left. Kari told them about Danny's tooth and his cutting two more. The doctor said he was exactly the right weight and development for his age. He also gave him his second immunization. "That's wonderful," Camille replied. "And guess what," "What?" Joe and Camille asked together, "I am now officially Danny's mother. Daniel surprised me the other day with the news and the judge pronounced me the mother of Daniel Lee Meyers (Danny). I almost jumped with joy." Joe said, "Kari that is wonderful." Camille came over, hugged and kissed her and said "That means we are grandparents, you know." Kari laughed, "I hadn't really thought of that, but yes, you are."

Daniel came in about that time and they all greeted one another and enjoyed their togetherness for a while. Daniel said, "Kari, I smell something great from the kitchen, is dinner ready?" "Oh yes, and Daniel, I was able to make dinner today. Camille, help me set the table and let the men chat for a while." They prepared the table and set the meal out, it did smell wonderful. Kari had already put some frozen rolls in the oven and they were almost ready. When they had made coffee and fixed the water glasses, dinner was indeed ready. Both men came into the kitchen and sat down. They blessed the food and thanked God for their safe trip and the wonderful care He had given to all of them. Then they proceeded to eat. Danny awoke right on cue; Kari got up to get him and Daniel stood up too, "You are not to lift him remember?" "Well, yes I can, Dr. Little gave me a clean bill of health today." Daniel hugged her and said that was great, but he would help her just the same. Of course Danny needed changing and clean clothing. When that was completed, Daniel and Kari came out, with Kari carrying Danny. They presented a beautiful picture. Camille said, "Okay, it's my turn to hold my grandson." Daniel, Kari and Joe started laughing, seems Kari had told them about the adoption and they were thrilled. Daniel replied; "So am I."

They finished dinner and all three of the adults told Kari how much they enjoyed it. They took Danny into the great room and, although his pallet was there, Camille chose to rock him and play. Danny began to want on his pallet; he had to show off his skills too! He would pick up a toy, talk to it, and toss it; roll over and perform the same act with another toy. Camille said; "He is brilliant!" Kari said; "He's just like his father, but don't brag on them too much, they may not mind me." Daniel spoke up and said; "Not a chance, my beautiful red-head has a way of keeping us both in check. At least that's what my Chief says." They laughed and talked a while and Kari noticed that Camille and Joe were getting tired, for that matter, so was she. She told them to go on to bed; she and Daniel would tidy everything and get Danny to sleep. They gave no objection and hugged them all and went to their room.

Daniel and Kari tidied the kitchen, put the dishwasher on, and Kari took some large muffins out of the freezer to pop in the oven in the morning. She then fixed Danny's bottle and cereal and Daniel brought Danny into her and she fed him. Daniel said, "Honey, you know I'll have to sleep on the couch tonight." "I know Kari replied, but I don't particularly like it." They chatted a bit and Kari told Daniel about the doctor's report on her and Danny. She told him that Dr. Little said she was healed, but the vaginal vault was still a bit tight. "My dearest Kari, that is fine; stop worrying about me. We will make love when you want to and feel you are ready, not before." Kari took the now sleeping Danny to his crib and Daniel followed to get his couch sheet and pillow out of the closet. They held each other and kissed good night. "I love you," they both said at the same time.

Daniel went into the great room to the couch. He thanked God for the doctor's good report and for the safe arrival of Camille and Joe. He would get some fellows he knew to help unload the U-Haul when Camille and Joe decided on the house they wanted. They had two that they both liked, but needed to look at them both in order to determine which they wanted. Daniel finally fell asleep and Kari did as well, but neither rested as well as if Daniel and she were on the same bed. Thankfully, the wedding was a bit over a week away. Kari had told him about the vocalist at Sadie's Church and that she would be the only one. The organist and pianist at Daniel's church would play a few pieces of music. She also asked Daniel if they could walk down the aisle together, without any of the formality of 'giving away' the bride. That was fine with him.

The next morning Kari had awakened before even Danny had, she prepared breakfast of eggs with green onion and bread crumbs in muffin tins with some cheese on top, Canadian bacon, and the muffins she had put out the night before. Everything smelled so good; it soon brought everyone to the kitchen. Daniel had awakened when Kari went to the kitchen. He checked on Danny who was awake and ready for his day. Daniel gave him a bath and Danny seemed to want to eat his duck, but Daniel told him to let him swim, that's what ducks do. Danny threw the duck in the bath water and Daniel finished his bath, wrapped him in a big towel and found his clothing and diapers and dressed him; he also put his boots on. Danny seemed to talk to Daniel, but was getting ready to eat. Kari heard them stirring and prepared Danny's breakfast. She fed him and they put him in his swing. Camille and Joe came out about that time and both told Kari of the wonderful smell in the kitchen. "Well sit down at the table and I'll have the food ready shortly."

They looked at Danny and Joe saw the boots first, "Don't tell me, Daniel that you boys go hunting yet." Daniel and Kari laughed and said "No," but Danny liked his boots and could swing easily with them on. Danny had his teething ring and other toys and was enjoying himself. They all ate breakfast and Joe told Kari and Daniel that he and Camille had an appointment to see the houses at ten o'clock. Kari said, "Well, take my car and leave yours parked here." "Thanks," Joe answered. They finished another cup of coffee and went to dress for their appointment. Daniel helped Kari tidy the kitchen and gave her a big kiss and hug before he hit the shower. He came out of the bedroom, dressed and ready for work.

Sadie soon arrived and Daniel left for work. Kari told Sadie about Joe and Camille checking the houses and when they decided on one that Daniel would get some of the guys he knew to help them move in. Sadie said, "That's good of Daniel, seems like Joe and Camille have been through quite a lot since she saw them last." Kari said, "Probably so, but Camille has not talked with me much about it".

Sadie showed Kari some of her thoughts on the cake and goodies for the reception. They looked great and Kari showed Sadie the pictures she had made of the Church and reception room. "I know Camille will want to help and you know, Sadie, I've got a good bill of health now." "I know," Sadie replied, "But Danny is still trying to get those two teeth through and will still have periods of fretfulness. You need to care for him and do what you can to make, dinner and laundry and all that entails. Camille and I will make you happy with the décor and reception." "I know," Kari replied, "And I'm deeply grateful to both of you. Daniel and I have decided to walk down the aisle together. I expect the wedding ceremony and salt covenant to be rather short and a blessing to all in attendance." "Oh my word, Sadie, I have forgotten to send out invitations and now it's too late." "Oh, nonsense," Sadie replied. "You do that today, while I tidy up and look after Daniel." "Sadie, I cannot believe I made such a mistake; seems like I'm getting better and then something as important as sending invitations on time, I forget. Will I ever become my normal self?" Sadie answered, "Of course you will, Kari, but you must stop so much worry about protocol and focus on the important things, like getting your dress and choosing a bouquet to carry."

"The wedding and reception have been planned and all that remains is to get the Church decorated and the reception hall fixed with tablecloth, plates, forks, and napkins, as well as, deciding what type punch the two of you like. I've got a pretty punch bowl and glasses and nice little serving plates. I told you I do this kind of thing for most of the girls at my Church." "One day the beginning of the week Daniel and I are going to get my dress; he insisted on seeing me in it when I try it on. I know he had very little or no input in his first wedding."

Danny was ready to get out of his swing and go to the pallet for a while; he was also becoming fretful again. Sadie said, "I'll get Danny settled and you write your invitations and we'll mail them today. That will be only two to three days late and that matters very little to the people who you especially want at the wedding; but I can tell you, there will be a number of people you haven't yet met who will be there. Daniel is pretty well known in the entire community and people love him, and they will want to see him happy." "Oh, that's fine Sadie, thanks."

Sadie went to attend to Danny and Kari completed the invitations and had them ready to mail. She told Sadie she was going to walk down to the mail box and put them in the mail. "The fresh air will do you good, but put a heavy jacket on, it's cold out there." Kari took the invitations to the mail box and took a short walk. It felt wonderful to have some of the burden she felt lifted. She thanked the Lord for Daniel, Danny, Sadie, Camille and Joe, as well as, the number of people who had helped her since she had moved. She felt sure that all would go well and soon she and Daniel would be married. She soon went back into the house and began preparations for dinner. She was making 'chicken in a sack' with roasted vegetables and a 'mac and cheese casserole'. She had everything prepared and Sadie called her to prepare Danny's lunch. He was hungry and she would give him a sponge bath and change his clothing and Kari could handle his food and the rocking chair. Sadie would tidy the house and do laundry and whatever else needed attention. Kari sat at the table and fed Danny his cereal and bottle and carried him to the rocking chair; soon he was asleep. Sadie reminded Kari that she too needed a rest, so Kari took a rest period too.

Danny slept and Kari rested a while, but was soon up to finish preparations for dinner and make chocolate cake and they would have ice cream and strawberries on top. Sadie had completed the laundry and tidying the rest of the house. She made sure Danny's pallet had been cleaned well and the swing had been wiped down. Danny was a messy little fellow with food and toys mixed with his teething ring. Danny awoke about the time Kari was elbow deep in making the cake so Sadie went to get him and dried him and brought him to the swing. He played a few minutes and decided he didn't like swinging anymore, seemed he wanted to eat. Kari fixed some baby-food peas and his formula. He immediately spit out the peas. She tried again and Danny spit and cried and definitely did not want any peas. So Kari picked him up out of the swing and sponged him off and put a clean shirt and diaper on him; all the while Danny is 'yelling' attempting to eat his teething ring. Kari felt his gums and called Sadie. Sadie came into the room and Kari said; "I believe he has cut another tooth, this time the top one." Sadie felt his gums and he bit down on her finger, Sadie laughed and said, "Yep, he's got a top tooth and bottom tooth, but they are not matched." They both laughed and Danny yelled. "Okay, my darling, come on and mama will feed you and rub the other gum and maybe give you some drops." He did feel a bit warm and was extremely cranky. She fed him his bottle and he had begun to want to hold it himself, but each time he tried, he would miss his mouth and yell. Finally, Kari said, "I'll do the feeding for now, young man." She gave him his bottle and rocked him and he was soon ready to play. She put him on his pallet and watched him scoot toward his toys. He seemed fine and Kari went back to her chores.

WEDDING PREPARATIONS

Sadie had made a pretty table setting and she turned to Kari and reminded her that she hadn't eaten lunch, and you are loosing too much weight, Kari. Kari said she would eat a muffin and apple with some coffee if Sadie would join her. "Okay," Sadie replied, she had already made fresh coffee. They talked a little bit about the wedding and how everything was going as planned. Sadie told her that she would bring her own cake pans, etc. for the wedding cake and treats; make them here and put all of the stuff into the freezer until the time came for the wedding. Kari had installed a very large freezer when she had the house built, and there was plenty of room. She asked Kari to make a list of what she needed for the wedding stuff and she would make a list of groceries and things she needed. Daniel would take time to get everything they needed. "He has been so good about bringing in whatever I needed to run the house and make meals. I'm thankful for him and somewhat bewildered; you see, Frank never did anything like that; he told me what he wanted and if he was having a dinner party for his friends, and I did it and worked in the evenings." Sadie said; "Kari, Don't confuse Daniel with Frank; they are two entirely different men. Frank is gone and Daniel does not ever need to hear what you just told me. You see, Daniel is very sensitive to insuring your happiness and he loves to do things for you. He is not a selfish, spoiled man, you see, he has also been 'burned' with a former spouse." That was the closest Sadie had ever come to rebuking Kari for anything. "Oh, Sadie, you are so right; I love you for reminding me of that. You can bet Danny's boots I won't make that mistake again." "Good Kari, now why is your son so quiet?" They went into the great room and Danny was asleep on his pallet with his teething ring and toys in a pile. It seemed like he had arranged everything to his liking and gone to sleep. They both laughed gently and left him to finish his nap.

It was about time for Daniel to be in from work, so Sadie told Kari she would go home and check her recipes and make a list of needs and bring them in the morning for Daniel. Kari was also making her list and said, "that's fine, Sadie." Before Sadie could get her coat and prepare to go home, Joe and Camille came in. Sadie told them she was glad to see them and that Kari would not be alone, until Daniel came in. "That's our pleasure," they assured Sadie and glanced at the sleeping Danny. "We will go into the kitchen and visit some with Kari and tell her what we've decided on." "That's great", Sadie replied. Camille hugged Sadie and said, "We'll talk tomorrow".

Daniel came in from work and looked tired. He kissed Kari and said a very quiet hi to Danny, then greeted Joe and Camille. Kari told him that dinner was almost ready, for him to wash up and take a little rest on the couch. "I believe I will," he said. Kari, Joe and Camille noticed his fatigue and knew when he was ready; he would tell them what he wanted to tell them. Joe and Camille wanted to tell Kari about the house they had decided on, but would take their cue from Daniel. Camille fixed the water glasses and put the hot rolls in the container, while Kari put the 'chicken sacks' on a platter, as well as the roasted vegetables. They heard Daniel come back to the great room and Joe went in to briefly talk with him. Daniel already seemed more relaxed; seems seeing Kari and Danny had done as much to refresh him as a splash of water on his face. They talked quietly for a little while and Kari called them into dinner. Daniel said, "Wow, whatever you have cooked smells wonderful." Kari told them that dinner was now served. After they ate a while, Daniel said, "Joe, we've had another alcohol poisoning. We must do something to give the younger kids a place to go that is safe; seems this same 'Joe' came to see another group of high school kids and challenged them to a drinking contest. One of the girls died today. A girl is dead; no chance to live or to fulfill God's plan. Naturally, her parents are in deep shock and anger is replacing some of the shock. How could this happen in this town?"

Joe said, "Daniel, I don't know. We must have a special prayer for the parents of this girl, as well as the other kids drinking. Who knows but what this guy is scoping out this territory to start another drug dealership." Daniel said; "He and the Chief had started to believe the same thing.

Chief has already put some of his best detectives on this activity and if necessary will involve the SBI. He and I decided to become more active around the Middle and High Schools, with the Principals and School Board being made aware. Perhaps, we can stop this negative influence before it gets a 'foot hold'."

Joe told Daniel and the others, that he also had a degree in counseling. When he and Camille got settled a bit, he would offer his services to some of the high schools. I haven't been led to another Church and besides, at this time I'm more needed in this avenue. Daniel said; "I believe that's right."

"Now, tell us about your house." Camille spoke up and said, "Daniel, it is perfect for us. We can hardly wait for you and Kari to see it." Daniel said he had lined up some fellows to help them move in and get the heavy stuff set up where Camille wanted it. It seems like Joe is left out of the arranging, except of course for his office. They laughed and Kari took up now empty plates and served chocolate cake with ice cream and strawberries on top. Camille poured them all coffee.

After they had their coffee and dessert, they went into the great room. Danny chose that time to begin his fussing and crankiness. He had spit up on his clothing and the pallet and smelled none to pleasant. Kari picked him up and cooed with him, gave him a good warm bath and dressed him in pajamas. None of her cooing and loving made much difference. Danny was not a 'happy boy'. "Oh, I forgot he is teething, but he also had another immunization. I guess the little darling feels pretty bad." She handed him to Daniel to hold and talked to him, while she fixed him half formula and half Pedialyte. She came back into the great room with some medicine and drops to rub his gums and he bit her. "My-oh-my, young man, you bit your mama again." It looked like the other tooth had come through. Kari rubbed his gums and felt another bump on the opposite side on his top gum. Danny was still fussing and she gave him the drops the doctor ordered and fed him his bottle. In the meantime, Daniel had taken the soiled clothes and pallet to the washer. Kari fed him, talked softly to him and soon he was asleep. She continued to rock him, until she felt his little body completely relax; then she put him in his crib.

Joe, Camille, Kari and Daniel sat together and prayed for the parents and kids to be comforted by the Lord's Holy Spirit. They continued to ask

God's direction for each of them and to prepare a place in which the kids could have a place of refuge, play sports, study and be introduced to some college courses that would direct them in their future careers. They asked that Parents, the Community College and the High Schools might be receptive to the idea. The local Churches might assist with funding, but most of the kids on the street would not go to a Church. When they had finished their praying, they all felt better and began to talk about their house and the upcoming wedding.

Sadie would bring her own cake pans, serving dishes and punch bowl over here and keep everything in one place until time for the wedding. They could store things that did not need refrigeration on Kari's balcony. She and Camille would decorate the reception hall and determine where the flowers would be placed, as well as the punch bowl and cake. The serving dishes could be stacked as needed on the table.

Daniel told them he would put his house on the market tomorrow with an agent he knew. He would get everything the ladies had listed for him, and contact the fellows to help Joe and Camille move their belongings into their own home. Joe told him that would be great since they signed the agreement today, and had permission to move in. No one had lived there in quite a while. Camille piped up and said, "The house was just right. It has two bedrooms and an arch way to a library off the living room. It is old, but we fell in love with it as soon as we saw it. The plaster walls are great, but I might want some painting done in the kitchen and perhaps a nicer countertop. The entire house needs a good cleaning, so I hired a cleaning crew to come in the morning to get that done. Then Joe and some of the fellows Daniel spoke about can complete the rest."

It seemed that things were moving forward like a locomotive. There was the wedding, Daniel's house up for sale, Joe and Camille would be moving into their new home, Sadie was doing the majority of the cooking. Kari was feeling overwhelmed and anxiety was taking over her thinking. She could help Sadie with the cooking and look after Danny, but was she able to also help Camille get settled? She was beginning to feel unworthy and useless again. She stayed pretty quite for a while and then Danny piped up with a yell and grumble. Kari went to get him and she gave him a sponge bath and changed him into clean clothing. He wasn't happy and began to spit up and soon another diaper change was necessary. That other tooth must be coming in. She went to get his bottle mixed with gator-aid and fed him; she also gave him some medicine. She rubbed his gums and there were now two reddened swollen areas, "Poor darling, I'll get your teething ring and we'll just rock a while." She did and the others asked if he was alright. Kari replied, "Yes, just some teething issues."

Kari decided to rock Danny in her room and let the others talk a while. She and Danny were getting tired, so she rocked and Danny fell asleep and Kari was much more relaxed. She heard the others talking about going to bed and didn't venture out to say good night, Daniel could handle that. He did and then came in and sat down on the bed. "What's wrong, Kari?" "Nothing really," she said, "I'm just feeling a bit useless with all the things happening at once, or within the new week. I still haven't bought my dress, or found a new outfit for Danny. I can help Sadie with the cooking, but I'm of no use to Camille and Joe." Daniel said, "Is that why you became so quite?" "I guess so," Kari replied. Daniel said, "Kari you are definitely useful and a real blessing to everyone who meets you. I know you are tired and feeling overwhelmed and so am I a bit. However, you and I can go get your dress Tuesday and pick up an outfit for Danny. I also need a new suit and shirt, so we can spend the day, just the two of us. I'm sure Sadie will keep Danny with no problem. I'll do the laundry tonight and have it ready to be put away tomorrow morning. By the way, dinner was excellent." "Thanks, Daniel. I guess I'm a bit nervous about our wedding too. Did I tell you I sent an invitation to my aunt and uncle for the wedding?" "No, you didn't darling, but that is great, I hope they can come."

Kari got up and put the sleeping Danny in his crib. She asked if everyone was comfortable and Daniel said, "Yes." "I'll help tidy the kitchen, but first, could you hold me a few minutes?" "Oh dear Kari, of course and it's my pleasure." They held each other and kissed and Kari said, "Well, we'd better get the kitchen straight." "Okay," Daniel replied. They worked together and Daniel put the clothes in the washer and they sat down in the kitchen and began to help clear Kari's head. They both had a cup of hot tea and quite enjoyed themselves. Daniel said, "Kari, I think you might take one of the pills that Dr. Little prescribed for you." "Okay, but you know what?" "What," he asked. "As much as I love Joe and Camille, I'll be glad when we can get some routine back in our own lives." Daniel laughed, "You mean me sleeping on the covers with you?" "Yep," she answered. Daniel whispered; "Me too. Now take your pill while I finish up the laundry." Kari took her pill and was soon very relaxed and a bit sleepy. Daniel finished the laundry and took Kari to her bed and got his sheet and pillow from the closet. They both soon fell asleep.

Daniel and Kari awoke early and started breakfast. Kari had made a bread pudding the night before and had it ready to go into the oven. She also had some baked sweet potatoes sliced and ready for service. Daniel made the coffee and set the table and soon Danny made himself heard. Kari and Daniel went into the room and Danny had spit up and had diarrhea; so that entailed a complete bath and sheet change. Daniel bathed him and wrapped him in a large towel and brought him into the bedroom for a clean diaper and pajamas. Kari had mixed formula with 'gator-aid' and gave it to him, as well as some medicine. She got his teething ring and he chewed on it for a while and Kari continued rocking him. Daniel put his boots on him and they put him in the swing. He was at peace for a while.

They were finishing making breakfast when Joe and Camille came out. They all sat down to eat, blessed the food and began general conversation. Camille said that she needed to go to their house and supervise the cleaners and Joe needed to bring the U-Haul so the guys could unload it and Joe could take it the U-Haul place in town. Daniel agreed and said he had already contacted a few of the officers that were off duty and they would be glad to help. It shouldn't take very long. Camille said, "You all have been wonderful, but we can't wait to get into our own home." "That's great," Kari said, "But I can't do much to help you Camille; you see Danny is cutting some more teeth and is cranky today." Camille replied, "That's quite okay, Kari. Joe and I can do the beds and linens, now stop worrying about us!" Kari said, "All right, but we will have dinner prepared anyway, because you will be tired and can't possibly have groceries or even the cookware unpacked." "That would be great; Kari, but we will be spending our first night in our new home. We have already planned to go grocery shopping and get any items we need, tomorrow." They all enjoyed breakfast and of course, bragged on Kari's cooking. It was good.

As soon as breakfast and another coffee were finished, they played with Danny a few minutes and kissed him and got ready to leave. Camille and Joe left and Daniel made sure the guys could help Joe after lunch. They were glad to. By that time the cleaners would have finished the general cleaning and have things ready for Joe and Camille to tell them where to put the beds and furniture that was theirs. There weren't many pieces of furniture, just the beds and lamps stands and the boxes with books and linens and household things. Camille could show them where to put the things for the kitchen and Joe knew what would go into the bathroom. They had purchased a small dinette set and it would go into the dining room. They did have a china cabinet that was theirs, with some pretty china ware that they had collected over the years.

They hadn't been gone long when Danny became cranky and no longer wanted his swing. Daniel took his to dry him and insure his bottom wasn't red and dressed him again in clean pajamas, plus his boots! Kari had made some formula with a tiny bit of cereal which she fed him. He was more interested in the bottle than the cereal. He finished and seemed to want to play.

Kari took him to his pallet and lay down with him to play with him. They were both pretty happy. Daniel had begun tidying the kitchen and put a load of clothes on to wash. He came in to the great room and asked if he could play too. Of course he could, Kari said, but Daniel asked about Danny's opinion? "He told me he was glad daddy got his boots, he could now move about more easily." He could too. It looked like he could crawl to Daniel. "Oh, he can a little bit," Kari answered. Daniel lay beside Kari and they watched Danny. Soon they began to hug and kiss good morning. Daniel held Kari tightly, "I love you so much, I could almost eat you," he said. Kari hugged him back and said, "Well, that might be a problem; I don't want to be eaten, just kissed and hugged a lot." They both started laughing for the first time in several days. The doorbell rang and Daniel got up to answer it.

Sadie came in and looked about and asked where Danny had gone. Neither Kari nor Daniel had noticed Danny had crawled into Camille's room, and he was pulling on the bedspread. "Oh my word, how did he do that so quickly? We were all three playing on his pallet and Daniel and I got a bit involved with our wedding plans and he just quietly crawled in there. Sadie, he's almost on his feet," Kari said. "Well, it's about time for him to start pulling himself up and before you know it, he'll be crawling and pulling up to walk beside the couch." Sadie noted that Daniel's bed had been slept in. She asked where Camille and Joe were. "They've gone to their new house to supervise the cleaning crew and then the men that Daniel hired will move the rest of their belongings into the house. Sadie; it's Saturday, what do you need us to do?" She said, "Nothing I just wanted to check on you all. Kari, you looked a bit 'down' yesterday and I wondered if you were sick." "No, I'm not sick, but I was feeling a bit nervous. You see, Sadie, I'm not able to look after Danny and make dinner and have time to help Camille with her bed-making or lining shelves or anything." Sadie said, "I've got an idea, why don't the four of us ride over to the house and drop in with sandwiches for all of them; check to see if Camille and Joe are okay?"

Daniel said, "That's a great idea and I will keep an eye on Danny, lest he crawl up the balcony steps. We also might go get one of those baby gates Kari told me about." Kari said, "Oh Sadie, how dear you are; I love you and would very much like to make the whole gang some sandwiches and cupcakes for desert. You'll find some lunch bags in that last cupboard in front of the washer and dryer. Also, Daniel put a load of clothes in to wash and I haven't dried them yet. I've still been a bit overwhelmed, how will we get everything done on time?" Sadie and Daniel spoke up together and told her firmly, "It will all be done in time and up to your standards." They both smiled at her and Sadie went to put the clothes in the dryer, got a cup of coffee and asked Daniel if he would bring in the boxes she had in her car. "Sure I will, but would you keep your eye on Danny, I had no idea he could move that fast." Sadie laughed and said, "I can imagine it; I've seen him scoot pretty fast."

They decided to put Danny in his swing until Daniel got the boxes out of Sadie's car. "Do you mean it takes all these pans to make a cake, and there are tablecloths and small dishes and stuff I'm not familier with!" Sadie said, "Yep, you need it all to make things perfect." "Well, you ladies know best." "Kari, how can I help with the sandwiches?" "Nothing at this point, I'm making some cupcakes for dessert. Then we'll have an assembly line for sandwiches. I've got some baked chicken, some ham and turkey breast in the refrigerator, it will need to be warmed, but that's no problem; they all go in the oven at one time. I have plenty of good bread and a sauce for any sandwich that seems a little dry." "You can get the waxed paper out and tear sheets about twelve inches square to wrap the sandwiches in." Daniel turned to Sadie and said, "You know, Sadie, I'm learning more and more about my future wife. The wedding is less than a week away now and frankly, I was getting a little concerned that we wouldn't please Kari. Thank you more than you know, Sadie."

He bent to kiss her cheek and she smiled at him. About that time, Danny let out a roar. "My goodness young man, just because you can crawl, you have not become our master. Now hold on a minute and I'll fix your bottle," but Danny did not hush. Daniel said, "Do you all think he will ever obey?" "Oh yes, Daniel, he doesn't feel well and it is his own way of letting us know he needs something." Sadie picked him up and sure enough he needed another bath and change of clothes. Daniel shook his head and finished folding the laundry. Kari had the muffins made and put into the cups and into the oven. She set the timer and went into where Sadie, Daniel and Danny were. Danny saw her and reached for her. Kari cooed at him and told him in a minute he would have his bottle and mama would rock him. He quieted a little bit and decided he would quarrel with his mama. She put his teething ring in his hand and picked up the now clean and sweet-smelling Danny and took him to the rocking chair. She gave him his medicine and rubbed his gums and fed him his bottle. He didn't know whether to chew or drink his bottle; seems he decided to hold the ring and take his bottle. Kari rocked him and soon he was drowsy. She quietly put him in his crib and he seemed to rest and go to sleep, holding his teething ring.

Now back to the sandwiches, muffins, and new pot of coffee. "Daniel look under the cupboard beside the washer and you will find a large container that keeps things hot or cold." Daniel found it and proceeded to tear the sheets of waxed paper twelve inches square. Sadie was slicing the large pieces of meat and Kari was warming a spicy white sauce and reducing it down. They put out about twelve pieces of bread and Sadie started putting the meat on the bread. Kari used the sauce on the turkey and Sadie used mayonnaise and mustard on the other sandwiches. Kari then sliced a large tomato and put a slice on each sandwich with some basil leaves and lettuce. They then put the top bread on and Sadie and Kari wrapped the sandwiches in the waxed paper. Daniel didn't know what to do, so Kari asked him to rinse with very hot water the thermos and pour the large pot of coffee into the thermos. She also had frosted the muffins with some chocolate frosting and began wrapping them. Things were now ready to be packed and taken to Camille's house. Daniel got the now sleeping Danny and wrapped him well and put him in the car seat. He packed the boxes where Sadie and Kari told him to and they were soon off. Kari had prepared the diaper bag, medicine and drops, as well as his formula and put it in the car.

When they got to the house, the cleaners were just leaving and Camille had paid them. When she saw Kari, Sadie, Daniel and Danny, she started crying. The guys had just gotten there and she didn't have a clue what to feed them. Kari said, "Stop that crying and sniff, what do you smell in the box?" Camille did stop crying and gave Kari and Sadie a big hug. Daniel said; "I helped; I tore the paper to wrap the sandwiches in," and started to laugh. Camille hugged him too. Joe came in about that time and said; "Who is this kissing my wife? Do you think we can trust this guy, boys?" The boys were the officers who were to help unload. "Well, she's mighty pretty; I'd keep a watch on him," they laughed. Kari hadn't met them and she smiled at all of them and said; "You better believe you can. I'll have to have a strong speech with him." Daniel came over and introduced her to the guys and they smiled at her and said, Daniel, "How did you get so lucky?" "The Good Lord was looking after me," Daniel answered.

Camille said; "You guys can eat prior to unloading that U-Haul, Kari is a great cook and she and Sadie made some sandwiches and coffee." "Is that what we smelled?" "Sure is," Joe replied. "That would be great." So Kari showed them Danny and they couldn't believe how he had grown and how healthy he is. Daniel says, "He doesn't obey me, but quiets down when Sadie or Kari speak with him. I guess they know 'baby-talk'." Kari said, "Well we had better go, to buy a baby gate to keep him from crawling up the balcony."

They left, but before they got out the door, Camille had written down their new phone number. "We'll call before we come over this evening." Sadie, Kari, and Daniel got Danny settled and headed to the baby needs store. When they finished with that, Kari said, "I need to get some fresh meat that isn't frozen in order to make dinner on time. I have fresh vegetables and rolls; but I need a cake or pie for dessert, as well as some salad." "That'll be fine, Kari." Sadie said, "Kari, are you sure you can do all that cooking alone? It's about two-thirty now." Kari answered, "I think I can and Daniel can set the table and help with the vegetables. Sadie, you know I love you, but you don't have to do everything for me, unless you will have supper with us." Sadie said, "No, honey, I was just making sure you are not getting depressed and too tired. I've got to do a few things at my house and prepare for my Church tomorrow. I'll check again with my pastor and the vocalist you want, to be sure that part of the wedding is complete." "Thank you, Sadie. Please get yourself some rest. Tomorrow morning comes early, according to Danny."

Sadie left and said she would see them Monday morning. "Oh, wait Sadie, I forgot your check. Sleep well and we will see you Monday." Again, Daniel had paid her too much, but he had told her that he wanted to; that he knew he could depend on her to love and help Kari and Danny.

She went home and Kari got busy with the pork loin. She put several pieces of garlic in the meat, salted it and put some rosemary, sage, and vinegar in the pot she would use. She browned the loin and put it in the oven with vegetables and cooked it. She made slaw and a few roasted vegetables. She put the roasted vegetables in her other oven. She was really glad she had such a big kitchen. She had placed the rolls on a sheet pan to let them rise and would bake them when Camille and Joe got there.

She made a large pitcher of tea and coffee ready to brew. By this time Danny was tired of crawling or scooting or anything. Seemed he needed a clean diaper and clothing. Daniel had already picked him up and sure enough, he had another loose stool. He put him in the bathtub and bathed him, wrapped him in a large towel and dressed him in clean clothing. He took Danny into Kari and asked if his formula needed dilution with 'gator-aid'; "Probably," Kari answered. "I'll be so glad when the little darling stops teething for a while. He is so miserable and it hurts me to see him in any discomfort." Daniel smiled and noticed that when Kari took him, he quieted a little bit. He brought Kari the baby's bottle and teething ring. This time, he brought the medicine too. Kari rubbed his gums and said one of them was almost through the skin. She rocked him and Daniel sat with them. His heart was swollen with love and pride for his two loves. When Danny was asleep, Kari took him to the crib and he slept soundly.

She and Daniel went back to the kitchen and while Kari checked the food, Daniel set the table and had picked up some fresh flowers at the grocery store. He asked Kari if the flowers were the right height. "They are fine, Daniel." While the dinner was cooking, they both got a glass of tea and went into the great room on the couch. They lay together and sipped the tea and talked about how quickly things were moving. When the tea was finished, Kari put their glasses on the floor and hugged and kissed Daniel until he thought he might lose control. "Darling, I love this, but it's time to stop now. I can't take much more without squeezing you too hard. I love you so much." She said, "Okay, I too am getting out of control." They decided they needed to watch the news for a while.

Pretty soon the phone rang; it was Camille and she said, "Is the offer of dinner still open?" "You bet," Kari replied. She and Daniel went back into the kitchen and Daniel had to wash his face and hands, "Do you mind if I do it in the kitchen?" "Of course not!" He told Kari that she had better check her lipstick, it was now gone. She giggled and went to freshen up. She came back to the kitchen and she put the rolls in the oven. She took the pork loin out to let it rest, before slicing it. She also got the platters and bowls she needed and put them on the counter. Daniel put the glasses out ready for ice, and coffee cups ready for coffee.

The door bell rang in a few minutes and Joe and Camille came in. They both looked tired, but happy. Kari said, "Well let's eat and you tell Daniel and me about the work you've done." Joe thanked Daniel first for the officers who helped him set up the furniture; they were great and they wanted everything like Camille wanted it. I had told them for all practical purposes, this was Camille's first house.

The house was spic and span clean and it was easy to set the beds up and put the chests where she told them. Camille then thanked Kari for the sandwiches, cupcakes and coffee. The officers said, "That chaplain is one lucky man; seems he got a beauty this time, but one who really cares about him and the baby." One of the men told them that Daniel had it rough for a while; not knowing what may happen. He seems almost giddy about his Kari and Danny. None of us had seen him so at ease in a long time.

Camille told them that the linens fit; she had already washed them and towels, etc. before they moved. The boys even set up the washer and dryer and the refrigerator before they left. They made sure the electric meter was correct and the fire alarm had perfect batteries and anything else they could think of that might need attention. "I tell you Daniel, they were great."

They will be a big help with the youth camp/retreat. One of them knew of an old school house with a gym and classrooms and a kitchen. It seems the county is trying to sell it and put a new school closer into town. The school sits on quite a bit of property, so you all might think about that for the kids. There is room for gardening and the other things the Chief mentioned to us. Because the officers were on patrol, they would see problem kids before others might. "But, remember, Daniel, these kids won't enter a regular church; it seems they don't have what they call, 'proper clothes' and don't want those fancy duds."

Camille stopped talking long enough to eat dinner and Joe took up the conversation. It seems the Chief had told his officers to be on the look-out for some adequate property. This seems ideal. There will need to be chaperons around the clock to help with anyone who has been kicked out from home. Some of the kids simply need focus on what is good for them while others are a bit rougher, but they would get along, because each one had something the others didn't have. Plus, most young people enjoyed sports, and there was also a baseball yard, basketball gym and with a little help they could put in a swimming pool; plus the rooms for education would be ideal. If the Community College was in agreement, they would offer one instructor two times per week and determine what the kids were interested in. There was room for an auto repair shop and the Community College and high school wanted to get involved with that project. Chief has already talked with the Commissioners and they seemed to accept the idea. They would set a formal meeting with the Chief, Daniel and Joe, as well as the College and High School Superintendents.

Daniel interrupted and said; "You two learned all this today?" "Yes," Camille answered, "It seemed we just started talking about how some of the kids in this community had been led by the wrong types, who were older than themselves. They began to tell us what the Chief had planned with County Commissioners and School Board Superintendent, he knew you would be thrilled Daniel, but first we have to get you two married with a nice honeymoon. Sadie and I will keep Danny right here in his home. Sadie will stay at night and I will stay during the day, while you all are gone. Joe will hang around with the Chief and learn all he can. It seems the Lord is making this project into a 'work of art'." All Daniel could say was, "Wow, I had no idea how affected the Chief was by my distress over the alcohol poisonings and drive-by shootings that were beginning."

Camille said, "Daniel, I think the Chief wanted to tell you himself, but Joe called him and told him what the officers said and how much they had helped them today, so he said, go ahead and tell Daniel; maybe that will get him married and back to work in full force." Kari spoke up and said, "You know Camille, I've known you and Joe for a long time, but I had no idea you were both such fast workers and fireballs, to find out all this. Thank you so much." Daniel looked so amazed he looked like he might cry.

Daniel told Joe and Camille how much he appreciated them and that he loved them. "I had no idea the Chief was so secretive and was working behind the scenes. That is wonderful news. I've put my house on the market and the money from that can be used for the project, except for some remodeling here. Kari said she wanted two more bedrooms on top of the two we have; but I thought about off-setting the bedrooms backward a little way and have a balcony with railing and open air windows, for sitting to view the beautiful sunsets. Also, I can study out there in springtime." He looked at Kari and said, "I didn't mean to assume you would like that idea, but it seems it would really be pretty." Kari spoke up and said, "It's a great idea, I just hadn't thought of that."

"By the way, Camille, how did you and Sadie decide on a way to make sure Danny would be safe and cared for? I didn't hear you discussing it." "Well, of course you didn't, we decided this on the phone," Camille said giggling like a school girl. Joe just grinned and told Kari that this had been planned as long as they knew the two of you were serious about marriage. "Oh, we are definitely serious. Thank you again. What else can Daniel or I do to help?" "Just take care of one another until we can get you married."

Daniel spoke up and said; he needed Tuesday off, because he and Kari were going shopping for her dress and him a new suit, as well as a suit for Danny. They had all eaten and had coffee and cupcakes in the great room. They chatted more and in a few minutes, Camille told Kari, she was sorry not to help tidy the kitchen, but they were pretty tired. They had already made their bed and had fresh towels out. They thought about going to Church tomorrow, but they really needed to get groceries and a few things for the house. Camille said, "It feels so comfortable, Kari, you all have got to come to dinner one night after your honeymoon. I'm sure by that time I'll have my refrigerator and freezer well stocked. Thank you both so much for dinner and for all you've done for us. We love you both and of course, Danny is our grandson too." They hugged goodnight and left to sleep in their own bed.

Danny had slept a good while, but looked like he was down for the night. Daniel and Kari tidied the kitchen, put another load of laundry in and had another cup of hot tea. Daniel said, "Kari, I love you with all my being; thank you for loving me and Danny. I'm still shocked at how much the

Chief and Joe and Camille have done. Also, I paid the officers double time, but they almost wouldn't take the money. I said, guys, I appreciate this, but you have left families on a weekend to help me and you must let me show my appreciation; go buy your wives dinner on me." "Okay, boss," they replied. They are all a good group and will certainly do what they told Chief about keeping an eye out for the kids, especially those they saw visiting bars.

"It's been a wonderful day," Kari said, "But I'm pretty tired and a little nervous tonight. We did a good thing by loving Sadie, Camille and Joe; but we need to get some sleep too." "You're right, darling, but let me put the clothes in the dryer, while you get ready for bed." "Remember, you know your place now." "Yes," he replied. By the time Kari was finished changing and washed her face, she was worn out and her leg began to hurt. She went into the kitchen and told Daniel her leg was hurting and she was a bit keyed-up. "Well, take one of those pills the doctor prescribed and a couple aspirin." She did and dragged her left leg to the bed. Had she been on it too long today? Of course, she was feeling so much better; she didn't think she needed to rest during the daytime anymore. She started to rub her hip and upper leg and Daniel came in at that time. "Listen Kari, I can do that, but I'm aggravated with myself because I didn't realize until now that you haven't had any rest all day. Now, move over a bit and I'll rub your leg and hip and you try to sleep." She said, "I will but kiss me goodnight." He obliged and began a slow massage of her hip and upper thigh. She was soon asleep and seemed quite relaxed. Daniel chastised himself for not remembering to insist on her resting. He held her and soon he too was asleep.

As usual Danny woke them up fairly early. Seemed like he was feverish and had loose stools. Kari got up and ran the bath water and Daniel undressed him and put him in the water and dried him with a big towel. Kari stripped his crib sheet and the other things that needed washing, while Daniel dressed Danny. Daniel told Kari, "I believe he is feverish today." Kari said, "Probably so." All at once Daniel said, "Ouch, he bit me Kari." Kari took him and saw the tiny tooth on his upper gum and two other little bumps on the lower gum. "Those little teeth are sharp." Kari looked and Daniel's finger had a drop of blood on it. "My two poor, poor babies," Kari said laughing. Daniel looked up and couldn't believe the baby was quieting down.

Kari had rubbed his gums and gave him some medicine and then half formula and half 'gator-aid'. After he ate he wanted on his pallet, Daniel said, "Do you think I should put his boots on?" "Yes, that's a good idea."

Daniel went to put up the gate, just in case he could walk or crawl up the steps. Kari put Danny down and Daniel put his boots on. Kari went to make coffee and breakfast. "Daniel what specifically, would you like to do today?" "Specifically, I can't say; but I would like to look at a catalogue with dresses in it with you." "Oh, well I have one that I've been looking at and I'd like you to see it." They had their breakfast and both noticed about the same time that Danny was quiet. They checked and he had scooted or crawled toward the door to his room, holding his teething ring and sound asleep. "I know the floor is clean, but should I put him in his crib?" Daniel said, "No, we'll sit in here and watch the news and him."

"Sadie gave me a list of things she needed to make our cakes and you gave me your list; is there anything else you want me to pick up." "Not that I can think of right now." "In that case, let's look at the catalogue." She brought it to him and sat beside him and they looked at all kinds of dresses. Kari said, "Turn to page sixty-seven and let me know what you like or dislike about those." He kissed Kari and looked at the four dresses on the two pages. He looked and looked and finally said, "I really like this one, it looks like you." Kari grabbed him and kissed him until he was again breathless. "Kari, honey, your kisses are wonderful, but this almost makes me lose control. I really rather wait until we are married; because that's the right thing to do." Kari said, "I know, but sometimes I want you right now. I told you I'm not a patient person. So you will have to be patient for both of us." "Okay," he said laughing. Back to the catalogue, "That is my favorite too, Daniel, but I wanted you to pick one out for me. That will be so much more precious to me. Now I really do have to pick out the underwear, because I don't think you realize that can be very difficult with my shape. My top is quite a bit larger than my bottom part. I have to buy different sized blouses or sweaters, from jeans and slacks." "Oh, well, can I see when you take it off?" "I guess so because we will be married then."

"Kari, where would you like to go on our honeymoon? I'd really not given it a thought; but we do need some time with just the two of us to see the sights and walk and view historical things, if you like that kind of thing." "I sure do", Kari replied, "Only, I really can't walk a long time at once." "I know, darling. I was thinking about the mountains with creeks running and the walks would be short and we could sit and watch the water and trees and just relax. It seems like I'm wound as tight as an over wound clock. I've been that way for quite some time, but I relax more with you and Danny than with anyone. I like the three of us together, but I really want some time with just you."

"It seems that is already arranged by Sadie and Camille. They plan to dress the Church and reception room on Wednesday and Thursday. I'll help Sadie begin some baking tomorrow and we'll store the food in the freezer. Then she will be here with Danny and finish the cooking while he and I take a nap. Tuesday, she'll stay with Danny while you and I go shopping. That seems like we are rushing and it makes me tired and somewhat useless except I can help Sadie cook."

"Kari, my dear, you are not useless and I don't want you to speak of yourself like that. It hurts me, because I know better. You see, you aren't over all the traumas and sometimes your mind gets tired just like your body. Now kiss me and let's see what we can make for dinner, while our son is resting."

"Okay, what would you like Daniel?" "Well, let's see what's in the refrigerator and freezer." They went to check and Daniel spotted pork chops; "Oh, I really like these." "Could we put them out to thaw and maybe put some sweet potatoes in the oven?" "That's a great idea, Daniel. I like that myself and maybe some creamed spinach. There's also some coconut pie in the freezer." "Great," he said. "I'll go ahead and set the table and dry the laundry and put it away. You go lay on my couch and I'll be there in a few minutes." "Okay," Kari said. Daniel came in with one of her pills and some juice and she took the pill. They lay on the couch and talked a good while. Kari was almost asleep and Daniel told her to get her bed clothes on. She and Danny need some rest.

Daniel had been watching Kari while she cooked and he thought he could do the roasted vegetables and put the sweet potatoes in to bake. He had no idea how to make creamed spinach, but knew it had to be defrosted, so he took it out of the freezer and put it in a bowl with a kitchen towel underneath it. He knew enough to know there was lots of water in frozen spinach. The chops were already in the sink. Kari could cook them when she got up. He began to review in his mind what Joe and the officers said to him today. That school would be perfect. It was old, but made of oak and pine and stood the test of time.

He had almost dozed off to sleep when he heard Danny. He went to get him and Danny had another loose stool and still seemed a bit feverish. He bathed him and clothed him and put him on Kari's bed while he striped the crib sheets off.   As he was doing that, he saw Danny turn over and crawl up to where Kari usually lay. Danny looked at his daddy and started crying, none too softly. Daniel picked him up and talked softly; he told him that mommy was asleep. Let's you and me be quiet and go to the pallet. Danny had quieted down until he saw Kari asleep. He reached for her and Kari turned over and said, "What are you doing, darling?" Daniel told her what had happened and that mommy was asleep. "He quieted down and I was going to take him to the pallet and play with him there, but when he saw you, well, you know what happened."

Kari got up and fixed his formula half with 'gator-aid and got his medicine and teething drops as well as his teething ring. She fed him and put him in the swing while she prepared dinner. He seemed happy enough if he could see her. Daniel said; "I don't understand why you can know what to do and when you pick him up, he is happy and when I pick him up, he only tolerates it." "Well, one thing, I'm still a nurse and secondly, I'm softer than you." "Oh, that makes sense." He said, as he put the spinach out and the chops and wanted to help her with dinner. "Okay, dear, but there isn't that much to do since you've already put the vegetables and sweet potatoes in the oven. We need to squeeze the water out of the spinach and your hands are stronger than mine, so squeeze the water through that towel until they are dry. I'll use a little pork edging to sauté them in and add the cream and cheese later." She put the chops in some buttermilk and then rolled them in flour and put them in a sizzling pan. They were done quite soon.   She then took the vegetables out of the oven and put some more olive oil on them and put them on a platter. She steamed the spinach a bit more and put the cream and cheese in it and served it in a bowl. The chops were then ready and she put them on a platter. She got the potatoes out of the oven and sliced them and put a pat of butter on them.   They had some left over rolls and she nuked them and dinner was ready. They already had tea and coffee ready. Daniel said, "I love you, Kari and not just because you cook so well. You are one of the smartest women I know, full of love and compassion for anyone you meet. I'm so glad God put us together." "Daniel I am too; I think you might have saved my life. I love you with all my being. Now let's eat."

Danny occasionally spoke up and talked to both of them. They all had a wonderful dinner. Daniel took Danny out of his swing and put him on his pallet and Kari and he played with him. They watched him scoot around, quarrel with his toys and then begin crawling to Camille's bed.

He made an attempt to stand up and after several tries, he did stand up. He didn't seem to know what to do next, so he just stood there, looking at his mommy and daddy. He had hold of the spread but all of a sudden his legs didn't know how to move so he sat down. He twisted and turned and finally turned over onto his knees and began to crawl toward them, like he had really done something big. They laughed and bragged on him and Daniel held him and squeezed him. "You are a scamp, young man." Kari reached over and kissed him and they played for quite a while. Pretty soon it was time for bed and they dried him and gave him his formula and Kari rocked him to sleep.

Daniel tidied the kitchen and completed the laundry and he too went into the great room and lay down on the couch. Kari soon put him down and said he'll be out for the night. She joined Daniel on the couch and they watched TV and smooched a bit. When the news was off, Daniel sent Kari to bed; she reminded him where he belonged and he smiled and said, "Yes dear!"

The next morning was Monday and it was a good thing that Danny was such a good alarm. Kari's gown was damp and Daniel thought she was delectable. He had Danny in the bath when Sadie rang the bell. Kari got her robe and answered the door. Sadie came in and had picked up some extra things she thought they may need for wedding preparation. She saw coffee was not made, or breakfast started, so she began that. Kari said, "I'm sorry Sadie, you see Danny was up a lot last night, and Daniel has him in the bath now. He is having loose stools again; do think I might need to take him to the doctor." Sadie said, "I'll check him too when Daniel brings him out." Daniel put his clean diaper and pajamas on and brought Danny into the kitchen. He said, "Honey, I think he might be really sick." Kari and Sadie came over and checked him. They were both nurses, but Sadie was less connected to Danny. She told Daniel and Kari that the baby must be teething again and he might have a GI infection. Her suggestion was to give him Pedialyte and 'gator-aid' for several hours today and watch for any elevated temp or irritability.

Daniel said, "Okay, but you let me know if he doesn't improve by noon. We will take him to see Dr. Lee. I won't be able to work or see the florist or much of anything until I know both my loves are all right. You see Sadie, last night Kari was limping and nervous and I realized she had not taken even one break that day. I insisted on her taking aspirin and the pill Dr. Little prescribed and she finally was able to sleep. Danny was up and down several times, and I don't think Kari was too upset when I had him before he really yelled. So please let me know by lunchtime how they are doing." "I will," Sadie said; "Will you be at the office?" "Yes, I will, but I might ask Sandy to stop by here at her lunch break and get an idea of the flowers and greens that you all had planned for the wedding. That way they will deliver them, so you and Kari and Camille can instruct them where to place whatever you need." "That's fine, Daniel, now hit the shower, you look like you've been drug through a wrinkle machine." "I will," he answered.

Daniel showered and dressed and came back into the kitchen. "No breakfast for me, I'll get some coffee and Danish at the office." "Okay, just this once," Kari said. He kissed Kari and Danny and gave Sadie a hug. "Now on with the baking; and Kari don't you forget to eat or rest today." "She won't forget," Sadie answered. "That man worries too much about me, Sadie, I did have a rough night, but I really didn't know he was so worried." She finished feeding Danny his mixture and gave him his medicine. They rocked a while and Danny got quiet. Kari took him to her bed and lay down with him. They had both gone to sleep when Sadie checked them. She had a cup of coffee and began to measure the ingredients for two cakes. She also washed the small serving plates and placed dollies on each of them; then stacked them on the other end of the counter.

She called Daniel like she said she would. He asked immediately if they were okay. "Of course," Sadie said; "They are curled up on Kari's bed, both sleeping like babies. They will be up in a little bit, because their tummies will awaken them. Kari must have been more exhausted than I thought, Daniel, as soon as Danny got sleepy, she carried him into her bed and they haven't moved to my knowledge." "Well," Daniel replied, "Is it all right then, to send Sandy over to check on the florist and the arrangements you all want?" "Certainly, if they are still asleep; I will awaken them, but I'm sure they will be awake in a few minutes. I've got one cake baked and cooling and will make a light lunch so Kari can eat something." "Thank you Sadie, I've been worried about both of them." Sadie told Daniel that Danny was teething and that Kari had just become emotionally and physically fatigued.

The doorbell rang as they were hanging up and Sadie said, "I bet that's Sandy now." It was. She came in with two large journals of arrangements for them to view. Sandy asked if all was okay and Sadie told her about Danny teething and Kari being emotionally and physically fatigued. "Kari is still having some flashbacks regarding the traumas she had endured and I think she is afraid to believe we all love her and want the best for her."

Sandy said, "That's probably true, but we will get her through this and the Church will be beautiful no matter which arrangement she chooses." "I know, Sandy, I've used them before and they are wonderful to try to fulfill any request." "Well, I'll be going and will pick up the books whenever you all have decided, just give me a call." Kari came out about that time, dressed in jeans and a sweat shirt. "Hi Sandy, thanks for bringing the books over. How are you today?" Sandy told her fine, but she must get back to the office.

Danny awoke then and Kari checked on him and naturally he needed changing, but he hadn't had another stool. She changed him and put clean pajamas on him and brought him into Sadie. "I think I'll fix us some sandwiches, Sadie." "That's fine," Sadie replied. Kari set about fixing sandwiches and Sadie had already made fresh coffee. Sadie put Danny in his swing, but he was not happy one bit. "Oh, dear me," Kari said, "I didn't feed him. You know I don't think he has any fever now, just hungry." She fixed his bottle and Kari fed Danny. She felt for a new tooth and sure enough one of them had popped through. She told Sadie, that maybe he could rest better now. After half formula and half gator-aid, she put him in his swing and he was quite satisfied for the present. Kari and Sadie had sandwiches and coffee; Sadie brought the books from the florist over to Kari.

She told Kari she had used this florist several times and was familiar with their work. Kari looked at the books and saw what she thought would be really good for the Church and reception. She showed them to Sadie and she smiled yes, they will be. "Do you want to show them to Daniel and see if he likes them?"

"Yes I do," Kari replied. "We're going shopping tomorrow for our clothes and I hope you can watch Danny for us." "You know I can and I already have one cake done and the ingredients ready for the second cake. The first one is on the counter there, waiting for the frosting." Kari said, "It is beautiful, Sadie. Can I help you with the smaller ones or anything else for the reception?" "No, can't think of a thing, except play with Danny and the two of you rest as much as possible." "Okay," Kari replied. She and Danny went into great room and Sadie brought in Danny's swing. "Now the two of you have your instructions from Daniel and me." "Danny, did you hear that they are giving us orders; shall we let them for time being?" Danny gurgled and jabbered and Kari took that as yes. So they played and rested and watched TV for a while.

After a while, Danny began crawling toward the TV and then to the couch. He worked and worked trying to stand up. Soon he stood up, but didn't seem to know what to do next. Kari took his feet and showed him how to put one foot in front of the other. She pressed down on the foot that stayed on the floor and picked up and moved the other foot for Danny. He soon got tired and sat on the floor. He then tried again; this time Kari stayed where she was and encouraged Danny to walk along the couch. He managed to put one foot in front, but got the other tangled in his pajamas and sat down hard. Kari clapped for him and showed him how to clap his hands. That soon became a game that he liked. They both grew tired of playing and Danny seemed hungry. Kari gave him his formula and he was soon asleep. Kari left him on his pallet and went into the kitchen to help Sadie. She told Sadie it wouldn't be long before he could walk. Sadie said, "Yes, I heard the commotion. That's great, but his bones are not quite ready to walk yet, however he is learning fast."

Kari asked how the other cake was coming along and Sadie said; "See what you think of it." That cake was also done, and set on the counter to cool. Sadie had also made some mini cupcakes that were cooling. She was beginning to frost the first cake with white frosting which topped the red velvet cake she had first made. "That will be beautiful," Kari said. Sadie carried on with the first cake and the next cake was chocolate which she planned a caramel frosting for, if that's okay. "It is terrific Sadie."

Kari began to get things out to make dinner. She decided on a beef roast with potatoes, carrots, and spices. She would have a side dish of kale and turnip greens. They had some ice cream in the freezer, so she made some bran muffins that could also serve as breakfast the next morning. She then made a cake of cornbread to go with dinner. After she had things cooking, she decided she better rest a while, so she went to the pallet with Danny, only she got a pillow from the couch to rest on.

Sadie continued with her chores and watched the cooking that Kari had started. When she checked, she found both of them asleep on the pallet. Poor Kari, she did not realize how fatigued she was, and had not paid attention to her leg after she assumed Dr. Little had given her a clean bill of health. Being a nurse, Kari thought she could bounce back quickly, but that was not the case. She had not allowed herself time to grieve over the baby she lost; Sadie knew she was thinking about it at times, because she got that far-away look in her eyes and seemed to go to another place. Sadie never mentioned it to her, but she believed that Kari still had not reconciled herself to the miscarriage, the move and new home; and now a new husband and baby. That was enough to make anyone fatigued and nervous. Sadie planned on mentioning that to Daniel when she could get him alone a few minutes.

Daniel came in quietly and went into the kitchen with Sadie, after he saw Kari and Danny asleep on the pallet. "Sadie, wonder why Kari has become so fatigued and nervous of late?" Sadie told him what she had been thinking, that Kari had not allowed herself to grieve over the baby she lost, or the traumas she had suffered. "She sometimes gets that far away look as though she went somewhere in her head." Daniel said, "I've noticed that too, but have no idea how to approach her regarding the same things you mentioned." "Well, when the two of you go shopping tomorrow, why don't you go slowly and have a long lunch somewhere just with the two of you and ask her if she was thinking about her past. It doesn't matter how much she loves you, Danny, Camille, Joe and me, she needs to have quiet time to reflect and it often helps with someone she trusts. I think you will notice tomorrow. Just stay close to her and take her wherever she needs or wants to go, you will find that eventually she will open up and talk. Sometimes, that too is very important. It helps her think and speak about her pain. Then you will be able to understand her moods and still know she loves you and trusts you; maybe not herself yet, but definitely you."

"Sadie, I don't know what I would do without your help. You are a wise and wonderful woman. I barely remember my parents, they were killed in a car crash and I lived in foster care, actually several until I was old enough to be on my own. Your sweet character reminds me of my mother, as much as a three-year old can remember." "Oh Daniel, that's the sweetest compliment you could give me." Daniel looked somewhat shocked, but said, "Well it's true. I love you, Sadie."

Kari heard talking in the kitchen and got up to see what was going on. "Oh, Daniel, I didn't realize you were home. Look what Sadie had done today, she showed him the cakes and mini-muffins and he seemed to think that was awesome. She's also planning on making some little cake squares with decoration on the --- wait a minute, Sadie, did you tell me that or was I dreaming?" "You must have been dreaming, darling, but that's a great idea." Kari looked at her and said; "Sadie, I'm putting too much work on you." "Nonsense," Sadie replied, "Look at all I've accomplished in one day, while you and Danny rested and played. Frankly, I've had a great day." "Thank you, Sadie," Kari said; "You know Daniel and I are going to buy some clothes tomorrow, or did I assume I told you?" "You told me Kari, and that's a terrific idea. You also might show Daniel what you think about the florist pictures." "That's a great idea. Daniel, come look at these and see if you can decide and if it is the one I like." "Kari, you are a little witch, don't expect me to read your mind, although, I have a pretty good idea of what you like," he said, laughing.

Sadie went back to frosting the second cake and keeping check on Kari's dinner. It smelled good. Daniel took the books and looked at them, "Before I decide; could I have a cup of coffee?" "Of course," Kari replied. She got the coffee and they sat down to look at the florist's arrangements. Daniel had a feeling he was being 'set-up' because he caught Kari and Sadie grinning at each other. He flipped to the back of the book and started forward; suddenly he stopped and really looked at two pages of arrangements. They were very much alike, but he thought one of them would go well with the Church. "I like this one," Daniel said. Kari and Sadie burst out laughing, "What's so funny?" "Well, it just so happens that is the one I picked and Sadie said she had worked with this florist many times and they would fix it most any way we want." Daniel hugged Kari and said; "That's great! Now what is that mouth-watering food I smell?" Kari said, "Dinner and the cakes, but you can't have any cake. That's for Saturday, our wedding day." Sadie said, "Kari, I made a small one for the two of you to sample tonight." "You did?" "Yes," Sadie said, "Now that supper is finished, you two better eat and I'll see you both tomorrow."

Daniel stood up and took Kari in his arms and almost kissed her senseless. "You are one terrific lady and I love you." Kari was breathless and said, "Wow, you really are a good kisser." They laughed and Daniel set the table and Kari put the food on their plates, poured tea and they sat down to eat. Right on cue, Danny awoke, needing attention. "Coming right up, son," Daniel said. He got Danny up and talked to him and changed him. Daniel told him if he was a good boy, he could eat with mommy and daddy. Danny talked back to daddy with a gurgle and babble. He reached for Daniel's face and gave him a wet, slippery face. Daniel assumed that must be a kiss. Kari said, "Of course it is." She had prepared his formula, but waited on the cereal until tonight, just in case his tummy wasn't quite up to eating solids yet. They sat at the table and Kari ate between Danny's bottle and jabber. The food was good and Danny finished his bottle and reached for Kari's plate. They waited to see what he would take, as it turned out, he simply wanted to check out what he hadn't seen before. It was definitely time for his swing. Daniel was laughing hard and Danny imitated him, while Kari washed her hands and got some more food. She ate quietly and when she finished, she poured them both coffee and found the little cake that Sadie had stowed for them to sample. It was extremely moist and delicious. "Daniel, this will be perfect for the wedding or your birthday. Which do you want for your birthday?" "This one is good, but I'd like to try that caramel colored one for my birthday." "That's what I was thinking," Kari said.

They finished their cake and coffee and Kari said, "Daniel, I need to talk to you about something." He said, "Okay, let's get another coffee." He poured the coffee and noticed that Kari seemed a bit nervous. She sipped her coffee and said Daniel, "I haven't talked to you about my feelings for a good while, but now I think I can tell you something. You see, I still think about my baby that I lost. I keep wondering if it was a boy or girl, not that it matters, but I never even saw the remains of the baby. I had felt it move twice and then no more. I thought it might be too early for a lot of movement, but now I realize the little thing was dead, before I miscarried."

"Do you think I might have done something to cause that? Although I was violently raped and got pregnant, do you think I might have subconsciously wanted to lose the child? I've prayed about this and can't seem to get peace about it. I sometimes feel so unworthy about everything wonderful that has happened to me; you and Danny, Sadie, Camille and Joe, what did I do to deserve all of this?"

"Kari, you have not done anything wrong! God knows your heart and He has not only blessed you, but also me and all the ones you've just mentioned. He has a plan for each life and if the little one you lost was meant to be, you would not have miscarried, plus have you ever thought what might have happened had you carried the baby to term? Do you think the man who did this would ever let us live in peace? I don't think so. I believe rape is a matter of violence rather than anything else, therefore had you carried the babe to term, he would have then known and never let you rest again, for fear he would steal the baby and sell it or whatever. God does know the beginning from the end, and He took that little one back to Himself, where it will grow in the things of God and be happy and content; and yes it will know it's mother."

"Daniel, how did you get so wise? I really hadn't thought of those things, but you have really blessed me tonight. I think you are absolutely right. I think the love of money makes people focus on their wants at the moment with no thought of God or His precious work on Calvary. Thank you, Daniel for trusting me more than I trust myself in decision-making. I can think more clearly now and I love you."

Danny was beginning to grow tired of not being played with, his toys were not sufficient and he wanted their attention. He began his form of talk and quarreling and they both laughed. Daniel picked him up and they went into the great room. They played with him a bit and caught up on the news. Soon they missed Danny; they looked around and found him in the kitchen exploring anything he could pull up on. He still had not mastered the walking yet and he became most impatient and crawled somewhere else and tried again. Soon he screamed at the cupboards, as if they were to blame for his inability to move like he wanted to. Kari and Daniel watched him and soon he was wet and tired and cranky. Kari couldn't watch anymore she went in and picked him up and bragged on him, you are a smart little boy, but your bones aren't firm enough to actually walk. You must keep trying and mama will help, okay? Danny looked at her and started talking, at least his talking. She handed him to Daniel and prepared his dinner, and while she was doing that Daniel changed him and put his pajamas on him. It was bedtime and Danny ate his cereal and drank his formula. Kari rocked him a little while and Danny was out for the night.

Daniel told Kari it was time for her to go to bed as well. "I know you rested well today, but you still haven't caught up. So change and get into bed." "I will, but don't boss me." "Sorry," Daniel laughed, "I didn't think I was bossy." She went to change and came back for goodnight kiss and hug.

"You're forgiven for bossing me." "Okay, I'm so glad," he said, smiling at her. She looked up at Daniel and said, "We don't fit, I can't reach you to kiss you and you have to bend down to kiss me, what can we do about that?" Daniel lifted her up to a stool and now she was looking down at him. She hugged and kissed him until he put her back on the floor. "Kari, you are absolutely the most desirous woman I've ever known, but I cannot keep control with all this. Please go to bed and I'll find my place in a few minutes." "Okay," Kari replied, "I love you Daniel." In a little while Daniel came in and of course, lay on top of the covers. Soon they both went to sleep.

Danny again was their alarm clock. He was wrestling with one of his toys and tossed it. He would scoot to another and repeat the process; he soon grew tired of play and decided he needed to have attention from mommy and daddy. So he began to argue with them; they pretended to sleep on and Danny then became louder. "Okay, okay, little man," Daniel said. He got up to give him his bath and Kari went to start their breakfast and fix Danny's formula and cereal. Kari had taken the muffins out of the freezer last night and popped them in the oven to warm and made the coffee. Daniel brought the clean, dressed Danny in one arm to Kari and tossed the sheets and towels into the washer. Kari fed Danny and put him in his swing. They ate breakfast in peace and Daniel went to shower and dress first. Kari tidied the kitchen and put some salmon fillets in the refrigerator to thaw for dinner tonight.

Sadie came in about that time and Kari told her how wonderful the cake was that she fixed for them yesterday. "That's good," Sadie answered. "How is Danny today?" "He seems fine today, no crying or restlessness and he ate cereal and formula for breakfast. He's been playing in his swing since breakfast. Daniel is getting showered and ready for us to go shopping. I'll get showered and dressed afterward. We've decided to make a day of it and will drop off the books at the florist so they will know what arrangements we want." Sadie told her that was a great idea. She and Danny would make some little cakes and a few other things, put them in serving dishes, wrap with plastic wrap and box them up. She would leave the cakes in the freezer for Saturday. She would also make a good punch and put it in the refrigerator.

Sadie and Camille had decided to go to the Church today and talk with the pastor about them decorating early. Pastor Chuck said there were no

Church plans for the week and they were welcome to decorate. Sadie also told him about a photographer that she had used before and asked if he could take pictures before the wedding. That way they would have everything taken care of for Daniel and Kari. He told them that would be fine and his wife had volunteered to help any way she could. "That would be wonderful," Sadie said.

Daniel came out dressed and sat down for another coffee with Sadie. He also thanked her for the cake and asked if the caramel cake could be his birthday cake since Kari had insisted on celebrating both their wedding and his birthday. "Certainly," Sadie replied. Kari had already gone into to shower and got dressed for a day of shopping. She washed her hair and dried it and it looked like spun copper when she finished; she didn't think she would have time to have it cut before the wedding. She put her make-up on and came out to the kitchen. Daniel said, "Wow, Kari, I had no idea how long and beautiful your hair is. It looks great and I love it." Sadie said; "Daniel you better stay close to this girl today or someone might steal her from you." "Oh, I will stay close. I can't believe her hair is that long; she always has it in some kind of up-do." "Well, I haven't had time to have it cut and styled, so I hope I don't look like a little girl." "Absolutely not!" Daniel replied; "It is beautiful as is all of you. I hope you don't cut it, unless it is too much trouble." "No trouble," Kari replied.

They both kissed Danny and told Sadie they would take the books back to the florist and show them what they liked. "Good idea," answered Sadie. "Do you want me to prepare lunch for you or will you eat out?" Daniel said; "I've picked a nice place where we can dine and talk and rest a bit." They got into the car and headed for town. Daniel took her to the bridal shop and they looked at several dresses. Kari looked at one a while and asked if she might try this dress on. "Yes," the clerk remarked, "I'll help you with it." It was a pale yellow with a sweetheart neckline and sleeves to the elbow. When Kari had it on, she didn't like it as much as she thought she might. The waist was too large and it was too snug at the top. The skirt flared a bit more than she liked. Well Daniel said he wanted to see everything she tried on. She went out onto the platform and turned around for him to see all the dress. "Do you like it, darling?" "Well I thought I did, but it doesn't feel right." The clerk said; "It is too big in the waist and too snug across the bust, that's why you don't care for it. I noticed as soon as you put it on, the dress was not right for you."

"Perhaps you need to look in the other section of the store." "I didn't know there was another section." "Oh yes, that's our catalogue section, but we can have one you choose ready within twenty-four hours." Kari went back to change out of this dress, put a large robe on, and went into the next section. She looked and Daniel sat on the cushioned couch. Kari saw the very dress she had seen in the catalogue. "I'd like to try this one on," she said. "Of course," the clerk replied. The clerk took the dress into the fitting room and helped Kari get it on. It looked perfect, maybe a little loose in the waist, but it felt right. She went out onto the round stage and Daniel looked shocked. It was perfect for her coloring and her figure. She looked like an angel in the dress. It was a beautiful cream color and he really liked it. He didn't make a comment until Kari put her hands on her hips and said, "Well"? Daniel grinned and said, "Kari, that looks like you. Do you like it?" "Oh yes, I do." She twilled around like a school girl in a prom dress. She whispered to Daniel and the clerk, "It's so expensive do you really like it this much? Daniel laughed and said; "I like it this much," stretching his arms wide. "Okay then," she said to the clerk, "I'll take it."

"However, I also need some shoes to match and they will have to be low heels. I injured my hip a few months ago and can't wear high heels." The clerk said, "I think we have just the thing for you." They went into another department and Kari tried on several pair and finally picked one that was really pretty and would go well with her dress. Daniel agreed. Kari said, "Now, Daniel you can't see the other things I need." She told the clerk she needed new underwear. "Oh, that's fine, we have a wide selection." "Well that's good," Kari thought. She bought a couple of bras, panties, and a camisole, and tried them on with her dress. "You are quite pretty," the clerk remarked. "Thank you," Kari responded. They went out for Daniel to see the completed outfit. Daniel exclaimed "Kari, you are absolutely the most beautiful woman I've seen." The clerk took everything up to the check-out counter and tallied the bill. Kari reached for her checkbook and Daniel touched her arm; "No, Kari, this is mine and I'll hear nothing else." "Well Daniel, I didn't even think that you wanted to do this. Thank you." They had everything wrapped and Daniel took the box to the car, but before he even got there, he reached down and kissed Kari there on the street. The clerk was still watching and some fellow across the street let out a whistle! They both smiled and got into the car.

When they got into the car, Daniel said, "Do you want to eat or can we go get my suit? I'm not so difficult to fit as long as I go to the big man's shop." Daniel was tall with a large frame, so it seemed natural to go there. Daniel went to the suit he wanted and asked to try it on. "Certainly sir," the salesman said, "The dressing room is this way." He put it on and it fit him perfectly; now I need some shoes too. Kari said; "You didn't let me see you." "Honey, I didn't think that would matter to you, I'm sorry." "Well you are forgiven, but some evening would you let me see you in it?" "Of course I will," he said. He tried on his shoes and bought the first pair he tried, along with several pair of socks. He paid for everything and took the box to the car. "Now, can we go eat?" "Yes, I guess so," Kari laughed. "We still haven't got Danny's new outfit." "I'm sure that won't take long," Daniel replied. They headed out of town and Kari asked where they were going? "That's a surprise; we eat, sit, talk and walk a little way down this path I know." "That's great, Daniel." They stopped at a quaint little restaurant and went inside. It was quiet and peaceful and Kari said; "I didn't even know this place was here. I've passed by on this road, but I guess I was in no shape to notice. It is beautiful!"

They ordered soup, steak with a pepper sauce and vegetables, as well as a dessert. "Do you expect me to eat all this," Kari asked. "Well, I wish you could, but I doubt that will happen; however as you can see, we have the place to ourselves." Kari asked, "Did you arrange this, Daniel?" "Yes, I sure did. I told you I wanted to spend the day with you and Chief thought that was an excellent idea." Kari put down her fork.

She said, "Daniel, you know almost everything about me, but do you realize I know hardly anything about you; how you grew up, where your parents are and what your upbringing was like." Daniel said, "Are you sure you want to know?" "Yes I am," she replied. "Well, my parents were killed in a car accident when I was about three. I remember very little about them, except I noticed Sadie smile the other day and it reminded me that my mother smiled like that."

"Anyway, there were no relatives who wanted to rear a child that wasn't their own and so I was placed in foster care. I was shifted from one home to another and when I got big enough, I ran away. I would never depend on another person, ever, I said to myself. I lied about my age and education and went to work for a broker house. I climbed the ladder rather easily and made an excellent salary and stock in the company. Then one day, a man came to see me about his stock portfolio and I advised him to steer clear of too much stock. Invest in property or gold; those are two things that rarely, if ever, decrease in value. I never played the market myself, I didn't trust it. The man who came to see me was Chuck. He was such a decent man and he asked me to dinner that night with him. I said fine, and we became friends. Later on I found out he was a pastor, but at the time I didn't care. I figured people needed something to do and believe in. By this time I met Kelly who, for whatever reason took a liking to me, (I think she knew my bank account) because her dad was a broker who worked with me. Anyway, she was attractive and seemed nice enough and soon we married. You know the rest, except, Chuck had been praying for me to come to the Lord."

"He knew I believed in nothing except myself, but he still stayed my friend and could talk about anything. One day, he asked me if I knew where I'd go when I died? I said, I never thought about that. He then told me about Jesus, God's son, who had died to forgive my sins. I replied, Chuck, I'm as good a man as I know how to be, why would God do that? Chuck explained how we are all born in sin because of the fall of Adam and Eve, thus we need sinless blood to redeem us. He explained about blood sacrifices in the Old Testament and how Christ had paid the final sacrifice with His own life. He gave me a Bible and asked me to read John in the New Testament and we would talk again. I told him I would and I did. It wasn't too many months before I began to understand what he said, and I asked him how I could know that I'd go to heaven. He led me to Christ and my life has never been the same since. In a short time, I left the broker business and asked Chuck if he knew about any job available? He introduced me to Chief. I took some courses and the rest you know."

Kari asked, "Did you love Kelly or think it was time to marry and she was anxious?" "I never knew love, before you, but I liked her all right until the real Kelly came out. By that time I figured she would change her mind about the baby, she didn't. That was when any liking her or tolerating her was nearly impossible. If it hadn't been for Chuck, I don't know what I would have done. Kari, she did not want children ever, but that's not what she said early on. She was determined to abort this 'thing' that I was responsible for. She didn't like me and had never loved me. I begged her to have the baby and give it to me."

"Until I mentioned a huge sum of money, she wouldn't even listen. The money got her attention and I told her she would have to have prenatal care which I would pay for and she must make it legal that the child was mine. She was glad to do that and oh, by the way, I want an annulment. That was fine with me. That whole eight or nine months I prayed with Chuck and by myself every day and sometimes during the day. I was almost at the end of my rope, until Wayne had everything in order. I still did not trust her that she wouldn't abort the baby. I never touched her again, the thought of her made me sick. Kari, I know that my telling you this might make you doubt that I do or can love you. But, Kari, God knows my heart; long before I ever told you, I loved you. When I saw how protective you were about Danny, I knew you were not that kind of woman. The more I saw you, the more I loved you, and I will until the day I die."

Kari said, "Daniel I have no doubt you love me and I hope you know that I do love you. We seemed to have a similar background, but look what God has made of us. You are such a dear man, I don't know really know how you stood Kelly."

"I had a feeling that if I didn't keep the baby until his daddy picked him up, she might have abandoned him. I hope that's not true, but I did feel it rather strongly. The little fellow was smelly and had a very red bottom. The stuff for him was dirty, with only a few pieces of clothes and the bottles were filled with sour milk. I had found out that day that I was pregnant, so I had bought some clothes and diapers and blankets, plus some Pedialyte. I had forgotten the Pedialyte, so I mixed gator-aid with distilled water and fed him after a warm bath and put petroleum jelly on his bottom. That was to keep urine from burning him. I never told you, because you would have wanted to know where the clean clothes came from. I couldn't lift the boxes, but I pulled them inside until I was able to put them in the trash. I fed him with the new bottles I had bought after sterilizing them. She was dressed well and had her nails done, but the baby looked ready for a trash can. I know you probably think I'm exaggerating, but I truly am not."

Daniel was crying silently, and Kari said; "Let's go for a walk." He got up and left a hundred dollar bill on the table and they headed out to take a walk. "Kari, I'll never be able to thank you enough." They were on the path and he hugged her so tight and wiped his eyes with his hands and kissed her very deeply. "I don't doubt you for a second, but I know had she done that I would have killed her and turned myself in. I thank God you were at the right place at the right time and had a heart for the little guy."

They kissed again and Daniel said; "I'm not impotent because of her as you well know, but please understand why I want to wait for physical intimacy until we are married. By the way, that's only days away." "I know, but can we kiss some?" "That is my pleasure," he said smiling. "Now how is your leg feeling?" "A bit tired, but let's get Danny's outfit and drive around a little while. I really enjoy being out with you, seems like I've been in for quite a while."

They went into a baby shop and got the cutest outfit for Danny and some new shoes. "He won't like them like his boots, but he will wear them," Kari said. They had everything wrapped and Daniel put the box in the car. They went riding in the country and Kari saw a creek. "Stop Daniel, I want to look at that creek." He pulled off the road and they walked down to look at the creek. It was shallow, but the water was flowing down stream from them and it was clear. "I can't figure out why my creek is still muddy", Kari said. "Well honey, maybe some beavers need a home upstream." They got back in the car and Kari realized it was getting late. "Daniel we have to go home, it's almost time for Danny's feeding and preparation for bed." "Yes," Daniel replied, "It seems like we've only been out a short time, but it is almost his bedtime. I love you my precious Kari." "And I love you, Daniel."

They drove back home and Daniel unloaded all the boxes and put them in the second bedroom. Sadie looked at them and said, "Did you buy out the stores?" "Pretty much," Kari said. "You should see my dress Sadie, well you will, but not this evening, I'm a bit tired, but we had fun and Daniel showed me some of the country side. This is a pretty county, Sadie." "I've always thought so," she replied. "How did Danny behave today?" "Just like the angel he is," she replied. "He has had his evening bath, but he's getting ready for food. No loose stools or spit up, so I guess the other teeth are through. I haven't really looked, because we played and he played in his swing and took his formula and had a good nap. I've finished the small cakes and decorated the mini-muffins and put them all in the freezer. I'll decorate the small cakes tomorrow. Camille and I plan to decorate the Church and reception area. Chuck said his wife would be glad to help, so we should have everything ready for Saturday."

"Oh, by the way, I asked Pastor Chuck if the photographer from my church could come and take pictures of the Church before others came in." He said, "Absolutely, there are no services planned this week until Saturday."

"I've pressed the tablecloths and prepared them for the tables. You and Danny are welcome to come, but you are not to do anything except supervise." "Okay," Kari replied.

"Daniel, we didn't ask you, but we thought you would like the decorations too, since you helped pick out everything." "Oh, I'm sure I will." "Sadie, you won't believe how beautiful Kari looks in her dress. I was so amazed, I know she's beautiful, but she looks like an angel. Danny's suit is pretty and we got him some dress shoes, Kari said he wouldn't like them like his boots, but he needed to dress for this occasion. Sadie, thank you for everything you've done today. I hope you rest well." "Kari, I made the side dishes you had planned for dinner; all you will need to do is broil the salmon. Also, I made the two of you a small birthday cake for Daniel, just to see if you approve." "Oh, we will," Daniel replied.

Kari and Daniel changed clothes into sweats and played with Danny a while. He was soon ready for his dinner and Kari fed him his cereal and formula; rocked him a while and he was down for the night. Kari dressed the salmon with a special seasoning and broiled them and put a spicy sauce on them. They ate well and enjoyed themselves. Then Kari made some coffee and found Daniel's birthday cake that Sadie had made for them. It was small, just right for two people. It was really good and Daniel said; "I really like this for my birthday cake."

They took another cup of coffee into the great room and caught up on the news. Kari lay on the couch and Daniel sat beside her in his chair. Kari was relaxed and then she began to rub her thigh and hip. "That hurts you, doesn't it," Daniel asked. "Yes, a little, but it will be okay in a little bit." Daniel went and got some aspirin and one of the pills that Dr. Little had prescribed. Kari took them without fussing and pretty soon she was relaxed and sleepy. Daniel said; "Honey, can you sleep in your sweats or do you think you should change into your bedclothes?" "I think I'd better change," Kari replied. She went into the bedroom and put her nightwear on and came back to the couch. Daniel looked at his watch; it was time for all of them to go to bed. He picked Kari up and carried her to bed, hugged and kissed her and she fell asleep almost at once. He thought of all Kari had told him today. He asked God's forgiveness for his hatred for Kelly. "Please, Lord, forgive my unforgiving spirit; YOU know she did a terrible thing, but YOU worked it out for good. Thank You."

He got up and went to lie on top of the covers, as usual. Kari turned over and hugged him and kissed him and she wasn't really awake, thankfully, because he could barely keep control of himself. He said, "Kari, turn over honey," and she did, never waking up. He soon drifted off to sleep, too. They had a good night of rest and as usual, Danny woke them up early.

Seems he was getting hungry and did not like wet clothes. Daniel got up and gave him a warm bath, wrapped him in a large towel and put clean clothes on him. Kari awoke and kissed Danny and asked him if he was ready for breakfast. He gurgled and jabbered at her and she took that for a yes. She went into the kitchen and made coffee and put some muffins in the oven, then made his cereal and formula. Daniel brought him in and Kari proceeded to feed him. He really ate this morning, perhaps she better try some fruit with his breakfast. She put some peaches in his cereal and mixed it together and he ate that too. "Well, young man, if you eat anymore now, you will pop. You are going to swing some and work off some of your calories." Daniel had put his boots on and Danny began to play and 'talk' to his toys. Daniel and Kari finished their breakfast and Daniel went to the shower. He showered and shaved and came out dressed for work. About that time Sadie and Camille came in. They all greeted one another and they told Kari and Daniel what was on the agenda today. "Well, that's good," Daniel replied; "That way I have an excuse to come see my two darlings." Daniel kissed everyone goodbye and went to work. Kari told them to come have some coffee, she wanted to show them the dress and hang Daniel's suit in the guest bedroom, as well as Danny's. "That would be great," they both replied. "It's really cold outside and there might be a light snow tomorrow." When they went into the bedroom to hang the new clothing up, Camille and Sadie were thrilled with Kari's dress and of the boy's things. Kari showed them her shoes, as well as, her dress; "You know I still can't wear high heels because of my leg. It really hurt last night, but Daniel insisted I take aspirin and one of the pills Dr. Little prescribed. It soon stopped and I slept like a baby just as though I was Danny."

"Honey, everything is beautiful and Sadie and I will have the Church done in short order, because the florist will help us. Sadie has a photographer to come and take some pictures before the big day, when it might be a bit hectic." Sadie said, "Now your orders for today are to take care of Danny and yourself. You must be careful with that leg, no matter if it is healed, the fact that it sometimes hurts, means you've put too much stress on it."

"I know," Kari answered. "I will rest when Danny rests, and get dinner ready."

Camille and Sadie soon left for the Church and set up tables in the reception hall first of all. The tables were pretty and Sadie had brought the small serving plates that she had prepared with doilies. Camille commented on how well Sadie had done. Sadie said; "It does look pretty, doesn't it? I have the red punch in the freezer as well as the large cakes and mini-muffins. I've still got to decorate the small cakes." Camille said, "I am going to make some savory small things and some cheese straws as well as nuts of all kinds." "That's great," Sadie said. In a little while the florist arrived with the arrangements that Daniel and Kari had chosen. They began to arrange them and wove different white/cream flowers into the greenery. They had also brought large candles sticks and candles to go into them. They asked Sadie and Camille if the window sills needed some decoration and they both answered "Yes." By the time the photographer got there, the Church and reception area were beautiful. The chairs had been arranged in semi-circles in the reception hall so everyone would be involved with the festivities. It was later in the afternoon when everything was set up. Camille called Pastor Chuck into the Church to see it and the reception hall. "Do you think the kids will like this?" Chuck said, "They will love this; it is beautiful and you ladies are to be commended for your love and devotion to them. I appreciate it so much."

Daniel had dropped by home with some sandwiches for the two of them and they ate. They talked a while and played with Danny who was now on his pallet. Daniel soon hugged and kissed Kari and told her that he needed to see the Chief about something, he wasn't sure what, but he would see her tonight. "I love you and take care of you both for me." "Ditto," Kari laughed.

Camille and Sadie came in about one-thirty and told Kari how pretty everything looked and that Pastor Chuck thought so as well. They asked Kari if she wanted them to press her dress or Danny's suit. She said, "Yes, but I don't think they need pressing now, since I hung all of the things when we got home." Sadie and Camille went to check for themselves. "They look good," they told Kari. Sadie and Camille commented on something smelling wonderful in the kitchen. Kari said she had made a pork loin roast, roasted potatoes with garlic and some mixed greens as a side dish. She told them she had not made a dessert, because neither of them needed one today. She told them about Danny eating his cereal mixed with peaches this morning and took his formula. He has been a 'rounder' today. He crawls just about everywhere he goes and is pulling up on his feet several times when near the couch or bed. He also crawled in the kitchen and I almost stepped on him, before I realized he was there. I sure do feel better today and have had a good time with him. There is plenty of supper for all of us; I know the two of you must be tired. You can call Joe and tell him to come out too. "No, not tonight darling," Sadie and Camille said.

We need to get home and do some things we need to do; so they told Kari and Danny good night and Kari told them how much she did appreciate both of them for the hard work. "I can hardly wait to see it." "Well, not tonight, young lady. Your man will be home soon and he will be hungry." They all hugged and Camille and Sadie left.

Daniel came in so tired, but equally excited. He told Kari that the Chief had given him a lot of information this afternoon, but he was hungry. Kari laughed and said; "Dinner is coming right up, now go wash up and it will be on the table when you get back." She set the table and carved the roast which she had resting. She loaded the bowls with the rest of the food and poured tea. Daniel came in and kissed her and said, "I'll eat and talk if that's okay." "That's fine," she said. Daniel began to eat his dinner and looked over at Danny who was standing up by his swing. Daniel asked Kari, "How long has he been standing so long?" "I don't really know, but he has crawled all over this house today, I saw him one time at the baby gate, looking like he was a bit confused. He couldn't crawl on it or stand with it. He soon became interested in the pallet and off he went. He had only one long nap today, but otherwise we have played. He will be walking before long and I don't know how I'll keep up with him," she said laughing. She and Daniel finished their meal and Danny decided he needed in the swing. So Kari put him in the swing and he played with his tools.

Daniel told Kari how great dinner was and he loved her. She said, "I know; now tell me what the Chief said, that has you so pleased." "The Chief is something else," Daniel exclaimed. "He met with the City Counsel Members, the School Board and the Community College regarding the old school that they had wanted to sell. He told them that would be the ideal place for the center. It seems they had heard about the whole community being aware and afraid of the possible gang influence here. They all agreed to set aside some of their budget to help purchase the property and the High School and College would give two days to the center for teaching the different projects we mentioned."

"I'm planning to talk to Chuck tomorrow as well as Sadie's pastor about putting aside some mission money to aid the center. I can't wait for my house to sell, because as soon as it does, we'll start adding on to our house here and use the majority of the other to fund the center for at least a year. If all goes well, the center should be ready to open after Christmas. Isn't that wonderful news?" "Oh yes, my darling, but you know I can help with our remodeling and that too will help." "I know, Kari, but I want to do the remodeling, because then I will feel like it belongs to both of us. I know you don't mind, but humor me." "Okay, beloved, but know we are in this together; oh, by the way, we haven't put your name on the deed yet. I'll call Wayne tomorrow to arrange the paper work." "Kari, I didn't mean you needed to do that." "I know," Kari said, "But I had already thought about it and then 'my muddy mind' kicked in and I forgot."

By the time dinner was over, Danny decided it was time for him to eat again and he wanted out of the swing. Daniel went to get him, sponged him down and put clean pajamas on him. They came back to the kitchen and Kari had formula and cereal ready. He ate everything and seemed to quarrel with Kari. "Oh, you little scamp, you've worked hard today and still feel hungry"; Danny seemed to agree, so Kari gave him a very small serving of peaches and he was satisfied. She took him into the great room and rocked him until he fell asleep. She put him in his crib. Then she went to put her night clothes on because she was tired. She came out of the bathroom. She stopped to stare at her beautiful baby, she really loved him and of course, his daddy. Daniel had watched from the door and noticed Kari smiling at the sleeping Danny. Kari glanced up and came and gave Daniel a big kiss and hug and they went into the great room to catch the news.

They both lay on the couch and soon became involved with each other until Daniel said, "Excuse me honey." Kari wondered what in the world had happened to Daniel, and then she realized her gown was damp. "Oh, my word." She went in and changed her nightgown and went back to the couch. "Daniel, I'm sorry, I got carried away." "No, my darling, I got carried away and didn't pay close enough attention. Please forgive me." "My darling Daniel, there is nothing to forgive, but perhaps you had better sit in the chair and let me rest a bit and watch TV." "You're right, sweetheart. I do love you so much." "Me too," Kari replied. Pretty soon, she was almost asleep and Daniel picked her up and put her to bed. He kissed her goodnight and went back to lie on the couch a while. He reflected on all the day, what the Chief had told him, how much Danny was able to do and his precious Kari. "Dear Father, Thank you for this day and the blessings YOU have given. I'm so grateful to YOU for Kari and Danny and for the upcoming wedding. Thank YOU for Sadie and Camille, Chuck and Joe and Sadie's pastor. You are God our Provider, Protector and God of all things." He soon got up and went to lie beside Kari, who was restless, but seemed asleep. He wrapped his arms around Kari and soon drifted to sleep.

The next morning Danny awoke as usual; he played with his toes and toys and then decided he needed more attention. Daniel got up and put him in the tub and gave him a warm bath and dressed him, while Kari made breakfast for them and Danny. She mixed some formula with cereal, and put some biscuits with sausage in the microwave for her and Daniel. Daniel brought Danny in, clean and dry and quarreling with his daddy. Daniel laughed at him and Danny looked at Kari and reached for her. She took the biscuits out of the oven and asked Daniel to pour coffee, while she fed Danny. Danny ate like he hadn't had food before; Kari said, "Daniel the doctor told me that Danny was the perfect size for his length and age, but I can't understand why he seems hungry so often." "Well, it could be because he is so active now and burns the calories pretty quickly. We know he isn't sick because we've been through that before." No, he isn't sick; I guess he really does get hungry. He ate his cereal and Kari had put a bit of peach in the cereal and fed him his formula. After wiping his mouth and chin, Kari put him in the swing. He began to play and 'talk'. Daniel and Kari ate breakfast and had a second cup of coffee. Daniel said, "I need to hit the shower and get ready for work." He kissed Kari and headed to the shower.

Sadie came in about the time the shower was running. "How are you all this beautiful morning?" Kari told her fine, but she though Danny might eat them out of house and home. She told Sadie how Danny moved so quickly and ate so much for a baby, but told her the doctor said he was the perfect weight for his length and age. "Of course he is," Sadie said. "He's going to be a big boy, just like his daddy." "I think you're right Sadie. Now, what's our plan for today?" Sadie told her she was going to finish decorating the small cakes with wedding rings on top. "Oh, Sadie, I have forgotten to get Daniel a wedding ring." Sadie said, "Don't worry, when he goes to work and when you and Danny are ready, I'll take you to the jewelry store." "I'm really not sure what size he wears." Sadie said, "I am; you see Kelly got his wedding ring off the dresser and gave it to me. She said, maybe someone you know can use this; he thinks nothing of it and never wears it anymore. I took the ring and kept it for such a time that he might want it." Kari said, "Sadie, I want his size, not that wedding ring." Sadie said, "I know honey, I wasn't thinking except how Kelly looked when she gave me the ring. We'll go by my house and pick it up and you can have an idea of the size and get something entirely different; maybe you want something engraved inside the ring." "I do," Kari replied. Daniel came out of the bedroom dressed and ready to go to work. "You all be good while I'm gone," and gave Kari a kiss. "Yes, darling, we will." Daniel grinned and left for work.

"Sadie, are you sure you have time for this? I know you still want to decorate the small cakes, but I can help with those." "Yes Kari, I'm sure we have time and besides I want you to see the Church if you feel like it; we must not let you get too tired with that leg of yours. I'll carry Danny when we go to the jewelry store and in the Church. I'd also like to stop by a grocery and pick up some cream cheese and red food coloring." "Okay then," Kari said; "I'll go get dressed and then dress Danny." "Put a heavy jacket on both of you; the weather is cold today." They were all dressed fairly quickly and Sadie carried Danny and put him in the car seat. Kari took the diaper bag with the usual things inside it; she did put a bottle of water that she could mix with dry formula.

They went to Sadie's house and she said, "I'll be back in a minute, so you two stay warm." Sadie came out with a box and handed it to Kari. Kari looked at it and had an estimate of the size, but would take it with her to be sure, when she picked out what she wanted. She looked at many men's wedding bands; then she saw exactly what she wanted. It was a broad band of platinum with a thin ring of gold around the edges. She said, "Sadie, I like this one; What do you think? Will Daniel think it is sissy with the gold bands?" "No, Kari, he will love it and the band is large enough to have whatever you want engraved." Kari took the old band out and measured it to the one she wanted for Daniel. It looked like a fit to her. The saleslady said it was the same size. Kari put the old ring back in the box and handed it back to Sadie. Kari told the saleslady she wanted this ring, engraved with a message: 'Daniel and Kari until death parts us.' She asked for an appraisal and the ability to return it if needed. "Of course," the saleslady told her; "Do you have a special box you like?" "Yes," Kari answered, "I want this one." It had a beautiful interlocked ring on top of black velvet and the inside was black satin. They engraved it while they waited and Sadie looked at some rings that resemble birthstones. Kari asked Sadie when her birthday was and Sadie told her. Kari put that date in her 'long-term memory bank' and they looked at some more jewelry. The saleslady came out with Daniel's ring and Kari and Sadie looked at it. "It is beautiful Kari," Sadie said. Kari looked like she could cry, but instead a big smile broke out on her face. She leaned over and kissed Sadie. "Thank you so much, this means so much to me."

They then called Pastor Chuck and asked if they could come see the Church and reception hall. "Of course," he said, "But I can tell you it is absolutely beautiful." Kari said "Thanks and we'll be there soon." They walked into the Church and Pastor Chuck was waiting at the altar (like he was going to be when the wedding was performed), and said to Kari; "I'm standing in for Pastor Joe today." Kari said, "Oh my goodness, I knew it would be beautiful but this is beyond anything I expected." The windows had greenery and white blooms interwoven with one cream candle in the center of each. Kari asked Sadie if she was sure the photographer had pictures of this beautiful scene. Sadie replied; "He took more than one picture, there are a bunch of them." "Now, could I see the reception hall?" "Of course," Chuck said. Again, Kari looked like she would cry, "Oh Sadie, thank you so much. I know you and Camille worked very hard on this and the florist did as well." Kari looked at Chuck and said, "Chuck, I have no idea the amount for a gratuity to give all of you, please give me a figure." Chuck smiled deeply and said, "Kari, you and Daniel owe me a kiss and hug; well, I can do without the kiss from Daniel. It is time, young lady that you don't have to pay people to love you and want to do things for you. Now, if you are finished looking, I think you better look at your son; he seems very interested in the tablecloth and those flowers." "Oh my goodness," Sadie exclaimed; "I only put him down a moment ago." Kari started laughing; "Yes I put him down yesterday for a minute to load the dishwasher and he had crawled into the kitchen and I almost stepped on him. I don't know how he can be so quiet when he's busy and so noisy when he needs attention." Sadie had picked him up and they thanked Chuck and Kari gave him a hug and kiss on the cheek. "Who is kissing my husband?" Chuck's wife (Sharon) asked, laughing. Kari said, "Chuck said I owed him a hug and kiss and Daniel only owed him a hug." She said; "You are something else, Kari. Daniel has a wonderful wife to be; it is only two days away." "I know," said Kari. "Thank you both for all you've done and for loving Daniel and me."

Sadie, Kari, and Danny left and went by the grocery store. Sadie asked if there was anything Kari needed while she was there. "I don't think so Sadie, but thank you." She and Danny waited for Sadie to come out of the store and then they headed home. Danny was getting a bit cranky and Kari knew he was ready for a change and his lunch. They drove up in the driveway and Daniel's car was there. Sadie got Danny out of the car seat and Kari went in to find Daniel writing her a note. He had come in to have lunch with them and had brought enough sandwiches for all of them. "Hi, my darlings, where have you been?" Kari answered and said, "We had some errands to do and Sadie needed some supplies for decorating the small cakes." "Well, I'm glad you got back before I left." Kari said; "We also went by the Church and honey you really ought to see it. It is absolutely the prettiest thing I have seen and it is for our wedding." "Well how did you manage that?" "I called Pastor Chuck and asked if I could see it. He of course said yes. I had no idea of the gratuity one pays for the Church and reception or for Chuck and Sadie's pastor and the vocalist. Chuck didn't tell me a price, except we owed him a hug and kiss; well he can do without your kiss, but I gave him a smacker and a hug and his wife caught me. At first, I thought she was angry, but then she was laughing so hard, I guess at my expression. Anyway, you still owe him your hug." "All right, I'll see what I can do. Now, I suggest you feed that quarreling son of yours and let Sadie get some rest." He gave them all a hug and left to go back to work.

Kari fixed Danny's cereal and formula, dried him, and then fed him. Meanwhile, Sadie had made some tea and put the sandwiches on the plates. After they put Danny down for his nap, Sadie and Kari ate the sandwiches. "That was good," Kari said. "I know, now you take a nap while Danny does, because you've been up a good while." "Well, I believe I will lie down a bit." After Sadie got the kitchen tidy, she checked on the two of them and they were both asleep. Sadie went back to the kitchen and prepared the frosting for the small cakes. They did look pretty and she put them in the freezer until Saturday. She kept two out for Kari and Daniel for dessert.

About three-thirty Kari got up and started dinner. She had prepared the makings for Salisbury steak, green beans for a side and a salad. Sadie showed her the small cakes and Kari thought they were beautiful. Kari asked Sadie if she thought she might have Daniel try his ring on to be sure it fit. Sadie said, "That was a good idea. You're still wearing your engagement ring, but I don't know if Daniel thought to get a wedding band." "I didn't even ask him," Kari replied. Sadie and Kari talked about several things and Sadie set the table and made some tea and prepared the coffee pot, just needed to be turned on. Sadie asked Kari if she was sure that she wanted Sadie to keep Daniel's old wedding band. "Of course I am," Kari responded, "Keep it, sell it or whatever; it is yours." Sadie told Kari that she had a niece who was getting married in about two months and the two of them had very little money, but she knew they really loved one another and she would probably give it to her niece for her to give to her husband to be. "That would be terrific, Sadie. Now that I'm rested, you can have dinner with us or go home and get rest. You know tomorrow and Saturday might be a bit hectic. It seems I've forgotten something, but I cannot remember what it is." Sadie said, "Nothing has been forgotten you are a bit nervous about the wedding." "I guess so," Kari replied. "Well, I think I will go home then, if you are sure you will be all right." "I'm positive," Kari replied. "Thank you for today, Sadie." Sadie said, "You are welcome. Now, I forgot to tell you that Camille will be over tomorrow with some savory things for the reception. She and I will go ahead and put them out on the table and be sure the flowers have enough water." "That's great, Sadie, now goodnight."

Daniel came in from work and was still excited about the Chief's report. Seems some citizens who wished to remain anonymous have set up a fund to be used for the center. Chief Carl is on the job with his investigators regarding checking for new young people in the area, especially those who frequent bars. "Daniel that is wonderful. I told you about going to see the Church and reception room, didn't I?" "Yes honey you did." "Listen, dinner is almost ready and the table is set. Sadie helped me fix it and I took a nap with Danny. He's still asleep, but we had better have our dinner before he starts yelling." Daniel fixed the glasses of tea and Kari put the food on the plates. They ate and Daniel noticed that Kari was a little nervous. They finished the meal and Kari asked to turn the coffee on and he already had. She got out the two little cakes that Sadie kept out for them to try. He said; "These are really good." Kari said, "They surely are good and smell good too."

Kari said, "Daniel?" He asked, "What, Sweetheart?" "Well I did something without your permission or knowledge today." "What might that be," Daniel asked? Kari kept stalling and looked like she might cry or run away. Daniel came over and knelt beside her and said, "Kari you can do nothing that would make me mad at you, we will soon be one, anyway. So what did you do that you are so afraid to tell me." "Well, Daniel I bought you a wedding band and I don't know if you will like it. You see, Kelly gave your old wedding band to Sadie (Sadie took care of her while she was pregnant) and I don't know who paid her; however, Sadie kept the ring and I said, I don't want that ring, I need it to see if I can get one that fits you. Sadie took me by her house and brought the ring out; seemed Kelly told Sadie she could do with it what she wanted, you never wore it, so Sadie kept it. I took it into the store with me and simply looked until I found a ring that I think is beautiful, but I don't know if you will like it or not. Oh by the way, I gave the other ring to Sadie, because she has a niece getting married in a couple months and they don't have much money. I told her you would be glad for her to do with it what she wanted."

"But, you see Daniel; I never asked you if the ring meant anything to you, before I gave it to Sadie. And you haven't mentioned whether you want a wedding band, and I'm afraid you will think it sissy." Daniel started laughing. "My dearest Kari, no the ring means nothing to me and I'm thankful Sadie can use it. Now; how do you know whether it fits or whether I like it until I see the ring?" Kari got up to go get it; she still had a worried look on her face, and Daniel stood up and hugged her and kissed her and assured her that she could do nothing that he would not like. Kari went into the bedroom and came back with a beautiful box and handed it to him.

"Wait, my darling, the box is beautiful, but I'd like you to take it out of the box and let me see it." Kari looked him straight in the eye for a minute; then with trembling hands opened the box. There was the most beautiful wedding band he had ever seen. She asked, "Can I try it on your finger?" "Oh yes," he laughed. It fit perfectly and was really a fine piece of jewelry. Kari told him then, that there was writing inside the band and if he did not like it, she had the appraisal and the option of returning it. Daniel took the ring off and read the inscription; he stood speechless. "Kari, please stand right there." He went into Camille's bedroom and got the box that Kari's ring had been in and took the wedding band out. He said, "Look inside the band." Kari almost dropped the ring. "We said the same thing and neither of us knew what the other was doing." "Yes, my dearest darling, don't you understand God brought us together. I love my ring and can barely wait until Saturday for you to put it on my hand." They began to hug and kiss and about that time, Danny decided to make himself known. "Okay, young man, daddy will change you and don't pee on his left hand." Danny gurgled and jabbered. Kari went to fix his formula and food and Daniel brought the clean dry pajama clad Danny to his mommy.

Kari began to feed Danny and noticed Daniel still had his ring on and was really looking at it. "Kari it is so beautiful and what did you say about it being sissy?" "Well, I didn't know what you would think with platinum and gold mixed." "I love this ring and after you put it on me at our wedding; I will never take it off again." "That is what I had planned too," she said. Danny ate like he was starving. "You little rascal, I know what I fed you for lunch, and now your dinner is almost gone. Do you have a hollow leg to put all that food in?" Danny gurgled and babbled and started to twist; he wanted on the floor. Kari took him to his pallet and they watched him play a while. He found his truck and tried to imitate Kari, but it didn't come out right. He threw the truck away and grabbed one of the other toys, talked to it and threw it away. "What is with his throwing, do you think Daniel?" "I don't know for sure, but when I was a very little boy, I'd throw things away if I got mad at them. Maybe that behavior is genetic. Whether it is or not, we will have to teach him some manners at some point."

"He is so precious, if I sound like I'm scolding him, he looks so pitiful, I pick him up, hug and kiss him and he returns the favor; except he spits all over my face." Daniel knew Kari was tired and he went into the kitchen to tidy everything up. He came back and asked where the two of them had gone. Kari said, "We're in here at his crib." Daniel looked and Danny would hold the slats and take about two or three steps (with Kari's help) and then plop down on his bottom; crawl back and start again. "He is definitely a handful now, isn't he?" "Yes, but aren't you thankful he is so healthy and happy?" "Yes my love, I am, and it is thanks to my beautiful bride. I do love you Kari until death parts us." Kari hugged him and kissed him and told him the same. "Now do you want to put our wedding rings together, so we won't forget them Saturday?" "Yes, I think that is a good idea; but where will we put them Saturday, since we walk down the aisle together." "I don't know, but Sadie or Camille will know." He put the box on Camille's dresser.

Danny had crawled nearly everywhere in the house. He was beginning to tire now and Kari thought it might be time to give him a bottle of water and rock him to sleep. As much as he has worked since dinner, water will probably be all he needs. She got him a bottle of distilled water and flavored it a bit with 'gator-aid' and he took it while she rocked him. He was soon asleep and they put him in the crib.

"You know Kari, I've been thinking about something. Why don't we have Camille walk down the aisle beside of you and Sadie beside of me? Then they can keep the rings and hand them to us when the time comes." "That is great!" Daniel went to put on his sweats and then Kari went to put on her bedclothes. Daniel sat on his chair and Kari lay down on the couch. Pretty soon, Daniel noticed her rubbing her leg and hip while they were watching TV. Daniel noticed the time and realized they needed to go to bed. He went into the kitchen and got two aspirin and a pill that Dr. Little prescribed and gave them to Kari and she took them. He began to massage her hip and leg and soon she was sleepy. Daniel picked her up and took her to bed. He kissed her and said; "I'll be in after a while." He lay down on the couch and watched TV and almost went to sleep. He heard Kari calling, "Where are you Daniel? Have you left?" "No," he said; "I'll be right there." Kari was standing in the doorway and didn't really seem to be awake. He said; "I'm right here darling." He put his arms around her and kissed her and she went to sleep with restlessness. Daniel wondered why Kari sometimes acted afraid if she went to sleep and woke up without him beside her. She really was never fully awake, but she was afraid. I guess her 'muddy creek' was bothering her. He prayed silently and asked God to please let her rest and not be afraid. He knew she had been through a lot, but God you know the ins and outs of everything. You know I'd give my life for her; so please give her peace.

The next day was Friday and the day before her wedding and Kari awoke before Daniel or Danny. She went in to make bacon and scrambled eggs with some cheese in them. She prepared the toast and then prepared the food for Danny. She heard him squirming around and went to get him before he awoke Daniel. She gave him a warm bath, wrapped him in a towel and brought him back and put him on the bed to dress him. Danny was tired of waiting for his food and started to cry. Daniel sat up and said, "I'll be right there son." Kari said, "No need, we've had our bath and the breakfast is ready for you, me, and Danny." "How did I sleep through all that, Kari? I'm so sorry; I want to take as much off you as possible." "You usually do, but I think you were pretty tired last night as well." "I was," he said. "Well, my loves come into the kitchen and mommy will feed you both." Daniel started laughing and joined her in the kitchen. Danny was not ready to greet anyone, just his bottle and food. Kari had mixed the peaches and cereal together and his formula. He ate everything and turned to Kari and smiled. "You are my good boy, Daniel would you hand me that damp hand towel, so I can clean his face?" Daniel did and Danny looked up at him and smiled too. Then Danny clapped his hands. Daniel asked, "When did that start?" "A few days ago we were playing and clapping hands, he hasn't done it again, so I thought he had forgotten." Daniel kissed them both and went to the shower, dressed and came back in the kitchen, to find Sadie all ready there. They all three chatted about Danny's clapping and smiling and taking a few steps. Then Camille came in and after everyone was greeted, Daniel had to go to work.

Daniel decided to go to Sadie's Pastor and pay him for his services as well as the vocalist. He told them how much Sadie meant to them and how much they loved her. She was a God-send to us, especially when Kari was still so sick. "We are so pleased to do that and for the invitations to the wedding. When Sadie told us how much she loved the two of you, we kept it quiet from her, but I expect there will be quite a few from our Church." "That's great! Sadie doesn't know it yet, but she will walk down the aisle on my side with my wedding band and Camille will walk down on Kari's side with her wedding band. That way we won't lose them." "That's a good idea," he said. Daniel said, "Thank you so much for coming to our wedding, neither one of us have close family."

Daniel left and went by the florist and paid them for the beautiful arrangements. They said that's fine, the Church is quite pretty. "Why don't you call Pastor Chuck and go see it?" "I think I might," he answered. He went on to work and asked the Chief if they had anything pressing to do this morning. Chief said, "No, I don't believe we do." "Good, will you come with me to see the Church? It has been decorated, but I haven't seen it yet. It will give you a chance to meet my pastor, Chuck. You might also at some point check with him about setting aside money for the center." Chief started laughing; "Daniel you are getting married tomorrow and it seems you are still determined to get the center open after Christmas. I will contact him and invite him to our next meeting, but you are not invited. You must take some time to get to know your new wife and enjoy yourselves. You know you haven't taken a vacation in over three years. Now I expect and the officers expect you to take three weeks off. We have the best officers around and whether you knew it or not, we had scheduled an officer to keep a close eye on Kari. I swore Wayne to secrecy, lest he told you. These guys know you and love you; you need not be too surprised if a number of them show up at the Church. I did contact Chuck to see if there was room for some of us". He said, "Absolutely; and I've already spoken to him about the center. So let's see the Church and you go home and help the ladies that I know cannot lift all that stuff." They went into the Church and Daniel stopped short; "Chief, I've never seen anything so pretty. I paid the florist today and spoke to Sadie's pastor and the vocalist. They love Sadie as much as we do. She and Camille have worked so hard with them and I can't believe how beautiful it is, without all that gaudy stuff I've seen before." Chuck had come up behind them and said, "Daniel, please don't ever let Kari know how gaudy your first wedding was. I know I wasn't good enough to marry you and I'm glad you didn't ask, but Kari is different."

The Chief spoke up and said essentially the same thing. "Well, I appreciate you both for your advice." Chuck said, "Come on into the reception area. Your jaw might drop", Chuck said, laughing. It was indeed beautiful. Chuck said the other day when Sadie and Kari came by, Sadie put Danny down for a moment and he became very interested in the tablecloth and flowers. Sadie and Kari couldn't believe how quick the little ones can be when they see something they like that's new to them. Daniel could hardly believe what he saw, it is truly beautiful and so like Kari, simple, but stunning. "Thanks Chuck and give Sharon my hug for you." They all laughed and Daniel and the Chief went back to the office. "Now I mean it Daniel, you go home and help your women with stuff needing doing, if nothing else, keep Danny out from under their feet." "Okay, I will."

When Daniel got home, all three of the women looked at him and asked if he felt all right. "Yes I do, but you won't believe what the Chief and Chuck told me to do. Go home from work; we don't want to see you until the wedding. I am to do whatever any of you say. I'm being bossed by my boss and pastor," he said grinning. "Daniel I'm so glad to see you. Danny is asleep and Sadie and Camille don't need my help right now. Can we take a walk?" "Of course, honey," he said hugging her and looking over her head at Camille and Sadie. They mouthed, she needs out of the house for a while. Daniel said, "Go get your coat it's cold outside and we'll take a walk and perhaps a drive." "That's a good idea Daniel, she's been nervous and not exactly herself today." "Is she sick?" "No, I'm not sick; can I not go for a walk with my husband to be and perhaps a drive?" "Yes, you may my darling. I like that idea too."

They left to take a walk and naturally went down to Kari's creek. It was still a bit muddy, but perhaps there really was a little dam upstream or downstream for that matter. Kari shivered and Daniel said, "Let's take a ride around the country side and let me tell you about my day." "That would be a good idea," she said. "Well, first of all I went to see Sadie's pastor and the vocalist to pay them; they didn't want to take it, but I insisted. They told me that Sadie didn't know it, but quite a few from Church would be coming to the wedding". I talked to Pastor Chuck to check the room and he said there is plenty of room. I went to work and checked to see if there was anything pushing this morning. Chief said no, and I asked him to go to the Church with me to see the decorations and meet Chuck. Kari, the Church is decorated so beautifully, I thought I might cry in front of the Chief and Chuck; I managed to control myself. Did you see the windows?" Kari smiled and said "Yes, I did, and I love it too. Did you see the reception area?" "Yes, honey and it is just as beautiful. I can hardly believe everything is perfect for us. When we started to go I told Chuck he could give Sharon my hug and kiss." "Gladly," he said. He told me about Danny trying to get to the tablecloth and flowers. He was laughing at how quickly you and Sadie grabbed him up. Chief was very serious about not seeing me until the wedding and said a number of officers would be there."

CAUGHT SMOOCHING!

They drove on for a while looking at the scenery and Kari said; "Daniel you know I love you and I know you love me, but are you absolutely sure you are happy with our wedding? "I told you, I can barely remember my first wedding; it felt cold. But I love the whole idea of our wedding. Please help me believe this is for real and we won't have any fancy junk that blurs my memory." "Oh, my dearest darling, I remember bits and pieces of my previous wedding, but what I remember I did not like. It too was cold and planned to the 'teeth' and all she needed from me was the money to pay for it."

He pulled the car off the road into a small side road and reached for Kari and hugged her and kissed her until she was breathless. "You listen to me my darling; I love everything about our wedding. It is like us and nothing could be more fitting. Please believe me; I couldn't bear it if you thought I would lie to you. I do believe you, but today I started thinking that maybe I was pushing too much of me onto the wedding and I began to worry that you wouldn't want some of it." "Please believe me; Daniel, I do believe you and I'm deeply thankful that I could talk to you about my fears and you don't think I'm silly." "Darling, you are not silly in any way. You are the only woman I've ever loved or ever will love." This time Kari smiling; grabbed him and kissed him until he was breathless. "We better stop," he said, "I think we've fogged up the windows. Some officer might come this way and find their chaplain making out with a beautiful red-head." "Daniel, thank you, thank you, thank you, and now lets go tell Camille and Sadie our plan for them to walk us down the aisle." Daniel laughed and said, "You are definitely welcome my love."

They headed back home and sure enough an officer followed them. "Oh I'll never hear the end of this honey." They both went into the kitchen and Kari started talking about everything they wanted and how they were smooching a bit and an officer followed them home. "Daniel says he will never hear the end of this. I think it is funny." Sadie and Camille said; it was. Daniel spoke up and asked them about walking down the aisle with them to keep their wedding bands separate and to let people know how much we love you. Sadie said, "Daniel, are you sure you want me?" "Absolutely! And before you ask Camille, Yes, I want you too." They both agreed and looked at the two of them. "Could we see the rings, just in case we can't tell the largest from the smallest?" "Yes," Daniel laughed and went to get the rings. "They are both beautiful and I think we can get the right ring to the right person." They were all laughing and suddenly, Kari said; "Where is Danny? Did he crawl outdoors when we left?" "No, Danny is exploring the cupboards over there." He sure was, in a minute he hit a pot with a wooden spoon and thought that was so funny. He looked up at all of them, as though he needed applause, which of course he got.

It was getting late and Daniel asked if they wanted him to put the cakes in the car, since it would be cold tonight. "That's a good idea," Sadie said. Camille said, "We made your dinner because we didn't know how long you would be gone and besides neither of you need to cook tonight." Daniel started taking the boxes out to the car and the punch with the punch bowl and cups. Everything Sadie had done was now in the car. Camille said, "My stuff is already in my car and Sadie and I will place it on the tables in the morning."

"I put the boxes in my car, Sadie. Don't you want me to take you and lift the boxes out for you?" "No," Sadie said, "They aren't that heavy, but you were getting 'antsy' because the Chief said you better help us. Well you have. We will see you both here about twelve-thirty. We can help Kari get dressed and dress Danny and I assume you can dress yourself, Daniel." He laughed and said, "I've been doing it for many years now. Look in the refrigerator for Kari's flowers and see what you think of them. Oh, I got a flower for me, but I forgot what the saleslady said it was. I also got flowers for you and Sadie. If they are not to your liking, the lady said I could exchange them in the morning." Sadie and Camille looked in the refrigerator and could not imagine when he put them there. "They are just right Daniel, look Kari, they are beautiful." Kari started jumping up and down and said, "They really are perfect." Daniel took hold of her arm and said, "No jumping in the house." "Well you better tell your son that too." Danny was trying to imitate Kari. They all laughed and Camille and Sadie said, "We'll see you about twelve-thirty tomorrow." They both left smiling.

Danny was beginning to get cranky. "Oh, my dear baby, you are hungry aren't you?" Danny 'talked' back to her. She said, "Okay, Mommy will fix your dinner." While Kari was doing that Daniel picked Danny up and gave him a sponge bath and changed him into his pajamas. It was past his bedtime; so Kari fed him cereal with peaches and his formula and rocked him a while and Danny was out 'like a light turned off'. Kari put him in his crib for the night.

Daniel had set the table and got the food out of the warmer and fixed their plates. The food was good, he had not realized he hadn't eaten today and doubted Kari had either. They enjoyed their dinner and Daniel told Kari to get her night clothes on and he would tidy the kitchen, which he did. Kari changed and lay down on the couch. She realized she really was tired, but did not in any way seem sleepy. Daniel came into the great room and Kari said, "I'm tired, but I can't go to sleep. You know tomorrow is our wedding day and I can't think of anything but that." Daniel said, "I'm the same way, but you must take these pills and then we'll go to bed." He turned the TV on for a little while and pretty soon, Kari was rubbing her leg. He rubbed her leg and hip for her and soon she was sleepy. He picked her up and took her to bed, kissed her and told her he would be in shortly. She had gone to sleep almost as soon as her head met the pillow. Daniel finished watching the news and turned the TV off and thanked the Lord for the day and the wonderful things He had done for all of them. Please bless this wedding and all who attend, Daniel prayed. He then got up and took his place beside Kari. When he put his arm around her, she sighed and slept soundly.

As was the usual routine, Danny awoke and began his babbling, he then got louder and rolled over and crawled to the side of the crib that Kari was on. He had never learned words yet, but Kari tried to teach him to say dada and mama, but he hadn't said words. He began his 'talk' and said; "dada." Daniel sat up and said, "Did he really say that?" Kari answered, "Yes, we've been trying to talk. He can say mama, but hasn't got that right, yet." "He will," Daniel said. "Did you teach him dada?" Kari answered, "Of course."

Daniel got up and gave Danny his bath and they played a bit and then wrapped in a large towel; Daniel took him into the room and dressed him in clean pajamas. It would be a while before he would dress for their wedding. Kari went into the kitchen and made them a healthy breakfast; natural cereal and scrambled eggs with toast. She made the coffee and had Danny's breakfast ready. As usual, he had cereal with peaches and formula. He was then ready to play. Daniel put him in his swing and turned and hugged Kari. "Hello, my beautiful bride, I love you", and he kissed her. Kari said, "Yep, we really are getting married." She hugged him and kissed him too. "Your son gave you your birthday present, but you will have to settle for me for your birthday, this year. I couldn't think of anything you had mentioned that I could get, so I present my rumpled self to you this morning. I love you, Daniel." Daniel held her and told her how precious his gift was. They sat down to have breakfast and enjoyed the coffee and watched Danny play.

Soon Daniel said, "I'll go take my shower first and I'll shave close so I won't have a 'five o'clock' shadow by three o'clock." "Okay," Kari answered, "But put on something that won't be soiled, running after Danny." He said he would and went to shower and shave. He was thrilled that today they would be able to be a family with God's blessings. He came out to the kitchen and found Danny crawling around Kari's feet, while she was trying to prepare a lunch for them. She knew they would need something light to eat before the wedding. Danny pulled up on her gown and stood a minute and reached for the cupboard door. He managed one step and got the handle of the cupboard door. Kari said, "Are you now going to help me cook or are you going to play drums?" Danny looked up at her; "You want your spoon don't you?" She handed him a spoon and pot and he began to bang. Daniel was at the door and neither of them had seen him. Daniel said; "You really like drums in the morning?" Kari said, "It's a wooden spoon, but he likes to play in the cupboards now; he can actually get a pot out of the cupboard."

"Daniel", said Kari, "He is learning and moving so fast, how will we ever be able to catch up?" "Oh, we'll be fine and so will our darling."

While Daniel was in the shower, Kari had called Wayne to ask him to have the necessary papers for Daniel to become co-owner of the house. "I'm sorry I waited so long, Wayne, but I kept forgetting. Do you think you can do that by the wedding?" "I believe I can," Wayne replied. "Oh, good'" Kari replied, "Just bring them to the wedding and since we'll be signing papers after the wedding, Daniel can sign that too." "Okay," Wayne replied. "Is Daniel as nervous as you sound?" "I didn't think I was nervous, but I guess he feels about like I do; we want the wedding and all the festivities that Sadie and Camille have planned, but it will be a big day and I wonder if I can stay up all day without becoming so exhausted that my leg will really act up." "Kari, take some advice from your lawyer, who happens to care for both of you, make yourself take a rest about mid-morning, that way you will be rested and won't have difficulty with your leg." "Okay, Wayne, I guess I need to do that." Daniel had heard part of her conversation and waited until after breakfast and taking care of Danny to ask her what she and Wayne were talking about. "Well Daniel, I had forgotten again to see Wayne about having you sign as co-owner of the house. He said he would bring the papers to Church today and since we will be signing everything for the wedding, he'll have you sign that as well." Daniel said, "Honey you don't have to do this, you know it means a lot, but it can certainly wait a while." "Not for me", Kari replied. "He also told me that I needed to take a good rest sometime this morning, because otherwise my leg might not hold up to all the activity." Daniel said, "We will make sure; you need to take a pill that Dr. Little gave you and go to bed a while." "That will make me feel better, darling. I can take care of Danny and finish lunch. I'll wake you before Camille and Sadie get here. I don't want anything to mar our wedding; so please take the pill now." "Well I guess I better, seems my leg hurts when I've been on it all day. I must have a kiss first." "Oh, very well," Daniel said, "If I must, you must, you rascal you." Daniel hugged and kissed her and laughing got her pills and gave them to her and then kissed her again. He took her to the bed, he had straightened and she went to bed. Soon she was asleep.

Daniel went into the kitchen to finish the lunch that Kari had started and he and Danny talked and played. About lunch time, Danny became cranky and Daniel looked at his watch; where did the time go, it was twelve noon. He went to wake Kari and she had just awakened. Daniel said, "Honey, I forgot the time while Danny and I were playing, but he became cranky and I realized he wants his lunch." "Well good," Kari replied.

Daniel said, "Sweetheart, please put your robe on; not only for my sanity, but because Sadie and Camille will be here soon". She did and then fixed Danny's lunch. He was now yelling, not just cranky. Kari fed him cereal with some applesauce and his formula. He tasted the cereal and swallowed, but looked at Kari with a funny expression. Kari said, "Danny, we have to start different solid foods now, I know how you feel about peas, but the applesauce is good." Danny ate and took his formula and was ready for Kari to rock him. He was soon asleep. She put him in his crib and asked Daniel how they had done while she was asleep. "Well, I thought we were doing well, until he got cranky and I knew I had changed him, so I didn't know what to do, until I looked at my watch. I realized you needed to get up and Danny needed his food. I finished our lunch and we can eat while he is asleep. One more time before Sadie and Camille get here, I want you to know I really love you and our wedding." "Thank you, Daniel, I do too." They ate lunch and were having a cup of coffee and Sadie and Camille came in.

Sadie looked at Daniel and Kari and said, "Daniel, any last requests?" "Yeah, let's get on with the wedding." She and Camille started laughing, we thought so, they both said. "Kari, I meant to tell you to please rest this morning and I simply forgot." "Oh, that's okay, Daniel gave me a pill and some aspirin and I went to sleep until twelve o'clock when Danny decided it was time to eat, he is none too quiet when he is hungry. He's had lunch and is now asleep."

Kari and Daniel noticed that Camille and Sadie were already dressed and really looked pretty. "You girls look pretty today, are you ready to walk with us." "Yes, but not like you guys look at the moment." Daniel said, "I showered and shaved this morning, but Kari needed to sleep so I wore this garb, because Danny can be messy." "That's a good idea," Sadie said.

Camille and Sadie asked if Kari needed to shower and she said, "Yes. I shampooed my hair yesterday, so I won't need to dry it; it is becoming so long, and I didn't realize it until it was too late to have it styled." "Your hair is beautiful, but it might need to be combed," Sadie said. Kari said, "Well, here I go to the shower; I'm going to use the one in your room Camille." She had put her underwear out the night before and had her make-up in that bathroom.

She showered and dried well and put her underwear on and then her robe. "I'm putting my make-up on, but I need you two to help me pack my suitcase. I forgot to do it this past week. All the things I need are in the dresser drawers and the suitcase is over there." She put her make-up on and combed and styled her long hair and came out of the bathroom. Sadie and Camille both let out a whistle and said; "You have beautiful clothing for the next couple weeks. Then you might need to find a washer for some of the unmentionables." Kari laughed so hard, she could hardly catch her breath. "I haven't heard the word 'unmentionables' in I can't remember when," she said.

Everything was packed in two suitcases. She put her pantyhose on and Sadie and Camille helped her with her dress. "Do I look all right?" "Beautiful," Daniel said from the door. Sadie asked, "Are you supposed to see your bride before the wedding?" "I guess I can since I was with her when she picked it out. Kari, you really are beautiful inside and outside. Do you ladies need me to put the suitcases in the car?" "Yes we do," they said, "And did you get your things packed?" "Yes I did and that suitcase is already in the car." He picked up the suitcases and took them to his car. He said quietly, "Thank you, Lord, for Kari and Danny and for our dear friends. Please bless this union and keep Kari well."

When all that was done, they sat down for a cup of coffee and told Kari and Daniel how beautiful everything looked. We have Pastor Chuck standing guard over the food and Sharon will take over when you all are ready. Then she will take her seat. "You all have planned everything and we do appreciate you." "You are both welcome, it was our pleasure," they said.

Danny chose that time to start his music. He needed or wanted attention. Daniel said, "I'll get him, but Kari will you fix that bottle of water and 'gator-aid'? He seems to like it and it will hold him over until his suppertime." "Now are you and Camille sure you have things worked out that won't cause you too much to do while we are gone." "We absolutely do; now scoot and bring your son to me," Sadie said. Danny went immediately to Sadie, who fed him and then she and Camille put a clean diaper and his little suit on him. They put his new shoes on, but he did not seem to like them. He saw his boots and wanted them. Sadie said; "We'll put boots on after mommy and daddy are gone." That seemed to satisfy him, but he decided he wanted his teething ring. They had him dressed and Kari said, "Daniel, he looks like you and he is beautiful." "Thank you, Kari. Now it's about time we get to the Church. Who will hold Danny while you two walk us down the aisle?" "Joe has already decided he will and if they decide to take a walk, well, they will take a walk."

THE WEDDING AND RECEPTION

Daniel and Kari drove to Church together and Sadie, Camille and Danny followed. "Kari, I want you to know you have made me the happiest man in the world. It feels like we have already married, long ago, but this just makes it legal." Kari said, "You know Daniel, I feel the same way, except now you don't have to sleep on top of the covers." They both laughed and the Church was in sight. They were shocked at the number of cars there. "How many invitations did you send, honey?" "About twelve, I think," Kari replied. "Well, Chief, Chuck, and Sadie's pastor must have thought that wasn't enough to ensure we were properly 'tied'," he laughed. Joe met them at the door and took Danny. They walked around the Church to the side door and walked down the halls a bit, hoping to get Danny a little tired. Camille told Joe that the diaper bag with water and dry formula was in the car.

Camille handed Kari her bouquet and Sadie pinned Daniel's flower on his lapel. A voice called them and they turned around to see who it was and several pictures were taken of them in moments. Sadie said, "He's already done the inside of the Church and reception hall and will take pictures after the wedding." Daniel and Kari stepped inside in the vestibule and to one side. Daniel reached down and kissed Kari and they both heard a voice, say, "Well, what is this, did I miss the wedding?" They looked up the stairs and Chuck and Sharon were coming down, along with Joe, dressed in a dark suit. Sadie's pastor was with Joe and they heard music playing. They were lined up ready to go into the sanctuary from the vestibule, Kari said, "Daniel where is Danny?" "Oh," Sadie said, "I introduced him to my niece the other day and they were best friends quickly, so she has him and is seated near the side door in case they need to go out."

They heard the piece of music by Strauss that Kari had asked to be played instead of the usual 'Here comes the Bride'. Joe and Chuck had gone down the hall from the vestibule and had taken their place at the front. Daniel with Sadie at his side and Camille at Kari's side started slowly down the aisle. They got to the altar and the vocalist sang the most beautiful rendition of 'The Lord's Prayer' that Kari had ever heard. Then it was time for Joe to marry them; he told the congregation that they may be seated and this marriage might be a bit different from the ones they normally attended. So the marriage began and when Joe said they could exchange rings, Sadie handed Daniel the ring for Kari and he put it on her finger but first slipped the engagement ring off her finger and put it in front of the wedding band. Then Camille handed Kari Daniel's ring and she slipped it on his left hand. He had already pronounced them husband and wife. Then he said; "We have another part to this ceremony." Chuck came to front from the side and Joe stepped to the side and Chuck explained about the 'salt covenant'. He asked Daniel to reach into the bag of salt and get a pinch; then he opened the bag for Kari to get a pinch. Then he asked them both to drop the salt back into the bag and he gently shook it. Then he said; "Just as neither of them can get the exact salt crystal they picked up, they are forever joined in this covenant." He then said, "Daniel, you may kiss your bride."

The music began to play, Daniel and Kari turned to go down the aisle as husband and wife; the photographer took several more shots of them. They got to the vestibule and Sadie and Camille escorted the bride and groom into the reception hall. Soon the room was filled with officers, people Kari had never seen from Sadie's Church, and then she saw Joey and Leslie. They smiled at her. Sadie explained that today was also Daniel's birthday and the caramel cake was his birthday cake and the red velvet with creamed cheese frosting was what they both wanted for their wedding cake.

"Now each of you may come greet the bride and groom and then get some refreshments, but first, Daniel and Kari have to cut their cake and give each other a bite." Everyone laughed as it was easy for Daniel to get the bite in Kari's mouth, but she had to reach far up and then missed part of his mouth. He laughed, got a napkin, wiped his mouth and kissed his bride again. Everyone clapped and came in a line to greet the couple. Nearly everyone kissed Kari on the cheek and some even got Daniel's cheek. When Joey and Leslie got to them, Kari grabbed and kissed Joey and Leslie and introduced Daniel to them both. Joey whispered to Kari, "You were right, thank you and I love you." Daniel said; "Did you just tell my wife you loved her?" "Boys, have you ever heard such a thing," laughing all the while. One of the officers said, "We were all going to do the same, but you are bigger than we are." Joey turned and said; "Kari has been like a sister to me for several years, and just as bossy as a sister." The entire reception group laughed and Joey and Leslie moved on down the row for refreshments. Everyone was soon past so Kari and Daniel took a bite of his birthday cake and said he had an announcement; "Kari and I are married and very grateful for all of you attending; and boys," looking directly at the officers, "I don't expect to be followed anymore, if I want to kiss my wife in the car; you all did notice I pulled off the road and made it safe for other drivers." They all laughed and clapped because they knew he had spotted them. He turned to Sadie's pastor and thanked him for keeping this wonderful surprise from Sadie. "We love her as much as you do." After mingling a bit with the guests, Joe and Wayne came to get Kari and Daniel; "Sorry folks, it 'ain't' over till the paper work is complete." Daniel said, "We know, but could we introduce our son; you all know that my first wife chose to not to keep any tie to the baby, but when he was about six weeks old, she dropped him off at Kari's and said I'd pick him up after work. My now angel wife adopted him long before we got married. So here comes our son, Danny." Danny looked around at everyone and then saw the red cake. He began to reach for it and Kari gave him a tiny bite. That didn't seem enough. Kari said, "We'll be back darling and you can mess up your pretty suit with your own cake". They went with Joe and Wayne and signed all the papers, plus Daniel signed where Kari and Wayne pointed. "Honey, this is not necessary," he said. "Yes, it is; now sign!" Joe and Wayne both started laughing as Daniel very obediently signed the paper. "You have one terrific wife, Daniel, she will keep you straight." "I'm finding that out," he laughed.

Soon the guests were leaving and Daniel and Kari left for their honeymoon. "Where are we going," asked Kari. "I'll tell you later. It's a surprise." They chatted about how beautiful the wedding was and what a surprise that so many people came. Daniel said, "Well, I knew the people from Sadie's Church were coming because her pastor told me; I told him that was great, but please keep it a surprise from Sadie. He assured me they had.

By the way, when Sadie saw all her Church people, she whispered to me, you scamp, but I love you." "You know, Daniel, I had no idea so many people would bring us gifts; I certainly did not expect that." "Me either," he said, "But Camille said she and Sadie would take them to the house. We can write thank notes when we get back." Kari picked up Daniel's left hand and kissed it; "Thank you for liking the ring, Daniel." "I love the ring, Kari, and I might say the same for you," as he picked up her left hand and kissed it."

THE HONEYMOOM

They drove on a good while and suddenly Kari's stomach started grumbling. "Oh my," Kari said. "Well that's good because we are almost to our destination." They drove up a small hill on the side of a larger mountain and came to a stop in front of a lodge. "There aren't any cars, Daniel, are you sure they are open?" "I'm sure," he said. They parked the car and went inside the lodge. It was huge with a gigantic fireplace in the center of the dinning room. Almost as soon as they got into the door, a man came out of the back room and said; "Welcome Mr. and Mrs. Meyers". Kari looked up at Daniel, and said; "Daniel did you do this?" "Yep, I sure did. Carlos, my wife is starving, could we have dinner now?" "Of course, of course, sit anywhere you like. We'll have dinner out soon." Kari said; "Did you order too? You are such a charmer, Daniel. How did I get so blessed?" "We both are, honey. By the way, did I tell you I love you?" "Well, you might have mentioned it a time or two." "I really do love you to; now could we sit near the fireplace?" Kari replied, "I was thinking the same thing, there is something about a fireplace that relaxes me and the warmth is just right." They sat down near the fireplace and Daniel watched the light shining on her hair; it was like spun copper with waves of gold interspersed. She was a beauty to behold and she still had her wedding dress on. "You are so beautiful, Kari." "Thank you, kind sir; and, may I say; you are one handsome dude!"

Carlos came out with a huge cart with flowers and silver domes with food inside that smelled wonderful. He had a bottle of sparking water in a wine bucket. When he lifted the domes, there was lobster, steak, shrimp and various side dishes. "Are we supposed to eat all this food?" Carlos answered, "Yes, but save some room for the beautiful dessert."

When Carlos left, they bowed their head and gave God thanks for the food and everything He had done for them. Then Kari picked up her fork and put it down, "Where are the lobster clamps?" "Just lift the shell with your fork," it came off beautifully. Carlos came back out and begged forgiveness for not bringing their bib for the lobster, because it had some butter on it. He put bibs on Daniel and Kari. They thanked him and Kari started laughing. "You look like Danny," she said.

Daniel was laughing too and as he took a bite, he realized he did need a bib. Kari began eating lobster and some of the shrimp and steak. She enjoyed the mixed green salad and went back to the lobster. She ate as much as she could, and Daniel ate a bit more. He got up to pour their coffee and some sparkling water. They enjoyed it all. Kari took another bite of her steak and lobster and said, "Daniel, I cannot finish this beautiful dinner." "That's okay. If you get hungry later, there is room service, and I assure you the food will appear pretty soon after you order." "Daniel, I just realized, you rented this entire lodge for us. There aren't any other people here and I saw no cars outside." He looked at her and said simply, "I did."

About that time Carlos came out with another cart and moved the other away and opened the dome. He lighted it and it flamed beautifully and smelled wonderful. "Daniel, how did you know this is my favorite dessert, I know I haven't told you." Carlos smiled at them and left them to serve themselves when they wished. Daniel got up and served their plates and poured another coffee. Kari dipped her fork in and took a bite before he could take his seat. Daniel laughed out loud. "I guessed about the dessert, but I like it too. If you had not liked it, there are several others he will make." "No, this is perfect and taste so good, I can't wait for you to taste yours." "That's great," he said and took a bite; sure enough it was delicious. They ate their entire serving and this time, Kari put her fork down, and said, "Daniel if I eat anything else, I'll be sick." "Well, we will watch the fire and go over to that couch on the other side of the fireplace." "That's totally great!" Kari replied.

They went to the other side of the open fireplace and the couch really looked inviting, so they both sat down and Daniel got a stool for Kari's feet. "Now relax, no more talking about Danny, he is fine! Let's just enjoy each other and the fireplace." "That sounds great," Kari said, and leaned over on Daniel's chest. Carlos came to tidy up the dinner ware and told them goodnight. "If you need anything during the nighttime there will be someone to assist you. Just call the extension I told you, Mr. Meyers." "Thanks," Daniel said. They relaxed and talked about the wedding and how great it was. Kari said, "I was so glad to see Joey and Leslie." "I was too", Daniel said. "He looks like a fine young man and Leslie looks like she has an inner strength that will help him." "She does," Kari said. They talked some more and the fireplace slowly began to dim.

Daniel said, "Let's go to our suite, there is a fireplace there too and it's been lit." They went up to their suite and it was beautiful. Kari was about to jump and realized she better not. Daniel kissed her and told her he was going to get their suitcases. He came back with his and Carlos came back carrying her two. "Would you like me to send one of the ladies to help you unpack, Mrs. Meyers?" Kari said, "No, thank you, I think we can manage." "Well have a wonderful night, if the fireplace is too warm, Daniel can turn it down." He left and Kari said, "He always called you Mr. Meyers downstairs and just then he called you Daniel." "I know sweetheart, I got Carlos out of some trouble a long time ago; because he wasn't guilty and most always if there is someone around, He calls me Mr. Meyers." "You are a good man, Daniel Meyers, and I love you. I also appreciate this place and the flowers in every room. You are so special."

They lay down on the large couch in front of the fireplace. They snuggled, hugged and kissed for some time. "Sweetheart, it's almost eleven-thirty. Don't you think we should get out of wedding clothes?" "I sure do, I'd like to keep this dress." "I'd like that too, Daniel replied. "Which room did you put our bags in?" "The room over here; it's got a king sized bed and a fireplace; the other has a queen sized bed, but no fireplace." "You made the right choice." They darkened most of the lights in the living room.

Daniel checked the refrigerator to ensure there was juice and soft drinks. He also turned the fireplace down some in the living room. Then he went into their bedroom and Kari was waiting for him. The bed had been turned down, with chocolates on the pillow and roses on the night stand with a small lamp. "Daniel, could we leave the bathroom light on with the door almost shut, that way there will be a light all night, or will that keep you awake?" "That's a good idea."

Kari said, "I need to take my dress off and hang it up." Daniel said "I'll take my jacket off and hang it, but I draw the line at you taking your dress off. I would like to do that." "Oh, okay, but I'll take your shirt and tie off." She reached up to take his tie off and couldn't get it off. He said, "Honey the tie goes like this" and he moved it loose enough that she took it off and pulled it over his head. She unbuttoned his shirt and pulled it out of his trousers and then hugged him and rubbed his chest and back and tried to reach him for a kiss. He kissed her and then said; "Now it's my turn." The lamps were still on and the fireplace was to her back. Daniel simply looked at her for a long while and then very gently unzipped the back of her dress. He rubbed her back and gently took the dress off her shoulders. He looked at the most beautiful woman he had ever seen. He lowered her dress and hung it up in the closet. When he turned around, she took his belt off and started to undo his trousers, but he said; "Better not right now."

He told her to sit down and he would take her pantyhose off. She did and he picked her up and gazed at her beauty. He caressed her and then tried to remove her bra. "There are so many hooks, what if I scratch you? And do you have to go through this everyday?" Kari laughed, she said; "I told you I was a bit bigger at the top and yes, I do it everyday. I'm much more use to it than you are. Let me show you how." She started at the bottom hook and worked upward the whole four hooks. Daniel looked at her back and said, "I did hurt you, there's a red spot where I tried." "It will go away, honey." He took the straps down onto her arms and gazed at her beautifully perfect breasts. "I really want to touch them, is that okay?" "Of course, darling, but how about another kiss?" "Coming right up," he said. He kissed her and fondled her breasts, they were soft and at the same time firm. He took the bra off of her shoulders, he was about to lose his breath. "Okay," Kari said, she took his belt off and loosed his trousers and let them fall, and bent down and hung them in the closet. She then took his underwear off and put it on the foot of the bed.

"Oh, you are a scamp. Well, my shoes need to come off you know and seems like there is another garment on my person." Daniel relaxed and realized she was teasing him in the sweetest way. He bent down and took her shoes off and put them at the end of the bed. "Now what," he asked, "Well, what else do you see on me?" "I see some very pretty panties can I remove those as well?" "There doesn't seem to be anything else left, now does there?" Daniel could not believe she was still teasing him, when he was about to squeeze her hard. "Can we at least lie down, Kari, I'm about to lose my breath and balance." "Well, in that case we might both lie down." He took her in his arms and Kari said, "The fireplace feels good, but you feel better." Daniel said, "Honey, are you sure you're ready for this"? "I'm absolutely ready and feel here." She placed his hand under her left upper arm and, Daniel asked; "What are those?" She reminded him of her doctor ordering birth control until she was ready for a baby. "Those little capsules have measured doses of birth control medicine." Daniel said "I thought birth control came in little pills." "Some do, but at that time and even now, I might forget them and mess up my whole system."

Also, Dr. Little said I might be tight with the first few times I had sex, but not to worry; they had to mend my whole pelvic floor when I was raped. "Thankfully, I'm healed, but I wanted you to know, well, so you would know." They hugged, snuggled, and kissed until Daniel thought he would lose all control. Kari said, "Daniel, are you going to make love to me or must I attack you?" He chuckled and said, "No attack needed; tell me when you are ready." "I've been ready, and I really want you now. I'm not really patient, you know." He kissed her and she kissed him. He held himself up off her chest and entered her slowly. She started kissing him and as he moved gently, Kari trembled and asked; "What was that?" Daniel whispered; "That was your orgasm." "Really, that's great, let's do it again." "I'll try but I'm not sure I can wait much longer," Daniel said. "Darling I love you now make love to me, like you mean it." Daniel moved more and deeper and Kari hung on and wrapped her legs around his buttocks and kissed him deeply. About that time, they both had an orgasm. Daniel's breathing was so short and this time they couldn't tell which one was the most shaken. "My darling Kari, that was wonderful." They were lying on their side facing one another and Daniel asked, "Did you never have an orgasm with Frank?" "No, he was always in a hurry, so I just went along with whatever he wanted." "My dearest Kari, I'm so sorry about that, but I will do my best to wait until you are ready before making love." They stayed facing one another and Kari dozed a little and Daniel had to go the bathroom. He had blood all over himself, he must have hurt her. He took a warm bath cloth and went into the bedroom and started wiping her down; there was blood on her legs as well. He rinsed the bath cloth and kept it as warm as possible and put on her. Kari awoke and Daniel told her what happened and he was so sorry. Kari said, "Daniel

I'm fine; I told you what Dr. Little said, there's no harm done unless you were really rough with me, AND YOU DEFINITELY WERE NOT. Now stop worrying and come hold me a while." "I will sweetheart, but appease me, come to the bathroom and check yourself to be sure you are all right." "I will, but I'm telling you, Daniel, I'm fine." They both went into the bathroom and Kari said, "I'm fine, but I will use some of that cream Dr. Little gave me." Daniel stood watch over her and she looked up at him with the most brilliant smile. "Now may we go to bed and you hold me, under the covers." "All right," but Kari knew he was still worried. "Okay Daniel, the next time I feel like making love, I will get on top of you and you can see my face and my entire body. That way, you will know that I am fine." "That would make me feel better, Kari. You've been through so much trauma, thinking I might have added to it makes me sick." "Well don't worry my place is on top next time, besides your chest feels good on me and your stomach as well." They finally went to sleep for a few hours.

In a few hours, Kari had to go to the bathroom. As she was coming out Daniel sat up and said, "Me too." "It is now free," she laughed. When he came out of the bathroom, after washing his hands, he went to the refrigerator and brought them both a bottle of juice. "I don't know how I could be thirsty after that huge dinner, but I am," Kari said. "Is there anything else in there," she asked? "Yes, some fruit and cheese, soft drinks, chocolates, Oh and some pasta salad." "You're kidding," Kari exclaimed. "Nope, see for yourself." Kari ran into the kitchen, with her cute little butt showing and got a small serving of pasta salad. She gave Daniel a bite and herself a bite. Now how did he know I like pasta salad, no need to tell me, you told him. "Yep," Daniel said, smiling at her. She was sitting 'Indian style' and fed him and herself. The small bowl was finished and he took it and put it on his light stand.

"Kari I can't tell you what you mean to me, but you are the dearest person I've ever known." "Well you just might have to be still and I'll show you what you mean to me. No touching, except my touch." She lay up on his chest and started kissing all over his face, except his lips; then she kissed his 'Adams apple' and down his neck and kissed every little spot on his neck and upper arms and then down his chest; he started to grab her and hug her and she said, "Nope, my moves only." Daniel didn't know how he could stand this loving and teasing; she kissed his tummy and belly button and then scooted down to his thighs and knees and started working herself back up the big Daniel. He was trembling and breathing hard; "Kari, I can't stand this", "You can a little bit longer," then she was on top of him and kissed around his mouth and finally his lips. "You may hug me now if you want," "Oh, I want!" He began kissing her and her neck and breasts; Kari put her arms around his neck and kissed him very softly and said, "Ready or not, here I come." He started kissing her and gently lifted her on top of him. She had been right, this felt wonderful with skin to skin, breast to chest, stomach to stomach. She felt his erection and slowly let him enter her. She was very still absorbing every nuance of feeling. She slowly began to move and Daniel hugged her and kissed her until she was now breathless and didn't realize until it happened that she had been moving. She had an orgasm and lay on his chest and stomach for a few moments; "Happened again, didn't it?" "Yes my darling, now kiss me again." She started kissing him and he pressed down on her buttocks and hugged her tightly and kissed so deeply and she felt his release. Daniel rubbed her back and buttocks with one hand and with the other massaged and kissed her breasts. Then she scooted from off top of him and lay snuggled in his arms. She said, "I can't move but I need the cover on my back." He reached down and brought the covers over her. Soon she was asleep and he was getting sleepy. Never had he experienced anything like what just happened.

Oh, how he loved her; for a girl who hadn't had much experience, she was a fast learner. He kept thinking of her sensual movements and thought, I better count sheep or goats or something. My goodness, just thinking about her made him want her again. He positioned himself a bit more on his side and finally dozed off. She awakened the next morning, positioned more on her back, but rested and comfortable. She eased out of bed and went to the bathroom. She found herself a bit sore today. She took a warm bath cloth and washed herself and put some more cream on herself. She then cleaned her face with a new bath cloth and quietly brushed her teeth. My, what a lovely night, she had. She wondered if Daniel felt the same way. Oh how she loved him. She brushed her hair and realized it had curled more and was difficult to brush; Oh well, she combed it the best she could and went back to the bedroom. She thought Daniel was asleep, so she went to make coffee. She looked out the window and a light snow covered everything. She turned up the fireplace and got some coffee and lay down on the couch with a throw wrapped over her. She almost dozed off again and drank her coffee and did drift off to sleep.

Daniel had heard her brushing her teeth and washing her face, but he dozed back off again; until he smelled coffee. He went to the bathroom, cleaned himself and brushed his teeth. He wondered where Kari had gone; he found her asleep on the couch with her empty coffee cup about to hit the floor and noticed the fireplace up and the coverlet over her. He went back into the bedroom and ordered breakfast for two. He put underwear on and a robe and slippers. That way he could answer the door without waking Kari. She looked like the angel she was.

Pretty soon there was a knock on the door and Daniel opened the door and Carlos came in with a cart filled with domes. "If you need anything else, let me know." "Thanks Carlos and I'll put the cart outside the room door. It seems to have snowed last night." "It did and more is predicted for today." Kari had awakened when she heard talking and realized she better be still; she still hadn't dressed. She stayed snuggled down until Carlos had gone. She put her coffee cup on the floor, she had almost dropped it.

Daniel brought the cart over to the small table and started to set out breakfast. "Wake up, sleepy head; breakfast is served, although I see you've had coffee." "Yes, but I'd like some more." She looked at the table and couldn't believe her eyes, French toast, eggs, hash browns, muffins and various kinds of jellies and spreads. "My word, Daniel, they must think we eat like road workers." "Well, we are hungry this morning, aren't we?" "Yes, we are," "Did you know it snowed last night?" Daniel said, "Yes I noticed when I came looking for you; I found you with the fireplace burning more brightly and the throw wrapped around you and your coffee cup almost on the floor." "I guess I was still sleepy. "Did you rest well, Daniel?" "I sure did my darling."

They started eating and Kari looked around at everything in their suite. Things were as beautiful as she thought the night before. Daniel asked; "Are you all right?" "You better believe it," she said; "Okay, a bit sore, but the cream has helped." "I was afraid of that," Daniel said. "Are you daring me to make love to you by force sometime today?" "No, never that," Daniel laughed. "Well fill your mouth with food and let me enjoy mine," she said, smiling at him. "You really are a worry-wart, aren't you?" "Well, sometimes, maybe a little." "Sweetheart, I will tell you if I'm not up to love-making or anything else." "Thank you, darling."

They had a leisurely breakfast and extra coffee and Kari said, "I think I need a shower and some clothing on." "Okay, sweetheart. I'm going to glance at the paper while you shower. There is supposed to be more snow today, so I doubt we can do what I had planned, but there are other days left." After Kari showered, she put on sweat clothes and socks. She came back to find Daniel really studying the paper. He looked up and said, "Honey, the Chief of Police and his deputy have been arrested and jailed for drug distribution in the town you lived in; but another one of the officers there was found shot to death. I'm sorry; I hope that doesn't upset you." "No, Daniel, you see I found out that Frank had lied to me all along. He was up to his eyeballs in drug dealing and smuggling. It's hard for me to believe I was so gullible, but I believed what ever he told me. I'm sorry he was killed that way and I'm sorry this other officer was killed. However, I hope the Chief and his deputy will spend a lot of years in jail, because one or both of them had Frank killed and I would think they still have outside contacts that got rid of the officer who was found dead today." "My sweet Kari, you did have to grow up suddenly and in a terrible way; however you did grow up and became far less gullible. Your being a trusting person, is not a crime, but it can get one in trouble at times. It seems your house was really searched again and there were some missing boxes, but the house has now been sold. You will need to close on it around Thanksgiving, but there is no need to see any judge; only your realtor and I would like Wayne to go with you." "Well you too," she answered. "That money will help with the center and Daniel, I've been thinking about something." "What," he asked? "Well, why could we not have a place within all that building for rehab services for kids who have become addicted?" "I hadn't really thought of that, Kari, but it's a great idea. The only problem I see is that I don't know a therapist." "I don't either, but I know someone at the hospital would know a good therapist who deals with addiction; both in treatment and group sessions."

"Do you want to read the paper," he asked Kari? "Nope, just remind me that we really are married and that you love me." "Oh yes, my darling Kari; we are married forever and I definitely love you forever." They both looked at their rings almost at the same time. Kari said, "You know Daniel, Sadie was with me when I got the ring; oh, I've already told you about that, but I worried that you wouldn't like it. I think it's beautiful, but I didn't know if you would like it or wear it." "Sweetheart;" it has not been off my finger since you put it on, I love it and most of all I love the fact that you picked it out for me." Kari replied, "Well you know how much I love mine, seems like in one sense I've known you all my life and loved you all my life; that does sound strange, I expect, but I feel safe and comfortable with you. Thank you for that, my sweet Daniel."

Daniel said, "We'll have a wonderful life together, serving God and each other, as well as the ones who need our help. Now this stuff is deep, I would like to have some fun, but we can't go as far as I'd planned to ski or sled. I know we must be careful with your leg; but we can stay here and watch TV, eat and love one another in front of the fireplace." "Daniel, I'll gain a hundred pounds with all this food." Daniel said, "No you won't, maybe a pound or two; stop worrying about all this stuff that means very little, except to your health." "Okay," she said.

"Would you like to take a walk in the snow? I certainly packed enough and I hope you did." "Yes, I packed enough and I think a good walk would be wonderful; did you bring a heavy coat?" "No, Daniel, I brought my down coat, not heavy, just super warm." Daniel laughed and said; "I see you have decided to tease me all day." "Yep, just like you do." "Well can I at least have a good morning kiss?" Daniel asked. "I'd like that, but I must not be too eager to kiss you, I get too carried away." Daniel chuckled; "Sometimes I do too, but we should go outside and see some of God's beauty, before it begins to snow again." "Well, it seems one of us isn't ready for the cold, and it's not me," Kari retorted. "Well, seems you are right, as usual." I'll shower and change; and I'll be out in a flash. Kari poured another coffee and sat on the couch with her legs drawn up on the couch. It seemed he meant what he said; it wasn't long before Daniel came out dressed in sweats and boots. "Ready?" he asked. "Just as soon as I get my boots and coat on," she replied. While Kari was getting her boots and coat, Daniel tidied the table and put the cart into the hall. They went down to the lobby and Carlos asked them if their breakfast was to their liking. "It was terrific," Kari said. "Thank you, Carlos." Daniel spoke up and told him, we're going for a walk unless it has already started snowing again. "No it hasn't," he said, "But it is rather chilly and more snow is predicted this afternoon." "Thanks," they both said, and left the lodge.

They walked along some paths and Kari said, "We really are the only guests here; no other footprints are present. Where does Carlos live?" "He and his family live in a large apartment on the lowest level of the lodge. I think he has a couple of girls and his wife. They attend the lodge and own it, but in a busy season, he hires another chef and helpers. I've never been here when it was not perfectly clean and welcoming." "How often do you come out here Daniel?" "Well, honey, I serve as his monitor, mentor and I must check him at least once a month; he was never guilty of any crime, but he was with a group that was into drugs and other things. I went to see him in jail, and told the Chief I would assume responsibility for him for as long as it took for them to believe he was clean. I personally think the other guys lied about him, because they thought a Hispanic man, in this part of the country, was guilty of the same crimes. He wasn't. I read people pretty well and have for a long time; I risked my own reputation for Carlos and he has never let me down. He had worked in saw-milling and was able to put down a small payment to buy this lodge; that was to be torn down. I helped him some and he pays me back every month. I have repeatedly told him that was not necessary, but he and his wife insist. You'll meet Maria, if you ask to meet his wonderful wife." "I sure will," Kari replied. "The lodge is very clean and polished and I wondered who helped him keep it so neat."

"Daniel did you bring Kelly here on your honeymoon?" "Absolutely not! That was not her style, she wanted to go to a big city and I didn't care where we went, as long as I could be back in a week. And before you ask; no, she was not a virgin; she had a number of previous lovers; which I found out later. Now Kari; I'm going to scold you---please do not ever think of Kelly again; I never loved her, I came to hate her, and I've asked God to take away the hatred, because it is wrong and I wanted nothing to interfere with our marriage. Now, do you understand why I love you so much; I don't seem to do anything that you hate. I truly hope I never do." "Now you listen, Daniel; I do believe you and I should have known better, simply because when I saw her, she was only interested in me taking the baby until his daddy came home."

"I don't think she is prettier than me or better than me or any of those things that some women think about. You see; I want to be the only one you love, I mean woman; and I don't want to do or say anything that would hurt you. I know the difference between true love and sympathy or lust. Please forgive me and realize sometimes I do wonder or think that I must do whatever to please you Daniel. I had a hard time pleasing other people in my life."

"Did you notice my aunt and uncle did not come to the wedding?" "Yes, honey, I did. Now, quiet, There is nothing to forgive and I want to kiss you and I can't kiss and listen at the same time." Kari said, "You could've fooled me. You do very well at kissing, hugging and listening. I love you, Daniel. Am I forgiven for stupidity?" "You are not stupid, Kari! Now I'm going to kiss you until you know the real Daniel and kiss you again until you can barely breathe and kiss you again, until I can hardly breathe." Bu---she never finished her 'but'; because Daniel began to kiss her and hug and fondle her until she drew her head back and took a deep breath. She smiled at him and he chuckled and began kissing her again. He had to get a big breath this time; they both started laughing and began their walk a little farther.

It was really beautiful with the fresh fallen snow. They came upon a lake that looked large; it was very pretty with what seemed like fog hovering over it. "I was planning to take us boating, but with the promise of more snow, I think we'd better not try that." "I think you're right, darling." They walked a little farther and found another little path. "I wonder what's down there," Kari asked. "I don't know; do you want to go see?" "Yes, I'd like to," she said. They walked on a short way and the wind started blowing a bit harder and the clouds looked like it really might start snowing. Daniel said, "I think we'd better head back to the lodge." Kari shivered and said, "Me too!" They turned and headed back to the lodge, passed the lake and snow was gently falling, so they did not linger at the lake. They made it to the lodge just as it really started to snow.

Carlos met them at the door and said, "Look, your hot chocolate is ready at the table near the fireplace." He smiled broadly and said; "I knew it was going to snow, but I didn't know the two of you would get caught out in it". "That's okay, Carlos, we had a wonderful walk down past the lake. It is really pretty," Kari said. "We'll go have some hot chocolate in front of the fireplace." They got to the fireplace and a lady had brought out a rolling table with hot chocolate and twice-baked cookies, some cheese and crackers and grapes. She smiled shyly, and Carlos said to Kari; "I'd like you to meet my wonderful wife, Maria." "It's so nice to meet you," Kari said and smiled warmly at Maria. "Thank you so much," Maria replied and went back to the kitchen. "Now the two of you enjoy your chocolate," Carlos said, and he too went back to the kitchen.

They took their coats off and sat down in front of the fireplace and sipped the hot chocolate. It was really good with some spice to it. "This is great," Kari said. "You might remember I like spicy food." "Yes, I seem to remember," Daniel laughed. "I like spicy food, as well as my spicy red-head. Did you get too cold, Kari?" "No," she said, "But I was glad to be back in front of a fireplace. This cookie is spicy too, Daniel, taste it." "Yes it is good." They drank their chocolate and had another cookie and some grapes and cheese and decided that was enough food for a while. Daniel called out to Carlos, "Thank you for the food; we'll probably call for a late lunch or early dinner. No need to make lunch, the snack filled us." They went back to their suite and snuggled on the couch. Daniel noticed that Kari was rubbing her leg a bit. Daniel said, "Kari, why didn't you tell me your leg was hurting?" "Well it isn't much, but I probably need to stretch out for a while; but not without you." "Very well, if I must," Daniel said smiling. Kari took her bra off and left her sweats on and climbed into bed. It had been freshly made and turned down; again with a fresh rose bud on her side of the bed and some chocolates. She lay down on her right side and Daniel massaged her hip and upper thigh. "Your hands are warm and that feels good," she said. Daniel could tell she was sleepy and so he said, "Yes it does and I love you sweetheart." Kari drifted off to sleep and Daniel, not being used to napping during the day, spent some time in silent prayer and holding Kari. He soon became drowsy and must have dozed, because the next thing he remembered was Kari turning over and wrapping her arms around his neck and kissing him on his cheek. She was not fully awake, but Daniel was. He lay looking at his bride and realized she was still rather fragile emotionally and physically. He would let her sleep her nap out and then find out if she was hungry. He would then call Carlos and order an early dinner. Kari seemed so relaxed and when he put his other arm around her, he found she had removed that terrible bra. That's why she was so much more relaxed, at least he thought so.

In about an hour, Kari awoke and seemed so refreshed. She said; "Did you rest too, Daniel?" "Yes, honey I did." "Good, I wouldn't have liked to leave you all alone while I slept." He swept her up in his arms and she was almost on top of him. He smiled and said, "Have you always had to have a bra like that to hold your breasts up?" "Well about as long as I developed breasts; about thirteen or fourteen, I outgrew my friends and some of them were not very nice." Daniel said, "Honey, they were just jealous. I bet the boys noticed." "Yes, they seemed to, but I was busy with my studies and paid them little attention. I certainly found out my friends were not friends at all and I definitely wasn't interested in boys, but as an odd specimen." Daniel laughed out loud, "A specimen, you consider me a specimen?" "Oh no! That's not what I meant. You see boys never looked in my eyes, they always gazed at my breasts; I figured I looked like a freak and they were no better.

Besides science was my real love as well as anatomy. I'd stay in the lab for hours and I guess that's why I did well in nursing school. I began to study diseases before I ever went to nursing school." "You mean you didn't go to a prom or any outside school functions?" "I went with a boy on the football team to the prom, but found out he liked to dance because he could hold me closer than I wanted to be held. So I decided you cannot be close friends with anyone. I know that sounds mean; but I found out that is pretty well true."

"Then I met this big man, banging on my door, who awakened me. I grabbed my crutch and went to the door. I really wasn't able to stay by myself; let alone a poor little baby, that was dirty and smelly and fretful. That big man knocking on my door was impatient and I decided he would have to knock me down before he got that baby. I really didn't know if you were trustworthy or not until you showed me your identification with a picture. I didn't realize you were a chaplain. By the time I had stood in the cold doorway, I was about to fall and figured if you were going to hurt me you would have done so. So I think I motioned you in; my you were big and I thought; well he could squash me like a bug and never even break a sweat. But when you sat down where I told you too, and let me hold the baby, I began to realize you were not going to beat me up or anything else. I just watched you, not trusting, but certainly not fearful as I probably should have been. I'd been through so much, I figured, what's one more beating?"

"You picked Danny up so gently with your big hands, I thought, well he might be your baby; I have to admit, I was sorry and thought I might never get to see him again. I think I fell in love with that baby, the moment I saw him in that pitiful state, but I definitely did not like his mother one bit. She put the boxes of his clothes on the porch and when she left, I had to drag them into the house. They were all dirty and smelly and I knew I would not put anything like that on this precious little one. Anyway, that day I had found out I was pregnant and had stopped after seeing Dr. Little and bought several things my baby would need. I put the new things in the dryer with a sheet to make them soft, then, I went into my room where I had placed the little one. I gave him a warm bath and realized he would cry a little bit and hush. His little neck was smelly and his bottom was really reddened. I got some petroleum jelly and coated his little bottom and wrapped him a warm towel and went to the dryer, carrying him. I got out some clothes and a diaper out of the closets that I had put my baby's clothes into. I dressed the little darling and kept him warm in one of the blankets and fed him distilled water with a little 'gator-aid" and rocked him. I was so tired, I put the now sleeping baby beside me on the bed and we both slept. I really don't know how long, but I was still tired and weak, when this big man showed up. Daniel, I'm sorry; I just realized I've told you this before. I was as angry as I was scared, but no one would have that little baby until I knew who he belonged to." Daniel spoke up when he realized Kari was experiencing the same feelings she had that day; "Dearest Kari, you did tell me, but it only makes me love you more. I realized when I saw you, with fire in your eyes and propped on a crutch; that you acted like a mother hen. I did not mean to frighten you; but knowing Kelly, she had left a note that the baby was mine and she would leave him with the lady up the hill. I didn't really know who was up there, but I knew Kelly would leave the baby on the porch if I didn't get there quick. Thank God, you had a heart for a dear little one you had never seen and one whose parent seemed uninterested; and you took him, cleaned him and put what you planned for your own baby's clothes on him. I did not smell anything when I got in to your room, except some slight smell of soap and your sweet smell. You had a mark on your cheek, so I knew you had been asleep, but I had no idea of what you had been through. I will be eternally grateful for you and what you did for our baby."

Kari said, "I know we were not going to talk about Danny, but while I was asleep, I dreamed I was back on that porch. I awoke and found my husband who was smiling at me. I love you Daniel for staying with me, because I still have bad flashbacks of things that have happened and I become confused for a time; between now and then." "You are most welcome! Now, can I have a kiss?" "Yep, coming right up," and she kissed him until he was almost out of breath.

He hugged her and kissed her back. They were soon deeply involved with each other. Daniel said, "Are you too sore to make love?" "Of course not and if you don't, I will attack you." He laughed out loud, "Well, I like that too." Anyway, she removed his sweats and he removed her top and stopped to kiss each breast, over and over again. She reached down and

removed his bottom clothing and said, "Your turn to help get mine off."
"Gladly," Daniel said. He removed her bottoms and continued to kiss
nearly every part of her. "Daniel you better find your place, I want you
now, and you know I don't like to wait." "Yes, my dear." He held most of
his weight off Kari, and entered her very slowly. They kissed and hugged
one another until Daniel lifted Kari's bottom upward and moved and
they both had orgasms nearly together. Daniel was perspiring and Kari
was plenty warm. He pulled the sheet over them and they lay quietly in
each other's arms.

Daniel said, "I love you, my wife; let me know when you get hungry." Kari
said, "Okay," and yawned. They both dozed a while and Daniel awoke and
looked at his watch. Kari woke up too and asked, what was the matter?
Daniel said, "I didn't know it was this late and the snow is falling pretty
heavily." "What time is it Daniel?" "About five-thirty," Daniel replied.
"You mean I've slept all day?" "Well not quite, my dearest. You put my
lights out for a good while too." They both put their sweats back on and
went into the living room in front of that fireplace. Daniel said, "I'm going
to call Carlos and have dinner brought up about seven o'clock if that's
okay with you." "That's perfect," Kari responded. Daniel made the call
and they sat down to watch some news and it seemed the entire week was
going to have snow about every day.

Kari said, "Well, that's fine. We have things to read, TV and another habit
I've acclimated to rather easily." Daniel said, "I do declare, I think you
are right." They watched the TV news and another show or two and soon
there was a knock on the door. Daniel got up and opened the door and
Carlos brought in dinner and set it up on the table for them. Daniel said
"Thank you, Carlos and I'll put the cart out after we eat. Good night."

They looked at their dinner and it looked great. Carlos had brought them
some chips and salsa, burritos, and a small steak, with a very different kind
of sauce; one that Kari had never tasted. There was Mexican dish that
Kari was unfamiliar with, as well, but it tasted great. They ate and Kari
tried one of the almond paste cookies. "That is very good. I wonder if I
could get the recipe from Maria." They also enjoyed the green salad with
peppers, corn and tomatoes. The coffee had some kind of spice and that
too was good. "Have you had enough to eat?" Daniel asked. "Yes and it
was delicious." Daniel got up and put the things back on the cart and put
it outside the door.

They looked at news after dinner. The weather report said that snow was expected all week. Kari said, "Daniel, does that means we can't go for walks or drive anywhere?" "Well I think that's pretty much it," he answered. Daniel asked "Are you already bored with me?" "Of course not, you darling man, I sometimes get afraid, if I think I cannot get away. I'm sorry for complaining. That really does not mean that I'm tired of you. The fact is, I like having you close by, you are my snuggle bunny, as well as I like eating with you and kissing, among other things." "Me too," he said.

"Listen Kari, I didn't order the snow, but in one way it is very good. I'd like to show you around the lodge and let you get to know Maria and Carlos and their girls. There is also a library here that you won't believe. So we are not choked up in this room. Also, we can take brief walks as long as we're careful." Kari said, "A library, where is it and is it in Spanish or English?" "You see one of the girls is in college in town where we live and she might be interested in making some extra money, working at the youth center. I think she is planning to be a counselor when she graduates and she plans to go on to get her masters and doctorate. I imagine she will; she is just like Carlos. The younger girl is very interested in nursing. We'll talk to Carlos tomorrow and ask if we could have a conversation with all of them." "That would be wonderful." "Besides, I have a four wheel drive and we could get out, but Chief would have my skin, if I came back too early. He reminded me that I haven't taken a vacation in some three years. He also said; you've been on a sharp razor's edge for quite a while. You and Kari have both been through a lot and you need some inner quietness, especially Kari."

Kari said, "Oh, Daniel you are so wonderful and you have a great boss and I have the best husband. Now I won't fret about the snow and we can go walking in the morning if it isn't too deep. I'm especially interested in seeing the lodge. Do you think Carlos would mind if we looked around some." "I don't think so, but I'll call him and see if we can, at least, see the library." "Daniel that would be great, I'd really love to see it. I had a library put in the house at home, with a bathroom and outside steps; but I haven't been able to go up the balcony without fear of falling." Daniel called Carlos and asked him if they could look at the library and he said, "Of course, of course."

They put on jeans and sweaters and went downstairs. Carlos was waiting for them and all of his family was there. They said, "We'll be glad to show you around any where you would like to see." "That would be great, but I wonder if I might talk to all of you later; nothing serious, but I'd really like to hear about your school plans; (and Maria, if you give out recipes, I'd really like that mixture you made with the almond paste)." Maria smiled broadly and said she would be happy to share. "Most young women don't seem interesting in cooking, but I see you are." "Oh yes, I love to cook, but can't always remember when I make one and sometimes double it the next night." "Oh, I see," Maria said. "Well you all may go to the library or anywhere you want and the girls and I will have some refreshments ready when you finish looking." "Thank you, Maria."

They went with Carlos up a flight of stairs on the other side of the entrance. He opened a huge, heavy door and Kari saw the most beautiful library she had seen in many a day. She really loved any library, especially ones with ladders and wall to wall books. "Daniel, even if snowed in, we can come here each day, if that is all right with Carlos." "Most certainly, it is all right with me. I'll lock it after you leave, but stay as long as you wish. You see, I love a library as well." "Thank you again Carlos," and she gave him a hug. He blushed and looked at Daniel, who said, "You must get used to this precious woman, she hugs everyone she sees, but I'm always there." Carlos laughed and left them to the library.

Kari started looking at the books and some were classics, some were historical and some were novels. There was also a set of topical sheets. "This is wonderful." She went on around and found some science and math books that looked fairly new. She saw music books with history of major composers. "This is ideal, Daniel, don't you think so?" "Honey, I sure do. It is rather late and we did make an appointment with Carlos and Maria and the girls for a chat." "Yes we did. Daniel, I wasn't pushing myself into their private lives was I?" "Not at all, Carlos knows as much about me as you do and he's had a lot of hard knocks; but he is a perfect gentleman." They went downstairs to the table beside the fireplace and there Carlos and Maria sat. "The girls have to study. One is training to be a therapist and one is training to be a nurse." "That's wonderful," Kari said.

"Now, what can Maria and I do for you?" "Carlos, as you know, I've wanted to find a center for the youth and young adults in our county. There has been a drive-by shooting and two alcohol poisonings in the last six months. That is not acceptable to me. The Chief is helping, as are the Commissioners, the local school, officers on patrol and the high school.

We found an old school house that is in good shape with heart pine and oak floors and banisters. It sits on quite a bit of land and Joe and Camille (Kari's former pastors) are willing to help and several others. Kari told me last night that she was interested in opening a rehab center on the property for drying-out those addicted and for groups to meet to aid each other; however, we don't yet know a good counselor."

"We also need someone who could stay at night so that if a kid comes in, he will have a place to lie down; no judgmental attitudes or abuse from any worker. The officers are eager to help and the Board of Commissioners, the hospital and the Community College has already agreed. We also wanted to teach skills, such as gardening, cooking, automotive work, and things the guys are interested in. Camille is/was a school teacher and many other things that I've forgotten to mention. Our question is do you know a couple who could stay at night and assist if someone gets out of hand?"

"The county near us just had the police chief and his deputy arrested and jailed, but another officer was found dead yesterday morning. Does the name Frank mean anything to you Carlos?" "It certainly does, he hasn't come around in a while, but he tried to get my girls into that stuff. He also wanted me to carry it from the border over here, because I'm Hispanic. Daniel, you must not mess with this man, he is very involved with getting kids hooked and then he owns them; anything from selling drugs on the school campus or the high school. Daniel, don't bother this man, he is a bad man." Daniel told him the police chief and deputy are in jail and again Carlos said, "Don't believe them Daniel, they have contacts everywhere." Maria spoke up and said, "I spent much time in prayer for my girls and asked the Father to pray as well. If one is Hispanic or Italian, that person is targeted to be pushers." Kari spoke up and said, "Maria and Carlos, Frank is dead and another officer was killed yesterday. I was married to Frank and had absolutely no idea of such a thing going on. Our little town was fairly safe, I thought. I worked in the emergency room and saw the results of drugs, but had no inkling it was so bad. The first time I saw Daniel at my door, I thought he had come to kill me, because one man said, you are next. I moved here and tried to keep quiet about my past, but I had to have a lawyer I could trust, so I got on line and Wayne's group was large and clean and no scent of anything wrong they might have done. I called him and made an appointment with him for some advice. He has been one of the dearest men I know."

Carlos said, "I'm sorry for your loss, but you are so beautiful, he would have you involved before long. The fact that you worked in the ER only made him more believable. "Carlos, I thought I loved him and had been alone so much, I figured I might as well, but I soon realized I had made a big mistake. I'm sorry he died as he did, but I'm mostly sorry for what he did to others."

Daniel stood up from the table and told Maria how good the snack was. "We didn't realize how late it is; if we get hungry I will ring you by nine o'clock." "That's fine; we don't go to bed until eleven o'clock, and even if it's later, we make something for you. You might check your refrigerator; there is fruit, cheese, all kinds of goodies to eat." "Thank You Carlos, now you two try to think of someone who might wish to come here and live at the center.

Goodnight and thanks for the snacks; everything is good." Kari said, "I might want to watch you cook some tomorrow, if you don't mind." "That would be nice, Kari."

They went to their room and undressed and turned the fireplace up in the living room and checked that it was warm enough for Kari in the bedroom. In a few minutes, Kari went to the refrigerator to get something to drink and saw every kind of fruit, cheese and cookies and biscuits. "Daniel, do you want a bottle of water?" "No sweetheart, I might get some later." Kari sat down beside him and asked "What is the matter Daniel?" Daniel said, "You know Kari, they might have relatives who could come up and help, with the center. If there are any, you can bet Carlos will find them." He took a sip of her water and smiled at her, "You know, darling, you didn't have to tell Carlos or Maria about Frank, but I admire the fact that you did. You know he would not stop, so God let his buddies stop him. I know it was a shock to you to look up and see your husband on that stretcher, but you came through that okay." "Yes and I learned that I had no idea of what or who he was. The Priest did a beautiful service, but I honestly don't remember much about it. At that time the only person I trusted was Joey. I know he thinks of me as a bossy sister, but he loves me too."

"I didn't mean for us to get so deep tonight. We are still on our honeymoon and it is getting late. So share your water with me and let's go to bed. We might get a good start at staying in the library and you did ask Maria to let you see her cook." "I will enjoy that. I love to cook and I like learning new ways to cook."

He took her hand and they went to bed, but they hadn't forgotten to remove clothing, just in case. "Daniel, you really are a scamp and I adore you." Kari lifted her breast up onto Daniel's chest. She began to kiss him slowly and about everywhere she could reach. "Must I still keep my hands where they are?" "Yes, for a while; let's hope it's not too long." "You know Kari you turn me on, sometimes, with your smile." "Good now stay still; I haven't finished what I started." She kissed his tummy, chest and erection and that's where Daniel drew the line; "No, I can't stand that my sweet." He lifted her to his tummy and chest and started kissing her. She kissed him back and he said, "No, not now." "But Daniel I don't like being patient, now let me at least kiss you, okay?" "If you must." He did not expect the kiss he got; her lips were so soft on his face and his neck and back to his lips, like butterfly wing kisses. He picked her up and set her on his erection, She just lay there and gave him angel kisses and then she moved, a bit differently than before and he knew he was losing control; at the last second she moved gently and kissed him hard and moved hard. He tried to hold on and did until he felt her nipple pinch up and her slight tremble and then he lifted her and moved in her and she felt his release. She slid to his side, but he still held her and kissed her with butterfly kisses. "Do you know how sensual that is?" "No, but I'm finding out." They petted and kissed and soon Kari felt Daniel's erection again. "Did I do that too?" Kari asked. "Yes as matter of fact, I want you again, if you are up to it." "Watch this cowboy," she pushed down on him and slowly back up all the while with butterfly kisses all over him. He held her buttock and helped her move in just the right way. She shivered and began to perspire and then she did go to work on Daniel and felt his release in just a moment. He hugged her and kissed her and told her how much he loved her. "Indeed, loving you is my pleasure." They both chuckled and then headed for the bathroom. Again, Daniel had blood on himself, he looked at Kari and she said, "Yep, that's what it is all right." She smiled up at him and he knew he had totally lost his heart to his little red-haired wife. She was absolutely stunning. He got a clean warm bath cloth and handed it to her. She tidied herself and got up. She got up and tried to brush her hair; "Oh phooey, hand me that comb Daniel." "Please," he said. "Please," she parroted back. Daniel took her comb and started at the ends of her hair and soon all the tangles were out. He put the comb down and they went into the kitchen. Kari got some cheese and crackers, some cookies and a soft drink. "Honey, it's only eighty thirty, I can call Carlos and get a warm dinner." "Nope, I'm perfectly okay. You can have some, but I'm not going to peel your grapes." He started laughing and said, "That won't be necessary." He got some fruit and cheese and cheese straws and a soft drink. "This is good. Does making love spend many calories?" Daniel laughed and said, "I have no idea."

They sat and watched TV and caught the news and weather. The snow would lighten up tomorrow. "That's okay," Kari said, "Maria said I could watch her cook and I am really excited about exploring the library." "Well, we can sleep late you know." "I know," she said, "Danny's daddy doesn't start gurgling or jabbering early." Thus became their routine, they would make love when they wanted to and eat and explore the library.

Maria did indeed let Kari watch her make tortillas and burritos, and a spicy dish; that Kari could not pronounce. "It's like your gumbo, except without crayfish." "This is better, Maria." "Thanks," Maria answered. They sat down for a cup of coffee and Maria said, "You know Kari, I think of what you and Daniel were speaking about. I have a sister who has just lost her husband and our brother has lost his wife. Neither of them have children, but they both cook and speak English. I'll have to speak to Carlos about them and he can let Daniel know that they are trustworthy and good people. We do love Daniel; he was the only person who believed Carlos and he put his own career on the line for Carlos and us. We will never forget that kindness." "Thank you, Maria, now may I go to the library a while." "Of course, I have a key in my pocket and I'll take you up there." "I really love books," Kari told her.

Kari spent about two hours in the library. It was indeed a library with many types of books and graphics. Some were historical and others were religious. She read and read; then she thought about Daniel; where was he? She went to the door of the library and saw Carlos and Daniel talking in front of the fireplace. Kari went back to the library for a while. Soon Daniel came looking for her. "Here you are you little scamp. I was wondering if you would ever come out of here." "Hi Sweetie; Daniel you won't believe this wonderful library. I've so enjoyed it and the big chairs are so inviting." "Well, honey, that's great, but Carlos has lunch prepared and waiting on us in front of the fireplace down the steps." Kari said, "Is it that late"? "Yes," Daniel said "It's about one o'clock. "My goodness, I got carried away in the library." "I know," Daniel replied. "I've never met anyone so interested in libraries or books of all kinds." "Well, books were my friends for a long time."

They got up and went downstairs to the fireplace and Daniel served their lunch. Part of it was what Maria had shown Kari this morning. "She is such a nice lady, Daniel. I enjoyed visiting with her and watching her cook." "They are good people, Daniel replied. Now, let me have your plate, I'll put a bit of everything on it and then on mine." They said their blessing and began to eat. Everything was delicious. They had hot coffee with some small fried, bread that was sugar and cinnamon flavored. "Oh my; Daniel, I will weigh a ton if I don't watch my intake." Daniel laughed and said, "Well let's go put our warm clothes on and take a walk for a bit. "That would be great!" They headed up to their room and Daniel called out and told Maria and Carlos, that Kari loved lunch; and so did I. Carlos came out smiling and they told him they were going to walk. "Good, the snow has stopped."

KARI GETS HURT AND TO HOSPITAL

Kari and Daniel got to their room and started to change clothes; got a bit carried away; and Daniel said, "We better take our walk, before I ravage you." "Okay," Kari laughed. They put their heavy clothing on and went outside. Sure enough the snow had stopped and the sun was beginning to shine. They walked the path they had been on and then took another path in a different direction, upward. They walked and talked and laughed and enjoyed so much being together and looking at the beauty around them. Kari stopped a few minutes and looked at Daniel; "Do you realize our first week is nearly over?" "Yes, darling, I do." "Well, it seems to me it has flown by; but I have enjoyed it so much." "I have too, Kari." They walked on a bit and Kari began to walk slower. Daniel realized she was getting tired, and about that time she stumbled and almost fell. Daniel could have kicked himself; they had walked almost two hours and he didn't realize how tired she must be. He quickly picked her up and started to carry her all the way back to the lodge. Kari would not have it; "Daniel, I can walk, just a bit slower than before; now put me down!"

"Are you sure walking some more to the lodge will not harm your leg?" "I'm sure," she replied. They walked slowly back to the lodge and when they were in sight of the lodge, Kari stumbled again and Daniel left her no choice. He picked her up and kicked on the door of the lodge. Carlos came immediately. "What is wrong; Daniel?" He looked at Kari and saw how pale she was and called Maria out and they went to the room with them. Maria said, "I noticed you favored your left leg this morning, but I didn't know why." The bed had already been made fresh and Daniel laid Kari down on the bed. He turned the fireplace up and asked Maria if she had some aspirin. "Yes, yes I do, and I have some pain medicine the doctor gave me last week when I pulled my back. I'll bring what you need Kari." "Daniel, please don't make such a fuss." Carlos said, "Kari I'm terribly sorry you fell, that path is a bit tricky even without the snow covering it. I'll go, but Maria will help you and don't worry, the medicine is what the doctor ordered for her, but she didn't need much of it." About that time, Maria came back with fresh juice and the pills and gave them to Kari. Maria said, "Please rest now Kari; we will have dinner up when Daniel calls us." "Thanks Maria, but I think I'll be fine; this is the leg that was injured not too long ago and it takes very little to lose control of my balance. Now I'll be fine."

Daniel undressed her and put a warm nightgown on her and lay beside her and rubbed her hip and leg. There didn't seem to be any swelling or ankle swelling, but he continued to hold her and rub her hip and leg. Kari said; "Honey, I'm sorry I ruined our walk; I guess I'll have to pay more attention to this leg; you see; I'd just as soon forget it." Daniel said, "I know honey, but I should have been more observant. Now please be quiet and let the medicine work. I personally checked the bottle and the doctor and pharmacy and it is real." "Daniel, I never doubted that." "Okay, now I'm going to kiss you goodnight and I expect you to sleep. I'll be right here, until you are asleep and then I'll still be here in the room." "Well, I'm feeling better," she said. Daniel knew she was about asleep. He continued to rub her leg and hip, until he knew she was completely relaxed and asleep.

He gently got up and went into the living room and called Carlos to let him know how much he appreciated their help and Kari is asleep. "Thank Maria for her wonderful help and patience to let Kari observe her cooking. Kari said she enjoyed that so much." Carlos said, "I will; now call when you are ready for dinner. The pain pill is supposed to last four to six hours. She should sleep a good while." Daniel said, "Thanks again, Carlos."

Daniel kept a check on Kari, who had not moved. She was sleeping peacefully. He turned the TV on low and watched the news and weather report for the weekend and next week. They usually predicted the weather accurately and it seemed like there would be a heavy snow starting on Sunday night. He planned to get them home before the heavy snow fell. He continued to keep the news on low and dozed on the couch. In a few minutes (it seemed to him) he heard Kari cry out. He ran into the bedroom and she was looking afraid, then he realized he had inadvertently turned the bathroom light out and when she woke up, she was afraid. He ran to put her in his arms and said, "I'm right here, baby, I'm right here." "It seems I turned the light off in the bathroom and it is dark now." Kari awoke completely as he reached over and turned the lamp on beside their bed. Kari grabbed him and held him so tightly. She said, "Did I yell at you?" "No, I heard you cry out and I came in quickly and realized what had happened. You are fine, honey." "No, I'm not; sometimes I think I'll never be all right again. What time is it?" Daniel said, "About eight o'clock; sorry but I dozed off too." She started to kiss him and reached for him and her stomach let out a loud rumble. "My word, it seems I can never get enough food." Daniel laughed and said, "Carlos told me you would sleep awhile, like his Maria, and he would have dinner prepared as soon as I let him know when you were awake and ready to eat." "Well, I guess I'm ready."

"I need to go to the bathroom and splash some water on my face." Daniel watched her walk to the bathroom and followed her inside. "You don't seem to favor your leg as much." "I'm not," Kari said; "Once I'm off of it a few hours, I'm as good as new." "Good, now I'll call Carlos for our dinner." "Daniel, do I need to dress?" "Nope, just a robe, please, so I can enjoy my dinner too."

In a few minutes there was a knock on the door and Carlos brought in a table with domes stacked. There was fresh coffee like Kari liked (she could smell the spice) and Carlos began to get the table spread. Daniel said, "Thank you Carlos, I'll put the cart outside after we're finished." "How is your mistress, Daniel?" "Oh she slept most of the afternoon after Maria's med got to working. She says she is fine, except her stomach is grumbling." They both laughed and Carlos told him to enjoy dinner and let us know if you need anything. "I will," Daniel replied.

They began to eat all kinds of wonderful things; some that Maria had shown her how to make; and some more lobster with spicy cream sauce. Kari had mentioned how much she liked that lobster the other day, when cooking with Maria. Kari really ate well and asked Daniel if Carlos had spoken to him about Maria's brother and sister. Daniel said, "Yes, and I plan to tell the Chief and Commissioners, as well as the School and College. I'd bet my career on those two and any recommendation they give me." They finished eating and Daniel served dessert; it looked like a gooey butter cake with something underneath that had spices in it. Kari tasted it and said it was delicious. "You know Daniel I recognize the spices and I can probably make this." "Of course you can he replied." When they both finished, Daniel put everything on the cart and put it outside their door.

Daniel said; "Kari, I hate to tell you this, but I watched the news and long-term weather report, and the weather will be heavy snow, beginning Sunday night. I know we've only had a week of honeymoon, but I really think we need to go home Sunday morning." "Of course we can, Daniel. We can still have a honeymoon at home and you don't have to tell the Chief that you were not out of town. That way, we can get all your clothing and things you like out of your house and prepare it for selling." "You are so wise and wonderful," Daniel replied; "I thought you might be upset, because we can't safely stay another two weeks." "Well," Kari answered, "I'm not in the least upset, to tell you the truth, as much as I've grown to love Maria and Carlos; I'm ready to go home." "I can barely wait to see Danny." "I'm glad too; because as you said, we can get my clothes from the old house and move into yours and prep it for sale."

"The house is ours, Daniel, as well as Danny's." "Thank you honey, now would you like to watch TV a little while and let me check for sure about the weather?" "That will be fine, but your place is beside me on the couch." Daniel laughed; "Now where else would I be?" They caught up on the news and the weather forecast had not changed, except there might be eight to ten inches of accumulated snow. "Yep, we better go home," Kari said. "Well, not tonight," Daniel replied. "How does your leg feel?" "Much, much better," Kari answered. Daniel looked at his watch and it was pretty late. "Honey, we had better go to bed, don't you think?" "Yes I do!" Daniel said, "No lovemaking tonight, I might hurt your hip." "OH yeah", Kari said, "We'll see about that, but you will have to help me, while I attack you." Daniel started laughing; "You really are a scrapper, aren't you?" "Yes I am, when I see something I want and I certainly want you." "Okay, young woman, you better tell me if you feel pain." "I will," Kari said. They got up and Daniel turned the living room fireplace low and left a small light on, in case Kari awoke and he had forgotten the bathroom light again. He so hated he forgot that. He didn't understand why Kari was afraid of the dark, and it really didn't matter, except he had to be sure a light was left on somewhere in the house. They did make love and both of them slept soundly.

The next morning was Saturday and Daniel called Carlos and ordered breakfast. He also told Carlos that the two of them would be going home in the morning, because of the predicted snow storm. Carlos said, "I wish you could stay longer, but you are right, it looks like this one might be rough." In a few minutes, there was a knock on the door. Carlos came in with a beautiful breakfast that he lay out on the table. They ate well and it was really good. As usual, Maria was a wonderful cook and everything was great. Daniel tidied the table and put the cart outside the door. They chatted over another cup of coffee and Daniel said, "Why don't you put on some sweats and enjoy the library a while before we have to pack." "I think I will, but will you settle up with Carlos and join me in the library?" "Certainly, but it's already been settled; I will have to ask him if he will unlock the library for us." "Okay," Kari answered and went to get dressed. This time dressing took a while longer; her leg seemed rather stiff today. She dressed and Daniel had already dressed and they went down to find the library open. They both enjoyed reading a while and exploring different titles and authors that Kari especially liked. He noticed, but said nothing; however, he kept a note in his head about a wedding present that he would have delivered to Kari at the house, today.

He went down to ask Carlos where the nearest book store was and Carlos told him. "May I ask why you need a book store?" Daniel said, he wanted to surprise Kari with some of her favorite authors and books that could be delivered to day; she would be very surprised tomorrow to see the package. "Oh, I see; was there anything specific that you noticed she stayed near?" "Well yes, it is a graphic of the Holy Land, but I will order it." "No need," Carlos smiled; "I would like to present it to your beautiful bride." "Carlos, I'm surprised; that was not why I asked you about a bookstore." "Oh, Daniel, I know that, but Maria and I were talking last night about something special we could do for her. Maria has a cookbook already prepared and I would be so pleased if you would let us present her with the graphics and the cookbook. She seems like a wonderful wife for you, Daniel." "Carlos, I've never been happier in my life; she adopted Danny before we were married and has loved him as her own. I know God has blessed this union and I would be honored to accept your gift. Thank you from the bottom of my heart." Carlos gave him a big grin and said; "No problem."

Daniel and Kari read and enjoyed the library for quite some time and then Daniel said; "Honey, we'd better go pack so we'll be ready to leave in the morning, before the heavy snow sets in." "Okay," she replied. Daniel noticed she still favored her left leg some, but when he asked her how she was feeling, she said, fine. They went back to the room to start packing and the phone rang. Daniel picked it up and said, "Yes, Carlos, we've finished in the library and we are packing, because we need to leave in the morning." "Well, Maria and I would like to come say goodbye." "Okay," Daniel replied. He told Kari that Carlos and Maria wanted to come tell them goodbye. "That's great," Kari replied. "Now could you please reach my suitcase and put it on the bed?" "Surely," he said. They both began to pack and there was a knock at the door.

Daniel went to answer and Kari came out with him. There stool Carlos and Maria with wrapped packages in their arms. "Come in," Daniel said. Carlos said, "Please allow us the honor of giving you this small gift as a token of our esteem for both of you." Maria handed Kari her gift and Kari asked; "May I open it?" "Certainly," Maria said. Kari opened the package and there was one of Maria's personal cookbooks. Kari gave Maria a big hug and said "Thank you so much. I love cookbooks and this is so special. Thank you, Maria." Then Carlos handed Daniel a package and smiled and Daniel presented it to Kari. "Honey, that's your package." Maria just smiled the beautiful smile she had. Kari opened the package and her mouth fell open, she was speechless. Daniel said, "Well, what do you say when someone presents you with a gift?" Kari began to cry and tell Carlos how much she loved it. "I would never have asked this from you; however, it is so beautiful, I've almost memorized it since I've been here." She gave Carlos and Maria a double hug. Carlos blushed a bit and Maria started laughing; "You see Carlos is macho, as we say in Spanish, and has never received a hug from someone so beautiful." Kari said, "I absolutely love the gifts and I'll treasure the two of you in my heart, as well as the gifts." Daniel shook Carlos' hand warmly and gave Maria a hug and kiss on the cheek. "Thank you both so much," he said. "If it isn't too late could we have dinner about nine o'clock tonight?" "Absolutely yes," they said. Maria said; "I fix you a special".

Daniel and Kari went up to their room and finished packing, except some toiletries. Kari sat down on the bed and stretched her leg. "You know, Daniel, those two people are so special, wonder how we can help them." "Kari, they don't expect anything except what you did. You paid them a great honor by accepting so graciously their gift to you."

"Daniel, you are so wonderful and I love you with all my heart. I'm glad we're going home tomorrow; I love this place and the people, but I miss our home and Danny and all the others." "I do too," Daniel replied; "But we will keep Sadie during the day to look after Danny. I can handle him at night, but until we have a doctor check your leg, I won't be at ease." "Daniel, I don't need a doctor." "Humor me he said. You know I worry until I know you are all right." "Well, okay then, my sweet worry-wart." At a little past nine there was a knock on the door. Daniel answered and Carlos came in and brought a cart loaded with food. He set it out on the table and quietly left. Daniel followed him to the door and told him thank you again, and he would put the cart outside the door when they finished. "We'll probably be leaving about nine o'clock in the morning, so we will make it home before the heavy snow starts." "Good idea, we will have breakfast ready." "That will be great."

Daniel and Kari ate dinner and it was, as usual, fantastic. They drank another cup of coffee and then Daniel asked her to put on night clothes, so she could get comfortable and they would watch a little TV. "Okay, I will." "Don't stay too long. I'll probably make you take some pills Maria left." "I don't think I'll need them, but I will take one after a while. You must remember; don't boss me!" "I promise," he said, laughing and putting his hand over his heart. "Good," the little scamp said; as she went into the bedroom to change into night wear. She came out and Daniel was standing exactly where he was when she went to change; "I didn't go anywhere see, same spot." Kari started laughing and they hugged and kissed and semi watched TV. When the news and weather came on, the report was even more detailed than this morning. The snow might follow them home. "Kari, I told Carlos we might leave around nine o'clock." "That's a good idea," Kari replied. Shortly they went to bed and made love very gently and both of them slept well. The phone rang about eight o'clock and Carlos told them he would be bringing up breakfast in a few minutes. Daniel said, "Great." Kari got up, showered, and tried to comb her hair. She got the tangles out, but curly hair could be a mess. Daniel came in and said breakfast was here and they needed to have a good breakfast today. "It will take us about three hours or more to get home, but the snow will only follow us." They still managed a good morning kiss and ate their breakfast. As usual, Maria had done a fantastic job. The food was good and the spiced coffee was delicious.

When they finished, they both dressed in heavy clothing and Daniel took their bags out. While he was gone, Kari wrote a note to Carlos and Maria thanking them for a wonderful stay, food, and the precious gifts. Daniel came back and they went down together to head for the car. Carlos came out and wished them God-speed and a safe journey. They shook hands and said goodbye. Carlos said, "I'll keep you posted, about Maria's brother and sister." "Thanks Carlos."

They got in the car and headed home. It was cold and the wind was blowing, but Daniel seemed to have no problem driving. "Our trip will take about three hours, maybe a bit more, but we should miss the heavy snow." They had brought some juice and water with them. Kari began to rub her leg, but didn't seem aware of it. Daniel said, "Honey please take one of those pills Maria gave you. She said they would not hurt you and gave them to me. They are in my jacket pocket." "All right," Kari said, but I might go to sleep." "That's fine," Daniel said. She took one pill and drank some juice and pretty soon, Daniel noticed she was no longer rubbing her leg; in about thirty minutes, she was asleep with her head on a pillow that he had put in the car. Kari slept and Daniel drove.

It seemed only minutes when the car stopped. She opened her eyes and they were home. "This seems impossible," Kari said. "We are already home." "Yep, we are," Daniel answered. They went into the house and Camille came running out of the kitchen to see them and hug them both tightly. "I was so afraid you all would get stuck somewhere and not be able to get home and all sorts of terrible things." Joe came out of the kitchen and they hugged him. Joe said, "I couldn't get her to relax since we saw the news last night." "Well, we are here, safe and sound. Kari might be a little fuzzy; you see she slipped when we were taking a walk the other day and Maria insisted I take these pills with me, just in case Kari needed one."

Kari said, "I probably did, because my leg doesn't hurt very much now. Where is my precious baby?" Just about that time Danny came crawling fast toward Kari. Camille picked him up and had Kari sit down and gave the squirming Danny to her. He seemed to be talking to her in not such a sweet voice. "Well," Kari said to him, "Mommy and daddy needed to be away a while, but Papa Joe and Mama Camille took good care of you, didn't they?" Danny seemed to agree; and "Didn't Mama Sadie stay with you at night?" Danny grinned and started to kiss Kari, well his kind of kissing. When Camille placed him in Kari's arms, Joe and Daniel brought in the bags. Daniel looked over at Kari and Danny and asked, "Don't I get a kiss?" Danny looked up and smiled broadly. Kari told Daniel to hold him while she put her sweats on. He did and Danny began giving him the same lecture that Kari had heard. Daniel said, "Danny, daddy can't understand like mommy, but we love you and missed you." Danny relaxed and seemed perfectly at ease.

Kari came out and lay down on Danny's pallet; he immediately wanted on the pallet as well. "Seems like he is happiest with Kari, doesn't it?" He asked Joe and Camille to come into the kitchen; he needed to tell them something.

He told them about Carlos and Maria and how her siblings had been left alone in Mexico. They both speak English and Spanish fluently and are interested in coming to live here. I told Carlos with his recommendation, I would tell you and the whole group dealing with the youth center about them. They would probably live upstairs in a couple rooms and act as chaperons and answer any call in the middle of the night. "I'd trust Carlos with my life and if he recommends someone to help, you can bet that person or persons will be exactly what he says. I can't go see the Chief or officers, because Chief would have my skin; no matter that the snow was to reach as much as ten inches where we were staying. He definitely told me that he did not want to see me for three weeks. So I'll leave the decision up to you, Joe, on whether to tell him or not. I'd prefer that Kari and I have some time to move my clothes and things I've treasured into this house. That way we can get some things done we want to do and still be on vacation."

"I will ask Sadie to stay with Kari and Danny during the day and help Kari with the cooking or whatever. But the two of you are probably tired of young Danny. I did not realize that he could move so fast." "He has been a joy to all of us. Those two are quiet, wonder if they are ok?" Daniel went to look in the great room and they were both asleep in front of the fireplace on Danny's pallet. "Well, let them sleep," Daniel said, "Kari had to take a pain pill before we got too far toward home and I think she is still sleeping." "That's fine Danny will wake them both when he gets hungry." Camille said. She had made dinner; she had a feeling you might come home today. "We will go pack up our things and get home before the snow comes here. It is predicted that we might get two to four inches. There is plenty of food in your freezer and ours, as well as, the refrigerator is filled with produce." Daniel said, "Thank you, but you did not have to do that." Camille spoke up and said, "The bill for all the food is on your tab at the grocery store, so stop worrying." "Thanks," Daniel said. Joe came out of the bedroom with their suitcase and told Daniel it was snowing a bit more heavily outside. "I think we might need to go home." "That's a good idea," Daniel said. They left and said they would keep in touch. "Thanks," Daniel replied. "We will talk with you all tomorrow."

Danny awoke and began talking to Kari. She awoke and said, "Hi, my sweet baby, but you don't smell so sweet. Are you hungry? Daniel will you lift Danny for me; he needs a bath and clean clothing?" Daniel came in and lifted him up and undressed him and put him in a warm tub of water with his special soap. Daniel wondered where that came from; it had a lot of bubbles and Danny would grab for the bubbles. Soon he was ready to leave the tub and Daniel wrapped him in a large towel, put a clean diaper on and his pajamas. He took him into the kitchen where Kari was preparing his dinner. Kari sat down and started feeding him his cereal and applesauce and formula. They talked a while and Kari asked Daniel to put him in his swing. Daniel did and said, "Kari, it doesn't take a genius to tell something happened to your hip the other day; I think it might be cracked." "Well, Daniel, I think you are right. I'll need to stay stretched out as much as possible, and I'm afraid you will need to put supper out." She started to sob and Danny did too. Kari tried to stop because she knew this was upsetting Danny, but she couldn't.

She told Daniel that she had slipped again in the shower this morning and felt like the split was open or there might be a crack there. "Kari, why did you not tell me when it happened?" "Because I knew we were coming home and I could rest here." He picked her up and put her on the bed. He picked the phone up and called Sadie. "Sadie, it's Daniel; could you please, come stay with Danny tonight? Kari and I had to come home early because of the snow promised where we were staying. It seems she slipped in the shower this morning and I'm going to take her to the emergency room for an x-ray." "Sure," Sadie said, "I was just on my way anyhow. I'll be there shortly. Daniel, "Did she hit her head"? "Sadie, I don't know; you know Kari won't say much when she is sick or injured. If I didn't know she was hurt; I'm afraid I might give her a tongue lashing. This is frightening, suppose we had not come home and stuck in inches of snow." "Well, the good thing is that you made it back and God protected you," Sadie replied; "Now let me off the phone so I can come over." "Okay," Daniel replied.

He went back to check on Kari and she was still crying softly. He picked her up and kissed the tears away and told her that Sadie was on the way over. "You and I are going to the emergency room and check that hip and leg with x-rays." "That's probably a good idea."

"Daniel, it hasn't hurt this badly in a long time; I'm so sorry I didn't tell you, but I thought it would be okay. It's not though." Daniel held her gently and kissed her and noticed that Danny had quieted down. He was talking to his toys or something, but not crying. In a few minutes, Sadie came in and came to look at Kari. "Kari, did you hit your head this morning?" "No, I caught myself with this left elbow. I don't know if I bruised it or not, but it's not hurting. But Sadie, I'm afraid I might have re-cracked this leg. It wants to "draw"; you know how a cracked or broken long bone does." "Yes honey, I do. Now Daniel you get a large blanket and take her to the ER and I'll make sure Danny is fine." He's had dinner and a bath Kari told Sadie. "Stop worrying about Danny; humor me Kari, and get that hip and leg x-rayed." "All right, I know that is best."

Daniel had already started the car and left the door open, so he could set her in the car and get to the ER. As usual, when they arrived, they greeted him and said, "What's up, Daniel, you all are supposed to be on your honeymoon." "It started snowing badly and we decided to come home early and I'm so glad we did. You don't have to tell Chief that I'm back, because I don't want to work for a couple weeks. He told me he didn't want to see my face for three weeks."

"Now can we please get Kari's hip and leg x-rayed?" The ER doctor came in and said, "Of course we can." He ordered the x-ray and looked at Kari's leg and foot. "Kari, how many times did you fall?" "Well, I slipped when Daniel and I were walking the other day, but I slipped and almost fell in the shower this morning. I felt like I might have cracked the leg again, but I didn't tell Daniel because he is such a 'worry-wart'; however, I think he has reason this time."

The doctor looked at Daniel and said, "Her foot is turned in and she may very well have broken that leg this morning. Now Kari, while you get the x-rays, I'm going to talk to Daniel, because you obviously think he'll worry. No back-talk my sweet red-head. I know how Daniel feels. My wife fell down slippery steps when she was five months pregnant and I could not get to her for two or three minutes. I picked her up and she also called me a 'worry-wart'. That must be a saying you women use when you think you are protecting your man. Now slide onto that stretcher and go with Mike to have the x-rays done."

He turned to Daniel and said, "Please don't worry; because my wife had no damage, however, I assume you know what happened to Kari before the two of you met." "Yes and the first time I saw her, she was pale as death, but fire in her eyes, and was using a crutch. I realized I needed to show my identification with a picture on it. She looked like she might fall. She said, please have a seat on the other side of the fireplace and let me rock the baby. I did, and managed to stay far enough not to scare her." "Well, she had been badly damaged with the rape itself, plus this must have been a big man, because Dr. Little and I thought her hip and back might be broken. They were not, but the leg is split and we chose not to put a plate in at that time. This time it might need one, and no matter how she yells, (I know she has a temper) because she yelled at me to save her baby. Daniel, the little thing was dead and had been some time; I told her Dr. Little would be here in a minute. She trusts Dr. Little because she is a woman and very smart. You know the rest."

"But if this leg is cracked again, we will have no option that I can think of to avoid a plate. The plate is a piece of steel that semi-wraps the bone and is screwed into place. She may still need crutches a while, but we will provide them. It is up to you to make sure she uses them. She is so fond of Danny (yes, she told Dr. Little about him) and Dr. Little told me. I'm an orthopedic surgeon and Dr. Little is a general surgeon as well as gynecologist."

In about five minutes, Mike the technician called the ER doctor (Dr. Smythe) and asked him to come take a look. Daniel said; "May I go with you?" "Of course," Dr. Smythe said. They went into the X-ray room and Mike had the pictures up and told Dr. Smythe that he had already put a call into Dr. Little. "Good, Good, Mike; she should be here in about fifteen minutes. Meanwhile, Daniel look at this," and he showed Daniel a seam that even he knew, what that meant.

Kari spoke up and said; "Gentlemen, please move, that's my leg and I want to see for myself." The gentlemen moved. Kari looked and knew she was in trouble. "Oh Daniel what will happen to Danny and you; I can't stay up long enough to cook and I certainly can't lift my Danny." "Kari, now you are a worry-wart. You know Sadie is a nurse and is already with Danny and remember she stayed with you too when you first got here. Besides Mama Camille and Papa Joe will tan your little butt, even if you are on crutches unless we have the same arrangement; and contrary to your sweet wonderful self, I'm man enough to keep the ghosts away." "You are right, Daniel, but this might have to be done tonight." "It will," said Dr. Little and Smythe almost together. "You will also be staying overnight so we can keep you somewhat sedated until we're sure there won't be too much bleeding." "Oh FUDGE," Kari said. Dr. Little asked how long it had been since she ate. "I don't know," Kari said. Daniel said, "A good twelve hours. She had some juice about five hours ago." "That's fine. Call the OR staff in and we will get underway."

"This might take a couple hours, Daniel." As soon as they prepped Kari and headed for the OR, Daniel followed to the doors, bent down and kissed Kari and told her he would be waiting. When he got to the waiting room, he called Sadie and told her that Kari had to have surgery to put a plate in. Sadie said, "I thought as much." Daniel said, "Kari did too. She kept looking at her foot and she told me how it was feeling. Sadie would you please call your pastor and ask them for prayer for Kari; and give me Camille and Joe's number so I can let them know. My brain doesn't seem to work well tonight and I need Chuck's number as well." Sadie gave him all the numbers he needed and Daniel thanked her. Sadie said, "Daniel, you know I'm a nurse and this surgery will be over in a couple hours. She might have to stay in hospital overnight for observation, but please stop worrying about all of us; just pray for yourself as well as Kari."

"I know you pretty well, Daniel, and you are so on edge; you can hardly stand it. I know our Lord will protect her. Now do you want me to call Camille and Joe for you?" "That might be best," Daniel replied. Daniel called Chuck to tell him about Kari. Chuck, being the perceptive man he was, told Daniel he would be over in a little bit. Daniel went into the bathroom and cried and prayed. He finally had himself under control and splashed water on his face and held a cold paper towel to his face. He didn't realize how red his face had become. It showed through his natural olive skin. He splashed more cold water on his face and then thought he looked presentable, and went back to the waiting room. In a few minutes Chuck came in and shortly thereafter, Camille and Joe came in. They sat with him and all of them prayed for him and Kari. Daniel said, "Thank you". Daniel began to tell them how Kari had slipped when they went for a walk, but he did not know she slipped so badly in the shower. They are going to put a plate in and it will be screwed into the bone and the bone will be stable. "You all please help me to ensure she uses her crutches until the doctor says she can stop using them." "We will," Camille assured him. "She will use them, especially after she knows how important it is for her well-being and yours."

Although it seemed like hours and hours, it was about two hours when Dr. Smythe and Dr. Little came out of the operating room. They said the surgery went well and only the outside of the leg needed a plate.

They said the surgery went well "We will keep her overnight to observe and see if there is any excess bleeding. Her vital signs are good and she is beginning to awaken. She thought I was Daniel and said, well, are you going to kiss me or not. I said, no, I'd better not; Daniel would have me boiled in oil." She said, "Oh, Dr. Smythe. Well, where is he?" I assured her I would go get you. Daniel got up quickly and went to the recovery room. She had all kinds of monitors on her, but she told him what each one was measuring. "I'm glad you are a nurse. I love you, Kari." "Well, act like it then and give me a kiss." He did. They came in to take Kari to her room and removed all the stuff hanging around her, except the IV bottle. They moved her out on the stretcher and Daniel was right beside them. He asked what room and they told him and as Joe came over, Daniel told him the room, but they would have to wait until they got her settled. Daniel asked one of them to call Sadie and let her know Kari was out of surgery and I'd be staying with her tonight. "That's fine; we'll make sure Sadie knows."

As soon as the OR staff had Kari settled, Daniel, Joe and Camille walked in. Daniel came out   and stood with Chuck until Camille and Joe had visited with Kari. She was still groggy, but alert enough to converse with them. "Now you all better go home and get rest; I've caused enough trouble for all of you." "Yes, dear, we will go home." They left the room grinning; Daniel said; "What happened"? "Same thing that usually happens when she gets her spunk back; she starts giving orders." "I have some sympathy for you, Daniel," Joe said, "That little red-head is feisty." "I know," Daniel said. He and Chuck went in to see Kari. She was drowsy, but knew each of them. She said, "Hi Chuck, thanks for coming over to stay with the love of my life." Daniel had stepped out of her sight, but he heard her. Chuck said, "Daniel will be fine, now that he knows you are."

"Thank you, Chuck. I made the ER and OR tape my rings on, because I wouldn't remove them." "I think that's fine Kari; now you have to rest some. Daniel will be here in a minute." Daniel walked up and said, "Hi honey, how do you feel?" "Like a heel, for making you all go through so much, but Daniel, I couldn't help slipping." "I know sweetheart, but both doctors said you would be fine and probably go home tomorrow." "Well you can go get some rest at home." "Nope, I've got permission to stay right here with you." "Good," she said, and was soon drifting off again. Daniel stepped out the door and told Camille, Joe, and Chuck that he was staying with her tonight and they could go home. "Thank you all for coming over here; and most of all for your prayers." "Our prayers will continue, but we will go home."

DISCHARGED

Daniel lay down beside Kari on the bed and she seemed to relax and slept deeply. Daniel prayed a while; he went to sleep. It was soon morning; the nurses had checked on Kari and were amazed at how such a large man could sleep in such a tiny place. The nurses came in and asked Kari if she wanted breakfast; she said, "No, but I would like some coffee." "How about you, Mr. Meyers?" "Yes, I'd like a cup too." The doctors came in and said; "She can go home; we did some more tests during the night and her blood count is fine. She will have some swelling and definitely need to use crutches." Daniel thanked them both and told Kari he would be back in a few minutes. Daniel came back with the heavy blanket and the nursing staff helped him put her on the stretcher. "Does your car have a back seat?" they asked Daniel. "Yes, it does and I've started the car and left it running to keep it warm for Kari." They went out to the car and Daniel picked her up so gently and put her in the back seat. After they thanked everyone, they headed home.

It wasn't very far, and he knew Sadie had fresh linen on the bed and her light on, and fireplace on. She had also pulled Danny's crib into the great room, near his pallet. "You all can still hear him, but he won't awaken Kari," Sadie had told him on the phone. She had also made breakfast and was ready for them to get home. They got home and Daniel carried Kari and placed her on the bed. He took the heavy blanket off and covered her with a softer blanket. By this time Kari was in pain; she asked Daniel if there was another pill in his pocket? "Yes honey and here it is." Sadie had already put some water by her bed and Kari took the medicine. Daniel told her he would be back soon, that he had to go to the drug store for

221

the prescription that Dr. Smythe wrote. "Fine," she said, "Now where are Danny and Sadie?" Sadie brought Danny in and he wanted Kari. Kari said, "Let him lie beside me for a while. He has to quarrel at me and then he will snuggle up and he too might go to sleep. Sadie, I thank you so much for caring for me, as well as Danny and Daniel. I'm sure Camille and Joe will be here soon."

Sure enough, Danny climbed on her chest and quarreled with her for a very few minutes. He then decided she needed his kisses. Slippery though they were; then Kari said, "Mommy loves you and needs you to lie beside her and talk." It was if Danny understood everything she said. He soon found his place and Kari started to feed him his bottle and he let her know he could help. He was almost ready to handle the bottle totally by himself. They finished with his bottle and he lay quietly beside Kari and soon they both went to sleep.

Sadie went to the kitchen and began to put a load of clothing in the washer and tidy the kitchen. She had prepared breakfast, but had not put the bowls, etc. in the dishwasher. She would wait until Daniel returned and ate his breakfast. It didn't take long for Daniel to get the prescription and whatever the pharmacist told him he might need to make Kari more comfortable. He came in and didn't see anyone; Sadie came out of the kitchen and motioned with her lips to be quiet. Daniel only looked into Kari's room and was rather surprised that Danny was snuggled with Kari and was asleep. Sadie said, "Daniel they have been like that since Danny decided to stop his 'talking' to Kari and she told him; I know honey, but mommy had to go to the hospital and she needed him to rest with her." "I had taken a bottle to them and Danny showed Kari how he could help her with the bottle and started 'kissing' her face and then snuggled close to Kari and they both went to sleep. It still amazes me at how well they understand one another's moods, especially since she didn't actually birth him." Daniel told Sadie that he was also amazed, "I think it's because his own mother's scent had been washed away, and Kari's scent became his mother's scent. They are bonded and I'm so thankful." "Well, now come eat some breakfast/lunch." "I believe I will." Sadie had some coffee with him and they chatted very quietly.

The washer finished and Sadie put the clothes in the dryer. About the time she had them folded; the doorbell rang. Daniel ran to the door and motioned them to be quiet. Camille and Joe came into the kitchen with

Daniel and Sadie and talked a while about how Kari was doing. Daniel said, "She had to take a pain pill, but she is sleeping peacefully with her son." Camille and Joe laughed and said, "They really are bonded." Sadie told them to have breakfast, but they had eaten and took a cup of coffee instead. They both asked Daniel how he was and he said, "Fine. I'd still like to impose on Sadie and Camille to help take care of Kari. She still must use the crutches for at least two weeks," he told Joe. "Oh Daniel, Sadie and I already planned that, to cook and clean and take care of Danny and Kari. We'll both leave at night because we know you can care for those two."

JOE TELLS DANIEL ABOUT THE YOUTH CENTER

Joe said; "Let's go for a walk, grab your jacket because it is cold outdoors." They went outside and started to walk down the path that Kari usually took. Joe said; "Daniel, the Chief knows you all are back and what happened to Kari. He said stop worrying about anything, the docs said Kari would be fine and you were to do whatever you wanted. He would like to talk to you sometime this week, if you have time." "I'll give him a call when we get back. I have some news for him regarding a couple who would be great as chaperons and teachers of Spanish, for the youth center." "I think that's something he wants to talk with you about, too." They walked on as Joe told him that he and the Chief had spent quite some time together. There seems to be good news about the center. Daniel told Joe, he had his house on the market and the realtor could show it as soon as I get some stuff out of there. "If you don't mind, Joe, I'd like you to see the house and give advice on anything we might need for the center or store, for future use." "Okay," Joe said; "We can go whenever you want." "Well, if you aren't busy today, I like to go over and get your input; however, I'll call Chief first and find out if I can see him this evening." "That sounds like a good idea," Joe said.

They came back to the house and Daniel asked about Kari and Danny. "They're still asleep," Sadie said. "Good, I have to make a phone call to the Chief and then Joe and I are going over to my house to get my clothing. Then we will check any furniture or things we can use for the center, or put in storage for later." "That's great," Camille responded. When Daniel got on the phone with the Chief, Chief asked him straight forward how

Kari was today. Daniel said the doctors said she would be fine, but would need crutches for two weeks, at least. "She is asleep right now due to a pain killer that doc prescribed." "Well, that's good. Could you pick up Joe and Wayne and come to my office?" "Sure, when do you want us there?" "What about three o'clock; if that's okay with you and the other guys." "That will be fine." Daniel called Wayne and asked him if he could meet with the Chief, Joe and himself at the Chief's office at three o'clock. "As a matter of fact, I can." "Good, Joe and I will pick you up in about twenty minutes." Daniel went quietly to the bedroom and saw his two sleeping loves. Then he and Joe went to pick Wayne up at his office to see the Chief. (Joe had told Sadie and Camille about the meeting), so they were not surprised when they left.

They picked up Wayne who was ready to go and they met with the Chief at about three o'clock. The Chief looked at Daniel and said, "Welcome back, but you still won't be working for three weeks. Now let me tell you all about what I've found out; as much as I can." They all sat down where Chief had other chairs brought into his office. Sadie's pastor was already there, so Daniel knew something big had happened. It seems with a little arm-twisting and 'down and dirty' facts, the Commissioners have agreed to sell the old school at a fraction of its value for the center. They requested that we do all the rest; for us to see about getting some furniture and chairs for the classrooms. They said they would leave the present furniture, but you all would have to have it cleaned well and prepared for inspection. The Hospital Administration will also supply a few medical people for a day or two a week; for those who needed medical care. They have a very good therapy department there and will give them a couple of days a week.

Now for the farming equipment and swimming pool you all want; you will have to sell cookies or something for that. The gymnasium is in pretty good shape. Since it is winter and will be cold a few more months, we might plan a "WINTER FESTIVAL" for the community to tell the community what this is all about. Now Chuck and Charles (Sadie's pastor) will have to make your church community aware and enlist any help they can give. The Commissioners also cleared this with the State and it is believed with a lot of elbow grease and some funding, the center can be opened somewhere around January 15. Do you guys think you can get your wives and ladies in the Church communities to make all the treats to be sold, as well as help with the "WINTER FESTIVAL?"

"Some of the farmers in the county will donate their tractors and plows a couple days a week with them and overseeing the use of their equipment. They can help prepare some fields for gardening like Camille wanted and the kitchen in the school will be fine, after inspection. Do all of you think we can get this done?" "Yes, we can," they replied, "With all the community's help and prayer, we will be ready by January 15." Daniel spoke up and said, "I am deeply grateful to each of you for all this work; it could not have been done without you all." The Chief said that some of the officer's wives had volunteered to oversee any stragglers or observe anyone who looked too interested. "It seems to me that women have more instinct than men, for that kind of thing. I believe that is a God-given talent He planted in the hearts of women (well, most women); I cannot thank you all enough." Chief said, "Daniel we all want what's best for our community; your constant nagging about the youth has paid off well." Daniel thought he might break down and cry; but he held back and said; "Thank you everyone." Chief said; "Now boys, it's time for me to go home to my Mrs. And hopefully, she has a good dinner for me."

They all laughed and left. When Wayne and Joe got back in the car, they headed home. They dropped Wayne at his office and Joe and Daniel went home. Daniel said; "You know Joe, we may never find out who put Kari through so much; but you know God really did turn everything around for good." Joe said, "Daniel, that's what He promised."

They got home and something smelled wonderful. Sadie and Camille had made a big dinner, Kari was up (using her crutches) and Danny was crawling toward his daddy. "We have such wonderful news! Absolutely wonderful!" All the women started laughing and said, "Well, tell us!" Sadie said, "First we all need to sit down and have dinner." She made everyone sit down and served plates and herself one and the men began to tell them the wonderful news that Chief had for them. They all prayed and thanked God for the more than abundant blessings. They thanked Him for Kari's surgery, for safety, and for the blessings of the community getting behind the youth center, and most of all for His Great LOVE.

CONCLUSION

The great news about community involvement regarding the youth center was wonderful. The major group in bringing the attention to the government: State, Education, Hospital Administration, Police Department, Social Services, and various inspectors were elated.

Kari was still on crutches and couldn't keep up with Danny and the housework and dinner every day. She still was much less depressed. Either: Daniel, Sadie, Camille or Joe would be with her every day. She reminded all of them, that while she couldn't do a lot of physical work; she could keep records and make leaflets, with the date for the WINTER FESTIVAL; as well as things needed for the center.

She would be able to find the history of the county and prepare a booklet describing it, (who the main people were who settled here and other interesting things about the county; so that those who went shopping or employees could pick one up to learn about where they lived).

She could also explain what the Youth Center and WINTER FESTIVAL were about. Kari could include the offer for anyone interested in helping would be welcome. There would be a need for lots of cakes, cookies, BBQ a pig in a pit or grill (probably need men to help with the BBQ), build a bon-fire and tend it; however women could make side dishes, and they would need help serving the guests. They would need a cashier to collect the monies, as well as someone to place costs on items. She could put the needed objects in the leaflet so those who picked one up could decide what they could do.

She would also keep records of expenses and those who needed receipts for taxes, for expensive objects.

Kari could also give her number for anyone interested to call; and she could assign them to a specific area they wanted or make suggestions on what the people might need. They might decide to have an auction, in which people could donate clothing, canned goods, toiletries, and most anything the youth might need, such as basketballs, baseballs, bats, indoor games, TV's and DVD's with a library of DVDs, and books.

The leaders were hiring a cleaning crew to come into the center and prepare it ready for inspection, as well as the electrical, air conditioning and heating companies and water companies. They had been assured that the State would send inspectors as well; because there would be residents twenty-four hours a day.

The furniture that would be needed was checked and be ordered as soon as they knew what might be donated. Such things as chairs, single beds, linens, bathroom supplies were needed (towels, bath cloths, soap, toilet tissue, etc.) They would order what they couldn't collect from the auction, on line. They would be delivered two days prior to the opening of the center WINTER FESTIVAL.

They had to insure that chaperons were obtained who were dependable and loving people. Joe and Daniel would be primarily responsible for interviews of chaperons. They would need to have people who lived at the center in order to take calls at night.

Many of the officers volunteered to help on their day off and very often volunteered their wives, whether wives knew or not. Of course they were glad to do what Daniel or Chief asked them to do.

The pastors would start the following Sunday asking the women and men to volunteer for assistance during the festival and prior to it's date to set up tables and place the foods to be sold, with the price of each. They would also need 'word-of-mouth' volunteers to phone those they knew and ask for support. They may have a group who are into crafts that could be sold, since Thanksgiving and Christmas was up-coming.

The Chief, Joe, Daniel, Wayne, Pastors, School Supervisors, as well as the Community College Board met regularly to insure progress was made and the correct needs and accessories were done.

As the days went by, Kari and Daniel became even closer, they were in truth becoming one. Daniel reminded Kari that mental work was as hard as physical work. Kari seemed less and less depressed and began laughing more and became her, wonderful outgoing self. Joe, Camille, Sadie and Wayne made sure that Daniel had noticed her improvement; he did. Danny was as happy as could be when one of Kari's caretakers took him to the site. He too was growing and about to walk. He was a charmer.

Daniel and Joe were pretty sure that Carlos' in-laws would be perfect to live there. They would also have another   group come in to help keep records at the center, as well as help cook and serve. The students would be given rotating jobs such as laundry, serving tables, and clean-up duty to insure those who wanted to learn to cook or become a chef had the basics instilled. The automotive shop would be maintained by the kids interested in automotive work, such as cleaning shop floors and tools and everything kept in place. There would also be groups of students who liked to work outside with gardening of vegetables and fruits. They too would be responsible for keeping tools clean and in the right place. There would be various chaperons to assist each group, but the groups would be responsible for the work. Each dorm room must be kept clean and uncluttered and would be inspected daily by one of the 'house-mothers'. There would be much time allotted for sports or other activities in which the students were interested. The same rules applied; "If you work here, you keep it clean."

The students were given one chance, if they decided to leave or not obey the rules. Structure was set up for every area of the center and each student must stay within the boundaries that had been set up. It would indeed be a center for youth who might be headed for prison or the grave to learn and become independent and good citizens.